# A KEY TO LOVE

*A Novel*
*Inspired by Historical Events*

## MARY JANE BUETTNER

authorHOUSE®

❧❦❧❦

# *YOU ARE INVITED*

*Will you journey with me through my initial novel,*
**A KEY TO LOVE?** *My goal is to deliver superb
characterization within a well-constructed plot with a
great sense of timing while delivering a solid emotional
punch, and of course, a happy ending. Although my
characters portrayed are fictitious and I have taken
some liberties with the story, there was a great chronicle
behind the history of the building of Saint John
Catholic Church in the 1860's. I felt compelled to tell
the story, as I imagined it, honoring the current parish
including the people who always have, and continue to
share their time, talent and treasure.*
<u>*Embellishments? Of course; it is a novel!*</u>
*But, I tried to follow a time line that paralleled many
of the actual events in Baltimore and Westminster,
Maryland, Gettysburg and Pittsburgh, Pennsylvania
during a time-honored segment of history.*

*Escape and be part of my adventure . . . Enjoy!*

❧❦❧❦

# Kudos

~∽~∽~∽

The following are opinions by readers, who like to escape,
now and then . . .

## *PEOPLE LIKE YOU*

who enjoy reading a book set in simpler times that weaves in
and out of history, with many interesting turns and twists of fate
resulting in a find of treasure, unlike any other!

"A unique literary work of imaginary characters backed-up
by seventy pages encompassing the Historical Chronicle. Each
"individual's" idiosyncrasies blossomed into unforgettable
characteristics presenting their emotional, intellectual and
moral qualities.
"A KEY TO LOVE allowed me to analyze just how you
used the facts to create the fiction, taking me on a delightful
experience—my own personal slip-away from everyday life."
Renee Taylor,
Teacher

"A compelling and well-researched piece of fiction . . .
"A journey into gentler times with a mix of mystery, romance
and finely crafted characters."
Nancy Latini
Director, Latini Communications Services

"The author's maiden voyage takes us to a time and place that
gently lulls us on the waves of fond memories, stories, loves, losses
and choices that become the hallmarks of any family's history.
This saga; as it unfolds; repeatedly reflects the giftedness of the
writer in bringing the characters to life while weaving a tapestry
of life's journey."
Mary Jo Hutson
Friend and Educator

8

"Great! . . . Story spans five generations.
"Terrific character development!"
Barbara Neukum, a voracious reader

"A KEY TO LOVE, illuminates the archetypical struggle of good vs. evil between siblings. Woven together, over generations, is the effect of this conflict. The impact to so many lives is not only far reaching, but revealing in the struggle and choices made by many individuals.
"I was captivated by the storyline and all of the "real" characters.
"Sequel? . . . I hope!"
Cecile Pickford, Malibu, California

"Unique story line, great detailing! Loved the historical photographs!"
Joseph Lee

"Amazing first book! . . .
"The story is powerful . . . I felt like I was right there witnessing the events. I can't believe you've been hiding your talented gift of writing, all these years."
Gail Myers
Friend and Nurse Program Mgr., Carroll County Health Dept.

"Spellbinding! . . . Wonderfully exciting!"
Pat Nash-Devereux

"I was thoroughly engaged in this exciting adventure. The unique tale immediately captured and held my attention throughout the entire text.
"I especially enjoyed the segments that often included familiar locations."
Reverend Bonnie S. Block

"Bravo! I just finished reading—A KEY TO LOVE.
"It fits together beautifully; the flow was wonderful!
"God has truly blessed you with your gift of writing and your faith; and you, in turn give homage to Him in this book."
Charlotte Rajotte

"Exciting, suspenseful . . . I loved the historical facts!"
Angie Diehlmann

"What a combination of family, history, adventure, suspense, religion, treasure and several beautiful love stories . . . all rolled up into one. Thoroughly enjoyed it!"
Robin Heart

"Reminiscent of stories, now classics, which I treasure! I could really see it. I felt like I was watching a movie!"
Linda Fay

"Standing in the turquoise blue, clear waters of the Caribbean Sea in Grand Cayman, while watching the fish swim around my feet; reading this book was a pleasure. It kept my interest with the twists and turns of the common thread of the keys. Everyone in their lives has at least touched a key and after reading this, I am now touched by keys. I think of them in a different way and wanted to keep going to see how the keys would touch the characters' lives.
"The colorful imagery and suspense makes you want to just keep reading . . . just keep reading . . . just keep reading . . ."
Deborah Alms, Cayman Islands

༄‑ঙ৹ঙ৹ঙ৹

*AuthorHouse*™
*1663 Liberty Drive*
*Bloomington, IN 47403*
*www.authorhouse.com*
*Phone: 1-800-839-8640*

*Cover artwork by Clara Nash*
*Back cover photography by Clara Nash*
*Interior design by Mary Jane Buettner*
*Manufactured in the United States of America*

*Certain characters in this work are historical figures, and certain events portrayed did take place. However, this is a work of fiction. All of the other characters, names, and events as well as all places, incidents, organizations, and dialogue in this novel are either the products of the author's imagination or are used fictitiously.*

*Published by AuthorHouse    12/20/2012*

*ISBN: 978-1-4772-4904-8 (sc)*
*ISBN: 978-1-4772-4902-4 (hc)*
*ISBN: 978-1-4772-4903-1 (e)*

*Library of Congress Control Number: 2012913084*

*This book is printed on acid-free paper.*

# SUCCESS

*DREAM BIG . . .*
*WORK HARD . . . BUT, FIRST . . .*

## TRUST IN GOD

*Mary Jane Buettner*

*Lovingly Dedicated*
*to*

*My parents*
*Margaret and Frank Trachta Sr.*

*Henry, my husband*
*My rock, my wings*
*and*
*My support*

*Jennifer, Michael,*
*Mackenzie, Madison*

*Diane, Joe, Kory, Kacy*
*and*
*Lee*

ॐক৯ॐক৯ॐক৯

# TABLE OF CONTENTS

ॐॐॐॐॐॐ

# ANDERSON FAMILY TREE

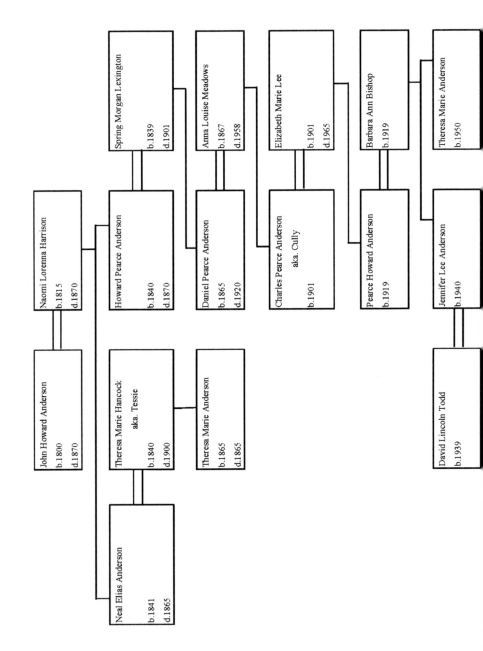

# FRANK FAMILY TREE

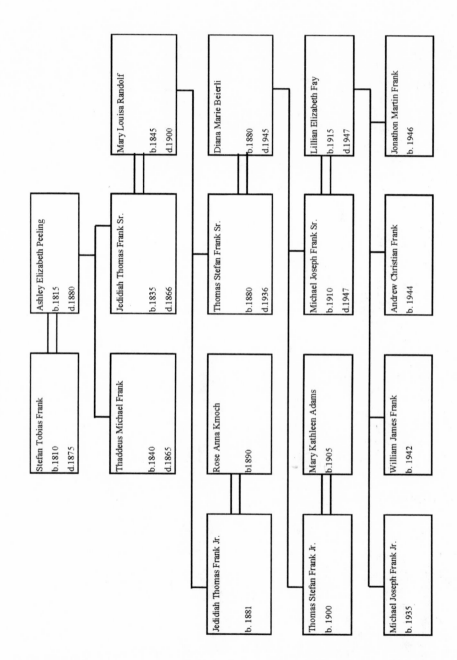

# A KEY TO LOVE

# PROLOGUE

❧❧❧❧

## MAY 1958

Suddenly, two boys bolted from the front, side door of the church as the smoke surged higher and higher from the choir loft floor while swirling and twisting, thicker and thicker.

Now, into the steeple it rose, escaping out through the louvers, threatening to still the reverberation of the bell which had summoned all from far and wide since the 1860's.

Hiding behind the tombstones as they ran through the adjacent graveyard, each of the boys looked from side to side hoping no one would see them, especially the inhabitants of the convent at the graveyard's edge.

They darted from behind the massive cross-shaped, marble monuments, hustling toward Green Street.

Fleeing over the bridge that arched the train tracks, they came down the hill on the other side, sliding down the grassy knoll on their backsides, finally reaching the ground.

After following the tracks for about a mile, running as fast as their legs could carry them, they stopped beneath an overpass and looked around to be sure that no one was watching.

Andrew, one of the youngsters, had both hands on his thighs, leaning forward as he looked back over his shoulder and into the sky.

"Oh my God!" he panted, turning now to fully face it, covering his mouth and chin with his hand while his eyes bugged out in a disbelieving stare.

His voice hitched.

"Look . . . Jonathon, the whole place . . . must be on fire."

Flames were now visible, dancing betwixt and between the gray and black billows of smoke. Up and up it rose, choking off the vision of the immense, ninety foot steeple.

The cross on the apex, the tallest point of the Westminster skyline, was the only part they could see. The church was obliterated by the distance with houses and trees between the boys and their parish buildings on Main Street.

Jonathon looked undeniably surprised. With a sneer in his voice, he said,

"It wasn't that bad when we left and, besides, the Fire Department is just up the block. They could've taken care of it."

"No, we should've gotten Father, should've told someone what was happening when we first saw the smoke," said his brother, Andrew, in a nervous voice, choking back tears.

"But we didn't! So I don't want to hear a thing about it. Got it? Not a thing! We'll be in reform school for sure if it leaks out. Reform school, I tell ya'. So nobody can know, just you and me."

Pleading, Andrew said,

"Jonathon, we should go back now, tell what happened. Monsignor will understand. We'll ask for forgiveness and . . ."

Before Andrew could finish, Jonathon grabbed him by the neck of his shirt and began to yell and swear,

"So help me, if you tell another living soul, I'll tell everyone it was *all your* fault. You being fourteen and the older brother—you should've known better. They'll say, '*How could you* put *your* little brother in harm's way like that? After all he's only twelve. *You're* the one that should be punished. Yeah, we should send *you* away. Away from your brothers and the Aunt and Uncle who raised you. Away from . . ."

"Okay, Okay, Jonathon, I won't tell," Andrew's voice trembled.

But Jonathon wasn't yet convinced that Andrew wouldn't talk.

"Gimme your hand," said Jonathon, "and prove to me that you won't squeal."

He took out his penknife and made a tiny slit in both his and his brother's finger. Jonathon made Andrew touch his slit to his own, like he had seen the *Lone Ranger* and *Tonto* do on their television show.

"Now, we are blood brothers," Jonathon said.

"But, Jonathon, we are already brothers," Andrew said through clenched teeth, the frustration building.

"But now, we are blood brothers and if you tell, you will be breaking a vow, *Kemosabe*."

Oblivious to the spectacle of the fire behind them, Jonathon dramatically spread his arms outward and upward and mimicked the actors he had seen, saying,

"I now summon the gods of my tribe to watch this brother, Andrew. If he tells our secret to anyone, let the gods be unhappy. Let the gods put him to death in a horrible way. Yes, if he makes the gods unhappy, let a spear pierce through his heart."

"Stop it, Jonathon, stop it. You're scaring me. Don't talk like that," Andrew cried.

Jonathon turned, arms still outstretched, looking up and away from Andrew like the portrayal of an Indian chief summoning a higher being. He was biting his lip, holding back the laughter bubbling in his throat and said under his breath,

"Andrew, you are such a wimp."

Sirens wailed into the midday quiet, breaking the exchange between the two brothers.

They were coming from everywhere it seemed. One fire engine crossed over the bridge above them, literally shaking its foundation. Two others came, one marked Reese Fire Company and the other, Reisterstown, from about fifteen miles away.

The boys sneaked back along the railroad tracks to get a closer look at the melee.

Red, yellow and blue flames totally engulfed the spot they had been in minutes before and the fire catapulted about fifty feet higher into the air.

Suddenly, to their amazement, the steeple toppled over, crashing into the main body of the gothic masterpiece.

And then, like dominoes falling, it continued bashing the rectory. Its copper cross, once stationed majestically atop it, was falling in the direction of the courtyard where the Monsignor usually sat at his metal table, daily, while saying his afternoon prayers.

They heard a scream, then the sound of more destruction.

Although they couldn't see where it landed, they gasped, turned, and ran away again.

# CHAPTER ONE

❧❧❧❧

## JULY 1966

$\mathcal{T}$here she was, walking down the path leading to Maggie Fischer's front door with something clutched close to her. The young girl strained to see the sign yet to be installed, leaning against a post and cocked at an angle, its black letters on white, partially concealed.

A puzzled look crossed her face as she halted her stride, wondering if she was in the right place.

She saw a few men and walked near them, deciding to ask them for help, and then realized they were preoccupied, struggling to pull multiple two-by-fours off their truck without disturbing sheets of faux wood paneling.

Carpenter jargon could be heard as she watched them hoist the lumber up onto their shoulders. One took the front and one the back, then they disappeared inside the house. On their second trip, while they were loaded down, she hesitantly queried only to receive an impatient, "not just now," response.

Considering she just might be getting in their way during their steady caravan of toting wood, she decided not to inquire further, turned and began retreating, squeezing her arm and the parcel gently toward her body.

"Wait," she heard someone say.

Turning around she saw a woman with smiling, brown eyes, her darker brown hair styled with full bangs and flipped-up edges captured with a wide headband, standing in the doorway that the men had just gone through.

Theresa scanned her outfit from toe to head and decided immediately she liked her look—from the soft, leather flats to the slim-fitting, black Capri pants—topped off with a loose fitting tunic top, buttons dotting its front. She formed an opinion right there, on the spot, that she was going to like this woman and thought that with her creamy, white skin and slim figure, she could be a double for

Laura Petri on the *Dick Van Dyke Show*.

"Are you wondering if we're open for business?

"We are, we are, well, sort of. Please, come in," Maggie said, motioning with her hand in a welcoming gesture to the teenager.

"Give me a minute to turn this radio volume down. The guys like their background music loud while they work."

While walking toward the radio she heard the announcer say, "And now, number five on the 'WTTR Top 40 Morning Show' for the summer of '66, The Mamas and the Papas'—'Monday, Monday.'"

She listened, hearing it play much softer, as she said,

"Now, that's better. Hi, I'm Maggie Fischer, and you are? Oh, wait. Move over here out of harm's way."

The pouch began to wiggle as the young girl said,

"Hi, I'm Theresa Anderson and this," she uncovered the hidden treasure, "is Bundles, my new puppy. Just got her about four weeks ago."

As the rest of the blanket was removed, a little ball of fur emerged. The pure white Maltese, with a solid black button nose, peeked out of dark, oval eyes right into Maggie's and she fell in love instantly.

Around her little neck, the puppy sported a tiny collar and a heart-shaped name tag, still blank, and Theresa held a rolled-up matching leash.

The dog's tail waggled as Maggie patted its slightly rounded head.

"Oh my, you are a cutie," she said through a wide grin and a giggle that emanated from deep within her throat.

"Is she registered?"

Theresa signaled with a nod,

"The names I submitted were Bundles of Crystal Threads and Bundles of Anderson Manor. I'm waiting for a reply from the American Kennel Club. Either one works for me."

More items were brought in from the truck—some drywall, the paneling and nails, drills, hammers and other assorted hand tools, not to mention a five-gallon bucket of paint.

The foreman, Brian, looked over to see the little puppy resembling one of his grandmother's powder puffs, the size of two fists, and couldn't resist. He walked over to Theresa and Maggie. Suddenly all the machismo melted and he stroked the dog while talking to it, his voice about two octaves higher. As the other workmen set down their items, they too walked over and turned to mush.

Maggie, somewhat of a people watcher, enjoyed seeing the transformation caused by 'Bundles', only to marvel at the change when they walked back into their work world with their tool belts flapping, oozing masculinity once again.

Theresa asked as she scratched her head, peering back at the workers she'd just met, still holding the animal close to her,

"Miss Fischer, I really wasn't sure if I was in the right place, couldn't make out the lettering on the sign leanin' against the wooden rail on the lawn. This is the *T.L.C. Grooming Salon*—right?"

"Oh, yes, yes it is, and I understand your hesitation. Brian, my carpenter, one of the men you just met, said he was waiting for the other thick post to come in to hang the sign on, so I guess I'd better tilt that sign to face the street temporarily, otherwise no one will see it. 'Course, if it did get shipped, and it's on their truck, maybe the guys will get to it today.

"I don't want to miss a new customer, that's for sure.

"Is she your first, Theresa?" asked Maggie, motioning toward the Maltese while anticipating her reply.

Theresa's head nodded.

"My father surprised me on my birthday, my sixteenth birthday, actually. I've been wanting a puppy for as long as I can remember . . . said now I'd be responsible enough to take care of my own. My older sister, Jennifer, has her own Springer spaniel, Roxy. She's had her about ten years and she lives with Jen and her husband in Ohio. It was her sixteenth birthday gift, too.

"I know this kind of dog needs grooming and Mom said I should set up an appointment to learn how to take care of her myself . . . in between times, she meant. Her hair is gonna' be long and silky, so I wanna' do it right."

That was music to Maggie's ears. The first customer and on the very same day the business was initially advertised in the *Carroll County Times*.

It was the first week of July, 1966, and the ad mentioned the grand opening in only two weeks, but Maggie was welcoming Theresa and her puppy business, today, ready or not, with open arms.

# CHAPTER TWO

❧✧❧✧

$\mathcal{M}$aggie told Theresa while guiding her to step toward the reception desk,

"Scoot on over here, but excuse the construction. Watch out . . . careful where you step. There's more wood stacked here and there, waiting for them to begin. This entrance is being converted to accommodate the business."

Theresa was surveying the space, spotting two ladders, smaller cans of paint, buckets of nails, molding and a large roll of linoleum and baseboard, as well as stacked wood furring strips, next to the pile of new items that the workmen had just unloaded.

"This foyer will be the reception area for the business, which means I get to create an addition and a new entrance for my house," Maggie told her. She shook her head questionably as she continued, "I only hope they get it finished in time for the grand opening in two weeks. We'll have dog sweaters, animal toys and leashes, but not until we get the grooming business going; and I wonder . . . how they will really get it done in time?"

She sighed as she turned around to scan the mess and while pushing one of the piles into a tighter pattern, left the young lady's presence for a few moments.

Curiously, Theresa took a few steps beyond the foyer, stuck her neck out and saw more of the house, but all of the furniture was covered with old sheets and tarps. She noticed two walls, straight ahead and to her right, filled with keys of all sizes, shapes and textures. Never had she seen a collection like this one, and she was drawn to the unique way they were all hung, facing in various directions. The background walls were painted off white and each key seemed to jut forward as if suspended in mid-air.

There were average keys but most of them had a novel quality about them in their composite, as well as their size and shape.

Many were brass, pewter and iron and there was even a glass ornamental key, all varying in size from two inches, up to designs about two feet long. These surprised Theresa, but she began to

notice very authentic looking specimens interspersed among them.
A matching pair had written inscriptions, one was hand-painted, yet
some were untouched, rusty and natural, signifying the aged metals.
One grouping sported old automobile keys and two were marked
"Ford" and "Dodge."

"Wow! That's a neat collection. Keys, humph! I would never
have thought to hang keys, but it is so cool! Where did you get them
all, and how many are there? Did you ever count 'em? Is that one
glass? Cool! How are they attached up there? Wow, that one's big.
We have a Ford. Did you paint that one?"

As she spoke, Theresa's head turned back and forth between
Maggie's direction and the keys, like she was watching a tennis
match.

At the end of the recitation, Maggie walked toward her as she
tried to remember all of the questions she was hearing, to answer
them one by one.

Maggie took a deep breath as she gazed at Theresa, then back
over her shoulder deciding whether the cacophony of carpentry
sounds would soon drown out their words.

Theresa smiled, licked one hand and slicked back little strands
of her tawny hair that had escaped her ponytail. Her green eyes
were surrounded by long, fluttery lashes, a perfect specimen of a
sixteen-year old in bell-bottomed jeans and a T-shirt.

She clutched her dog while waiting, watching Maggie like a
storyteller at the library. Her ears tuned into, 'These Boots Are Made
For Walkin', by Nancy Sinatra, barely audible, but loud enough to
stimulate her rhythm as she gently tapped her fingertips on Bundles'
back in keeping time with the music.

"Actually, the keys will be moved into my new entrance, but I'll
be happy to tell you about them," she said as she kept an eye on the
workmen's progress. Seeing them now doing quiet work, measuring
and marking with a carpenter's pencil just where to zip through with
the electric buzz saw, she decided to begin her saga.

She had told the story, oh, so many times, to anyone who had seen
the gallery walls and inquired. Since it was her passion, she always
enjoyed retelling it. After all, the keys numbering over two hundred
grew gradually from the first wooden key she and her husband, Jim,
received as a wedding present thirty years ago. It was one of those

ornamental keys meant to hold your house and car keys, somewhere near a door . . . one that little hooks are screwed into. In fact, the little hooks were in the box the key came in, but Maggie decided she liked it better without them. It was perfect to use ornamentally to fill in a small, open space on the wall.

After telling Theresa how it began, she continued, "One day we were antique-a-ling, a word my husband, Jim, made up for hunting down the neatest finds in old, out-of-the-way antique shops. We were in New Market, a little town that calls itself the "Antiques Capital of Maryland." We always stop there, on the way to Frederick, and stroll in and out of the buildings. Had just gotten back from our honeymoon a few months before and there wasn't much money in our budget for extras.

"But, suddenly I spied them, old iron keys, about ten altogether. Two were larger and looked much older than the others. The shopkeeper swore they were authentic jail keys and I believed him but wanted to know more, so I probed."

"'Not much I can tell ya' 'bout 'em 'cept these two were from an armory at Harper's Ferry, West Virginia, during the Civil War era. That town sat at the junction of them two rivers, Potomac and the Shenandoah,' he had said."

"Oh, I remember those rivers. Yeah, we read about the Civil War in school," Theresa blurted out.

"Yes, dear," Maggie answered unconsciously and then continued, "That was all I needed to hear. I wanted those keys. I'd find out more about them later. How much? I said. See, I had to lock in the price, then and there. Thought the more he'd tell me the higher his price would go."

"'Gimme five bucks for each of 'em and they're yours,' the owner said."

"I took both of the bigger keys he separated from the others, and, after inspecting them, laid them near his cash register.

"To try to lock in his sale, he said to me, 'There's a lot of history behind 'em, and as I thought about it, I knew he was right. But, I just waited, knowing if he had a need to chat, I'd offer a willing ear."

"And what did he tell ya'?" Theresa interjected.

"I remember exactly what he said and how he said it." She modulated her voice, "'If them there keys could talk we'd be hearin' some tales all right. Wonder who was captive in that old jail? Why, it could've been some important General, a Captain or some deserter. Heard it was abandoned and burned by a garrison about April of 1861. Makes my mind do flip-flops just a'thinkin' on it . . . only wish I knew more. The longer I have this shop the more I will find out about 'em and the more valuable they will become.'

"I knew that shopkeeper was right—they would become more valuable as time went on and my mind began to expand on his theories." Maggie looked dreamily into the space above Theresa's head while she accentuated each word. "My ideas involved side tales of romance and fantasy and intrigue."

She brought her attention back to Theresa who was staring at her.

"From that day on, whenever a key came into my possession, I investigated to find out as much of its background as possible, who had owned it and what part it had played in history. And now, I love telling the tales as much as having the collection."

"Cool," Theresa said enthusiastically.

Maggie looked back to discern if the men were working when she didn't see them. Then she heard the buzz saw they had set up outside, being fed by the electric current coming from their extension cord plugged into her house.

They talked a little louder now.

Maggie pointed to the wall, "Theresa, see that small key right there? I located it in a little shop right on the main drag of a charming, little town, St. Michael's, over on the eastern shore of the Chesapeake Bay. It fit an old trunk found in a mansion. That was how the antique dealer relayed the story to me and the stories always intrigued me, so I listened very intently as he set the time period and proceeded to explain how those trunks were used and he even named the old mansion it came from."

"Wow! Sooo cool! Really?" Theresa crooned, her eyes wide like saucers, with a grin from ear to ear lighting up her face.

Maggie changed her inflection again. "'They filled 'em with their shoes, clothes and underpinnings that would be used during their summer stay at one of those Eastern Shore, telescope houses.'

"I must have looked puzzled 'cause he interjected, 'You know, the house kept being added onto like a telescope opens up, only layin' on its side. The entire family from the city would move into their summer home. This particular trunk was left behind for one of the servant girls, whose family continued to care for it for the past ninety-two years. The servant girl's great-granddaughter just sold it to me, along with some other antiques . . . and would you believe it, just one week ago. And, here you are buying it with the original key in the lock, and I'm sure you'll keep it in your family for ninety-two more years, right?' He winked and grinned at me when he said that."

Maggie continued faking his drawl,

"'Look, I told you all I can tell about it—all that I know. Guess you'll just have to add your own thoughts to it and imagine the rest.'

"Yes, Theresa, that's exactly what he said to me and that's exactly what I did. In my mind I conjured up a family with a young maiden spending her last family summer on the *"Shore"*, before leaving for finishing school abroad. Of course, this lovely Miss would meet a ruggedly, handsome young man, Henry, Phillip or Todd would be his name, something strong and masculine. He would be working in the family seafood business. Crabbing with a trot line in the summer and harvesting oysters in winter creates a strong body with weathered skin."

Maggie's eyes shifted upward and her head tilted as she heaved a dreamlike sigh and continued, "The two of them would meet by chance. Her family would nix their relationship because of the difference in their social rank. But, somehow love would conquer."

Barely within earshot, and between the lulls in the shrill whirl of the buzz saw, Maggie could hear Percy Sledge recant his tale of woe in 'When a Man Loves a Woman.' Dramatically she drew her arms to her chest and closed her eyes, "They would fall into each other's arms, pledge their undying devotion to each other and . . ."

Before she could finish, Theresa interrupted Maggie's next thought and brought her back to reality.

"Where did that one with the metal tag on it come from?"

Shaking her head and focusing in, Maggie began,

"Oh. Oh, that one . . . that one's from Paris."

"Wow! You do have keys from all over the world." Theresa found this so exciting and as she listened she continued to chatter as soon as a thought popped into her head. "If I can find one, would you have room for another?"

Before Maggie could answer she said,

"Tell me about Paris."

"Okay . . . while in Paris, I stayed in a quaint, narrow hotel which was three stories high. The elevator, or lift as they call it, was so tiny only one person and two small pieces of luggage, piled on top of each other, would fit at one time."

"Wow!!! That *is* tiny. I've never seen an elevator *that* small," Theresa said emphatically, making Bundles, who had been relaxing, jump at the sound of the volume of her voice.

"I was with a group of twenty-five women for a week of intensive skin-care training. The bellman filled up the elevator, bowed with one hand at his waist and motioned with his other hand for each lady to enter, accompanying her bags. He then pushed the appropriate floor button and ran up a spiral staircase to meet the elevator as it arrived on the second or third floor. He escorted the guest to her room, then retrieved madam or mademoiselle's luggage and deposited it inside the door.

"Down he rode to refill it again and again and would then scamper up the stairs, humming and singing what sounded like a French folk song as he went. After his job was completed he was exhausted, but with heavy pockets full of tips from grateful Americans.

"That key fit the door to my tiny room which had wonderful, as we call them, French doors, that opened out onto a balcony overlooking a beautiful park with an elaborate fountain. It was a charming adventure, but I'll tell you more another time."

Theresa was giggling, "I love it. Tell me another one, *please*," she begged.

"Okay." Maggie was entertaining Theresa and enjoying every minute of it. So she went on with her tale and pointed to a small specimen. "That one is from a 1958 Classic Mercedes . . . belonged to a retired Admiral from the U.S. Navy living near San Diego. My husband and I met him and his wife while we were there on business.

"One day, while watching the Fourth of July parade on Orange Avenue in Coronado, my husband, struck up a conversation with the people sitting near to us. Before we knew what happened, we were being whisked around Point Loma and La Jolla by those two friendly souls. We had lunch at the historic Del Coronado hotel, full of opulence and grandeur."

"What's that? Grand door?"

"No honey," she accentuated her words, "Grandeur, full of beauty, an old, beautiful hotel . . . It was great!

"They became our private tour guides, telling us about the navy base and how they settled there after World War II, before the rest of the world found out about the charm of that southern, coastal city.

"Everywhere we went, the Admiral drove, and we were seated on the back seat like a king and queen.

"As we were getting to know each other quite well, I mentioned my collection of keys.

"We exchanged addresses and promised to keep in touch. And, believe it or not, within one week, a package arrived from Admiral Josephs. Can you imagine how surprised I was to find within it, one of his original keys to that vintage car. The note he enclosed said, 'Memories are made of this.'"

"Neat! Did you keep in touch?"

"Oh, absolutely! We fly out there and they come here about every other year and when we go to San Diego, he still drives us in that classic Mercedes. And, I might add, with as much precision as many younger drivers I know."

"One more, please, tell me about one more," Theresa pleaded.

"Sure, but then, we've got to take Bundles back for her mock grooming and set up an appointment. That *is* the reason you're here, remember?

"Okay, which one is enticing you?" Maggie asked with enthusiasm, continuing her show and tell with Theresa.

"That huge one near the center top of the wall . . . what did that key open, Miss Fischer?"

"Please call me, Miss Maggie, Theresa. The ceramic one you're pointing to really doesn't open anything, it's just an ornate key, but it does have a story."

Maggie grinned slyly as she recalled some details. "I was working as a hairdresser. My former boss made ceramics and gave me that one shaped like a key when she found out that I had a collection. The thing was so big that I had to build a design around it to make it work on the wall. That was about twenty years ago. She's now in jail for trying to defraud the Federal government. But, that's another story."

# CHAPTER THREE

∂∕∕∂∕∕∂∕∕∂∕

$\mathcal{B}$efore Theresa could persuade one more tale, Maggie said,
"Okay! Let's get started. C'mon back into the grooming salon. We will have a collage wall of *before* and *after* photos of our customers' pets, and though I know technically we aren't open for business, I am considering your puppy to be our first customer. Would it be alright if I start with Bundles today for her *before*? In her case, her coat will be growing longer and fuller with each photo we take."

Theresa agreed excitedly while Maggie walked into the living room and lifted a covering from her antique desk. She grabbed her camera and a framed picture, then walked over to the new grooming room and sat the photo on the floor at her feet. The puppy had all four paws firmly planted on the rubber mat of the brand new grooming table when Maggie snapped the Polaroid.

"Let me hold Bundles and we'll go through some of the motions, as if we were clipping her. Here, would you please hold the developing picture and this framed one I have right down here?"

She lifted it and gave it to Theresa.

"My daughter, Gretchen—there in the photo—does most of the grooming, and I know she will love taking care of your puppy and that Bundles will be very comfortable with her. I have to tell you, she does an incredible job, Theresa, and she'll show you how to brush her properly."

Theresa glanced at the picture recognizing Gretchen, but said nothing. She looked back over her shoulder at the few keys she could barely see and smiled, her head swimming with an idea that had just been born.

Maggie put the puppy back on the table and used the metal grooming brush gently on her tiny body. Clippers buzzed as they were held against Bundles to let her feel the vibration and to hear the hum of the motor. Then, Maggie used the shears, just a little, to let her hear another sound—the swish of the blades.

After each of the experiences, she kindly stroked Bundles and spoke high-pitched, baby talk, telling her she was such a good girl.

Her little tail went 'round and 'round like a propeller on a prop plane. It was easy to tell she liked this treatment.

As she finished, she incorporated a little mini-massage on the dog's whole body, and, with Theresa's permission, offered a special, tiny liver treat that Bundles gobbled up immediately.

Maggie then scooped her up and got lots of doggie kisses as she walked Theresa to the desk to secure an appointment . . . and, just in time.

Brian's workers were ready to use their hammers, but Maggie asked them to hold off 'til Theresa left.

"All of you banging at once would make *me* jump," she told them, "and I don't want to frighten that little puppy."

The men agreed and walked outside to take a break.

They looked at the finished photo and Maggie reminded Theresa to bring it on grooming day, and Bundles' photo could be the first picture on the "Look who we have as customers" wall, to which they would add the *after* photo.

Giving the puppy one last scratch on the head, she handed her back to Theresa and said,

"That's how I'll try to win them over, Theresa. If their first experience is good, they should always be happy to come here. Actually, they will all get a mini-massage before we put them in their crates. After brushing out tangles, shampooing, clipping nails, and blow drying, they have had some unpleasant happenings . . . it's just inevitable. It's amazing how that soothing touch will help them to relax and enjoy their experience here.

"And, it will be the last memory of their visit . . . a happy one," Maggie added.

As they walked toward the door, Theresa was ready to pay for today's visit, but Maggie would not accept it, not even a tip. She hoped this would encourage Theresa to become a permanent customer and that she would tell all of her friends about the *T.L.C. Grooming Salon.*

The new business would be on its way!

Maggie's generosity thrilled Theresa. She couldn't wait to investigate her idea, which she just knew she had to make happen.

She walked down the street, planning her strategy and giggling, knowing exactly whom she should talk to, whom she should ask to subsidize her whim . . .

# CHAPTER FOUR

❧❧❧❧

## JULY 1966

## A FEW DAYS LATER

As he looked into the bathroom mirror, Cully Anderson saw his granddaughter Theresa staring at his face, foamy with the shaving cream he had just applied. She had watched his every move as he stirred hot water into the soapy mug with a small-handled brush, then swirled lather on his bristly-white shadow of stubble.

He scraped the leather strop with his straight razor to bring up a sharper edge on the blade, stretched his face taut and prepared to behead each hair.

She liked to watch her Poppy (as she called him) do almost anything. When he worked in his basement using tools or when he tinkered in his garden, Theresa could be found nearby, listening and learning.

But today she was at his house exceptionally early before their weekly drive to Sunday Mass. She asked if she could watch him shave and, although she had seen him do that before, this time he sensed there was a special purpose to her inquiry.

Hair and foam disappeared as he contorted his face and stretched the skin under the blade until it looked pink and smooth again. When he covered his face with a hot cloth, even though Theresa hadn't said anything, he could just tell that she was setting her thoughts to prepare for a request.

While slapping on his Aqua Velva aftershave, he shooed her out of the bathroom so he could bathe and told her he would see her downstairs.

As the tub filled, he remembered Theresa telling him about a woman with a key collection and decided that her visit so early, before the ten-thirty service, had something to do with that.

He had laid out his clothes before she came and proceeded to put together one of his "Sunday best," completely color-coordinated, of course, but not subtle heathers or herringbone.

Today he sported white polyester pants and matching vinyl shoes, topped off by a silver-grey jacket covering most of a pale, pink shirt.

"My tie . . . which tie today?" he asked aloud.

"Here we go," he said, while choosing a foulard design in shades of silver and white with a touch of burgundy and hot pink. The handkerchief that he folded picked up the exact shades within the print of the tie, and he placed it into the breast pocket of his jacket, encouraging three edges to point upward, peeking out, just so.

As he walked past the dresser, he felt that his posture denied the mirrored reflection of a sixty-five year old man.

The frames on distinctive glasses that surrounded his steel-blue eyes slid into a handsome shock of his crowning glory—white hair, thick and full, presenting quite a dapper appearance.

He stood with his hands on his hips remembering what his neighbor had often told him, "Cully, I swear. The way you like to dress, you should own a men's clothing store, right here in our small town."

Many a time I'd tell him right back,

"After sixty-five years livin' here in Westminster, about the last thing I wanna' do is come out of retirement to open a haberdashery. But, thanks for the compliment."

And as he stood there thinking about it that great smile of his lit up his whole face.

Meanwhile, Theresa was downstairs watching the clock, planning and waiting. She knew he had a couple of old keys from aunts and uncles who had died but didn't know how or where he had gotten the rest of them. Many times she listened to his tales relating to antiques he had collected from Maryland, Pennsylvania, and Virginia, just as she had listened to Miss Maggie's stories a few days before. They were much like his, weaving in and out of history, nothing like the classes at school with boring dates and times she'd had to memorize.

She was determined . . . and she knew he would agree with her . . . if only she could convince him.

As his foot hit the bottom step and he turned into the room, Theresa put her arms around him and gave him a big hug.

"Oh, what's this?" he asked, smiling, as her actions were fulfilling his suspicion.

Theresa's words burst out, "Remember me telling you the other day about that lady, Maggie Fischer, and Bundles and everything?"

And through her exuberance he listened intently as she told him more of the story, repeating much of it word for word.

"Poppy, it's incredible. She has about two hundred keys and they are displayed on two walls at her business. She was so kind to me and Bundles, wouldn't let me pay her and wouldn't accept a tip!

"As I looked up at them, I remembered that you have some old keys. Couldn't forget about the time you showed all of them to me when you were telling me about our family and about great, great Uncle Neal who had worked at Saint John's Church and how he went off to serve the church and help with the injured. It made me so sad that he had to die when a sniper shot him and his friend, the priest. And you told me about his wife, great, great Aunt Tessie and how she helped by caring for the wounded and cooking big 'ol pots of stew and everything for the soldiers.

"See, I listened to all that you told me. Oh, and it was so much more that you said and I remember it all . . . every bit of it!

"Now I remember seeing those old keys too and, unless you don't want to part with them, could we give one of them to Miss Maggie Fischer as a little gift from me?"

She excitedly kept trying to persuade him, hardly taking a breath as she continued,

"I know she would treasure it and she would find a special place for it on one of her walls." I could see it every time I go there with Bundles, knowing it was from you. What do you think, Poppy? Would it be okay?"

He thought for a minute. "Describe Maggie Fischer to me. Do I know her?" he inquired.

"Poppy, I'm sure you have seen her at St. John's Church. She's tall and has very dark hair and she's always with her daughter who is twenty-six or twenty-seven. Her daughter has brown hair and they're both about the same height. They always sit on the left of the center aisle."

Then she proceeded to tell him of another connection to Maggie's daughter, Gretchen.

His eyebrows rose as he listened and he nodded as she spoke, remembering back a few years when his other granddaughter, Jennifer, was still in high school and the part that Maggie's daughter had played in Jennifer's quest to succeed on the basketball team.

He did have a couple of special keys in his antique collection, and he especially treasured the ones from his ancestors.

Cully Anderson wasn't a person to give up parts of his collection of old oddities, but whenever someone was kind to his granddaughters, on whom he doted, they were in his favor.

Theresa hadn't swayed him completely, and he didn't promise to relinquish a key; but he decided to look for Maggie Fischer that very morning.

As he opened the front door to leave, he saw Theresa waiting patiently outside by his car, looking so angelic. He hesitated, then turned and quickly climbed two flights of stairs to the attic. In a quick minute he was retracing his steps, and as he shut the door to his house, he patted something in his inside jacket pocket, nearest his heart.

# CHAPTER FIVE

❧✦❧✦

$\mathcal{B}$eing an usher, and always at the 10:30 a.m. Mass, Cully Anderson was able to scan the pews for Maggie Fischer. He saw her alone today, just where Theresa said she always sat, left of the center aisle.

His granddaughter was standing outside talking to some friends. Just as Theresa was about to enter the church, he walked over to her and told her not to let Maggie see them together because he had a plan worked out.

"The girls from my school are goin' down to the Twin Kiss for a Coke after Mass and they asked me to go along. If it's okay with you, Poppy, I'll scoot out with them and we'll go through the side door. Cecile's mother already said she'd give me a ride home, if I wanted to go. I'll walk over to your house later, okay?"

She thought, but didn't say . . . I hope you decide to give her a key and I'll be by to ask you about it then.

"Is that okay, Poppy?" she asked, finishing it off with a big cheeky kiss.

He agreed, and Theresa went inside, carefully staying behind people taller than her until she found her classmates sitting to the far right of the altar. Miss Maggie could barely be seen from that pew, but her grandfather was visible from there, standing in the back, and eyeing up her new-found friend. She said a little makeshift prayer that the two would meet.

As the congregation filed out through the vestibule, Maggie absent-mindedly took a weekly bulletin from a man, who surprised her by saying,

"Maggie Fischer, can you wait 'til I'm through. I have something to show you?"

She looked up at him bewildered, but said nothing. The crowd behind her kept moving forward, as she did. Wondering how he knew her name and what he could want to show her, she busied herself outside the church, talking to some other parishioners while continually watching him out of the corner of her eye.

Most of the crowd had dwindled as he walked outside. From his inside jacket pocket he retrieved a large key. Maggie spied it immediately and her interest heightened. She excused herself from the group and walked over to him.

"Hear you collect these things," he said, as he held it so she could see it.

"I sure do, I've got about two hundred of them, all hanging on two walls in my home, sort of like a gallery of keys . . . my private collection," she said.

"Yep, I know that," he responded emphatically.

Puzzled, she tilted her head as she looked at him. His statement caught her off guard, and she wondered how this church usher knew so much about her.

She opened her mouth and as she was about to ask, he said,

"Want it, Maggie Fischer?"

And before she could say yes, he put it directly into her hand.

Her eyes widened, her eyebrows arched expressively and she smiled. Under other circumstances, if she had met this man and heard his reference to the interior of her house, she would have been very leery of him, but her intuition told her to proceed.

Then he asked,

"So, you do want it?"

"Sure," she responded, "I love keys and I'll add it to my collection. But, why would you give it to me and how did you know my name and that I collect keys?"

"Bet you'll never guess what it used to lock," he continued, ignoring her questions.

Although she didn't have a clue, she did like the looks of it. Apparently very old, maybe from the mid or late 1800's, it was probably made of iron, which was often used back then because of its durability and strength.

She was intrigued and knew this man had more to tell her. Maggie even noticed a little grin on his face and a twinkle in his eye as he looked into hers.

Without warning, he reached for the key and took it back from her, holding it, twisting it and playing with it.

"I really would love to have it," she said quickly, as she looked at it in his hands, which were now covering most of it. He raised his fists, holding the key out in front of her, and as she reached for it, he released it, allowing it to fall back into her hands. She fumbled, but caught it before it fell to the ground and held on to it much tighter now as she didn't want to take a chance on him changing his mind.

He was toying with her, enjoying the little cat and mouse game, as he asked,

"Do you know I remember the first time I saw your family in church, after you moved here? Your daughter was goin' to Westminster High, same time one of my granddaughters, my Jennifer, was. Both of them played on the school basketball teams, varsity and j.v., and I watched your girl on the court . . . good sportsmanship. No superstar was she, but passed the ball off for the good of the team. Wife and I watched all the girls' games, seein' as how our granddaughter might be movin' up in her senior year. In fact, my Jennifer pointed you out to me one Sunday and told me how your girl helped her, showed her how to fake and dribble and kept encouragin' her to 'go for it' . . . the varsity, that is. And, my Jennifer did, and she made the team and I still think your daughter made all the difference, supported her, gave her confidence in herself!

"Ya' did a fine job with her and ya' know, the apple don't fall far from the tree, is what I always say.

"Now, I know I'm off in a different direction talkin' about your daughter and all, but I wanted you to know I observed all of that and because of it, I want you to have that old key you're holdin'."

Maggie looked down at the key and back at him as he continued.

"Ya' see, that key means a lot to me and I wouldn't give it away to just anybody. Somehow, I know you'll treasure it like you treasured your daughter all these years."

Maggie's eyes lit up as she said,

"I'd love to have it."

She felt flattered by his statement and didn't quite know how to respond to the part about her daughter, Gretchen. She also didn't know where the key came from originally but hoped she would find out if she played along.

"This church we worshipped in today, this modern church, it's not the one I grew up knowin', not the one my parents or my grandparents went to either. The old church was downtown on Main

Street where the Davis Library stands today. Rectory and school too, became part of the library."

He shook his head, deep in thought.

"Oh, Maggie, it sure was beautiful. Gothic, they call that style, standin' there, tall and imposin' against the sky. One-hundred and eighty-five feet tall from its base to the top of the eight foot copper cross that finished her off. Kinda' like a mini-cathedral. Had a steeple, ninety feet tall that could be seen from every part of the city and when you looked at it, you knew it was pointin', straight up to God."

"They have photos of it on the walls of the Davis library, don't they?" she asked. "Several of them actually."

He didn't respond to her but continued on, while leaning against the church, looking into the sky, almost painting the picture for her.

"It was like a church should be, full of that special church-type architecture. No pillars inside though, had a special roof designed to lean against the walls in wide arches, kinda' like a bridge is built to hold itself up. Beautiful statues and fourteen, hand-carved Stations of the Cross, hangin' there on the walls, a sanctuary lamp that was suspended about twenty feet down from the ceiling in the center of the altar area and a marble Communion railing."

Some of these things were new to Maggie. She listened in awe.

"In the back of the church were votive candles in wrought iron holders that stood about four feet high by about four feet wide. It resembled a cage, only the entire top held about three hundred glass cups with candles inside. Whenever you wanted a special prayer heard, you'd light a candle with a long, thin stick, after borrowin' a flame from another candle, already lit. To cover the cost of the candles, you would make an offering into a small metal box with a slit in it that was attached. Then you'd kneel down and ask for them special wishes. Didja' ever do that?"

"Why no, I'm not a Catholic."

"Not Catholic! But you're here at St. John's every week," he said while scratching his head.

"My husband is a Catholic and I promised to raise our daughter Gretchen in the Catholic faith. In the beginning, I would bring her to Mass when her Dad couldn't. Now I come because I like to," Maggie explained.

"Oh, I see," he said, obviously pleased.

"Well," he continued, "anyway, that traditional church on Main Street was very, very special and that's where this iron key was from. 'Course, don't even know why they had a key for it . . . never, ever locked the doors back then. 'Tis why it looks so new, nary a mark on it."

"It was? It is?" she asked, her voice rising in surprise, "From the original church on Main Street?"

Maggie was excited. She had heard about the old church and how beautiful it was from some of the salesladies at Mercer Floors when she picked out the linoleum for the grooming business, and now she was sure she had glanced at the pictures at the library a few weeks ago. If her memory served correctly, it had all the components of that traditional gothic style that he had mentioned, and she was sure it must have soaring ceilings, gilded trim that touched off the paintings within and chiseled, marble statues throughout. As she thought more about it, Maggie felt ecstatic and honored that he would want her to have that key. It wasn't just the key itself, but she could imagine the services that its door had been opened to . . . Christmas, Masses, weddings and funerals. If it could talk, the people and the stories that old church could tell and this key could unlock those tales.

Suddenly, there was that gleam in her eye and her mind began to wander, began to fantasize, just as it always did with each new acquisition.

She had to know more.

Maggie was enjoying his story and the way he was describing it, and she decided to tell him,

"Oh, I love hearing all of this, Mister . . . er . . . Mister, I'm sorry, I don't know your name."

"Cully, Cully Anderson. Just call me Cully." he said.

As parishioners continued to mill about, he motioned for her to move over near the cornerstone. He went on to tell her that he had the key because his grandparents had been the sextons of the original rectory, church and sacristy, very honorable positions. He revealed they had followed in their parents' footsteps. In fact, there was always an Anderson involved in caring for or working with St. John's from that original church and the little Oswego Chapel it grew from, even before that. His mother, Anna, washed, starched and ironed the altar cloths and vestments, scrubbed the marble sacristy on her hands and knees and swept through the entire church, prepared all the chalices and patens after the Reverend washed them, and polished the wooden pews.

"Maggie, she always said, 'I didn't wash the blessing off, just the dirt.'"

He continued.

"Over at the rectory, she cooked all the meals for the priests startin' off with fresh coffee every mornin'. Told me how the kitchen had one of two narrow staircases that were built in that house, and that one led up to a sittin' room just off the Reverends' bedrooms.

"Each and every day, she'd bake either a cake or maybe she'd fry fresh donuts and sprinkle powdered sugar on 'em, then maneuver 'em on a tray up that tiny stairwell and set 'em out on a table. Then she'd ring a little bell as a signal, before goin' downstairs.

"She'd start to laugh as she told how two of the priests, when they came downstairs, wore their powdered sugar on their black shirts, tellin' all who'd be seein' 'em of their sweet tooth . . . 'til she dusted 'em off and sent 'em on their way to save more souls. Before they'd leave they always gave her a blessing for her carin' ways.

"She died at ninety-one, God bless her. Well since retired from cleanin' the church and cookin', but continued her pressin' skills on the fabrics, at home as a labor of love, right up to the end.

"Now, my father, Daniel, was actually a jack-of-all-trades, workin' as often as needed, keepin' the kneelers from wobblin', repairin' the furnaces, shovelin' snow and securin' railings leadin' to the choir loft, whenever they became loose."

"Back even further . . . Civil War times, my grandfather, name was Howard and Great Aunt Tessie and Great Uncle Neal, all of them took care of the priests and the parish, same kinda' duties as I just mentioned, plus Aunt Tessie was carin' for the wounded as they'd bring 'em back from the battlefields . . . Johnny Rebs and Union boys alike. Don't know too much about my Grandmother, 'cept her name was Spring . . . pretty unusual name if'n you ask me.

"Gettysburg, Antietam, Hanover, Harper's Ferry . . . they are all around us, and back then at all a' those places, men were fallin' like flies.

"Sad, very sad . . . Neal lost his life on the very same day as the pastor and only priest who'd ever been assigned at that time to Saint John's parish. Ya' see, both of 'em were takin' a horse and buckboard to give out Communion to the troops and help bring back the injured when they themselves were mistakenly ambushed . . . shot dead in their tracks, up around Union Mills."

Maggie's eyes were as big as saucers and her mouth agape.

"Now, Aunt Tessie was with child and didn't know it, but the family helped her, though the baby died after two days. Name on her tombstone says Theresa . . . 'tis why my granddaughter has that name today!

"Why, they hadn't been married too long and I remember readin' one of Uncle Neal's journals. It said that before they got hitched he spent many a night after work pitchin' horseshoes, shootin' marbles and playin' checkers down in the rectory basement with the Reverend, Father Martin Ray . . . or was it Ray Martin, just can't remember . . . my Grandfather Howard, Thaddeus Frank and one or two others."

He puffed up his chest and repeated,

"Yep, I read all about it in one of Uncle Neal's many journals stuffed up there in my attic."

Maggie asked in awe,

"So, this key was from your parents' possessions?"

"No, actually it's from my Grandpa Howard and Grandma Spring's antiques, handed down to my parents and now to me."

"And you're willing to give it to me? Then I *am* honored!

"But, how did you even know I had a key collection?" she queried.

"Do you remember a new customer who came into your business last week, Theresa Anderson?"

"Sure, such a sweet girl . . . Anderson . . . Cully . . . Theresa . . . she's your granddaughter?" Maggie projected, smiling at her discovery.

"Yep, that's my granddaughter, and she told me how kind you were to her and her new puppy, little Bundles. And a'course, your daughter was to her sister, Jennifer, when they were back in high school.

"My little darlin' knew I had a coupl'a old keys. Why, she even cornered me this mornin' while I was shavin', tryin' to convince me.

"A lot like her Grandmother Elizabeth, my wife . . . God rest her soul. Wouldn't take no for an answer.

"So, I decided you would enjoy havin' it, 'specially with so much history attached, and your extensive collection she couldn't stop tellin' me about.

"Look here, this key has a date scratched right on it, right around the curve. It's small, but you can just about make it out.

"You will hang it up there on your wall, right? So my Theresa can see it every time she comes in?"

"Absolutely . . . April 18th, 1865! Wow, just think of the history behind this one!" Maggie said to Cully.

Images of that gothic church unfolded in her mind's eye as she fantasized, becoming more excited about having received the key.

As her perception grew, she became more determined to research both its visual history and anything that he would share with her.

Her thoughts intensified. Why, this key was carried at the time the Civil War was fought and Abraham Lincoln was President!

She contemplated. Now she remembered . . . Lincoln had been assassinated just a few days before that date. Now she wasn't sure. Research . . . yes. I'll have to research that, she thought.

Cully began to excuse himself, to lock up the church, he told her.

"Oh, Mr. Anderson . . . Cully, I must thank you for this wonderful gift!" she said.

"And please, sir . . . what happened to the church. How or why was it destroyed? Surely there are old photographs from your family that captured its beauty? And if you have them, can we get together? Will you show them to me? I . . . I . . . I just have to know more!"

Her thoughts rolled on with a challenge lain at her feet, and since she had never backed down from the chance to investigate any new addition to her collection before, this certainly was not going to be the exception.

# CHAPTER SIX

❧✦❧✦

$\mathcal{M}$aggie found herself sitting across the kitchen table from Cully Anderson only three days later. She had so much to do to prepare for the Grand Opening of the grooming salon in less than two weeks but this meeting took precedence.

He was up and down, nervously looking for snacks of some sort to offer her, but she just wanted to hear more of his story and see pictures . . . as many as possible.

While he searched in the drawers, she noticed he had on creased, dress pants and a crisp, white shirt with sleeves rolled up exactly three times. Yes, she thought, they *are* pressed that way. She chuckled to herself . . . his shoes were probably spit-shined and buffed every day of the week.

As she waited for him to settle in, she took in the whole room. Everything was immaculate and in tip-top shape.

The table had a three-inch wide band of chrome edging, which she imagined must have been as shiny as the first day he bought it. The legs, too, gleamed and were set off by the aqua, vinyl padding on the chairs and the same colored plastic-coated tabletop on which she rested her arms, while sipping a cold Coke through a straw from a short, green bottle.

Along the wall was a metal, freestanding cabinet with enamel shelves, holding a breadbox, which sat adjacent to the sink and drain-board.

Curtains at the windows, which she considered rather frilly for a man's taste, were clean, starched and ironed crisply, waving into deep ruffles against pale, yellow walls, painted with a glossy finish. And on a shelf over the sink were six unfilled ceramic planters. Each one was a little different and each one showed a delicate woman, smartly dressed and coiffed, her delicate face surrounded by pearls and matching earrings, topped by a chic hairstyle and hat, circa 1940's or '50's.

It reminded her of a scene from *Father Knows Best.*

He sat down again, putting a pink, Depression glass bowl filled with potato chips in front of her, and slid a paper napkin front and center.

Cully seemed uncomfortable, and she wondered if it was because he was unaccustomed to entertaining a woman, alone, in his home.

Sheepishly, he grinned and said,

"Couldn't find them old pictures I was lookin' for, might just be at my daughter's. Since my wife died it's hard to find things around here. Got boxes and boxes of old books up there in the attic where I was lookin', from my father, my grandfather and even from my great-grandfather and their wives. Have yet to go through 'em all.

"And papers . . . lordy, I've got papers that go back to the Civil War and beyond. My granddaughter, Jennifer, has been takin' a box at a time back to her house, but she's so busy and there's certainly no rush to go through 'em. They've been sittin' up there all this time."

Maggie interrupted, "Mr. Anderson, er . . . Cully, I hope you don't mind . . . would you mind if I use a tape recorder? It seems if I try to remember everything, my thoughts go into a blur."

"Well I certainly can understand that . . . had my share of thoughts blowin' in the wind. No, you go on, pull it out and I'll do my best to describe the old church and, hey now, wait a minute, I do have a photo. It was taken from the organ loft showin' the Christmas decorations. Can't believe I forgot about that one. I'll be right back. It's upstairs in my Bible."

Maggie set up the device and listened to her previous notes that she entered after their initial meeting outside Saint John's Church.

Three minutes later he was back, with two photos in hand, grinning from ear to ear while unfolding them ever so carefully. One was showing a snapshot of the interior of the old church, and the other, an overview of the parish dated 1910, showing the rectory, church and the school sitting at Main Street, then a dirt road, horses and buggies attesting to that.

"Will ya' look at this . . . can't believe I found both of these. We'll go over the inside, but let me start describing it from the outside first," he said as he put them down, a little to the side of her.

Maggie was captivated and her gut feeling told her this adventure would not be like any other that she had experienced before through her collection of keys.

"Let's see now," he began, "there were four buildings that made up the parish. If you was standin' across the street at Mather's Department Store on Main Street, you'd be seein' the church, between the school to the right and the rectory to the left. See, here they are . . ."

He pointed to each and said,

"Rectory . . . church . . . school. That there is the original school. See how small it was!

"Directly behind the church was our graveyard, and to the left of that was the convent, making up the fourth building. Why, every day you'd see all the nuns walkin', one-by-one in a row through that graveyard, on its windin', cement path, headin' for church to go to Mass early in the mornin' or to say vespers, that is, their night prayers.

"It always tickled me to see them walkin', one behind the other, but especially in the winter after it snowed. Those crisp, black habits and long black gowns zig-zaggin', kinda' looked like they was skatin' against all that white, or maybe like a train, especially with the steam comin' from their mouths and them movin' so fast. Didn't wear coats, just a black shawl. Guess I'd be movin' fast too . . . cold, very cold.

"The rectory was one of the buildings I spent a lot of time in, after my chores that is, just like my 'ol relatives. Down in the lower level they had a dirt floor so we'd have to use a rake to smooth it out and a spade to pat it down.

"Part of it held the 'ol coal bin, but next to it, me and the Reverends would shoot marbles, just like them old timers, and lit by several oil lamps just like they had used, no doubt.

"But a funny thing . . . sometimes I'd be usin' my taw—my shootin' marble as it was called—and I'd pop a marble out of its circle, and then I couldn't find it. Figured I didn't know my own strength and it must've shot into the coal bin. Father and me looked and looked, but it was dark and dusty. Gotta' say, lost quite a few marbles that way. Sure did have me shakin' my head, a'wonderin'!

"Never did get a chance on the next visit to find 'em . . . too busy, figured they went into the furnace with a shovel full of coal. Every once in a while I'd hear a pop or two when she got good and hot, and I'd swear it was one of my favorites that I had lost.

"Somethin' else, they also had pegs driven into the ground, about thirty-five to forty feet apart, so's we could pitch horseshoes. Only problem was, just a little past that peg on either end was a brick wall, and we tried not to fling 'em wild. But every once in a while, that 'ol horseshoe'd be bustin' off a chip of the brick or mortar.

"Well, I'll bet that those nicks are still there . . . that's if they didn't tear down that wall when they built the library. When they tore Saint John's down, the rectory building would have been the last to go, and I never did get to go into that there library building.

"Now back to the church. Here ya' go. See. Kinda' a mixture of designs—'Gothic' on the outside and 'Romanesque' on the inside, I heard it called.

"As you walked up to the double doors and looked up, there was a beautiful stained glass window, and then a steeple with its cross that took it up to one-hundred and eighty-five feet. It seemed colossal to people who had never had anything higher than forty or fifty feet in their neighborhood."

"I guess so," she said.

"When you opened up those big doors, inside was the vestibule, then the baptistery to the right in a little room. Votive lights—you know, the metal stand I told you about—were to the left, next to the confessional. Stairs there, too . . . led on up to a landing, then more steps up to the choir loft, the huge pipe organ and the ninety-foot steeple. Straight ahead were the pews. See, there they are," he said, pointing to the photo.

"In the 1920's, they used to rent pews."

"Rent? A pew . . . rent?" she questioned.

"Oh, families wanted to hold their special pew to sit in every time they came, and paid a sum to do just that. But, they did away with that, back then. Did seem kinda' unfair, didn't it?"

Before Maggie could answer, Cully went on.

"Straight ahead was the altar with two gates that swung open. See all the white marble?

"Italy . . . marble came from Italy. Used to be wooden, that railing, and they shifted it to the gallery way back near the steps that led to the choir loft. We always tried to re-use each and everything we could. Waste not, want not—right?"

She opened her mouth to answer, but Cully continued before Maggie could say a word.

"Ya' know what was really special about St. John's, Maggie? See, look at this. There were no columns or pillars inside. Everybody could see from the back row all the way forward to the altar. It had a tall ceiling, too, but somehow built without pillars. Remember, I started tellin' you about it on Sunday. I never could understand how they could do that, some kinda' arches or somethin."

He flipped over the photo,

"Oh, here it is, the explanation on the back of the photo. I must've written it down before, when somebody explained it, whilst I was tryin' to figure it out.

"Says . . .

*Made of heavy timber which formed a conical frame, cross-braced with heavy wooden beams. Designed so that the vaulted ceiling had no visible supports. The eight-sided surface was covered with thick slate roofing . . .*

"Yeah, that's what it was," he said as he shook his head, satisfied.

"Up in the back, in the choir loft, where this picture was taken, we had one beauty of an organ. The thing cost over ten-thousand dollars, back then. Got it from the Moeller Company. 'Course the gallery loft had to be braced with iron and steel girders, to bear such a great weight from her.

"Somebody said she had two-thousand pipes. Oh, that's right, my friend Charlie told me that. Now, that there is one talented man," he said, veering from the subject.

"When old Charlie played that organ, you thought you died and went to heaven. Why, I was always sure that the angels would be chimin' in at any moment when he tapped those keys just so. Did religious recitals, too! Oh, that's right, he played at the Mass just the other day, so you heard him.

"He always said acoustics were exceptional. In fact, he told me that they were so perfect in that old church, you could hear the priest if he decided to whisper on the altar.

"Now, if you went up the steps from the choir loft you would be all the way up in the steeple, and that there was a great place to see the town. Louvers on all sides to peek through . . . northeast and southwest were the best views . . . all the stores on Main Street and all the people walkin' by. Ya' see, the church faced northwest and if ya' looked farther out about six blocks, and more to the west, you could see Western Maryland College and ol' Baker Chapel sittin' up on the hill.

"If ya' looked out to the south you could see . . . oh, I told you already, the church graveyard and the convent on Green Street. Oh yeah, and also the railroad tracks and bridges over 'em, off to the right. Them tracks would take ya' over towards New Windsor and Union Bridge. Then the train would pull into Hagerstown, two hours later, if'n' you decided to go.

Maggie wasn't exactly following his directions and wondered what it was about men that allowed them to use the compass in their head to visualize east, west, north and south better than she and her friends could. She tried her best to follow.

"Should you wanta' look northwest, well you'd be seein' the top of the Albion Hotel and further out, B. F. Shriver's Cannery and all the rest of the packin' houses. Did ya' know, Carroll County was the first county in the world to produce canned corn? Well, anyway, them canneries would be right next to the train tracks—same tracks as before, but headin' ya' towards the Tannery borough and south into Reisterstown, then to Baltimore, about an hour later.

"Yep, same tracks, just depended on which way the engine was facin'.

"East, well east, on the same side of the street as the church, sat the rectory, then a sewin' factory and then, the fire department.

"Sometimes I would clear out bird feathers, old leaves and such, up there in the steeple . . . be amazed how far I could see.

"The old bell was up there, too. That thing weighed eleven-hundred pounds and it was cast in 1862, I believe, by the Joshua Register Foundry in Baltimore.

"My daddy and granddaddy before him rang that bell for the Angelus, special prayers said three times every day, at 6 in the mornin', 12 noon and then again at 6 in the evenin'.

"People would set their timepieces by them. The story goes, one day my daddy's watch ran slow and he was late ringin' that bell. People came from all over town to tell him about it—that's how much they depended on him.

"Oh, oh yeah, I just remembered what you said the other day, about not bein' Catholic. You probably don't know about those prayers. I'll explain. Whenever the bell rang, at those times, people actually stopped what they were doin' for a minute, bowed their heads, and some knelt down and said the Angelus prayer. Then they resumed their day.

"Not only did he ring the bell each day, he was responsible for shoveling snow and stokin', even repairing the furnace . . ."

Maggie didn't stop him even though she had heard this from him before.

"And repairin' wobbly kneelers.

"Why, he was responsible for keepin' the fires stoked in four locations—the church, rectory, convent and the school. And, it wasn't a matter of just flickin' on a switch on the wall. Oh no, he had to use wood and coal to heat up the places.

"Now, the wood he'd get that from the children in school. In September, he'd ask the students to bring along a piece of wood to school, once or twice a week. Had a spot back near the graveyard where they could pile it up. The children could bring kindlin' or whatever they could find.

"Some of us boys would walk along the railroad tracks and find scraps and some got theirs' on their farm. Branches were always fallin' here and there. Over near the tomato packin' house, up by Shrivers', some of us found old baskets and broke 'em up. Kinda' was fun, jumpin' on 'em and hearin' 'em crackle under your feet. Better have long pants on though, else your shins and ankles got all scraped up.

"By the beginning of October he'd have a fairly good-sized woodpile started, knowin' tweren't gonna be long before he'd be a needin' it.

"All the coal usually came from West Virginia mines, travelin' by railroad cars through track after track, endin' up only one block away from St. John's parish, at the station down the street, through the Western Maryland Railway—that's the one I just described to you a minute ago.

"When those trains of one-hundred cars or more loaded down with coal came through, the earth actually trembled. You could feel it shakin' in the school and in the church, which was only two-hundred feet away from the tracks. Couldn't put your fountain pen in your inkwell, you'd have a mess. Everybody just stopped talkin', 'cause they couldn't be heard . . . so the day just waited for a few minutes.

"Once the train stopped, each coal man hitched up his company wagon, just to the side of the huge coal cars and began shovelin' it into the back. The wagon sunk lower and lower . . . hard, hard work . . . bull work.

"After it was full, our coal man only had to move his horses up the street to St. John's with his big, ol' heavy wagon and deliver to each building.

"They would use a chute aimed into a coal bin to store it, usually in the basement. Together they worked as a team . . . the coal man above, shovelin' into the chute, nuggets bouncin' and rumblin' down that flume, black dust from coal particles fillin' the air and my father, guidin' it with his shovel and slightly movin' the chute to fill up the whole bin. When they finished it would be chock full of that 'black gold', as they called it.

"After that, my daddy would have to start each fire in four furnaces. usin' a wheelbarrow to move the coal around. He'd load up kindlin' from the woodpile, stackin' it just so, crossin' each piece, almost like a nest. Coal was stacked on top and all around it, but not too tight . . . it needed air to go between to create a draft. Fires flame higher if there's a draft.

"Come to think of it, that's probably what did-in old St. John's steeple."

Maggie stopped him.

"St. John's steeple! Was there a fire there?"

"Oh yeah, a humdinger! Why, that flame spread so fast, even the Westminster Fire Department, the one that sat just up the street, couldn't save her. I'm the one who reported it. Why, one minute I was walkin' through the church to oil the hinges on the Communion gates. Then I went out back to cut through the graveyard to go home, walkin' about a block and a half. Don't know why, but I looked back and saw smoke. I actually ran up the street to the fire department as fast as I could. It became a three-alarmer. Engine companies, volunteer and otherwise, were called in. Everybody wanted to help, wanted to save that beautiful church. But it was too late," he said sadly.

"Smoke was so thick, people in the towns of Union Mills, Silver Run, Taneytown and even up at the Mason-Dixon Line at Littlestown, headin' towards Gettysburg, could see the smoke and drove in to see what was on fire. She was a'blazin' alright.

"And, Maggie, it happened right in the middle of the afternoon, just before school let out, back in 1958. Good thing too, why if those children were walkin' up the street when it toppled, who knows what woulda' happened. See, the school was next to the church. As you face it, it would be on your right. It was the closest building to the railroad tracks.

"Am I repeatin' myself? Sorry, been doin' that a lot lately.

"Well, anyway, I'm thinkin' the wax residue they found after the fire was from them candles that sat in that votive contraption, with the little glass cups. And the air just fanned it, took the flames from the bottom level right on up and through, shootin' out through the slates or louvers, high up in the steeple.

"That huge steeple, 'course you can't see it on this picture, but it was towerin' into the sky, 'twas what did most of the harm. The granite pinnacles too. They were close to the base of the steeple, did a lot of damage, almost like four powerful arrows bein' shot straight down as it fell. Horrible, just horrible."

"It was there one minute, then a huge burst of flames shot up, some say as high as fifty feet, and she began to tumble. I saw it . . . standing right down the street from it. I screamed and then I cried, yep, I cried," he said with a melancholic voice.

"I remember sayin', 'Oh Lord, please don't let this be true.' But it was . . . it was."

"Oh, it must have been unbelievable," Maggie sadly agreed.

"It was, it was, but," his voice brightened, "on an up note, one miracle for sure . . . Monsignor Bollinger . . . every day, sat outside in the afternoon, took a little breather, and said the rosary. Now, it was just pure luck, I say, that he was not catchin' a little nap there like he done so often when he finished his prayers. Many a day I'd seen him with crossed arms on the table, his head restin' on 'em, catchin' twenty winks. 'Specially the way the afternoon sun came through and with a soft breeze that spun through the buildings. Warm and cool at the same time. It was his perfect hideaway.

"His mother was visitin' that day and called him inside to the kitchen. While he was in there, the fire started and the steeple toppled. And get this . . . it smashed through his bedroom and out directly across the spot where he usually sat, crushin' the metal table and chairs. Whew!

"Can you imagine if you was him? Seein' all of the destruction of your church and then seein' that exactly, not six inches one way or the other, but exactly, where you parked yourself every day, flattened to the ground. Some said the devil was after him. I say, God protected him by gettin' his butt up and outta' there and just in the nick of time. Lord, don't take ya' if you got more to do on this earth, and he must've had plenty more to do."

"Oh my God," she said, "what an incredible story!"

He kept going,

"After the fire was out, I got to go into the church. Yeah, ya see, they only let a couple of us who were mighty active at St. John's and Monsignor Bollinger trudge inside with the Fire Inspector, who watched over us. Maggie, it broke my heart!

"Charred ashes, singed pews, at least what was left of 'em and wet, soppy linens were strewn throughout.

"When the steeple fell, it crushed the organ loft and stairs and destroyed rows and rows of the pews and kneelers.

"It kept fallin' through the church on an angle. Amazingly, it missed the stained glass windows, but crushed the wall between two of them. And these," he said, as he pointed to objects dotted on the walls throughout the building, "these Stations of the Cross, the originals from the church of the 1860's, made in Germany around the mid 1700's. As big as they are, four feet by six feet, weren't even touched. Fourteen of 'em, and not a one was destroyed. Made of horsehair and wood paste and fastened to the wall with wooden pegs and heavy wire. I was surprised that they didn't scorch or crumble from the heat.

"See here, on the back of this Christmas photo, my beautiful wife Elizabeth, God rest her soul, wrote this . . ."

Maggie scrolled down and read aloud to him with great interest and anticipation, pausing as she spoke to visualize these things she had never seen before . . .

"Stations of the Cross, Munich, Germany, mid-1700's. Fourteen tableaus, four feet by six feet, each with twelve, eighteen and twenty-four inch statues within the interior box; some protruding six to twelve inches, creating a three-dimensional design. Depicts the story of the Condemnation, Passion and Crucifixion of Jesus Christ. Although made of horsehair for strength and wood paste for pliability, in creams, tans and other natural tones, in 1930 they were hand-painted by a liturgical artist, Piccolino.
They were classic examples of Gothic gables, pinnacles and pinnacles surrounded by removable finials and crockets topped off by a centered cross."

"Yes sir," he said, "That's exactly the way I'd say it, 'cept I'd be callin' it—all except for the cross mind ya'—yep, I'd be callin it gingerbread. Ya' know, all that fussiness up and around the top and sides. Most important part of it all ain't their trimmins,' but it's what inside and the look on them faces on the statues. Why, it just about breaks your heart seein' the pain and such on them figurines, lookin' so real.

"But, of all that was damaged, *the* most important, was the tabernacle. It was safe!

"Oh yeah, and the marble Communion railin' and the sanctuary lamp with its huge candle within was untouched, too. Wax melted all through the lamp parts though, and some hardened in long streams. Looked like somethin' from a horror movie.

"Smoke went into the vestry and all the vestments for the priests and the altar boys. Their cassocks and surplices had smoke damage and had to be tossed.

"See that pulpit, all made of twisted wrought iron rods? Kinda' matched the votive holder. Didn't melt or anything, but it was still warm to the touch, days later. 'Course, it was a hot day when we went inside," he reflected.

"But, the worst, and I can still smell it today, was the stench that the fire and its aftermath created, so full of death and destruction. In a Catholic church, usually there is a light, fragrant scent that floats through the air—the candles, flowers and incense. It almost hypnotizes you and once you smell it, it never leaves your memory. But, no more, no more," he said, as he shook his head from side to side, very slowly.

Maggie sat with her mouth opened, in awe of the story he was presenting. She had no idea there was so much of an unusual tale behind the old church of St. John's Parish, and the key, now *her* key. But she was very willing to hear it all, and she gave him her undivided attention.

"The Monsignor had a crew come in to see if they could save the church. The old-timers wanted to fix her up, save her, but they had to tear her down, yep, tear her down. When that clam bucket hit her again and again—excuse me, that wreckin' ball—tons of slate fell to the floor. It was like our hearts were bein' torn out . . . felt like I was bein' crushed every time it hit." His eyes began to fill as he pulled out a perfectly pressed handkerchief, blew his nose and said,

"Very emotional!

"We all cried. All of us, men and women alike, just cried when we got the news and then seein' it happenin' was ten times worse, seein' her ripped apart, I mean.

"And then, we had to build a new church. There wasn't any real money, not enough for a church like this with such fine detail," he said, smacking at the photo with the back of his hand.

"Back in the 1860's, the stone masons, painters and the like who settled here from Europe, agreed to work on the church . . . did all of the fine finishin' and then donated their work to boot.

"So, the powers that be decided on a modern church, cheaper, but certainly not better. Low ceilings, more efficient for air-conditionin', which we never had on Main Street, just sweated through the summer. Modern architecture, less costly, fewer statues, smaller windows.

"Everything was down-scaled.

"They kept sayin' this is all we could afford, but we all thought, just maybe, someday, we'll build another church like the St. John's that we knew and loved."

"How sad," Maggie said.

"Yep, and I forgot to tell ya'. Before they tore her down, we had to find a place for all the parts of the church that wouldn't fit in that modern building. Some went into the basement of the rectory, but only as an emergency holding spot.

"A man over in Manchester bought the marble altar rail. The front doors went to a winery, up near Silver Run. Two gates went to somebody on Mayberry Road, and other pieces of marble were divided up amongst parishioners. The Tabernacle lamp and chain and the pulpit went to St. Bartholomew's over in the town of Manchester, Maryland. Still in that church today.

"One lady that I know, Lucy, who lives up in Frizzellburg, paved a complete walkway from the street to her house using Saint John's bricks. Hauled 'em away herself.

"All the donations collected for these things went to the building fund of the new church, it's true, the round one we use today. But, I'll tell ya' one thing, some of us got mighty protective of her old parts, especially seein' her bein' taken apart.

"I salvaged a couple of altar cloths, although scorched and charred a bit . . . figured my mother probably put her hand to em', ironin' and foldin'. Tell ya' the truth, we used one of 'em. Actually, I gave one of the smaller ones to Jennifer to carry on her weddin' day.

"Packed away in the attic, I got a couple of candle holders, partially melted and lookin' kind of misshapen, and one block of marble. I'll pull 'em out and show you sometime.

"Then there were the bigger pieces that had to be stored. Ya' had to have lots of room.

"The stained glass windows are packed up real tight in my friend Lester's barn. Two angel statues, the wrought iron votive stand, the big, outdoor Nativity set, and the fourteen Stations of the Cross went to . . .

"Say, that's who you need to talk to. He's got to have old photos of St. John's. His family has been involved in St. John's church from the very beginnin', standing side-by-side with mine. Earlier when I mentioned Thaddeus Frank being a friend to my Great Uncle Neal and my Grandfather Howard and the three of them gettin' together with the Reverend from St. John's way back when the Civil War was goin' on, I just didn't give my own friend a thought or a mention to ya', though he's Thaddeus Frank's great-nephew!

"He's been an usher 'bout as long as I have, too. Tell you what. I'll call him and tell him to make time for you. Very busy; farm, produce business and all. But, I think he'll want to talk to you, Maggie.

"His name is Thomas Frank."

# CHAPTER SEVEN

❧❦❧❦

## JULY 1966

## A FEW DAYS LATER

𝓜aggie Fischer was anxious to find out more about the old St. John's Church and ready to investigate its history, now that she owned an original key for her collection.

It was intriguing to compile stories about each key's background, thinking about who owned it and what part it had played in history.

She had a good start on this one, having met with Cully Anderson, the owner of the old key. Now, with his help, she would find out more, perhaps through photographs. At the very least, she would hear about his friend's story.

How did that church touch the lives of this new family she was about to meet—the Thomas Frank family—and perhaps the whole town, the very town that she, her husband and daughter were living in?

And, to think that her key had been around since the 1860's when President Lincoln walked this earth. Why, that boggled her mind even more.

Yes, this time she just knew she could paint a more complete picture, with Thomas Frank's help, that is. But just how much could he, or would he, tell her?

Never knowing just where her lead would take her, as she cautiously walked up to the cottage she started to take it all in.

The path had cracked cement that was raised and lowered most probably from the previous winter's freeze and thaw. She noticed that great detail had originally been given to the gardens interspersed with natural stones though now, partially buried. Plants had become overdeveloped, creating mostly greens with very sparse, leggy flowers—the cottage was surrounded by overgrown perennials, evergreens and intertwined ivy sprouts—and any sense of a planned design of the yews was now lost in broken branches.

Through the open window, she heard a woman singing along to Dean Martin's hit from a few years before—'Everybody Loves Somebody'. She listened to the melody coming from a talented voice and hummed along. As the singing continued, Maggie sensed a house that had been created out of love and warmth and with no pretense.

Quietly, she turned around and viewed the images that this family could see each time they walked from their house to this spot on the porch. At the end of a dirt and gravel road she saw a huge barn jutting high into the sky. It was bigger than any which she had seen throughout Carroll County.

As Maggie turned and knocked, the radio volume became barely discernable, and a woman appeared. She introduced herself as Mrs. Frank and invited Maggie into the parlor.

After she motioned where Maggie should sit and glanced back over her shoulder once or twice, she called to her husband.

A huge, old regulator clock, like one she had seen at Penn Railroad Station in Baltimore, ticked in precise movement as she viewed her surroundings. Most of the furniture was oak and all of it was mismatched, but comfortable. The sofa's thick cushions invited a body to sink into them and were covered in beige twill with a burgundy-flecked print, which peeked through doilies that covered the back and the arm rests.

A channel-back chair with claw feet flanked the sofa while its wrap-around arms suggested a comforting spot to land. Odd lights, mimicking oil lamps, strayed far from the originals and a drum table waited across the room for a chair to be its partner. Displayed atop it in crowded, unmatched frames were photos of four boys ranging from infancy to manhood. The photo that was closest and therefore she thought probably the most recent showed Mrs. Frank with four men in various poses in front of a Christmas tree.

An ancient Victrola in a tall cabinet with carved edges stood next to the archway leading to the dining room, where odd chairs of varying height flanked the oak pedestal table. Light showed through the crocheted lace tablecloth, which hung down too far, and a bowl of waxed fruit sat upon it. Scatter rugs appeared throughout, underfoot at the sofa as well.

A bit of country, she thought, but that's what drew Maggie to land in Westminster. She liked the real feeling she got from the people who lived there—unpretentious, warm, friendly people—that's what she looked for when she and her husband moved there from the city. It wasn't what you had, but who you were and how you cared about your neighbor that mattered.

They had looked around for two years, on and off, but when they stopped at that last, *For Sale* sign, she knew she could make a life there in Carroll County.

Now it was her time. She was giving up her "book," her clients. Hairstyling had been good to her for thirty years and helped to send Gretchen, through college; but after the last big raise, her husband Jim's job was going to be able to support them comfortably.

Of course, once a hairdresser always a hairdresser. People still wanted to know if she made house calls. It did cross her mind, and she thought maybe she would once in a while, but only for special people that she really liked. After all, she would be with them steadily if she went to their homes, not intermingling two or three appointments at once, like the scheduling in a salon.

She nixed the idea and would continue to concentrate on remodeling her house to make room for Gretchen's venture, the dog grooming business. It would be great to spend more together time as her manager and receptionist, at least in the beginning, until she got it going.

"Sounds like fun," said Gretchen when she had approached her with the idea. Maggie loved dogs, all dogs, and they liked her. She had more wet noses nuzzle up to her than most people had in three lifetimes. And cats—they adored her. Whenever she heard people say how aloof cats were, she couldn't understand it because her friends' cats were always playful with her when she visited.

But, at least for now, Gretchen's business was strictly for grooming dogs, and Maggie was as excited as was her daughter. The house remodeling was coming along nicely—her transformation was working and the new entrance was almost finished.

All of her keys looked even more interesting with the new walls in place, and when Maggie would leave here today, she would be anxious to hang up the key from Cully Anderson that she had brought to show Thomas Frank, as promised.

She wondered why he would want to see the old key, but followed instructions to the letter, especially since he was as generous as he had been to see her so quickly.

Maggie was glad Cully Anderson had contacted this man to make the initial connection for her and was anxious and ready to meet him.

"Thank you for taking the time to share your memories with me," Maggie said to Thomas Frank as he walked toward her wearing heavy work boots, khaki pants and a tattersall plaid shirt.

He was ruggedly handsome, but not with perfect features. In fact, his nose tilted and his upper lip was much fuller than the bottom. Sandy brown hair mixed with grey had been sun-bleached and tousled, revealing a less than perfect haircut, but his clean-shaven face and the aroma of after-shave signaled that he had prepared to meet this woman that Cully had called him about, this Maggie Fischer.

She stood and outstretched her hand, which he took awkwardly, then lightly squeezed the tips of her four fingers. Such a strong man, whose frame of six feet, three inches, balanced by broad shoulders and a full chest, told her he could easily have given her a bone crushing handshake. But he was too sensitive of women's genteelness to deliver that, she thought.

And he proved her right by the way he walked with her, then motioned that she should take a seat while he sat adjacent in the channel-back chair, looking at her, straight on, trying to read her. He seemed so light on his feet, for such a big man. Maggie visualized him on the dance floor, maybe just a few years before.

"Cully Anderson explained that you were researchin' an old key that he gave you. He's my buddy—been together all our lives.

"What, an old key for a collection of some sort? Said it's from our old St. John's Church that had been downtown. Now, I didn't know he had that old key, although everythin' scattered when they tore down the place. Let me see it. You did bring it?"

Thomas' question was more like a statement.

Maggie produced the iron key from her purse. He took it from her and while looking it over a big, crooked smile crossed his lips.

"Oh, you've got the actual, old, original key! I see scratched right on here, though ever so small, 1865, just as clear as a bell!"

"Hey, wait a minute, why . . . what? . . . April 15<sup>th</sup>, 1865? Oh, I see, the date scratched on it was the day President Lincoln died and not the date that the church was opened; at least, that would be my guess.

He squeezed it tightly and touched it to his chin, while he reminisced,

"Such a beautiful church . . . steeped with so much tradition. So much of my family's history took place inside those walls. Humph, inside. I should say inside, outside, around and through those walls."

Her eyes squinted into a puzzled look. She said,

"What do you mean?"

"Before that church was ever built in the 1860's, well wait, here, I'm gonna' show you somethin'," he said as he walked briskly out of the room.

When he got up to leave, Mrs. Frank, who was making lemonade in the kitchen and listening to bits and pieces of their conversation, stopped to see what he was going for. He seemed anxious to comply with this stranger's needs—this slim, trim, younger visitor with perfect hair and make-up, whom she had never seen before.

She heard him fumbling through heavy books which produced a weighty thud while he re-stacked them.

He reappeared with several old scrapbooks of sorts. Some were bound with woven yarn, threaded through holes and tied to retain the pages, but others were bound books. All were very fragile; full of what she thought must be acidic paper. She had once heard an old-timer, who was a collector, say that old books with acidic paper resemble a smoldering fire inside, gradually burning themselves away. Without even being touched, the paper pages flake into oblivion, taking the written or photographic contents with them. Some of his books had that burnt brown appearance but were still intact. She felt uneasy touching them, knowing her touch could increase the probability of their destruction, but nevertheless followed his lead.

"Mr. Frank, I'm wondering if you would mind if I used a tape recorder for our meeting?

"Cully, er, Mr. Anderson didn't object and I was able to keep my notes straight."

"It's okay by me," he said.

# CHAPTER EIGHT

❧❦❧❦

𝒜s he gently laid back the cover of the scrapbook, there were hand-written notes and dates and a photo of a handlebar-mustached man standing next to a wagon full of bricks and a six-pack of mules that would have been pulling as a team. The picture was faded and somewhat crackled, and it was dated 1865.

Thomas puffed out his chest, cocked his head up and pointing with Maggie's key, he said,

"This here's my Grandfather Jed—Jedidiah Thomas Frank Sr., that is, on my father's side. Was a stone mason and owned a farm, six miles north of here, near Bachman Valley. The bricks you're seein' there, they were used to build that old church you're talkin' about. And, let me tell you somethin' about those bricks—*all* baked on that farm, 500,000 of 'em. I can just imagine the back-breakin' job of firin' up them bricks just so, then stackin' 'em on his wagon, hitchin' up the mules and then slowly bringin 'em to Main Street where they were unloaded and stacked for the masons puttin' her together. Half a million of them bricks!

"He wrote about how long it took in a notebook, but the papers got wet and the ink smeared . . . still got it though, up in the attic. There's nobody around anymore who read the thing so we just keep passin' down as much as we know and, sad to say, it ain't much. Wish I'da paid attention, to my mother—her name was Diana—when she was tellin' us all about it. Why, she could remember details about my father's family more than he could."

Thomas shook his head reminiscing while turning the page.

"Course I can't complain, I still have a few journals listin' other bits of background about him and other relatives.

"Just how much do you want to know, Miss Maggie?" He asked, massaging the key with the fingers from his other hand.

"Oh, just as much as you will share. You see, Mr. Frank, I have this key collection, the one Cully Anderson mentioned to you, and it's from all over the world. And, well, here are some pictures of it," she said as she pulled photos from her purse, letting him see both the close-ups and the full-view of over two hundred keys hanging on two walls she referred to as her gallery.

"Well, I'll be. Why keys?" he asked.

"I began gathering them almost thirty years ago. At first it was a way to fill up some wall space, but as soon as I started realizing the history behind them, I got hooked. My imagination took over. I began to think about the stories they could tell, if only they could talk. Just think of the great people who had them in their hands and took them wherever they went."

"True. Never thought about that, but you've got a point there. And just which ones are your favorites in the collection?"

Maggie was off, doing what she loved, telling the tales.

"One of my favorites, in my assortment to date, I got when I went to Paris. I negotiated with the innkeeper to keep my room key. Several francs and some pleading on my part captured a quizzical 'yes', although he shrugged his shoulders, obviously unsure why I would want it.

"That old place was originally from the eighteen hundreds. It sat only a few kilometers from Notre Dame Cathedral, across the Seine River. The fountain just down the block, at the main square, was shown in an old history book I had read. It had posts with rings attached to tie up horses while they drank from it. No doubt, it was the meeting place for the counts and countesses on their way to other parts of Paris.

"I arrived on May 1st, during their May Day celebration. Flowers were being sold on every corner of the street and everyone carried bouquets to give to their loved ones. I bought three bunches, not thinking about containers so I borrowed old milk bottles from the kitchen help. They became our vases, filling the room with fragrance and color."

As she rambled on about France, Thomas vaguely listened, but was disinterested in quite so many details, scanning his pages before him for the particulars that he wanted to discuss.

She informed him, "Why, I've got one key from Williamsburg that dates back to 1769, when it was still the capital of the Crown Colony. And I found out it fit an old trunk that belonged to one of the original families that settled there."

Now *that* he heard, and it captured his attention as he stopped scanning and looked at her finger pointing to the photo of one of the many treasures on her walls.

"Another key, my daughter acquired while at college in Delaware . . . came from an old farm on the Eastern Shore, across the way from Easton, Maryland. That one was from a dreary old tunnel, honeycombed with subterranean passages that emptied into nearby fields with an iron gate at its opening, hidden with brush and brambles. The lady she got it from told her that old mine was used to hide the slaves, many of 'em meetin' up with Harriet Tubman as they escaped during the Civil War, and the reason she knew all about it was because the passage was on her property. Her daughter roomed with Gretchen, my daughter, who did some part-time work for her. She helped her care for her bird collection, parrots and cockatiels, during her semester breaks from college. That woman gave the key to Gretchen for me, once she told her about my hobby.

"Isn't that great?" Maggie rattled on, unable to withhold her excitement.

Thomas was interested now. If there's one thing he liked it was American history, and this woman was bringing it to him in bits and pieces, with a unique twist and with real enthusiasm, but he wanted to show her his history, and that of St. John's Church.

"I see, I see. Well, let me turn the page, okay Miss Maggie?" He began, "This is an old picture of the church showin' the horses and buggies parked across from it. Not sure of the age, but it had to be before 1910 because Main Street was still a dirt road."

"Why, it's beautiful," she stated as her brown eyes viewed the picture, the same photo that Cully had shown her. She decided that old St. John's was almost like a mini-cathedral which surprised her considering the small farm-town it was nestled within. She saw a very symmetrical building with double doors and a steeple reaching far into the sky, with a cross atop it, just like Cully Anderson had said. In fact, it almost duplicated the size of the base of the building it sat upon. High in its eaves were slats to view the town through, she remembered.

Thomas saw her touch the slates where the bell sat.

"Bell inside there weighed eleven-hundred pounds. When that bell rang, all of Westminster knew it," he said.

In all, Maggie felt it was a perfect replica of any church she had ever seen in a Christmas garden, finished in complete detail and traditional in its shape and size, except for that oversized, towering steeple.

Thomas began explaining,

"Trees dotted the property, but that church dwarfed 'em. This is the way it was set up. The rectory sat to its left and the school to its right. See those school windows—we used to watch the train go by, less than two hundred feet away, for two of the four times a day it passed in the 1930's and '40's.

"Came through with cargo, coal mostly, from West Virginia and Western Maryland. Picked up crops here in town and took 'em in towards Baltimore to be put on the ships at the harbor for ports far, far away.

"Had a hard time hearin', either in school or in church, when she chugged by."

She remembered Cully saying that.

"Whoever was speakin', nun or priest, had to be quiet and wait it out. The train had to pick up speed to make it over the slight incline right at Main Street, so the noise became more intense. She'd been trackin' through town since Civil War days. Actually, was used to haul Union troops and supplies up to Westminster, and then they'd fill up wagons to get 'em to Gettysburg. Very important depot for the Civil War. She was part of the Western Maryland Railroad. Bet you'd like a key from one of those times. In fact . . ."

Before he could finish his sentence, she butt in,

"Oh yes, I would. Any really old keys just stir my imagination. Mr. Frank, another key I bought came from a jail in Harper's Ferry, West Virginia, from around the time of John Brown's raid. It's amazing, don't you think, just how much Civil War history is right here in our own backyard. I guess I feel privileged to own a part of our nation's heritage, even if it is only a key."

His voice rose with impatience and forcefulness,

"As I started to tell ya', you think *that's* somethin'—one of *my* relatives, Great Uncle Thaddeus on my father's side, was involved in the Lincoln funeral train procession right here in Maryland. Why, I've got a picture of him right here."

Maggie remembered Cully mentioning that name—Thaddeus.

Thomas Frank carefully turned the page to expose a man dressed in a railroad uniform and flat topped cap. A chain from what would be a pocket watch was visible, but what was in his hand caught Maggie's eye . . . a ring of keys!

"Mr. Frank, do you have any of those keys from Thaddeus' belongings?" Maggie asked, excitedly, pointing to the ring.

"I'm, I'm not sure . . . I'd, I'd have to think on it," he replied as he handed her key back to her hurriedly, sensing where she might be going.

"Well, if you do, please think of me. I'd love to have it. I'll buy it from you for my collection," she said, obviously without much thought.

Just then the telephone rang on the buffet in the next room and Mrs. Frank retrieved it.

"Sell it, why I don't think so, but . . ."

Thomas' attention was torn between Maggie Fischer and the sounds he heard his wife mumbling.

"Did you say? You did say, Lincoln, President Lincoln's funeral train?" Maggie asked as the words sank into her brain in questioning disbelief as she turned her attention from the key ring to look at Thomas.

His head turned back and forth, his thoughts interrupted.

"Ah, er yes, you heard me alright, and I'm about to tell ya' how it all came about. Uncle Thaddeus was an able-bodied young man with a few dollars to his name about to serve in the Civil War, but instead he hired a substitute and paid three hundred dollars so he didn't have to . . ."

"Thomas, Thomas," Mary Kathleen, his wife, intruded, nervously calling his name. "Come quickly, it's Mr. Codday, the lawyer from Pittsburgh, about Uncle Jay."

"Uncle Jay? Why I just left him three days ago, full of smiles and teasin' in his usual way. What could be goin' on?

"'Scuse me, Miss Maggie," he said as he slipped the book onto Maggie's legs, and he was off to take the receiver from his wife.

Maggie was left holding the old, tattered, golden-paged book and faced Uncle Thaddeus and his key ring. She had never heard about Civil War substitutes or the details of President Lincoln's funeral procession and just knew Mr. Frank could tell her the whole story. Patiently she waited, the keys on the ring continuing to stir her vivid imagination, conjuring thoughts of the railroad man and his part in history.

But before she could formulate too many ideas, suddenly, Mrs. Frank re-appeared and said,

"Maggie, we've just heard some bad news. My husband's Uncle Jay is very ill, possibly in critical condition. Thomas is very close to him, like his own son, he is. He lives in Pittsburgh so I know we'll be goin' out there today to see exactly what we can do for him. Why, if he dies it'll be like Thomas is losin' his own father, 'stead of his uncle."

Maggie sat the book down and its pages fluttered open to another spot, as she stood.

"I am so sorry. Please don't worry about me. But, what can I do? Can I do anything here at the farm? The animals . . . I've got a dog grooming business. Can I call anyone for you?"

"No, no, my nephews, I've got four of 'em, will stay at the house and take care of the animals. But, my, you are kind to offer to help us out."

Maggie left after being shown to the door by Mary Kathleen Frank, although she felt there was more she wanted to do.

Determined to help, she went home, sat the key on the mantle, and quickly whipped up a cinnamon-topped coffee cake, drizzled with butter, which needed only thirty minutes to bake. As it cooled, Maggie prepared a basket with cloth napkins and brewed a huge thermos of coffee. She wrapped the cut squares in waxed paper and neatly filled the tote with about twenty-four pieces of cake.

She thought she might be too late when she appeared at the Franks' door, basket in hand, but Thomas hadn't left. He awkwardly accepted it and a crooked smile of surprise changed the anxious expression she had immediately noticed on his face as he opened the door.

"These are for you . . . to take along," Maggie said.

"Thanks," was all he could say, obviously touched by this stranger's thoughtful gesture.

As the door shut, he looked down at the thermos and the cake and suspiciously wondered why someone he had just met would be so nice to him.

Whoa, so many strange things have been happening to me lately, he thought. He remembered pulling into the rest stop three days before, on his way home from Uncle Jay's. He recalled the feeling that came over him . . . haunting, eerie, and almost seductive and the sounds that surrounded him, light and melodic. He was sure it was the wind blowing through the trees, but none stirred. Then he thought he saw movement, heard a voice, quiet, yet powerful,

*"Build that new church, Thomas. Build it just as you dreamed it should be. Build it big, just as big as the money will allow. Bide your time, Thomas. There is a plan."*

Yes, all of that happening, and now here comes this stranger into my life who is asking me to bring up all of the old history of Saint John's. Showin' me a key, askin' me some questions I haven't thought about for eight years.

I swear, when I took that key into my hands a little while ago, I felt electricity flowin' through, but I put that thought off, said to myself, no way!

Can't wait to tell Uncle Jay, what's been goin' on. He's the only one I can tell it to, won't think I'm crazy.

He started to analyze. Could it be . . . could it be the right time to start . . . but it might be . . . no, no, not enough money . . . not enough money.

Her voice startled him, and he jumped as he heard,

"What'cha got there?" asked Mary Kathleen as Thomas put the thermos and all of the wrapped goodies onto a table. "That *woman* brought them back to you?

"Wow, you must have made a good impression."

Thomas didn't answer her as he ripped sheets of paper from his tan pocket journal and began to write instructions about the business for his nephews. He headed for the stairs to pack.

Mary Kathleen assumed she would be going along to Pittsburgh, but before she could follow him, he said,

"Give these papers to Michael and tell the boys to watch over the business 'til I get back. All the numbers are there for him to call for back-up."

"But . . . but, Thomas, I thought I would be going with you." she said.

"Now you know you've got to take care of the boys. I'll be back as soon as I can," he said matter-of-factly, and up the stairs he flew.

Although she said no more, Mary Kathleen sighed sadly and went back into the kitchen, taking both containers and the papers along. She began to pack a couple of sandwiches for him and again spied the thermos and coffee cake from Maggie Fischer.

"Won't be needin' all of these, now that I'm not goin' along," she said aloud and then opened one square of cake and gobbled it up. Hmmm, pretty good, she thought, as she opened another and unconsciously popped pieces into her mouth while packing her basket for Thomas.

A few minutes later he was in the kitchen ready to go. He scribbled a note, ripped it out of the same journal which he re-stuffed deep into his back pocket, and gave it to her. As she looked at it she was disappointed; all it had on it were additional specifics for the business.

"I'll call you just as soon as I find out what's goin' on," he said.

Mary Kathleen started puckering up her lips to kiss him good-bye, but instead, he gave her a quick peck on the forehead, turned and, with a slam of the screen door, was gone.

She sighed her sad sigh again, moistened her fingers and hen-pecked them on the waxed paper finishing off the crumbs left behind.

# CHAPTER NINE

🙟🙟🙟🙟

𝒪ℳary Kathleen thought about what Thomas had said, 'Take care of the boys.' Humph, the boys are men and can take care of themselves, she thought. After all, she had raised them since they were orphaned as little boys many years before, and she had taught them to be self-sufficient.

She began to reminisce . . . before they came, oh, before they came, how different it was then.

Thomas and she had time for each other, whenever they wanted it. Even with the farm chores, sometimes during the day, they made time to be together. And, on the weekends . . . how she looked forward to their weekends.

During the winter, they would drive to one of the grain mills nearby. She would use the chute for an ice slide, slipping down its turns to the bottom where Thomas would catch her flying off its edge.

During a hard freeze, they would join in the merriment of ice skating on a pond, which Mary Kathleen would try haphazardly, then fall into Thomas' arms, flirting and smiling into his eyes. Sometimes they would just listen to the radio, curled up in a blanket together, laughing at *The Bob Hope Show* or *Fibber McGee and Molly*.

When the weather was more agreeable, on Saturday nights they would drive into Westminster and park their truck along Main Street, joining many of their friends. They would catch up on the latest news and join in the ritual of walking hand-in-hand or arm-in-arm along a few blocks dotted with retail businesses on one side of the street and St. John's Catholic Church, the train station, a sewing factory and the fire department across from them. Sometimes they would buy a fountain Coke at the Rexall Drug Store for three cents, walk into, G. C. Murphy's Five and Ten Cent Store, or dream about owning a new Buick from the Davis Company as they walked by the showroom.

There were plays to be seen at the Opera House, movies like *Casablanca,* starring Bogie, at the State Theater. She remembered how these were always good for an arm around her shoulder. Thomas would buy a pack of Chesterfields for fifteen cents at the Smoke Shop and would light up as we walked along. She visualized herself and Thomas. He was tall, slim and broad shouldered and her figure was dainty and slender, her blond hair swept up and off her face. Red lipstick in a perfect bow and Max Factor rouge transformed the farm woman into a vision of loveliness.

She could still hear that clickety-clack of her high heels on the brick pavement as the echo ricocheted off the tunnel-like walls of the corridor leading to the rear of the Main Street businesses. Back there were the stairs that led up to Beard's, where they danced the night away to the music of a nickelodeon.

That stimulated the memory of driving west to Frederick to hear a special band. She had to chuckle as she remembered what happened toward the end of the night.

Some of the band members had been drinking, but the base fiddle player got drunk as a skunk. Right in the middle of a hot number, he suddenly disappeared . . . fell off the back of the stage and kept right on playin' while lyin' on his back. Everybody roared.

She giggled as her thoughts continued to drift back while she glided over to the old Victrola and put on a record. As she heard the tune, 'Take the "A" Train', with its upbeat tempo, definitely from the Swing era, she smiled, remembering. After rolling up the area rug, she started to jiggle and jive, the steps returning to her feet like it was yesterday instead of twenty years before, bringing more and more happy visions to light.

It seemed like the pace of the music was faster than it was yesterday though, and when it was over she was winded. She changed the record to something mellow.

Her mind pictured the entire chain of events as she heard the haunting strains of Artie Shaw's 'Stardust' . . . their song. Thomas took her by the hand and led her onto the floor. He spun her around, grabbing just the very tips of her fingers as he looked her up and down, ending by pulling her to him. They swayed in unison, their bodies close, the aroma of his Old Spice aftershave drifted back from her subconscious. He'd look into her eyes and, winking, he would say, "Let's get out of here."

Flying quickly behind him, she went down the stairs and out to the truck, where he grabbed her for a lingering kiss before starting the vehicle.

While she remained in a dreamlike state, the needle on the record player came full center, creating a swishing sound as it hit the paper label on the record, again and again, bringing her back to reality.

But, that was before the boys came, she thought. She walked over to remove the record and glanced into the kitchen, remembering how she had made formula and filled bottles. There, not far from the sink and stove was the basement door leading to the washer, where she had cleaned their diapers, shirts, pants and underwear and hung them outside to dry. Then, there was the cooking, canning and cleaning for four growing boys. It was no wonder she'd fall into bed exhausted after they came.

After turning off the Victrola and replacing the handle on its miniature stand, she unrolled the rug and walked into the hall area.

The mirror froze Mary Kathleen's reflection, which she had not taken time to study recently. She was no longer dainty and slender. Her hair, now graying, gave the blond an ashen appearance, and there were no red lips, pouty or otherwise. Her clothes were full and loose and one shoe had the back squished down. It was if she was seeing herself for the very first time.

She quickly pivoted from the mirror trying to erase the vision she had just witnessed, but to no avail. Into the kitchen she walked, grabbed two more pieces of coffee cake, dreamily sighed and shook her head in disgust. Her mind's eye saw Thomas on his way to Pittsburgh, and she popped a whole piece of cake into her mouth, making her cheeks puff out. As she carried the other wrapped piece through the hall, she kept her head down, avoiding the mirror. Then she went up the stairs, entered her bedroom and slammed the door.

# CHAPTER TEN

❧❦❧❦

$\mathcal{O}$he next morning Mary Kathleen followed her normal ritual. She made two huge pots of coffee and doubled her pancake recipe to accommodate the extra helpers that had come to fill in since Thomas was away in Pittsburgh.

Her nephew, Michael, who ran the produce delivery part of the business, liked to start off his day early at about 5 a.m. with a breakfast meeting while he gave out the daily rosters. By the time they loaded up the trucks, they made it to their destinations by 9 a.m.

When they cleared out, Mary Kathleen looked at the huge pile of dishes and silverware just like she did every other morning and began washing, drying and putting them away. As she did, she wondered why she couldn't have gone with Thomas to Pittsburgh the night before.

Humph! These men can make their own coffee and buy a doughnut or two for their breakfast meetings, she thought.

She resented being stuck at home with all the household duties, especially now that the boys were men.

It was different when they *were* boys and first came to live with them back in 1947. And although she loved Thomas' nephews like they were her own, they all fell into her lap at once, changing her life and her husband's forever.

The news was shocking. Both of them—Thomas' brother, Michael, and his sister-in-law, Lillian, parents to four boys—had been killed in an auto accident.

Thomas decided the four boys would come to live with them, and she agreed, but what choice did she have? Her husband made his mind up the very next day when they picked out the flowers for the caskets.

She loved him so much she would have done anything he asked of her. And those boys, those innocent little boys—Michael, a preteen, William, then five, Andrew, three, and Jonathon, only one. They were so adorable and so helpless with no one else to care for them, and they would have been placed in foster homes, which was unthinkable.

But she had no prior experience. Being an only child, there were no little siblings to observe. She jumped into it all cold turkey and soon found out the child-rearing responsibilities fell toward her daily routine, not Thomas'.

Yes, she had agreed, but oh, how she longed for their special alone times again—those picnics and the notes. Why, Thomas hasn't pulled out that daybook from his back pocket to write me a love note since those boys came, she thought sadly, and their picnics came to an end as well.

When Thomas and she first got married she loved her position as queen of the castle. They planted gardens with perennials and evergreens and placed stones just so to set a path to the circular flowerbed on the front lawn. Then another path led up to the porch with a swing suspended by white chain where they sat together on many soft, summer evenings.

She would awaken happy, humming or singing one of the latest hits by Doris Day or the Andrew Sisters as she washed her face and combed her golden hair up into a soft chignon.

While the hypnotic scent of their coffee was brewing, she'd set out two cups for her and Thomas. Quickly she would whip up a few muffins that would go with the sunny-side-up eggs that Thomas liked, and they would talk and laugh and smile into each other's eyes.

Then, off he'd go, shutting the door behind him, leaving her with a special good morning hug and kiss to warm her heart.

About once a week, as he left the little porch, he'd gently ring the large bell both of them had installed to the left side of the door. As she'd hear it ring, a smile would cross her lips, and she'd remember their little secret and what that signified between them.

She'd watch through the window as his tractor pulled away and as her household tasks progressed through the morning, she would occasionally glance out toward the field.

There she would see the clouds of dust stirred up by the tractor some distance from the house near the edge of the crops, and she would lovingly envision the time they would have later at eleven o'clock.

The morning played itself out with housecleaning and hanging laundry outside, but then it was time to prepare.

Just before lunch, Mary Kathleen would grab three face cloths and towels from the wicker basket. She'd use one to wash and refresh herself; the others, she'd pack for Thomas. She'd change into one of her soft, rayon house dresses with the buttons following its entire length.

The coffee would brew while she boiled water and made their favorite, a ham on rye with mustard and a few of her prize-winning dill pickles. Opening two thermos jugs, she'd fill each—one with coffee, cream and sugar and the other with the bubbling water.

All of it was packed with loving touches in the picnic basket, and when finished she would open the back door and pull the thick rope five times, which rang the large, loud dinner bell they had as a means to reach each other. It was her signal to Thomas.

As she closed the door, she'd sling a large woven coverlet across her arm and lift the basket, marking the beginning of their afternoon delight.

Thomas would hear the bell and watch for her, parking the tractor across the space between rows of corn. It was their special place, and he would sacrifice a couple of stalks by flattening them, giving them a place to spread out the blanket. The tall crop and tractor created a very private place for their lunch.

They would laugh together and use this time only for happy talk. No discussing impending problems—not now.

After he dusted off the morning's work from his clothes, he would flap the blanket, and then let the material fall completely, covering the earth, as Mary Kathleen would position the basket at one end of it. She'd remove the cloths and open the thermos of hot water, motioning for him to relax next to her. Kneeling near the edge, she would pour the steaming water onto the soap-filled cloth and shake it until it was tepid.

Looking into his eyes, she would gently hold his chin and wipe his brow, cheeks and lips. Next, she'd open the cloth to cleanse the back of his neck and slightly exposed chest. The part she enjoyed most was using the cloth to wipe away the dust of the morning's work from his strong, suntanned hands. Following the moist soapy wash, she'd pour more hot water on the second square and retrace her previous steps, rinsing his skin and patting him dry. Then she would kiss his fingertips, one by one.

Thomas looked forward to her tenderness, her loving touches she brought to everything she did. He would notice how pretty she was, how slim and trim she kept herself. He'd tell her so as he reached over to put his arm around her and lovingly pull her close.

Then, there were those notes . . . the notes he always managed to slip somewhere on her or in the basket that she'd carry back to the house. Sometime during the visit, Thomas would go back to the tractor and jot a quick note in his tan, leather-bound journal, then rip it out and hide it in one place or another in the items she had brought. Back at the house, it was fun guessing where it was hidden and checking to see if she was right. Sometimes it would be wrapped around the thermos bottle in a rubber band or scrunched up and tossed into the basket. Although the note may have been dusty and sometimes smudgy, Mary Kathleen would treasure it as if it was written on parchment.

After one tender session there was no note to be found, even though she had looked everywhere—in her pockets, and in and on the basket. She was sure that he had forgotten their ritual, but when Thomas came in, he showed her how he rolled it ever so tiny and stuck it in the leather strap which covered the handle of the basket. "Now, you know I wouldn't forget you," he had said.

Her mind continued to wander as she remembered when Thomas walked in from the field another time and heard her singing along to 'Stardust' playing on the radio.

When it first happened, she blushed, a bit embarrassed, and stopped.

Thomas told her, "Please don't stop. Keep singing. Your voice is so lovely."

He'd wanted to hug her, but was especially grungy and didn't want to get her dirty. Instead, he took hold of her fingertips and reached them over her head, twirling her gently, like she was a delicate doll he had found in a collector's shop. 'Round and 'round he gently led her, humming along to their song. She loved it and giggled playfully, winking at Thomas. He winked back and touched her chin, discontinuing the spin. Looking directly into her eyes, he had said,

"What a beauty you are inside and out. I'm a lucky, lucky man."

He'd pull her close, kiss her and say, "Honey, I'll always love you!"

That was one of the favorite phrases he would say to her over and over, and he would write it on his little love notes quite often. "Honey, I'll always love you."

Her mind repeated it, again and again . . . *Honey, I'll always love you . . . always love you.*

As she visualized that entire scene, she missed Thomas desperately and wanted him to come home. Tears streamed down her face and droplets fell into the soapy water. Her hands went back to the dishes while her mind continued to wander.

# CHAPTER ELEVEN

❧❧❧❧

As Thomas began the exhausting drive to Pittsburgh, his mind was racing with thoughts of Uncle Jay. What would he find when he got there?

His health had deteriorated in recent months. It was hard to accept—Uncle Jay was always so strong and virile, running-rings around his friends and even Thomas, himself. 'Course, now he is eighty-five years old, he reasoned, not that I'm getting' any older, but gosh, it seems like it was only yesterday . . .

Thoughts about his childhood surfaced, and he remembered how much a part his uncle had played in it. Even as a young boy, Thomas was very familiar with Pittsburgh—its cliffs, mountains and rivers—thanks to Uncle Jay and his wife, Aunt Rose, who lived most of their lives there. His uncle would call his brother—Thomas, Sr.—and tell him how he needed extra help. His father knew Thomas was the child Jay and Rose had always hoped for but wasn't blessed with, and he felt sorry for them. And, although difficult to lose another set of hands at the farm, his father would yield and put Thomas on the train to Pittsburgh.

When he'd come to stay for one or two weeks, Jay would make sure he could spend time with him. Aunt Rose would bake his favorite peanut butter cookies, which she'd take to the train station on the day he arrived, then day by day, she'd spoil him with all of her other specialties.

Thomas was very curious and enjoyed seeing how things were made, so Uncle Jay would take him to machine shops and factories, the kinds of places that little boys would find fascinating. One in particular had intricate systems of pulleys and levers, with ropes or chains attached. Workers would use them to hoist very cumbersome items, as if they weighed only a few pounds. The men would explain in detail how these worked, and Thomas would retain their instructions as he watched huge engines move with such ease they almost seemed to fly. Of all the many things that his Uncle would expose him to, this was to be his all-time favorite indoor activity.

Before long he would become just as accomplished at using the levers and pulleys as any of the men on the job.

But, Uncle Jay and Thomas did much more. They would ride on the funicular, the Duquesne and Monongahela Incline—cable cars that climbed up the side of Mount Washington. Sometimes they would go to Kennywood, an amusement park and ride the Figure Eight and the Racer.

Once they even climbed the Indian Trail steps from the Duquesne Incline to Duquesne Heights. Thomas remembered counting hundreds of wooden steps with their railings attached to the side of the cliff that twisted back and forth from the base to the top of the hill. At times he would get out of breath from running ahead of his uncle, taking those steps by twos. Uncle Jay would explain that these steps were used twice daily by hundreds of people who lived at the top of Mount Washington and worked below in the steel mills, the glass factories, and the paint and varnish works, and either chose not to ride or couldn't afford forty rides for one dollar to use the cable car.

Sometimes they would jump into his uncle's truck to go up the winding streets to Grandview Avenue, which overlooked the city. It presented a panoramic view of Pittsburgh through the soot and smog from the mills, looking down at the three rivers that came together—the Ohio, the Allegheny and the Monongahela. Some days, when the wind was just right, they could see for miles; when it wasn't, less than a few hundred feet.

There was nothing like this back on his father's farm in Westminster, Maryland. It was exciting, a little boy's dream come true, with so much to see and all of it happening at once. They would share a picnic lunch packed by Aunt Rose, watch the tug boats and barges, and hear the whistles from factories along the rivers. They'd see trucks, cars and trains crossing the numerous bridges. Once, Thomas told his uncle it was like seeing a miniature Christmas garden growing, right before his eyes.

They would have wonderful discussions about the past as Uncle Jay instilled strong work ethics in Thomas, explaining how he had traveled over on a boat from the old country, coming through Fells Point in Baltimore to be processed with immigration papers. Jay would tell him how he had first begun working in a tomato packing plant, then at age sixteen working' in a blue glass factory in South Baltimore where they made thick, navy-blue bottles for Bromo Seltzer. He shared that he had found his niche-at twenty-one while he was an apprentice at the glass works in Corning, New York, being only twenty-five when he moved to Pittsburgh to work with glass and machinery.

Thomas was like a sponge absorbing his Uncle's wisdom, asking questions, growing and learning. He always wanted to hear more, wanted to know what happened after that and after that and after that.

He remembered Uncle Jay describing his past projects.

*In 1910, at twenty nine, I started my own glass manufacturing company. Pittsburgh was the perfect city for it . . . had all the right components. Got the sand from the river and potash from the ash trees growin' at its edge. Then I could use all three rivers for transporting the glass once I got the business really growin'.*

Thomas recalled all of this, having heard it time and again, pulling out each detail from his memory. He shook his head lovingly. Uncle Jay . . . always said that God blessed him by allowing him to come to the United States of America and have these opportunities. I've always had a special love for my country and religion, and it was Uncle Jay who talked me into becoming an usher at St. John's Church many years ago.

Even though I professed my faith there, I kept thinkin' I was too busy, but I remember Uncle Jay sayin' to me,

*If God comes first, all the rest will fall into line.*

It amazed me then and still does. Seems like somehow, as busy as I am, when I follow my uncle's advice everything seems to get done. Uncle Jay had it right, by golly, and the man sure has been given his share of talent which he's made good use of. Could do just about anything he set his mind to.

Thomas cracked a couple of yawns.

Gosh, I remember one of my visits when Uncle Jay told me, *Thomas, in 1900, the very year you were born, me and your father built the barn you are still usin' today on the farm, back in Westminster.*

Couldn't believe it at the time, but I shoulda' known. I can see him sayin' it so proudly,

*Built that barn sixty-five feet straight up with a gambrel roof and
a cupola on the top with louvers for ventilation. One-hundred and
thirty feet long and sixty-five wide, perfect for the spot we put her
on. Bigger than most barns, don't 'cha' know. 'Course, we had the
help of a barn wright friend of mine from Lancaster and his friends,
but me and your father did most of the work.*

Thomas chuckled. Uncle Jay did like to have braggin' rights, for
sure.

He pulled off the road, stopped for a break at a filling station
and stretched out his legs and back, like his cat back home. After
replacing the cap on the gas tank of his pick-up truck, he was off
again and more than halfway there.

His thoughts ran into each other . . . maybe I should've called
him from back there at the pay phone, should've checked to see how
he's doin' . . . sure hope he's gonna' be alright.

"Oh, he's gonna be alright," he said aloud, reassuring himself,
"probably just playin' another joke on me, like he always did . . . one
of his games. He even pulled 'em on his buddies."

Thomas had seen first-hand and envisioned the time Uncle Jay
had set up an elaborate hoax with the men at the shop. Hid their
clothes in the wrong lockers; switched 'em while they were workin';
mixed up everything. They could've really let him have it, but they
laughed about it when he brought 'em each a cup of coffee and some
doughnuts while they sorted it all out. Each found a two dollar bill
amongst their things, and that smoothed out any of them that still
had ruffled feathers.

No doubt about it, he was the one who taught me all about a
good tease or riddle. 'Course I like to play games with the four boys
and Mary Kathleen. Like to watch 'em try to figure things out—all
innocent fun. Keeps 'em guessin' and on their toes.

Especially at Christmas, I love puttin' somethin' into a box with
Michael's name on it into a box with Andrew's name on it into a box
with William's name on it and finally, into a box with Jonathon's
name on the outside tag. I'd then do a switcheroo and mix 'em up
another way. It is fun to see 'em try to guess who is gonna' really
end up with it.

And at Easter, it was Uncle Jay who taught me to make clues for
the boys to follow to find their Easter baskets.

I still remember him showin' me how he had written a clue on a piece of paper and stuck it between two decorated eggs that said, *If you take Clue #1 to just the right spot, Clue #2 will 'pop up' in front of you.* The toaster held the next clue which read, *Take this clue for a walk and you will 'hear the talk'.* Then, under the old radio was the next clue. His clues were simple but the kids had to piece the puzzle together to find the last clue, which said, *Your basket is in the hall closet,* or under the basement steps, or wherever he hid it. The boys loved it, runnin' all over the place lookin' for that candy. Didn't cost him anything, just his time, energy, and sense of humor. And, it really made Mary Kathleen smile, just like it's makin' me smile just thinkin' about it.

Once he gave me a long, white envelope and told me to drop it in the collection plate at Mass.

"Even shocked me on that one," he muttered to himself.

He knew I would go into the counting room after church, just as I always did. When one of the ushers slid it open, inside that envelope were five crisp one-hundred dollar bills and a note which read . . . "For the building fund." No name, no other explanation. All of them were shocked and none of the ushers understood, except me, of course. I knew Uncle Jay had a dream for St. John's just as I did, but I never thought he'd come up with such a large anonymous gift. I kept a poker face through it all, but couldn't wait to tell Uncle Jay what had happened. I called him long distance just as soon as I got home, and we both had a good laugh on that one. Yeah, it took time to create those riddles and games, but Uncle Jay enjoyed it and I guess it rubbed off on me.

His mind drifted back to Mary Kathleen, smiling and happy at those times when the boys first came to live with them, and he started to remember other happy occasions they'd had together, before they came as well. He reached into his pocket for some gum as he recalled the notes he had written to her, and how he hid them in the picnic basket for her to find, many years before when they had their special times . . . their tender, private moments . . .

He thought of how magical their times in the cornfield had been. One day, she looked especially pretty walking toward me. I could barely stand it, and just as soon as she got there I jumped down off the tractor and took her into my . . .

Just then, a truck coming around a turn in the road swerved across the center line. Thomas blew his horn and, thinking quickly, twisted the steering wheel back and forth just enough to prevent the collision. It was scary and brought his full attention back to the road, back to his mission—to get to Uncle Jay's all in one piece!

# CHAPTER TWELVE

❧❧❧❧

*E*xhausted and drained, Thomas arrived back at his Westminster farm three days later at 11 p.m.

This trip was more difficult, as it was his second visit to Pittsburgh within two weeks, worsened by the added worry about Uncle Jay's health.

The doctors who had sent his uncle home from the hospital were amazed at his quick turn-around, telling Thomas that usually an eighty-five year old man didn't respond to treatment like he did and that, in just two days, his blood pressure was normal again, his heart strong and his lungs clear.

As he prepared to leave, Uncle Jay had called him over.

"Thomas," his Uncle whispered in his ear, "I've got another envelope upstairs in my underwear drawer for you to take. Be sure to get it before you go and put it with the rest."

He gave his uncle a good-bye hug and made him promise to take it easy and said to him,

"You did it again, Uncle Jay. Must have an angel on your shoulder, watchin' out for you; either that or you've got a horseshoe in your back pocket."

While they joked about it, Thomas said good-bye to the caretakers and his nurse who promised to call him at the mere sign of an impending problem. They exchanged telephone numbers, talked for a short time, and he left.

Now that he was finally back home, his mind began to classify the events of the past few days, and with each thought, adrenaline began pumping and sleep escaped Thomas Frank.

As his mind raced, he unpacked the truck and dropped his bags inside the farmhouse. He turned, holding the door so it wouldn't slam, and could see his old friend, the barn that Uncle Jay and his father had built so many years before, staring back at him while towering under a moonlit sky. He heard himself say,

"Gosh I love that 'ol barn. Don't matter if I'm greasin' the 'ol tractor, just pluckin' around out there or playin' around with my block and tackle—it just don't matter.

"Whenever I have a lot to sort out, that ol' barn is my hideaway and tonight I've got more to think about than usual. Just the sight of it makes me feel good."

As he walked down the dusty path, he remembered himself as a young boy, coming home from one of his visits from the machine shop in Pittsburgh excited and anxious to tell his father about the smooth, almost effortless movement that the block and tackle system allowed. He described how huge pieces of machinery were moved from place to place by the foreman and the workers explaining how they had taught him and that he could help with more chores if they had a system like the one at the factory.

Because his father could see its practical usage he agreed to install a basic system, but over the years Thomas created more and more elaborate combinations throughout the barn to use for his amusement.

He opened the heavy wooden barn doors. There was that familiar creak that made him feel as if an old friend was greeting him—a friend who was always there for him, uncomplicated and simple. Thomas said his silent prayers, as he always did when he first entered.

When he breathed-in a full breath, it hit him, the fragrance of hay and straw, oil, grease and barn siding. It welcomed him. He was home.

Lighting a lantern, he could barely see in the shadows above him several of the compound four-pulley systems that allowed him to manipulate almost anything from place to place in the barn.

After closing the door, he fired up more lantern wicks and re-examined his latest project, then began wrapping it with chain and attaching it to the massive hook. While he worked, his mind drifted back over the past, and he sorted out what changes would have to be made in the future. It seemed he could compartmentalize all his problems and work out the kinks while being out there.

He eyeballed where he wanted to reposition the box sitting in front of him, checked the chains and ropes again, and began. As he pulled, the ropes traveled through the pulley wheels. Because the four strands shared the force, his effort was one-quarter the weight of the load, making it very manageable. Several pieces were shifted as he progressed, and he remembered explaining this theory to his nephews who, as boys, would sit and watch him take out the tractor engine by hoisting it and allowing the gears and wheels to interchange as necessary. While still elevated, he would then guide the floating object left or right and lower it onto a rustic table to begin his tinkering.

Thomas loved machinery, and he had the innate talent to take it all apart, down to its smallest bit and screw, and easily see in his mind how each piece fit back together, fixing as he went.

The boys would watch and listen in awe. To them, he was their "Superman".

All four of them would watch him finish the repair, lift it again and swing it back into the vehicle easily. The engine would run as good as new.

But he wanted to show them more. He wanted to teach them the things he learned at Uncle Jay's glass factory, where the bottles were made, and at the machine shop, where the bottle caps had been formed.

As a boy, Thomas had felt right at home and happy to be in Pittsburgh, learning and doing. The workers couldn't believe that a youngster had such a mechanical mind . . . "born with it," they always said. And, he believed if he explained things just right, the boys would learn how and could then decide if they wanted to do something else rather than farming as he had been forced to do.

He didn't see himself as a farmer, but every time he broached the subject to start some kind of machine shop, his father had told him, *just use that talent of yours to keep all the farm equipment runnin' smooth. Don't want to hear about your headin' in some other direction . . . need you to keep this farm goin'.*

And he did. He had promised his father he would continue farming . . . would keep the land producing and in the family. That vow kept surfacing, and often his mind would wander to his special barn full of toys, full of his "what could have been" if he hadn't vowed to his father.

After the boys came he decided, once and for all, he wouldn't force them like he had been forced.

But, as life would have it, there was no choice; they had to help with the farm and the produce business that spawned from it.

# CHAPTER THIRTEEN

❧❧❧❧

𝒯homas reached into his pocket and retrieved the silver dollar, dated 1950 that he always carried on his left side. It triggered his memory . . .

What a day that was . . . can't believe it's been so many years!

Can see myself standing there, next to my truck parked on Route 140, melons in hand. 'Course I plopped 'em down next to a rock so they wouldn't roll again. Then I took off to runnin' my tail off to git back the rest of 'em; some still rollin' away from me, headin' for the gully. Musta' looked mighty funny . . . can laugh about it now.

Why, once those containers that I had everything sittin' up on shifted, the melons and corn started to tumble out. Then and there I said, *'Dear God, there's got to be a better way than sellin' my produce along the side of the road, here in Carroll County. Geez', if things keep goin' on this way and I gotta' wait for a car to stop and then sell 'em one or two things and only more if I'm lucky, then how am I ever gonna' meet all the bills each month?'*

"Know God heard me. He sure did," Thomas said aloud.

He continued reminiscing . . . probably a good thing it happened that way 'cause God sure helped me get started on the plan I had been shiftin' around in my head. I took off, there and then, for "Bal-mour" . . . thought I would give it a shot! Remember how I stopped and talked to a couple of restaurant managers down in the city while ordering somethin' from their menu.

In my change, I got this here silver dollar in Fells Point, first one in such a long time.

He flipped it, caught it, pushed it down deep in his pocket, patted it, and called it his good luck charm.

Worked hard to gain their trust. Told 'em how I raised fresh seasonal vegetables . . . lettuce, tomatoes, beans and the rest, and how I would bring them, myself, right to their door, nice and early.

I can't forget takin' two to three loads a week down there. Had heard good things about Haussner's Restaurant on Eastern Avenue and nosed around that area lookin' for other restaurants. Yep, that's how it all started.

Sure was glad when Michael was old enough to drive so I could get some sleep, 'cause growin', harvestin' and truckin' 'em too was real tough.

Findin' time to see Uncle Jay once a month, up in Pittsburgh was hard, and still volunteerin' at church through it all sure was a challenge.

Didn't have any time for Mary Kathleen and the boys, though. No time for them puzzles and riddles I liked to do, *no sirree-bob*! Had to catch myself, every so often, from bein' too darn grouchy . . . just tired.

Collectors breathin' down my neck . . . no choice . . . I had to do it . . . farm was at stake.

Thomas started up the antique tractor and listened for the purr of the engine, threw it into reverse and backed it out of the barn. After making an adjustment or two, he squeezed the oil can just a little, checked the tires, pulled it in, then shut it down, making sure he aligned the front, back and sides at just the right spot.

He jumped off and thought that lookin' back it wasn't so bad that the whole family had to pitch together. Taught 'em well, and hard work never hurt anyone. Kept 'em tight with each other, too.

As the boys continued to grow, maintainin' the cost of their food, clothin' and schoolin' escalated faster than I could make money, though. The food was the easiest . . . the farm supplied that. Raised those chickens, cattle and had that milk cow. Thank God, Mary Kathleen canned, when fruits and vegetables were in season, gettin' the boys help to peel, dice and fill the jars. I'll bet it was quite an assembly line. Never did git to see it, but I can remember Mary Kathleen describin' it all to me.

He reached into his pocket for the small packages of *Double Bubble* gum and popped two in his mouth at once. While chawin' away he replayed Mary Kathleen's version of the story in his mind.

But she and Thomas didn't quite know exactly how it really played out most of the time, behind the scenes, on canning days.

છ્જ-ઝ્જી-છ્જ-ઝ્જી

Since Michael was the oldest, he would carry in the baskets sitting them close to the sink. William would stand on a low stool and carefully wash off the dust and debris, piling the clean produce on the drain board so that the water droplets would run back into the sink. Andrew and Jonathon, the two youngest, would fill bowls with each piece, stacking as high as they could, but higher than they should. Top heavy pieces often would splat on the immaculately clean floor in Auntie's kitchen, juice, seeds and pulp going everywhere. They'd all scurry to clean it up before she saw it because they were warned over and over again, but Jonathon lit a fire under his brothers, especially Andrew, who stuck to Jonathon like glue. He would entice him, razz him and egg him on and Andrew always succumbed to the tease. Jonathon always seemed to skirt the trouble, but just barely; and that was exactly the part he enjoyed. Almost getting caught was really the fun of it all.

Once their aunt reprimanded them, and the older boys tried to explain that Jonathon was the instigator. But she had gone to get the canning jars and blue enamel pots in another room and thought they were picking on Jonathon and blaming him because he was the youngest.

She just couldn't catch on that while he was the youngest, he was also the foxiest.

He would bet his brothers a quarter from his allowance that he could carry a bowl stacked high with fruit or vegetables, balanced on one hand, from the sink to the kitchen table, then slide it off his palm onto the table, not letting one piece drop from it.

Jonathon mastered it and won three quarters, one from each of them. Even though they joined in, Michael and William shared mutual concern and must have been thinking the same thing as they looked at each other in dismay, and said in unison, *he always comes out ahead.*

ঌক৺৽ঌক৺৽

As Thomas pushed his tongue into his gum to soften it, he popped two small puffs of air and remembered that the cost of the boys' clothing had been another problem, with Michael always getting the new pieces and each boy, thereafter, wearing the hand-me-downs.

He smiled as he remembered Mary Kathleen making some of them, but she was not very proficient at the machine and he couldn't bring himself to tell her. Her pants were the worst, too full in the seat and legs and the bottoms never even, although she had four tries, one for each boy, to get the hem right.

His gum almost fell out of his mouth as he started to laugh quietly, recalling one incident when there was a good buy on corduroy at Mather's Department Store and Mary Kathleen made four matching pairs of pants. They all looked like a singing quartet in costume, gold and black hounds-tooth check. But worse, when they walked they sounded like the band that might back up the group . . . *voopah, voopah, voopah, voopah,* the sound of corduroy pants rubbing thigh to thigh.

Thomas shook his head and giggled while remembering that they sure hated those pants. Some of their buddies ridiculed 'em so much, they even tried hidin' 'em in different parts of the house. They stuffed 'em everywhere! Mary Kathleen always found 'em, steamed 'em and hung 'em all in a row on a clothesline, stretched across the rafters in the basement, getting' 'em ready for the next Sunday Mass at St. John's.

I can recall her voice, *boys, I finally found all of your corduroys. Don't worry though; I cleaned 'em all up and pressed 'em so they're ready to go.*

'Member it just like it happened yesterday. I can still see all of the boys as they looked at each other and cringed, makin' faces like they'd just sucked a lemon. They got me on the side and leveled with me . . . said they would rather wear the neighbors' cast-offs, but didn't want to hurt Auntie's feelins'.

Blowing a makeshift bubble he sighed.

Boy, I had to handle that one delicately; she tried so hard. I gently brought it up to her and finally, she had to agree. Even Mary Kathleen knew she had little talent at the sewing machine, so she bartered with Mrs. Nash, who worked at Grief's Sewing Factory and could sew so well she had several blue ribbons from the State Fair in Timonium, hangin' over her mantel. 'Course her taste was on target, too, pickin' the material that was more suitable for young boys.

Mrs. Nash was happy and willin' to trade fresh vegetables when in season. She especially liked Mary Kathleen's canned produce, particularly her peach and plum preserves and grape jelly, swapped for pants, shirts and even knitted socks that really fit.

Got to give it to 'em, the boys got smarter as time went on. Actually asked to help can the produce . . . didn't have to chase 'em down, knowin' it meant new clothes for 'em, includin' even hems at the right spot at the ankle.

As I think back, both of us knew schoolin' would be the toughest bill to scrape together—seventy-five cents a month for each boy—but we vowed our nephews would go to St. John's School.

What times they were . . . can still remember my knees knockin' as I met with the Mother Superior, one of the School Sisters of Notre Dame, with her black habit and all those robes.

As soon as he thought of her, he stopped chewing the gum and asked his tongue to tuck it tightly into his cheek.

The memories were impossible to forget.

She spoke fluent English but I heard her talkin' German to one of the other sisters before she walked into the room. I had remembered a few words that Gross Pop Jedidiah had taught me and decided to impress her. I tried a couple 'a words, but they just made her chuckle, though it broke the ice all the same, and I explained why I came. When I started I was still a little nervous at first and then, I finally relaxed and started my speech. Sat up though, straight and tall in my chair . . . I did do that.

I looked at her huge rosary hanging' from her waist, saw the crucifix and said a little prayer, cleared my throat and said,

*Mother Superior, my wife and I are raisin' our four nephews whose parents—that'd been my brother and his wife—were killed in a horrible car accident last year, over on the Eastern Shore. The oldest, Michael, is twelve and the next in line, William, is five, and we would like them to start their parochial schoolin' this fall. We're doin' our best at home to teach 'em right from wrong, but we want our boys to love their religion. You Nuns will go deeper, much deeper, into doctrine, but more important, you'll teach 'em to be honest, fair and just how a good Christian should act towards their fellow man.*

*I don't care what we have to do, all four of 'em will go on to do better than we both did in our schoolin' 'cause, even though I started at St. John's, never did finish past sixth grade. I'll work as*

*hard as need be, but I'm hopin' for a special arrangement if you think we can work it out.*

He whispered to himself,

"Man, my heart was in my throat."

He continued remembering his words.

*Here at the Convent you have what, twelve, maybe fourteen Sisters who teach, plus Sister Phamphilia, the cook? That's a lot of hungry mouths to feed, plus the food that's needed for the priests at the Rectory.*

*Sister, God's been real good to me. Gave me extra special dirt, and it seems I can grow anythin' in that soil of mine. My idea goes like this. Supposin' I bring all the vegetables and fruit you could need for each week that they're in season. Can offer you fresh eggs, too, and a 'course some fresh milk. I'm hopin' all of this would cover the boys tuition for school, and when the little ones, Andrew, who is three, then Jonathon, who's one, come on up, we'll see how it's been a 'workin'. I'll be as fair as I can, but you'll be lettin' me know if our arrangement is good from your side of the street.*

She slapped both hands together, looked up towards heaven and said, *Ach du lieber,* and didn't hesitate to agree.

*You can start the produce and dairy deliveries as soon as possible, Mr. Frank. Our cook will be elated to get the freshest fruit and vegetables, plus milk and eggs, and delivered right to our door!*

*You see, God always provides!*

*And to you, Mr. Frank . . .* she traced a cross on my forehead and I remember her sayin', *may God help you to fulfill your dreams today and every day of your life!*

I couldn't thank her enough and I remember sayin' to her, *You don't know just how much this all means to me, and to my wife, too.*

Then, I promised her to have the first crates there the next day by 7:30 a.m. including corn, string beans, peas and that new tomato I started growin' back then, the one that grew from seed that one of my customers had given me sent directly by his family from Italy.

I was so fired up I couldn't wait to tell Mary Kathleen. As I rushed in the door the look on her face told me she knew and didn't have to ask, but did anyway, *Sister said okay to your idea?*

My words were bubblin' out. *She not only said, okay, but she was crazy about the idea . . . asked me to start the deliveries as soon as I could, so I told her I'd be by tomorrow. If it works out, why we can bring all four boys on through school that way. As long as God grants us good weather and the crops are plentiful, we'll be fine, just fine.*

He started chewing again and blew his biggest and best, by far, as he continued to remember . . .

Yes indeed, year after year my prayers and Sister's were answered. God did send us good weather and good crops, the boys continued their education and all of them graduated from St. John's School through the twelfth grade. Yep . . . Michael first, then William and Andrew and finally, Jonathon.

And now, he thought, they are men. Michael is thirty-two and the manager of the business, William, my right hand man, is twenty-five; Andrew, about twenty-three and just returning from Vietnam, and now he is easing back into the farmin' end of the company. Can't believe it, but Jonathon is twenty-one already and has his own routes, responsible for deliverin' the fresh produce to our restaurant accounts.

He stopped the momentum of his thoughts and reached for one more, small package of gum, unwrapped it and added it to his wad.

Jonathon . . . now he's another story. If he can only keep his head on straight . . . just so different from the other three . . . can't figure out why.

"Oh, he'll be all right," he said convincing himself.

Thomas changed from that point of view and started to paint a picture of how it all had happened.

Pretty amazin' . . . what had started as a must-do operation to help save the farm has grown into a business that all the nephews seem to enjoy. Thanks to Michael, we're sellin' produce in the spring and summer with all the typical items—he counted each to himself as he held up his fingers—strawberries, asparagus, tomatoes, peas, green beans, corn, and cucumbers. And in the fall we're truckin' our apples, pumpkins and squash. December—trees are our staple load. Thankfully, some of our corn is even delivered to the Carroll County grain mills, ground into meal, packaged and sold, too. He just keeps comin' up with idea after idea and all of 'em profitable enough to keep the wolf away from the door.

Suddenly a mouse scampered by as a light went out; one of his lanterns had burned all of its kerosene. It jolted Thomas into realizing that he hadn't seen Torpedo, his cat, who normally raced over to see him whenever he walked into the barn. Wonder where he is tonight, he thought, as he opened the outer door and forced a special noise he made with lips and teeth, which usually produced his pet.

It was all too strange and he was concerned, so he decided to head back to the farmhouse to look for him, tossing his wet gum into a gopher hole not far from the barn door.

"That'll git ya', you varmint," he said. "You are one pesky rascal, even skirtin' Torpedo and his hunt and I don't want giant gopher holes around for the horses to break a leg. Cully told me that's how to git rid of you . . . sure is worth a try."

After he closed the barn doors he heard the crinkle of the envelope in his jacket pocket that Uncle Jay had told him to take.

*Put it with the rest,* he had said.

Forgot to tuck it away up in the loft . . . do it tomorrow, he thought, as he patted his hand over it, feeling its thickness. Tomorrow . . .

# CHAPTER FOURTEEN

❧❦❧❦

$O$nce inside the farmhouse Thomas tiptoed up the steps and cracked open the master bedroom door a few inches. Spying Mary Kathleen soundly asleep, he also saw Torpedo, who had been stretched out beside her. The cat scurried off the bed to hide under it, creating a cyclone of air that pulled with it a crisp note that had been on Thomas' pillow; a note that now fluttered to the floor. He was oblivious and missed the note altogether.

The cat then squeezed through the opening between his feet and Thomas watched him run down the stairs.

So there you are, he thought. Keepin' Mary Kathleen company, are ya'?

Thomas' stomach was growling. He realized it was late, but still he was not sleepy, and after quietly closing the bedroom door he headed for the stairs and the kitchen.

Zipping off his jacket, he hung it on a chair and proceeded to make his own midnight snack—peanut butter and apricot jelly on white bread, to be washed down by a glass of milk.

Torpedo began his nocturnal frenzy, sprinting through the downstairs rooms and vaulted from one piece of furniture to the next as if releasing pent-up energy.

"Go ahead, git it out of your system before I sit down with this snack," he said.

When he sat onto the sofa, Torpedo's stampede came to a halt at Thomas' feet as if the cat were applying brakes.

Thomas chuckled and ripped off a corner of his sandwich to toss to Torpedo, answering his meow. He wiped his fingertips on the side of his pants.

Torpedo arched his back and rubbed Thomas' legs, first on one side, then the other.

"Always here to welcome me, aren't ya'? That's my boy."

"Now will ya' look at this, Torpedo?"

Thomas saw one of the photo albums that he had pulled earlier in the week lying open on the end table. Leaning over, he saw pages of his father and Grandfather Jed first, and then backtracked to the pages of Great Uncle Thaddeus.

His thoughts returned to his meeting a few days before with the lady, Maggie Fischer, and how bold she was, trying to get him to part with one of his family's antiques, even though he hadn't seen it for years, hadn't cared about it that much. After all, it was only a key . . . wasn't like he had the small safe it opened or anything. Yet, it was part of the life of Uncle Thaddeus, part of his heritage and part of history.

When Uncle Jay got so sick, Maggie seemed so carin', bringin' over that cake and the coffee for me to take along. Is she bein' kindly or is she just after that old key, he now thought suspiciously.

He eyed up the kitchen and frowned. Hmmm, don't see any of that left-over cake just now. Guess the boys ate it all.

"Here ya' go, Torpedo. No more cake left for this milk to wash down," he said as he lay down his plate on the floor as a saucer. He poured the remaining milk while Torpedo's eyes glinted with anticipation before lapping it up.

Moving the old book to one side, he reached for another he had wanted to show Maggie Fischer. It held photos of the interior of old St. John's Church. This is actually why she came to see me in the first place, he thought, and he began looking at page after page of pictures showing the altars, statues, baptismal font and views of the Stations of the Cross . . . his Stations of the Cross.

There was the photo of the church at Christmas time, taken from the organ loft, with the evergreen trees he donated dotting the altar and the twenty-five foot pine, spruce and fir swags roped together and draped from side to side. On the side altar was the crèche with all of the figurines representing the birth of Christ . . . the Crèche he was caring for. He could see most of the tall stained-glass windows on the photo, although in black and white, and remembered how carefully they had crated 'em years before.

A photo of the vestibule showed the Armed Forces Memorial Plaque before it was destroyed, complete with all the names of the Veterans from the Westminster area who served in The Civil War, World War I, World War II and the Korean War. He also saw the votive candle holder with its black wrought iron rods which formed its legs and backbone and held it all together for the glass cups that sat within it. Now, all that was left of it was safely stored away.

Thomas turned to the back of the book and sadly saw the photos taken after the fire in that old treasure. There was a shot taken from a crane looking down into the church from what should have been the organ loft. The lens had stared at the crushed steeple, collapsed into the pews on an angle that caused the death and destruction of that beautiful Gothic masterpiece.

The photo of the altar showed the gold-trimmed sanctuary lamp, still hanging, and the wax candle within, melted down and re-hardened into stalactite-shaped forms like fingers from hell.

Another picture showed the hole where a wall had been between the thirteenth and fourteenth Station of the Cross. He thought it was so amazing to think that so much force from that huge steeple could come crashing down and spare fourteen, four-by-six foot, tableaus. He was moved to verbalize what he saw.

"Now will ya' look at this, Torpedo," he said, smacking the page with the back of his hand, "not even one of the . . . what . . . eighteen-inch tall and six to eight inch deep statues leanin' out of the box lost a hand or even a finger!"

The cat meowed on cue.

"And that gold stuff, gild or gilt, I think they call it, all along the edges of their border . . . can't believe it wasn't affected by the fire, and not one Station of the Cross was even singed.

"Amazin', yep truly amazin' that all fourteen of 'em still hung on what was left of them remainin' walls, depictin' the story of the death of Christ, from sentencin' to Crucifixion, in perfect condition; and yet they were facin' a deadly scene of ruin left by the fire . . . that demon fire!"

He slammed the book shut, not wanting to remember the horrific and shocking sight he had walked into after it was extinguished, but his heart still ached for the old church he loved so dearly, so much a part of him and his family.

"But they could've saved her," he said aloud, his eyes beginning to glisten. "If only they had tried, but the decision was to tear her down and build anew.

"Enough of this, enough of this," he said, as his head began to throb.

# CHAPTER FIFTEEN

✎✎✎✎

$\mathcal{H}$e slid the heavy book to the coffee table and reached for a calico-covered album he was sure would have lighter subject matter.

It contained pictures similar to the ones framed by Mary Kathleen that were sitting row by row on the drum table across the room.

Thomas smiled when he saw the first page, a photo of all four boys when they first came to live with them in 1947, after their parents' fatal accident . . . Jonathon, a babe in arms, held by Michael, then twelve . . . Andrew, three and William, five.

He pulled out the album he had shown to Maggie and then looked more intently at each album, the first and now this one. Thomas had never noticed until now, seeing both Michael and Great Uncle Thaddeus' photos side-by-side, just how much resemblance each had to the other. He remarked quietly,

"Thaddeus, sure wish you could talk to me . . . clue me in on just what it was like to live in the 1860's. Musta' been so much happenin' back then with the Civil War in full throws, railroads chuggin' along gettin' ya' everywhere you needed to go, and a church being built in the midst of it all, right in town on Main Street, then a dirt road. Your own brother Jed, supervisin' the bakin' of all them bricks on his farm, then bringin' 'em into town and seein' the masons build 'em into a church usin' lime mortar, long after the rectory was finished. Why I been a'wonderin' how many trips you had to make to transport half a million of 'em. Proud to say you're my relative. Yes sir, proud of it."

While looking back at the book and gently shaking his head, he spoke as if his nephew was in the room,

"Michael, you sure were the stronghold for the boys. Always made me proud too, and to this day never caused one lick 'a trouble. You pitched right in at sixteen, when you got your license in 1951, and started workin' one of the produce routes right away, after school and on Saturdays.

"Nuns never sent one letter home about you, Michael, and seems like you was always keepin' the other ones in line. Why, sometimes you acted more like their father than brother back then, and I sure was glad of that."

Thomas pushed back, feeling the sofa cushions against his lower spine, and began reminiscing further and further. He could see Michael's face when he ran the Baltimore drops, first introducing him to the owner of each restaurant whom Thomas had befriended, while offering outstanding customer service.

He talked directly to the photo.

"Some of them put their arm around you, Michael, welcomin' you, huggin' you side to side while lettin' you know what a tough act to follow I would be . . . heh, heh.

"I remember sayin', 'Oh yes sir, thanks, but you can be sure my nephew Michael will do as good a job as me. I guarantee it, ain't that right, Michael?'

"More than one of 'em seemed unsure, but then, Michael, you would reassure the man yourself. Your word was like gold, always was, and you told 'em, 'Yes sir, you will be getting only the best produce we've got to offer. I'll see to it and it will be here on time, every time. Thank you, sir.'"

He thought about how good he felt when, in the chain of command, the owner would summon his kitchen manager to make the introductions, explaining his acceptance of this new, young face. Then, by golly, the circle was completed.

And again, as if the photo could hear him,

"And, of course, I knew I could rely on your guarantee, Michael, knowin' you would not fail me or the owners. You're like me; don't know how to fail . . . that word ain't in your vocabulary. I knew it then and I know it now, my Michael's the kind of person who will do whatever it takes to complete a job. Stay up late, get up extra early, use superhuman strength to get the job done, and done right.

"But I have to admit that part of your determination revolved around your parents' death. You took over the role of mother and father to the younger boys, after that horrible accident, even though you were only twelve, and still the oldest. You were the one who first thought how ya' would raise the others even before Mary Kathleen and I made the announcement that all of ya' would come to live here at our farm."

He softened his words and said,

"I was so proud of you. Even in your little-boy mind, Michael, you told me you were quittin' school and gettin' a job, like your Daddy did.

"Told me, yep, I remember it so well, can hear it in my brain, how you talked about the many things you might do to take care of your brothers. You said, 'Maybe I'll work as an airplane pilot so I can take them all on trips, or I'll become a doctor so's I could make 'em better like that nice Dr. Goodman, Mommy took us to'.

"It was inborn, and being the elder, twelve year old, you needed to be responsible . . . strong for the others.

"Gosh, even in school, only A's were good enough for you, Michael. In the lower grades tweren't a problem, but as you moved up to high school you struggled, especially with the written word. I tried to help you there . . . words seemed to always come easy to me . . . loved writin' 'em down, but not with the correct grammar or spellin'. I just confused you more," he admitted.

"Numbers, yeah, numbers came easy . . . you could see them in your mind, could make them juggle into the correct categories. They were black or white."

Thomas nodded his head and thought—math, now that's where I really helped him.

"Michael, you graduated, ninth in your class from high school . . . seemed glad to be out though, and you couldn't wait to work the land and help me with the produce delivery business. Always had those big ideas about buildin' it bigger and better . . . guess that's where it started.

"Yes, I never had to worry about you, Michael, you're my rock . . . my rock," Thomas said, now in a whisper.

While he smiled at the pleasant memories of Michael growing into manhood, Thomas leaned his head back, sinking gradually deeper and deeper into the pillows of the sofa, until finally the sleep that had evaded him enveloped his entire body.

# CHAPTER SIXTEEN

### ❧❧❧❧

$\mathcal{H}$e heard his uncle stumble up the stairs, exit the bathroom and cause the box spring to creak as he got into bed.

Jonathon's clock showed 4 a.m. as he flicked the light on and off quickly. After lying in bed anticipating his next move, he waited for about twenty minutes, and then tiptoed down the stairs while the others slept and made his way to the cookie jar on top of the old Frigidaire. He knew his aunt used it to stash away canning and egg money if sales were good, and he helped himself to a five or ten spot at times. Tonight it was only full of paper receipts. The drawer in the living room—way in the back of it—that's where Unks puts his petty cash sometimes, he thought, and off he snuck to check it out.

As he was nosing around, he saw open scrapbooks lying on the Formica coffee table. He skimmed through one, looking for an old silver certificate five dollar bill or two that he knew his uncle had been saving. Instead he saw pictures of his mother and father . . . at least they'd told him that's who they were.

Jonathon thought, but why can't I remember them?

Her, I should remember *her* at least, shouldn't I? They always told me I was too young when it happened.

How could she do it? How could she leave me? It's probably not really her, he convinced himself, and flipped a couple of pages.

There was a photo of a bunch of the guys making a human pyramid at the Westminster city playground with all of their bikes parked beside them. On the margin above it his aunt had printed . . .

### 1957

**Andrew, 13, Bottom Left**                    **Jonathon, 11, Top**

Something in the photo made him sneer as he thought of one of his favorite memories and of how shifty he was back then. He stared into space, visualizing the entire scene, as some of his words, his brother Andrew's and his aunt's came back to him . . .

*C'mon bet me. What'sa matter, you scared to lose? I'll bet you a buck I can outrun ya'. No, two bucks to your one. If I win, you'll gimme' a dollar and if you win, I'll pay you two. C'mon, live a little. Take a chance. You know you're pretty fast. I'll probably lose and you'll have two bucks for your bank. I know how you love to feed that pig of yours in your bedroom.*

Jonathon thought how again and again he had tried to entice his brother Andrew to bet with him like before, but that time he wouldn't go for it.

He visualized Andrew speaking in a falsetto voice.

*No way, Jonathon! Maybe you don't mind losin' and tossin' your money away, but not me. I work too hard to earn it from Uncle Thomas and I'm gonna keep savin' it. I've been eyein' up that bike in town and I only need twenty more bucks, then I can get it. Aunt Mary Kathleen said I could buy it as long as I earn the money. Do ya' know how many months I've been workin' towards that bike?*

He remembered what he had said to Andrew, each and every word . . . *Yeah I know, you show it to me every time we walk past that place. Hey, I only need twenty bucks for a bike too, Andrew. But, you don't understand. No way am I gonna' work as hard as you. All I have to do is make some of the guys bet me on a couple of sure things. I'm fast and I know it, and I can outrun all of our friends. I just have to lie a little and tell them my leg is hurt . . . make 'em think I can't run as fast as usual. Do a couple of short races and bet real small wagers and lose to the guys, maybe two in a row. After I get 'em sure that I'll lose again, I'll bet 'em twice as much, double or nothing. They'll bet, we'll race, I'll turn on the speed and win. Then I'll walk away with their money. It can't lose. What a brilliant idea, if I say so myself!*

Jonathon relived how Andrew had shaken his head 'cause he couldn't believe I had said that and then he shot a look of disgust at me . . . like I cared, he thought sarcastically.

In his mind he mimicked Andrew's voice again . . . *Jonathon, how can you think that's such a great idea? You'll scheme to set up the whole thing, lyin' and takin' your friends money by being a cheater. It's a mean, nasty trick and your friends won't be friends for long if they find out you've set 'em up.*

Jonathon thought how he loved to get Andrew going when he told him,

*Set 'em up? Big deal! So what, I'll just get other friends. Besides, they can decide not to bet if they don't want to. I'm not forcin' 'em to play; am I? Their money is their money and they can do whatever they want with it. So butt out.*

Jonathon hitched a breath as he laughed and remembered that Andrew had almost called it exactly . . . I tricked my friends, won the race and pocketed their money. Except I was lucky—they didn't catch on, but I knew they wouldn't. And with the extra twenty dollars I needed to get a bike, deep in my pocket, I had convinced Aunt Mary Kathleen to drive me, right then and there, to J. Smith's Sporting Goods to buy it. She was proud of me for earning the cash, thinking I earned it from extra chores Uncle Thomas created for me, but not really knowing how I collected it.

It was a scream when she said,

*You can pick out whichever bike you have enough money for.*

I zeroed in immediately on the one I that I had always seen through the plate-glass window, the blue *Schwinn* with whitewalls and with silver streaks on the bar leading back to the seat . . . the bike with tasseled handlebars that 'ol brother Andrew swooned over, wanted with all his heart. It was the only one of its kind from a store with a small-town inventory.

*That's the one,* I said, as I pointed it out to her.

She shook her head up and down to the salesman while totally unaware of what I was doing. Man, she was sooo easy.

I couldn't wait to flaunt my prize. Andrew's eyes almost bugged out later when he saw me spit on a cloth that I used to shine up the handlebar and then press the horn button, blasting out a loud honk while I grinned slyly.

*Too bad Andy. I told you how. If you had done it first, you would be ridin' on the Silver Sky, the only one of its kind with red, white and blue plastic streamers that'll fly like the wind!*

Andrew hated me when I pulled a fast one on him like that. Wanted to grab me and punch me and tried, but I was fast, and slippery.

I heard him mumble,

*Humph, this time he has gone too far. Michael and William wouldn't do something like this to me. They would've helped me to earn what I needed to buy that prize bike . . . I just know it.*

Jonathon told himself they were chumps too, lookin' out for everybody else instead of numero uno. He grinned, remembering that was when the funniest part was about to happen.

As Andrew was about to tell Aunt Mary Kathleen what I did, conning the money and buying his dream bike out from under him, he knew she would take a switch to my bare behind . . . that's only if he could tell her. Heard him mumble again, how he had gotten the switch twice . . . hated it, but he knew I deserved it.

Coulda' told him . . . wasn't . . . gonna . . . get to tell her!

I saw him catch her arm as she walked into the kitchen and he blurted out to her,

*Wait 'til you hear what Jonathon did. He . . .*

Jonathon impersonated her and wagged his finger, recalling her words.

*Hold it. What did I tell you about tattling on your brother? It's wrong and I don't want to hear it. Understand?*

I'm crackin' up just thinkin' of it again, thought Jonathon, quietly giggling to himself now.

*But,* Andrew had started, *he . . .*

I can still see it. Andrew looked like he was gonna' cry, his lip comin' up as he said to her, *but . . . but . . . he . . .*

Auntie had put her finger over Andrew's lips.

*No buts about it. There will be no tattling.*

I was thinkin', go get 'em Auntie. You tell 'em. Then he remembered seeing Aunt Mary Kathleen's stare as she added her thumb to her finger in a twisting motion at her lips, signifying that Andrew should seal his lips and not say another word.

Yeah, I knew that look and how emphatically she meant business and good 'ol Andrew knew better than to even *consider* challengin' her.

Then I remember Auntie sayin' to him,

*Now, you march out of here young man, and keep that lip buttoned up! Find some chores, clean up your room, but don't bother me with this kind of nonsense again.*

I had seen it all as I watched from the upper stairwell, barely sneakin' a peak between the rungs of the banister, and I twisted my own lip to hold in all of the snickers I could before I would explode!

Jonathon popped out of his chair and headed to the kitchen.

Oh yeah, I remember the old days so well. Seems like I could always come up with a new twist . . . could always wiggle at just the right time. It's a gift, he thought, as he threw his hands into the air, full of pride in his uncanny sense of luck and deception.

After he poured a glass of milk and nabbed some cookies, he was about to return to the scrapbooks when he spied his uncle's jacket.

The entire house was asleep.

His hand slithered into each pocket until he heard the paper rustle and felt the smoothness of the envelope.

"Bingo", he said softly, knowing he could wake his aunt and uncle if he let his voice celebrate.

As he glanced inside, his demeanor lightened.

"Bing-ooo," he said as he counted out ten-fifties. He didn't give it a second thought or a bit of hesitation, but re-stuffed the envelope and glided it deep into his back pocket.

Grabbing his food, he headed back to the scrapbooks, all the while planning his next gambling jaunt.

"Cards, dice, the track? Hmm, haven't been to Pimlico or Laurel—which will it be," he muttered quietly.

# CHAPTER SEVENTEEN

❧❧❧❧

$\mathcal{J}$onathon chug-a-lugged the milk, washing down the cookies, and thumbed through more pages in the scrapbook, seeing himself in his cassock and surplice while holding the Crucifix and looking so angelic standing next to Father Bollinger.

He thought,

Boy, I remember serving Masses back then and skippin' out on 'em too. Wonder how many more times I could've weaseled out if I tried. Good thing Unks never found out. He would have swatted my hiney but good. But I pulled that one off on him, too.

He giggled. Man, I can hear Aunt Mary Kathleen yellin' up to me like it was yesterday . . . like it was yesterday.

*Come on Jonathon, get up. Your uncle is gonna' drop you off at St. John's for Mass this mornin'. Did you forget? You have altar duty today. It is ten after six and you better get movin.*

I heard her traipsin' up the stairs.

*He's out in the barn and he has a meetin' in town at six forty-five. You'll just have to go in early and wait in the back of the church 'til it's time to put on your cassock and surplice.*

Aunt Mary Kathleen was talkin' fast as she scurried me out of bed and into the bathroom. I could hear her continue as I started brushin' my teeth but started tunin' her out by runnin' the water faster, which caused the pipes to shimmy, then vibrate and screech.

After she left, I grimaced into the mirror, balancin' the bristles between my teeth like I was a monster attackin' her. Then I caught the foamy run-off with my fingertips, wiped it on my shirt, and then smeared my tooth-pasted face on the towel.

I was so angry. I was thinkin' . . .

Why do *I* have to serve Mass? Get up so early and then just sit there and wait. I wish they wouldn't make me do it. Probably one of the other guys will be there and Father can say Mass with only one server. Gee, why is it always *me*?

Then I hit the hay once more and tried to catch twenty winks, but just then I had heard Uncle Thomas downstairs, then outside on the porch, getting' things ready and askin' my aunt where I was. After all, he had called me before he went to the barn at five-thirty. I heard him yell for me into the morning air, but I just ignored him, snuck back into bed and went back to sleep.

Then that confounded screen door slammed.

Man, I remember, then, I had to rush. I shimmied into my pants and shirt and tied my shoes, rushin' like I was on fire.

Uncle Thomas didn't like to be kept waitin', especially if he had an important meetin', and that day the Grange members needed to decide on some co-op problems. And, I knew by them meetin' very early, it freed each of them to be back at home and out in their fields for the rest of the day, so he had to get goin'.

Yeah, I knew all of that, but who cared, Jonathon thought sarcastically.

His thoughts continued.

I heard him say a choice word or two and then I knew I was in trouble . . . counted three beats in my head, knowin' just how long it would take Unk's stride to reach the stairwell.

Quickly, I screeched off the hot and cold water, fakin' a bathroom visit and hit the stairs while meetin' the sound of Uncle Thomas yellin' up to me.

He remembered his uncle's deep voice.

*Jonathon, get down here now!*

*Yes sir*, I said. I knew when to pacify him and down the steps I flew, grabbin' my bag loaded with fruit and a cupcake for breakfast and a sandwich for lunch.

He reminded me that I couldn't eat, not because time wasn't available, but because I had to fast before Communion, from midnight the night before. Even though the days of fastin' were over, they made me do it anyway.

Both of us climbed inside and slammed the doors of the old pickup truck. The engine turned over and onward we drove, five miles to Route 140 towards town. Fifteen minutes later we would be at St. John's Church in the heart of Westminster.

Neither of us talked much. It was too early for conversation. We just made grunts and groans like every other morning.

As we drove south on Main Street, the steeple of the church became visible. After we crossed the railroad tracks and drove about

two-hundred and fifty feet, Unks pulled up to the front of the church
and he watched as I opened the huge door. I waved as the car door
closed, and I heard the engine sputter as he drove off. The priest
was not in the Confessional back there, so I started playin' with
the votive candles, wettin' my fingers with spit and sizzlin' 'em . . .
makin' the fire go out on each one. Couldn't hear the putter of the
truck anymore. I remember thinkin' I couldn't just stand there for
forty minutes 'til Mass starts, and out the door I went.

Walkin' along Main Street, I eyed up some of the sporting goods
at J. Smith's where I'd gotten my bike a few days before. Through
Baugher's window, I saw fruit piled high in bushel baskets and
flowers in large buckets of water in Dutterer's Flower Shop. As I
walked, I turned my head back toward St. John's to see if anyone
was seeing my escape, but all that I saw was the Westminster Fire
Department and the parish buildings.

I crossed the train tracks and kept walking, seein' Gear's
Hardware up ahead. Harry's Lunch was busy now, bacon and eggs
cookin' on the grill and that smell of fresh coffee comin' from the
doorway. Too, too much goin' on. I couldn't get in there to play
my nickels in the pinball machine at the end of the wooden booths,
as I'd hoped. Stu's Music Store was closed . . . too early to zip in
there to beat on the drums. Could see the State Theatre marquee, but
popcorn wasn't poppin' this early and the Treat Shop had all of their
candies under wraps 'til later. I didn't know what to do with myself
'til Mass started.

Thought about duckin' back into church to grab my sandwich so
I double-backed, and as I crossed the railroad tracks I saw someone
comin' out of the pool hall under the Albion Hotel. It was Whitey
Travis, one of the older guys.

*Hi Whitey; watcha' doin' down there?*

Umph, remember it so clearly like it was yesterday!

Whitey told me he was playing pool with some buddies and had
to get some fresh air.

*It's an all-nighter. I almost lost my shirt a few minutes ago, but
I pulled it out at the last second. Hit the last ball in, just before
the eight ball spun 'round and 'round and stopped just short of the
hole. I had twenty dollars ridin' on that shot alone, not countin' the
game.*

I asked him if I could come down and watch, but he warned against it.

*Now what is your mother and father gonna' say to that one if I take you down there, eh Jonathon?*

There it was again. He had forgotten Whitey had asked that back then, but he replayed his answer all over again in his mind, actually repeating aloud,

"My mother and father are dead." And as he said it now, the words stuck in his throat, like they always did.

Why did Whitey have to ask that? He hated to admit that. How could they be dead? How could they do that to me?

"Yes, how could they do that to me," he said in a whisper, reverting back to present day.

"And before I even got to know them. I was only a baby, one year old, when they left me," he finished in a melancholic tone.

His mind just couldn't let it go and it had resurfaced even more as he got older. He couldn't conjure any image of either of them, but he especially wanted to remember his mother. He hated that he couldn't. All three of his brothers remembered her, even Andrew, who was three when she died. He hated Andrew for remembering when he couldn't.

Fantasizing, he thought that maybe someday she would come to him again. Maybe then, yes then, he would see her . . . her eyes and lips . . . and feel that gentle feminine touch he was sure she must have had.

He shook his head to retreat from the hurt and again visualized Whitey Travis, embarrassed, sputtering,

*Oh sorry . . . sure, come on down. What's it gonna' hurt . . . right?*

Jonathon shook his head hard, as if to erase some of the bad thoughts.

Whitey slapped me on the back, tryin' to make everythin' alright, as he held open the door for me. How could I forget walkin' into that smoky room, all grey and blue, and seein' all the guys who were much older than me? Some of them were drinkin' beer from quart bottles with handles. They had filled 'em the night before at the tavern, keepin' 'em on ice, hidin' 'em, even though they were gradually goin' flat after the 2 a.m. liquor curfew.

Most of 'em didn't even look up as we came in, just kept on shootin' pool. I watched how they maneuvered the pool sticks, chalkin' the tips to create a soft buffer between the cue and the ball.

*Deuce in the corner pocket,* one of them had said and he delivered.

And another said, *ten and four off the side and in the north corner pocket.*

Perfect shot, and that's when I saw the man collect cash from his opponent. In fact, money was exchangin' hands quite readily.

I remember thinkin', Oh, so that's how it's played. Skill is important, but knowin' when to bet and on which shooter—that's the key. Wow even though I was young I always caught on fast, very fast, especially when it came to gamblin'. I was always so lucky and still am, and I would bet on the craziest happenings and win. It was like Lady Luck was always on my side, even if it was at other people's expense, heh, heh.

The guys let me shoot while they took a break. That was so neat—all those older guys taking me under their wings. Yeah, I really felt like a big shot back then. Whitey took a bathroom break, and I snuck a coupla' swigs of his beer, my first taste of the brew. Bitter, but interestin', and if all the guys liked it, it must be good, I thought, and stole another taste.

"How can a guy forget his first time," he sighed, remembering.

When Whitey came back in, and was tightening his belt buckle, he saw me drinkin' his brew and yelled at me.

*Hey, cut it out Jonathon. You wanna' get me in trouble with the law? Lucky I let you come down here, so don't push it.*

Man, I almost jumped out of my skin when he had said that and suddenly I realized the time. It was ten 'til nine. I had been there for almost an hour and, oh man, school was starting in ten minutes. I knocked over the spittoon as I hustled out of the door, ran up the stairs, around the corner and across the street, headin' straight for the school entrance. Just as I went for the door, Monsignor Bollinger was in front of me and I almost wet my pants.

I remember how I had cringed, and coiled back, then shot him a half-look. Almost passed out when he talked to me.

*Jonathon, I missed you at Mass today. Jim O'Connor was the only altar boy, and we had a crowd at 7:30 Mass because the train from Reisterstown was full of workers for all the farms, now that it's harvest time. Father Sanders had no one to hold the paten for him when he served Communion. I was worried about you, especially since . . .*

Before Monsignor Bollinger could finish his sentence, to cover my tracks I blurted out in my most angelic voice,

*We had a problem at the farm this mornin'. My Uncle Thomas was supposed to bring me into town, but he couldn't come so I had no way to get here. Everythin' is okay now, so you don't have to worry about Uncle Thomas or ask him anythin' about this mornin'. Okay? . . . Gee, I'm gonna' be late for school. Excuse me, please.*

I went around him, opened the school entrance door and off I ran, beatin' the bell as I flew into my classroom. The nun closed the door behind me as I grinned at her like an angel, sayin', *Good morning, Sister.*

He smirked.

Whoa! Just sneaked that one by him, alright—saved by the nun and just in the nick of time. Pretty swift, if I do say so myself, pullin' off that lie to Monsignor Bollinger.

He reveled as he skimmed through more pages.

Wow! Those were the days . . . nine years ago and I'm only getting better and better.

Then, suddenly, he shut the book.

He quietly tiptoed his way back upstairs. Once in the bathroom, he began his normal morning ritual of toothpaste and shaving cream, catching his reflection often, marveling at his cunning, catlike ways as he said to his image in the mirror,

"I could teach lessons in this stuff!"

ॐॐॐॐ

Although Jonathon thought that was where it ended, what he didn't know was that Monsignor Bollinger had found his lunch bag in the back of the church, still untouched. Inside was a little note from Aunt Mary Kathleen telling him how proud she was that he was such a good boy and would be serving at Mass that very morning. She included two quarters for him to use—one for the collection basket and one for a soda and potato chips to be bought after school.

The Monsignor read the paper, trying to find out whose lunch was in the bag. Father was ready to tell Jonathon about the note when the boy interrupted with his story. He also noticed a scent on Jonathon that reeked of smoke and beer. And he had a strong feeling that Jonathon was heading for trouble by searching out the wrong people to associate with, telling lies and hooking Mass. Then he decided to keep a close watch on his actions in the near future and would talk to Jonathon after school, confront him with his findings and expect an explanation as well as an apology.

But during that day, the Monsignor had been called to the hospital to visit a terminally ill patient. Then he'd headed into Baltimore for a meeting at the Basilica of the Assumption and just before school was dismissed, returned to St. John's but was pulled once again to another responsibility.

Jonathon got off scot-free. By the time the Monsignor could have addressed the problem, he was showing up for altar serving on time, every time. So the Reverend chalked it up to an error in judgment that had happened once, tossed the quarters into the poor box and decided to let it go.

∂◦⩗∂◦⩗

While Jonathon continued to admire himself in the bathroom mirror, his thoughts reverted back to his bike at the playground and his friends, stacked one on top of each other, in the photo. His mind would not go to the place he saw in the album just before he slammed it, however—the photos of St. John's Church after the fire.

# CHAPTER EIGHTEEN

❧❧❧❧

## JULY 1966

When Mary Kathleen awoke the next morning she reached over to feel for Thomas, touching his arm and back gently to reassure herself that he had returned safely from Pittsburgh.

He didn't wake her, to her recall, and there was no response whatsoever to her note—the note she had laid on his pillow . . . the love note she had written with the words, "Honey, I'll always love you." It was the very note she had hoped he would have found the night before that would have encouraged him to feel amorous and move on his intuition.

As she lay in bed she remembered earlier, while bathing in the tub, how she had planned it all.

When he comes home, Thomas will open the bedroom door and the light from the hall will shine in, just enough, to illuminate my special love note that I'll lay on his pillow in a crease, a gully that I'll fashion to hold the note in place.

He'll pick it up and take it to the bathroom where he'll smile as he reads it and then primp up a bit. Might even shave, splash on his Old Spice, and then he'll come lookin' for me . . . like before.

I'll feel his gentle touch, on my back first, perhaps. Thomas will then sit on the bed. I'll roll and then scoot over to make room, and we'll smile to each other. He'll tell me how much he'd missed me, how he wished I'd gone along, how next time I'd have to go . . . no "buts" about it . . . he wouldn't have it any other way.

My honey will lean down and give me a very special kiss that would let me know he meant it. Our feelings will escalate as we hold each other close, him pulling me up to him while he wraps my body with his strong arms.

I'll take his hand and kiss each and every finger, then his palm, while I'll adoringly look into his eyes. Both of us will gently encourage the other with all the tenderness of the loving couple we are.

Then he'll . . .

Thomas wheezed so loud and with such harshness that the bed vibrated and a shrill whistle emanated from within the snore, breaking the magic spell Mary Kathleen was under.

She looked at him, back in the reality of day, thinking how he was gone for days and not even a nudge, much less a goodnight kiss. Humph.

Her thoughts exploded while he slept, not suspecting a thing.

Well, he can stay away for all I care, she decided, then puffed up out of bed and walked out of the room in a huff.

She mumbled,

"Humph, he'll insist that I have to go with him. Humph, no 'buts' about it . . . he wouldn't have it any other way. Humph, that'll never happen. What a bunch of bull!"

Down the stairs she flew, like a vulture searching for prey, trying to find something to explain his actions . . . or inactions. She flicked on the light and the radio as she did every morning.

Laid over the chair was Thomas' jacket. His keys, thermos and crumpled paper bag with the waxed paper wrappers were on the coffee table.

From the radio she heard Frank Sinatra singing, 'Strangers in the Night,' and she cocked her ears to note the words.

Mary Kathleen couldn't hear them all but knew them well enough to remember that two strangers fall in love as they just look at each other.

She spied some newspapers from Pittsburgh and between two copies, just barely sticking out, something lavender. As she slid the top copy she saw some scribbled phone numbers with a foreign area code jotted onto pretty lavender lace-edged paper and the words, "Call me anytime," and just under that, "Laura."

The music seemed to grow louder as it continued, which intensified the moment. The words screamed into her head and she hyperventilated, feeling like she just might faint.

She looked at the dainty scribble again, heard a few more lines and then took a deeper breath while her cheeks took on the shade of crimson.

"I'll doobie, doobie, doo him when he gets down here."

Mary Kathleen sent the newspapers flying into the trash can along with the shredded lavender lace-edged paper and the word, "Laura," which was now undecipherable, torn into pieces.

She looked over at one of the scrapbooks opened to their wedding photograph. Storming over to it, she slammed it shut.

"Just wait 'til he gets up," she muttered, and continued stewing in her temper tantrum.

Mary Kathleen definitely acted first and the remorse followed. There was no stopping her, however, when she first got an idea in her head, whether right or wrong, and today was no different. Her mind was set as she twisted it into what she wanted to believe.

She bounded down the basement steps and began rooting through storage until she came across their special picnic basket with the thermos inside. Her eyes gazed at it for a few moments. Suddenly, boxes were being shoved, hangers filled with clothes were screeching across a ceiling pipe, and a crackling sound could be heard again and again. Only a few minutes passed until she was back in the kitchen standing at the door to the basement with tears streaming down her flushed face, tears of anger and tears of pain.

The thermos was intact, but the picnic basket lay crushed and broken in her hands with small, frayed pieces of the container left clinging onto her nightgown and anklet socks, her legs scratched up to her calves.

She trampled over to the outside door and launched her armful of debris to the wind, feeling the sting of the stiff breeze from an impending storm on her wet cheeks.

When the thermos hit the ground, glass fragments were heard shattering inside the tubular metal container, and the smashed sections of the picnic basket blew away in one forceful blast.

As she watched them blow, she stood rigid, frozen in a trance.

Suddenly during a strong gust, the door whipped from behind, smacking her on the rear end and then it slammed shut, delivering her on the porch only to see the dinner bell staring back at her.

It brought back the memories . . . she became sorrowful, then angry at its sight, which brought her out of her daze. She turned, went back into the house, and slammed the door even harder.

Thomas heard the door bang and sat up in bed. After stretching and scratching his stomach, he walked toward the bathroom yawning out loud, unaware of his impending fate.

Mary Kathleen's eyes shifted upward as she heard his shuffling feet. Her teeth compressed into each other, grinding as she waited, while her internal thermometer rose, degree by degree, flushing her face and neck again.

She squinted at the ceiling, listening, holding onto the ball at the end of the banister . . . squeezing and releasing. First, she tapped her foot to the beat of the regulator clock and then paced back and forth, like an unsettled tiger, waiting for Thomas to come down the steps. After her husband turned the squeaking faucets on and off for the twentieth time and finally shut the bathroom door, she knew he was on his way.

Before his foot hit the landing she was on him, making accusations, questioning him as to who was this Laura, charging him with high crimes of unfaithfulness and hanging him for the wrong that was in her mind.

He was astounded by her anger and allegations and half fell backward off his feet.

Where was all of this coming from, he thought? Uncle Jay was sick, very sick, and he had spent three days watching over him, visiting with doctors and nurses.

And Laura, who is this Laura she's talkin' about?

Now, he remembered. She was the nurse that came to the house to help Uncle Jay get settled from the hospital. Said she'd be the one the agency would send over every day to care for him. Seemed mighty nice to me . . . had a special way about her, kind and thoughtful. How in the world did Mary Kathleen find out about her?

He was just too tired to put it all together, but he told Mary Kathleen she had nothing to worry about, that Laura was Uncle Jay's nurse and that was that.

All she wanted was for Thomas to hold her, reassure her and kiss her full on the lips, like he did before, and take her away from the loneliness and ingratitude she was feeling.

Instead, he gave her a quick wave of the hand and said,

"Oh, cut this out. Now, the last thing I need is all of this to worry me, too."

He grabbed his jacket and out the door he went with a slam, pajamas and all, retreating from the unmistakable fury of this new-found judge, jury and would-be executioner.

Mary Kathleen was raging. She hadn't gotten the response from Thomas she wanted. In fact, he just dismissed her with a hand gesture and a quick exit, like he had so many other times before.

She felt so much pent up anger, she had to do something. Down the basement steps she flew again. She threw on an old house dress hanging in the rafters, grabbed her cleaning tools and headed all the way upstairs.

Mary Kathleen began her ritual. Everything in sight was getting rubbed and scrubbed. It helped her release her frustrations and at least she saw a positive change as she went. One thing she prided herself on was her housekeeping. She polished and buffed 'til each piece of furniture gleamed, all the while playing over and over in her mind the events that had just unfolded.

"I've got a right to question him," she said. "I'm not the one who said or did anything wrong."

Actually, she told herself, I think my temper is more under control, the older I get, totally dismissing her responsibility for the argument.

But, she couldn't explain Thomas' indifferent attitude, all of his recent visits to Pittsburgh and his lukewarm responses to her.

"I feel sure he has somethin' up his sleeve that is as crooked as a dogwood branch," she thought out loud.

Peering out the window, she could see Thomas' in his jacket as he stretched and yawned, facing the acres of corn in the fields, now shoulder high, the barn looming off to his left.

He quickly looked down from side to side, shuffling his feet over and over into the dirt as if he was searching for something.

"Why can't he be that wrapped-up lookin' for me?"

Her emotions bubbled over, tears welled into her eyes and flooded down her face as Thomas turned and disappeared into the barn which embraced him as she had hoped he would embrace her.

# CHAPTER NINETEEN

❧❧❧❧

## MAY 1958

## EIGHT YEARS EARLIER

𝒯here was a slight crispness to the air as Mary Kathleen hung the third load of wash outside, sheets from the five beds flapping and snapping in the breeze, tugging to escape the clothespins. She shivered and wished she had worn her flannel nightgown instead of her sweater over the cotton one she was wearing, which proved to be too light a covering.

She thought, This is May, isn't it? With a nip in the air like this I'd swear it was late September, readying itself for a frost. Well, at least everything will dry quickly, so's I can put 'em back on the beds.

As she stood at the sink, she watched the sleeves of Thomas' Sunday shirt wavin' to her, while the towels just got as stiff as usual, breeze or no breeze.

Piles of dishes she was washing seemed to go on forever as she methodically swished two plates at a time, rinsed them and tilted them on the drain board to dry. Knives, forks and spoons stood at attention in the strainer cup, elbow to elbow, all vying for the same space.

The pressure cooker valve was beginning to dance on the lid from a bare minimum to a hefty tap, signaling that it needed some watching and a lower flame to keep the pot roast going on a very slow simmer.

She flipped open the furnace door, planning to clean out the ashes and soot, but instead tucked in kindling wood and old newspapers, loosely stacking them.

Don't want too much heat, just enough to be takin' the chill off this linoleum, that my feet are hittin' right now, she analyzed. I'll be pullin' out the ashes tomorrow. Thomas said to toss 'em in the flower garden. It'll like it.

Off she trudged to the stairs, where she asked her feather duster to sneak in and out between the rungs and over the banister arm, then float across the stair treads as she made her way upstairs.

Her arm reached as high as it could while the tool stretched it out twenty-four more inches to gather any cobwebs that had accumulated over the week.

The mop led the way down the hall, dust bunnies scurrying for their last hurrah.

Thomas' and her room was first. All the dirt in the world didn't have a chance against Mary Kathleen. She worked and worked, using her pinkie to investigate every little nook and cranny. Next, she ordered the mop under the bed, finding her favorite slippers there as her toes wiggled into them, shooing out Thomas' extra shoes to neaten up their order.

Before her were the bed and the temptation to stretch out on it, even without the bedding covers. That'll be last, once they're dry, she thought, dismissing her tiredness and knowing all five beds had to be redressed. And only then, maybe twenty minutes of rest before she would dress too.

Off in the distance, even from across the room, she could see the huge barn that Thomas seemed to go to more and more. I'm beginning to hate that barn, she thought. Seems every time I need him, Thomas is out there diddlin' around. She heaved a heavy sigh of sadness, mixed with exhaustion, as she walked into the hallway.

Her methodical routine dictated the next hurdle—Andrew and Jonathon's bedroom. Only the Lord knows what I'll find in there, she thought.

She followed the usual cleaning ritual until she discovered a sticky mess on the top of Andrew's chest of drawers. A soda bottle, still at the scene, had toppled over, splashing the liquid onto the veneer and eating through the finish.

Mary Kathleen was furious and would have confronted him at once, had he not been in school.

Her anger escalated as she thought about his carelessness; after all, Andrew would be fourteen soon and should know better. She also knew there wasn't surplus cash to repair the chest.

"When he gets home," she said through clenched teeth, "Oooh, when he gets home . . . that Andrew!!!"

Her agitation brewed as she continued cleaning down the hall and into Michael and William's room.

The handle of the mop zoomed out from behind her and it rapped the stack of comic books near William's bed, now over three feet high, near the bottom as she turned. They slid on each other's shiny covers and spread out over the slippery linoleum floor to cover most of the room. She had warned him to put them away, but to him, stacking them was away.

"Every time I come in here there are comic books all over the floor. I'm tired of cleanin' 'em up," she said furiously.

As she looked at them surrounding her, she visualized the money wasted and, on top of the last mess that she had just encountered, she blew like the pressure cooker on the stove with the heat set too high.

Her hands became a set of claws grasping the comics together and stuffing them into an empty galvanized bucket. It became a ritual of filling up the pail, marching down the steps, and then tossing the contents into the seething embers of the furnace in the kitchen, relieving her exasperation.

Over and over her talons scrunched, *Superman* and *Flash*, the first issue of *Dick Tracy*, and the science-fiction anthology, *Alarming Tales*.

"*Alarming Tales, Dick Tracy, Superman* . . . what kind of garbage is William reading these days," she vented, as she crammed them together in a mash of paper.

At the bottom of the pile were *The Lone Ranger* and *Roy Rogers,* but even they didn't elude her grip as she marched them to the metal monster, who ate them unemotionally and burped up multi-colored flames from within its belly.

"There," she said, victoriously, at the end of the ceremony, "Now I won't have to re-stack them ever again!"

The house was overheated because of her tantrum, and she threw open the windows and doors to cool it as well as herself.

When William came home to a perfectly neat and empty room, he squealed. They had a terrible argument, but of course, Aunt Mary Kathleen won, assuring him it was 1958, and at the age of sixteen he was too old to be playing with comic books.

"Nothing is left of them, only black ash," she said vindictively, lashing out at him—a convenient recipient for her pent-up anger and exhaustion. She stood looking at him, arms folded.

"Now that will teach you to put things away when I tell you to. And, not another word, young man. Your Uncle will hear about the way you yelled at me . . . just you wait!"

Her anger made him withdraw, and although he felt like hitting her, he threw himself onto the mattress and punched the pillows on his bed, squeezing out all of his emotions through tears instead. It was a sad, rite of passage, and William never really forgave or trusted her again.

# CHAPTER TWENTY

❧◌❧◌❧◌❧

William asked himself, Why did she do that . . . what did I do to make her so angry with me?

While he cried on the bed that day he found it unbelievable, even more unbelievable than the fictional stories he digested in his collection of ten-cent folly, to think that all of his magazines were gone.

His hand pounded the bed in anger and then dropped loosely to the floor where his fingertips landed on a corner of glossy paper. As he slid the rectangular shape out from under his bed, the only survivor, *Archie,* one of his oldest "friends," looked up at him.

At least I still have you, he thought, and looked around to make sure he was alone. He wiped his blubbery face on his pillow and not hearing anyone in the house, sneaked down to the kitchen to snatch a piece of white butcher's paper.

He tiptoed up the far right sides of the stair treads to keep them from squeaking and thought that if anyone would hear him, *Archie,* too, would be *a goner.*

Back in the room behind closed doors, he wrapped the comic book as if it were a fine, antique manuscript. Then, while standing on a chair, he gently stashed it high in his closet near his other special treasures he had collected—his friend's old Boy Scout badges, rocks from the stream and a few other things.

Surely, Aunt Mary Kathleen wouldn't look up there, but, to be positive, he would be checking the spot daily to see if a piece of string he set up as a warning clue had been moved.

Andrew and Jonathon were home from school and had listened as William and Aunt Mary Kathleen quarreled, but they kept out sight. They had seen her blow-ups in the past and knew she was not to be taken lightly.

Later that night, Jonathon was kicking it around with Andrew. When they talked about William's comic books being burned in the kitchen furnace, Jonathon howled with laughter.

"I wish I could've seen the look on William's face when he walked into his room and . . . abracadabra," he motioned to Andrew like a magician would over the item he wanted to disappear. "Gone!"

"Aunt Mary Kathleen sure has a temper. I've seen her pop her cork. Gotta' watch out for it. Play her just right and you use that temper to your advantage. I always do. She's a cinch; been working on it for about eleven years."

"Jonathon, you're crazy. Why would you be so happy that William lost his comic collection? I feel sorry for him. He was buyin' 'em for a long time—for two years, since he was fourteen—and had 'em piled up this high," Andrew said, while reaching out about three feet. "Got the money cashin' in soda bottles for their deposit."

"So, what's the big deal? They weren't mine, were they?" he shot back at Andrew. "Well, there ya' go."

"But Jonathon . . . you should feel bad for him and . . ." before he could finish, Jonathon was up and dashing out of the room.

"See ya later alligator," he shot back to Andrew, "Gotta' catch some bugs and pin 'em up for school. They can be St. John's mascots . . . Rah, rah, rah, sis, boom, bah.

"Now, where oh where has that little bug gone," he started to chant to the tune of 'Where, Oh Where Has My Little Dog Gone', then shot down the stairs and out through the door.

A few hours later, while carrying the oblong box with a few small holes punched in it, Jonathon quietly knocked on Michael and William's bedroom door. He had seen them a little earlier down by the barn and expected no answer, so he eased his way in and shut the door. He snickered when he looked at the empty space next to William's bed, but kept moving toward Michael's dresser with only one thought.

His hands gently moved around, up and under, and in-between the neatly folded underwear and socks—nothing. On to the next drawer and the next and the next, each time carefully re-stacking everything very meticulously, so as not to mount any suspicion.

Zip . . . nothing, he thought.

He quietly glided over to William's closet, pulling a chair with him. Jonathon was ready to search the upper shelf when he saw the string laid out, just so, much like he had done in his own hideaways, to signal if an intruder had been there. Surveying just how it was attached, he removed it and slid his hand deep into the abyss and there it was—a carton of Lucky Strikes. Inside, he counted six packs, soon to be five, as he stuck one pack into his dungarees.

Who's William gonna' tell, he thought.

Hey, what's this, he said to himself, as he slipped out the white parcel. He neatly un-wrapped it on the bed and saw the red and blue colors with the word, *Archie*, printed on the cover.

So he did get to save one of 'em after all, he thought.

He carefully re-wrapped the comic book and set it on the bottom of the shelf. After stuffing the carton deep, he replaced everything just as it was, with the rocks and badges atop it. He then set the string into place as it had been, nestled between two and under one rock, placed the chair back, and closed the closet door. As he surveyed the room through a partially closed door, he saw it was as he had found it. Jonathon shut the door and left.

After going to his room, he walked outside. There was a bulge in his back pocket and, in his arms, a shoe box, its lid tightly affixed, with the name Diane printed on it, rattling as he shook it.

# CHAPTER TWENTY-ONE

❧◦❧◦❧◦❧

$\mathcal{D}$uring the afternoon of the very next day, Jonathon was anxious to watch what he thought would be pretty funny during Biology.

Diane, his classmate, had said the plan was for her to show the finished box project today, but school would be out soon and he was worried. When Sister Bernadette turned over the poster that was attached to the top of the blackboard frame to expose tall grasses and bugs, he was elated.

"Now," he whispered to himself with glee while rubbing his palms together under the top of his desk and looking over to his right to catch the eye of his accomplice, who nodded a smirk and a wink back.

"It's important that each of you pay attention to this project," said Sister Bernadette as she looked into the faces of her seventh grade class. She had most of their attention, but every time she turned toward the blackboard two of the pupils were quietly giggling, holding their lips together by sinking their upper teeth into their lower lips to squelch the sound of laughter which would get them into deep trouble. They half-listened to her knowing what she would find soon enough.

She held up two mesh cages as she continued,

"The praying mantis and the turtle experiments will be part of our biology grade this quarter. They must be cared for and while doing so we will keep daily records of the changes that we notice. Half of the class will be responsible for the praying mantis and the other half the amphibians.

"Your assignment tonight . . . read the chapters describing each and write at least three paragraphs telling how you think we should maintain their food, water and habitat," she continued as she nestled the cages on the ledge at the window and handed out homework papers to be taken that day.

When she turned her back she heard muffled laughter, but as soon as she spun around, Jonathon and his friend tightened their expressions into stone-faced stares. Sister frowned and her gimp surrounding her face and neck gapped, causing her bandeau to slide down and cover her eyebrows. She was about to address the problem when someone knocked at the door.

Sister Bernadette walked into the hall, and she and another teacher spoke in muffled voices. She tucked her head back into the room and said,

"Boys and girls, I need to go to the Principal's office for a few minutes. Study your spelling while I'm gone. Mary Jo, take names if anyone talks."

The door closed and just as soon as Sister walked down the hall, Jonathon and his buddy started to act up. His friend said,

"Hey, Jonathon, tell 'em what you said," laughing as he instigated. "Tell 'em . . . tell 'em about the," and he raised his arms and hands outstretched like Frankenstein, "praying mantis escape."

Jonathon kept the ball rolling, relating one funny scenario after the other involving Sister's praying mantis escaping. Tiny, baby praying mantis were being hatched out of their ball-shaped nest and Sister would be opening the classroom door one morning to find them covering the entire room . . . thousands of them everywhere, even finding their way into the girls' lunch boxes.

He continued. "I can see it all . . . waxed paper, crinkling and opening up . . . and between two pieces of white bread . . . ta-da, is a praying mantis . . . his eyeballs starin' at ya as you take a bite."

The girls screamed.

Mary Jo, all the while trying to copy down the names of those who talked, screamed too.

"Ah ha," Jonathon said. "I'm tellin' Sister you unbuttoned your lip, Mary Jo."

And the class roared.

Jonathon loved the attention.

When Sister's hand touched the knob, it was as if a magic spell descended on her pupils. All were sitting with both feet on the floor, hands folded together on top of the desk . . . eyes closed with lips mimicking letters as if in a Spelling Bee.

"Mary Jo, did anyone talk?" Sister Bernadette asked.

All eyes riveted on her.

"No, Sister," she lied.

"Good. Now, let's move on. Boys, go to the cloak room and get your jackets; then be-seated. Girls, put your sweaters on and bring out your shoe box projects and set them on your desks.

"After we are all ready, we'll take them outside to open them," Sister said.

When she assigned the project, Sister didn't quite expect it to be so misinterpreted. She had told them to bring in twenty-five different bugs in a perforated shoe box and be sure to print their names and species in their copybooks and on the containers.

She expected to see small branches, a few leaves and a rock or two for the bugs to perch on. They would take all the boxes outside to open them, reveal their collections and then release them in the grasses nearby. The pupils would have the species' names printed on the box and all would return inside to discuss them.

One of the girls, Diane, didn't like the idea of touching the bugs. She teased Jonathon into collecting them for her. He promised to bring the finished project to school the day it was due, but he made her promise not to open it until Sister asked for it.

The children were all standing at their desks waiting to line up when Diane accidentally knocked the project within the shoe box onto her seat. The lid opened as the box flipped over, and the contents poured out.

Diane screamed.

There on the floor and all over her shoes and socks were twenty-five bugs, all with straight pins that had originally been pushed into the cardboard of the box sticking through them, all alive and squirming; obviously in pain. They buzzed and wiggled, trying to crawl or fly away.

Many of the students tried to retrieve them, to eradicate the pins or to put them out of their misery. Kids were screaming as bugs were squashed under their feet.

"Jonathon, how could you do this to me," she yelled, while he and his friend, the other class clown, doubled-over in uproarious laughter. Both of them shot a glance toward each other as if to say that it was better than they thought it would be, as tears of laughter rolled down their cheeks.

Sister was not amused as she realized that Diane didn't do her own assignment, and there was no reason for Jonathon to cause pain to God's little creatures that way. It showed no compassion for them and their prolonged misery. She knew that Jonathon planned the whole idea with the goal of disrupting the class. She sent him to the Principal's office immediately.

"Only I get caught. He was in on it too, but me, only me. How come it is only me walkin' down this hall," he said as he kept playing it over and over in his mind.

As he got closer to the Principal's office, he could see it all. She would send him home with a note to be signed to insure that his aunt and uncle were notified.

Grounded . . . two weeks. No allowance. No Saturday movies. No skating at Sportsman Hall Roller Rink with the guys. Yeah, her temper would flare and Aunt Mary Kathleen would be such a killjoy.

He looked left to the Principal's office door, and then looked right to the exit door, which he swiftly took.

# CHAPTER TWENTY-TWO

❧❧❧❧

It was a cool breeze blowing on that perfect spring day. The sky was icy blue and dotted with marshmallowy clouds encircling the small town of Westminster, which housed Western Maryland College, but predominantly farms and canneries.

A saleslady for Mather's Department Store was dropped off at the traffic light near the old railroad station for the Western Maryland line. As she walked up Main Street, she passed the hotel and pool hall, the shoe store and the smoke shop and could see the Rexall Pharmacy and the bank farther up the tree-lined block. Diamond rings sparkled on a fancy, lazy-susan in David's Jewelry Store window and eye glasses were displayed in another shop.

The bakery clerk doled out samples of chocolate chip cookies to passers-by, and she couldn't resist the welcoming aroma as she popped a tiny piece into her mouth.

Strains of the song, 'Tequila', with its pop-Latin beat, poured out of the car's blaring radio as the driver slowly passed the saleslady once more. He threw her a kiss and waved good-bye again.

The reflections in the plate-glass windows mirrored her image as she checked her nylons for a straight seam and a slip that might be showing at the hem of her dress. She then walked inside to start her job.

A man glanced at his hat and a mother pushed a baby carriage, both seeing themselves as well as the image of St. John's Church with its steeple, the town's tallest landmark since the 1860's, repeated in the entire line of glass fronts opposite the structure.

As the parish had grown, the buildings also expanded, with the addition of a larger rectory and a school that went to the twelfth grade.

One of the earlier dismissal bells had rung, and the lower school's bell would ring in about thirty minutes.

A fourteen year old boy was walking in front of the church, when he heard some rustling sounds and turned his head in that direction.

"Hey, Andrew . . . psst . . . over here," whispered Jonathon, motioning his hand into the air toward his brother to come his way. He was hiding between two bushes, part of the landscaping of St. John's Church while Andrew was on his way to investigate how much lessons would cost at Stu's Music store nearby.

As he walked toward him, Jonathon continued quietly, yet emphatically,

"Don't look at me! Turn your head! Is there anyone near the school? Did you see Sister Bernadette anywhere?"

"Oh yeah, she's standing outside the side door of the school. You can't see her from here, but I just passed her as I walked up the street. She was talking to Monsignor Bollinger and looking mighty upset, too. But I can't see anybody else, now."

Jonathon jumped from the shrubs, firmly grabbed his brother's arm and ran around to the side of the old church with Andrew practically flying behind him like a kite.

They quickly ran inside and closed the door.

All was cool and quiet. The air inside was delicately scented with flowers and the lingering aroma of incense.

The hustle and bustle of the world was closed out and the serenity encompassing, as they stood perfectly still, just inside the front of the church.

They scanned the wooden pews, regimented one behind the other; solid and strong, hand-carved and polished to a high gloss shine.

Andrew and Jonathon seemed to be alone.

The white marble Communion railing, showing traces of a cream vein, was cold to the touch as both boys leapt over it, balancing their hands on it for leverage.

Only a small light was lit and the sunshine soaked the beautiful stained glass windows flickering primary and secondary colors—reds, blues, greens, and rich purples—outlined in blackened lead. As they ran toward the back, rainbows were angling through them, almost pointing to every sixth pew along the way. The shimmery, dream-like dust whirled in the wind behind their path.

"Follow me!" Jonathon ordered, as he took the stairs leading to the choir loft, two-by-two, with Andrew keeping close proximity.

Both of them landed behind the magnificent pipe organ, crouching at the bench, while huffing and puffing their breath in and out.

"What . . . what's going on?" Andrew managed to blow out.

"Let's just hang out here for a while," Jonathon said. "Sister's got a bee in her bonnet," he started, but before he could go further, he cracked up with laughter, rolling around on the wooden floor, tears squeezing out of his eyes.

"A bee," he chortled in a falsetto voice, "a bee in her bonnet!"

He could barely talk, but managed to tell Andrew about the praying mantis escape story and the bugs all crawling around with the pins in their backs after Diane dropped them and screamed.

"Get it! A bee in her bonnet!" Both of them started to breakup, laughing louder and louder, looking at each other, each time howling stronger until they both felt paralyzing tightness in their stomachs.

Jonathon got up, still half laughing, "I'll be right back," he said and flew down the stairs.

Near the vestibule was the wrought iron votive stand with red sparkles of light emanating from candles inside ruby glasses, lit earlier that day probably after the morning Mass. Within a small metal box filled with sand were long, thin wooden tapers for lighting the waiting wax.

As Jonathon maneuvered a lit candle that was partially burned from within the glass cup, he thought he heard someone inside the main church. He glanced around, but saw no one. Then he grabbed the longest taper and carried both upstairs, going slowly, eyeing the flame and shielding it with his hand to prevent it from becoming extinguished.

Seeing the lighted candle and the thin stick, Andrew shot a puzzled look his way.

From his shirt pocket, Jonathon retrieved a pack of cigarettes. He unfolded the silver paper that he'd carefully closed earlier to preserve freshness. Then he stuck out one finger and tapped the pack on it, coaxing a butt to slide out part of the way. He offered it to Andrew.

"Jonathon, are you crazy? We can't smoke in here. I can see it now. Father walks in and sees smoke signals from the choir loft, then goes out lookin' for the wagon train."

They both let out a nervous giggle.

"So, let's go up," said Jonathon, motioning to a doorway.

In a flash they were up the very narrow steps, hitting them two-by-two, until they reached the spot where the eleven-hundred pound bell and the louvers were, high in the steeple.

"We can blow the smoke out of the space between the slats. I do it all the time," Jonathon said as he used his hand to remove some of the dried twigs and leaves that the birds had deposited there.

Andrew lipped the white cylinder and put the taper to the candlelight, then dragged in air as he touched the flame to the exposed end of the cigarette.

Jonathon reached on top of his ear and pulled off his waiting cigarette, but used the lit end of Andrew's to coax the fire to the tip as he sucked air through the chamber.

Both of them sucked in all the tar and nicotine one puff would allow, then another and another, sputtering a cough every time while trying to fake enjoyment.

From this vantage point, through the thin spaces of light, they took turns describing to each other all of Main Street with Mather's Department Store and the Rexall Pharmacy directly across the street and part of the Post Office building half-a-block east. To the west, one-half block, was the Albion Hotel, the Western Maryland railroad tracks and the old train station.

Andrew said,

"Hey, look up there. It's Harry's Lunch, with the best pinball machine ever and Stu's Music, where I was headed earlier and the State Theatre, where we always spend a quarter to get into the Saturday matinee.

"Man, I can see Western Maryland College up on the hill about four blocks away, but I can only see the top of Baker Chapel."

They dragged more and more smoke in and hacked.

"Ready?" Jonathon asked holding out his cigarette.

Jonathon and Andrew both positioned their remaining butts between their thumbs and middle fingers and catapulted the cigarettes as far as they could make them go, each trying to beat the other's distance like they had done before in other places. This time they flipped them through the open space of the louver, and neither boy could see where they had gone, as the slats hid both of their contestants.

The boys did their secret handshake and called it a draw.

They were laughing and engaging in horseplay as they descended the steeple steps and started down the next set towards the church floor.

"Who goes there?" they heard.

It was Cully Anderson, their uncle's friend.

They stopped, as if petrified, for what seemed like an eternity. If they would move, surely one of the wooden steps would creak, giving them away.

Mr. Anderson stood and listened, turning his good ear towards different directions.

He waited. He turned. He listened.

Finally, he was satisfied that whatever he had heard must have come from outside the building. He tossed the oil can into his tool box and picked the box up from the floor. As he turned he began walking toward the door—each footstep echoing in the quiet church.

Cully genuflected on one knee in the center aisle and bowed his head, made the Sign of the Cross on his person and walked out.

The boys heard him leave as he closed the door.

Their hearts were in their throats and each could almost hear the other's beating.

They looked at each other, breathing a sigh of relief as they wiped their foreheads. In unison they said,

"Close call!"

Both boys crept, each against his own side wall, staying low under the fourteen Stations of the Cross The eighteen-inch, hand-painted statues within the stations protruded six to eight inches and the fingers, arms, knees and elbows of the statues seemed to reach out to them as they moved by. All seven on each side were solemn, frozen in time and circumstance of Christ's Crucifixion, which would only have increased the boys' feelings of guilt, fear and apprehension were they to look up—which they did not.

Finally they reached the front, near the Communion railing, and all was quiet.

They each faced the other and slowly dragged one foot and then the other, gradually coming closer and closer like two cartoon characters. As they met in the middle, after clowning around, they genuflected and gave a half-hearted Sign of the Cross while grinning like the *Cheshire Cat* in *Alice in Wonderland*. They knew they were now alone and home safe.

Both heard a crackling, popping sound.

Andrew spied the cause first.

"Look, Jonathon," he said in astonishment while pointing toward the organ loft.

Smoke was gently lifting upward. They saw no fire, just a little smoke, and they both ran for the door nearest them, each fumbling over the other's fingers for the knob to freedom. Each pushed the other out of the way, trying to be first out, as they distorted their faces in frightened grimaces.

Finally, the door flung open and smacked the outside wall, but as it swung back there were no bodies nearby to close the latch.

# CHAPTER TWENTY-THREE

❧✦❧✦

𝓜ary Kathleen looked up to see billows of smoke coming from the downtown area. Her stomach churned as she ran to the back porch, frantically ringing the bell over and over and over again.

Thomas heard the urgency in the repeated clang and turned toward the farmhouse. Over and above it and in the distance, he too saw that enormous grey and black cloud, surging and swelling high into the air. It was close . . . too close . . . to Main Street.

The boys, oh my God, the boys could be in danger, were his first thoughts as he ran back to the house cutting catty-corner through the field.

"I heard it on the radio," she screamed as he neared.

Both of them jumped into the truck and sped toward town while she continued with *what-ifs* to Thomas, who tried to calm her fears despite his own apprehension. As they got closer they could see that it *was* definitely something on Main Street on fire. They had to park four blocks away and run toward the smoke.

They were frantic.

"Oh, dear God," Thomas said, as he gasped in horror. "St. John's Church is on fire. Where could the boys be? Please, God, please let them be all right."

Mary Kathleen wanted to continue moving closer but the police officers were holding back the crowds.

"But officer, our boys could be in danger," she said in a tearful voice.

He reassured her that all of the children that had been in school were taken to the Armory on Longwell Avenue.

Off they ran toward the Armory to find all three of the boys, who would have been attending St. John's School that day.

First, they spied William, who attended the high school.

They grabbed him with gigantic hugs. Being sixteen, he initially was embarrassed by their outpouring of love, and then hugged back as he experienced the emotion too. With great anxiety they asked if he had seen Andrew and Jonathon.

"No, I didn't, but it's wild here. Everybody's been comin' in to pick up their kids. Is it just the church that's on fire?" he asked.

"I think so, the steeple is completely gone. It's hard to tell just how bad it is, but I know she's gone," Thomas said with trepidation.

Just then, Andrew and Jonathon came from the left, behind the businesses on Main Street that were across from the church, instead of the area to the right near the Armory and Post Office.

Mary Kathleen, Thomas and William all squealed with joy as they picked the twelve and fourteen year-old boys up off the ground in a united hug.

"Are you both all right?" they yelled over the noise of the area.

"Yeah, yeah, we're okay, aren't we Andrew. Tell 'em . . . tell 'em we're okay." said Jonathon.

"Okay . . . okay . . . yeah, we're okay," said Andrew while shooting a sideways glance to Jonathon and skirting the eyes of his aunt, uncle and brother.

"Thank God, here and now, that both of you are safe," said Mary Kathleen. She started praying aloud and was joined by her family for the next several minutes, seeing other families doing the same.

Both boys swallowed hard as they prayed and shot glances to each other as a sign of solidarity.

All of them stayed there, stunned, watching for hours. As they looked down the street, they could see the smoldering church, lying in ruins. Water from the firemen's hoses continued to pour out of the front door in a mini-waterfall, and as they walked out of the building in heavy helmets, coats and boots, the looks on their faces were solemn and sad.

Thomas cried more than once while he stood there aghast that something so horrible was happening right before his eyes.

So many of his friends and fellow parishioners were present and a look of shock could be read on every one of their faces.

Thomas saw Cully Anderson among the people, and both of them grabbed each other through the sadness of the moment.

"I was in the church just before the fire started," he yelled, "reported it to the fire department. Ran as fast as I could, not fast enough, I guess. Saw it from the graveyard—the smoke I mean.

"Remember those squeaky Communion gates? I was workin' on them with my oil can. Left by the side door and was on my way home. Turned back for just an instant and she was full of smoke. It was pouring out of the louvers near the bell. Was an evil sight! Evil!

"Saw the steeple go over after flames shot up into her for a few minutes and then she toppled." He grabbed his head as he shook it from side to side as he said,

"How could this have happened . . . dear God, how?"

As these two virile men sobbed their way through the information they had, all of the Frank family there at the time—Mary Kathleen, William, Andrew and Jonathon—watched.

Andrew put his hands to his eyes and started to choke up, too. Mary Kathleen turned to him and said,

"I know how hard it must be to have something you love so much taken away from you," referring to the church.

But he only heard Jonathon's voice in his head over and over again, yelling and swearing—*so help me, if you tell another living soul, I'll tell everyone it was all your fault. You being fourteen and the older brother should have known better. How could you put your little brother in harm's way like that? After all, he's only twelve. You're the one that should be punished. Yeah, we should send you away. Away from your brothers and the aunt and uncle who raised you. Away from . . . away from . . .*

The fear of losing his family terrorized Andrew. When just a little boy he had already lost both his mother and father, and he couldn't bear the thought of being sent away from the people he loved. He sobbed deeper, sucking air into his chest, hitching a breath now and then.

Mary Kathleen continued, "Andrew, but there was nothing you could do."

But he knew . . . there was something . . . in the beginning. He could have told Father or ran up the street to the Fire Department.

Andrew spurted out, "But, I should've . . ."

Before another sound, Jonathon leapt right in front of him and looked straight into his face, eyeball to eyeball, using his own type of intimidation, and said,

"But Andrew, you heard Aunt Mary Kathleen; there was *nothing* you could do . . . *nothing.*"

Andrew gulped back his words and said no more.

As the fire was extinguished, family upon family left the scene to go to their homes, still traumatized, yet somehow they'd try to pick-up their everyday routine.

Thomas had the business to run as well as the farm. Michael, who had been out on the route when it happened, was sincerely distressed and shocked by the news especially knowing how deeply St. John's history intertwined with their family background. He agreed to cover more of his uncle's responsibilities until Thomas could sort through this terrible tragedy.

The next morning, Monsignor Bollinger called an emergency meeting to discuss the damages with Thomas Frank, Cully Anderson, Charlie—the organist, and many of the other active parishioners.

During the gathering, the Monsignor told all of them what he knew of what had happened,

"My mother had been visiting, and she was out on the porch until she was called from inside the rectory—thank God for that. The fire came out of nowhere. We were in the kitchen and didn't even know it was ablaze. Suddenly, the steeple fell. It crashed through my bedroom and the cross came through to the garden, exactly to the very spot where I usually sit at my favorite table every afternoon . . . every afternoon! Why, if I had been there, if Mother and I had been there it would've . . ."

He gulped and didn't finish. He was white as a ghost while relaying the story. The men just shook their heads while patting his back, some gasping in disbelief.

Suddenly, as he began to piece things together, Thomas exclaimed,

"Oh my God . . . thank God that you're both okay! Is the rectory gonna' be okay? I guess with all of the commotion, I didn't realize. I walked out of here in shock, yesterday, I'm sorry, I should've thought, Monsignor, about where you'd stay . . . you can both stay with us at the farm, 'til we go inside to see just what has to be done to make it right for you and your Mother.

"And our beautiful church . . . maybe, just maybe, she can be saved!"

"I'll be fine, and thanks for the offer, but I'm staying upstairs over at Harry's Lunch, temporarily. It's close to the rectory and has fresh coffee every morning; plus I'm sure I'll be needed by the inspectors to answer a million questions. As for my mother, she's decided to return home and a friend is coming to stay with her."

෨෨෨෨

The same group of men met with the fire inspector who, after determining it to be safe, told them that the rectory could be repaired. Late the next afternoon, he led them in through the front, side door of the church to assess the damages. They stood at the altar peering back. Plaster dust, soot and ashes covered everything. They could see what was left of the steeple and how it had created a hole inside the floor, about fifty feet deep. The four granite pinnacles on the outside at the base of the bell tower had torpedoed into the floor, stabbing through charred wooden pews like arrows shot from a bow to a bull's-eye.

Miraculously the bell itself, weighing-in at eleven-hundred pounds, did not injure anyone, nor did it crack when it hit the ground.

The organ was a skeleton. Bricks were upon it and the pipes behind it had become blackened and melted into a grotesque shape. Charlie couldn't believe what he saw as tears streamed down his face.

As they looked directly above them, the tabernacle lantern, once containing a thick candle kept constantly burning, was now empty except for the hanging residue of wax that had oozed through a crack in the glass and there at their feet was a puddle of it's wax that had mounded, indiscriminately.

Surveying what was left, they could see that the tabernacle and the altars were untouched, the Communion railing was perfect, and the stained glass windows, miraculously, were not broken.

The fourteen Stations of the Cross were completely intact, which surprised Thomas because they were made of horsehair and wood paste. He was amazed they hadn't caught fire, especially those nearest the flames. As he looked at them he couldn't help but think that it was as if some of the facial expressions on the statues mirrored the feelings of all of the elders there at that moment.

"Will ya' look at that," Thomas said. "The steeple fell directly between Station thirteen and fourteen—took out the entire wall, missin' each of 'em by inches. God was certainly watchin' over 'em."

"It is truly a miracle," said Monsignor Bollinger, "That no one was hurt. Let's pray that throughout the clean-up phase, God blesses us and keeps everyone out of harm's way."

The group turned to leave, mumbling as they went. Only Thomas stayed on.

It was nearing dusk as he looked through the gaping hole where the steeple once was, and peered at the first stars in the blue sky amidst dotted fading clouds both so unaffected by the devastation below.

Now alone, he raised his right hand to God and swore an oath.

"Someday, God, if you give me the power and the ability and the fortitude, I will build a new church as magnificent as this one was, the one that was where I'm standing today.

It'll be a church like our forefathers built out of their sweat and blood, a church that will withstand the test of time through the wind, rain and snow and be a testament to your goodness and love for all of us.

"Somehow, someway, I swear I'll do it—so help me God!"

He made the Sign of the Cross on himself and, shedding tears once more, turned and left.

# CHAPTER TWENTY-FOUR

❧❧❧❧

## A FEW DAYS LATER

$\mathscr{T}$homas announced enthusiastically to Mary Kathleen and their nephews as he plopped down the telephone receiver,

"Comin' here tomorrow! Ain't that great?

"Uncle Jay and Aunt Rose are comin' for a visit!"

He returned to the dinner table and reached for the mashed potatoes.

"They're not takin' the train this time . . . using his truck. Can't understand why. Said he had somethin' to bring here. I shouldn't plan anything for two, maybe three days. Ya' just never know with Uncle Jay just what's up his sleeve. Did say he'd need help from some of you boys."

Thomas was smiling again and everyone was relieved.

"Hey, no problem, Unks," Michael chimed in, as William and Andrew nodded.

Thomas said,

"Remember last year for your eleventh birthday, Jonathon, he found out the circus was gonna' be in Westminster? I couldn't believe it. He paid the trainer to ride his elephant to the farm to perform, just to surprise you and the rest of us . . . brought along the clowns too. Seems like he loves to make a production of things . . . bring a smile to your day in a big way. Always did to me anyway."

Jonathon agreed with a big grin, as he remembered.

"Then there was the time he set up the hot-air balloon ride for you and me, Thomas, right here at the farm," Mary Kathleen said. "Your friend Lester was really surprised when we landed on his property, wasn't he?"

That too brought a couple of chuckles from her husband.

"Yeah, hope he liked that bottle we gave him for all his trouble," said Thomas. "Took down part of his fence which he and I fixed . . . was the worst thing."

"Now remember, Aunt Rose and Uncle Jay will be here tomorrow, and boys," he said, looking at Jonathon, William and Andrew, you'll see 'em both after school. Michael, you'll come home as soon as you can when you finish with the routes."

಄ೞ಄ೞ

Thomas heard the vehicle stop outside the barn and knew they had arrived. The screen door slammed at the farmhouse as Mary Kathleen came to welcome them and Uncle Jay was unpacking small items from his truck even before Thomas opened the huge barn doors to greet them.

"Good to see you, Uncle Jay. How ya' doin', Aunt Rose?" Thomas asked, as he gave her a pick-her-up kind of squeeze and patted Uncle Jay on his back, welcoming them while smiling from ear-to-ear.

"Glad you're here," said Mary Kathleen as she gave Aunt Rose a special look of trepidation. When she hugged her, Rose could tell Mary Kathleen was troubled.

Uncle Jay said,

"Just wish I could've been here sooner, to see how the church looked before they took her down. Happened so fast—seems she was there one minute and now, gone. Well I'll expect a full blow by blow, Thomas."

His voice evoked sorrow as he added,

"So many of our memories are wrapped up in that church; after all I grew up goin' to Mass at Saint John's and really missed her after I moved to Pittsburgh. I'm sad, really sad, to see her go. Drove by the spot on Main Street on the way here. Still can't believe it, but seein' that cleared lot between the rectory and the school brought it all home."

The four of them sat down at the oak dining table, drinking coffee and tea, and both Thomas and Mary Kathleen relayed the story of the fire.

As Thomas started, he literally trembled,

"It was a horrible sight . . . ain't never seen nothin' like it!"

Again and again they relived all the unbelievable details that had been swimming in their heads since the tragedy.

"The fire escalated too rapidly. Why, even two extra fire companies rushed to the blaze and couldn't save her even after pumpin' thousands of gallons of water through the roof and on the rest of the church."

"Shoulda' seen it—gushin' right out the front doors!" Mary Kathleen interjected.

"After a complete investigation, the fire marshal said it was wax catchin' fire from the open flames of votive candles that most probably started the blaze up in the choir loft near the organ area. Sure had me a wonderin'. Seems like he must've made a mistake. After all what would votive candles be doin' up there?

"Wait 'til you hear this. You know them little red glass cups that hold them candles there in the stand? Well wait, here, I'll show you—in the report it said . . ."

Thomas pulled a copy of the report from his papers on the buffet and read aloud.

"The twisted poles of the wrought iron stand at the rear vestibule were still intact. The red glass cups remained in their tulip-shaped holders, although thick, charred, wooden beams had smashed all around them on 75 and 90 degree angles."

"Wow!" Jay said in amazement as he read it too.

"Eek, kinda' spooky. How could that be?" said Rose.

"The inspectors said they had never seen anythin' like it," Thomas said. "Told me it was as if the items created with artistry and devotion were passed over by the demon fire.

"And I thought so too, Aunt Rose, and it happened the same way with the Stations of the Cross and the huge stained glass windows with all the Saints portrayed on 'em.

"Even the handcrafted pews with crosses carved on the end panels that sat in the front half of the church, although singed and blistered, were salvageable. Now the ones without the religious marks were all destroyed in the blaze."

"Ain't that somethin?" Mary Kathleen asked.

"Gives me the chills," Rose said as she shivered.

"Uncle Jay I knew you'd be interested in that, 'specially the part of the report about the glass, seein's how glass is somethin' you know so much about. Seems like they shoulda' melted or popped from the heat, don't ya' think? Seems like those windows coulda' cracked too.

"Am I right?"

He didn't wait for an answer but continued.

"Oh yeah, they're fine though. We stored 'em at Lester's farm, day before yesterday. Cully, me and a couple of the other ushers crated 'em up and took 'em there. We had to encase 'em in wooden frames to keep 'em supported, so they could be stacked one on top of the other . . . three piles of three and one besides.

"And Uncle Jay, were they ever heavy! 'Cause they're so big! You remember 'em, don't 'cha? Sure are beautiful!

"Four of us men had to carry each one round the back of Lester's corn crib and the silo, then over and down, past the breeze-way to his second barn. Laid each one on a thick bed of straw for cushionin' and stuffed some in between 'em on the frames too.

"And 'ya know, good thing he got rid of most of his Guernsey cows or he wouldn't have had enough room, but he did and he sure was glad.

"Yup, got 'em all tucked away, safe and sound.

"Now, where was I? Oh yeah, now I remember. Still, the inspectors said there was no way to save the church. In fact, it had to be demolished immediately, posin' a safety hazard to anyone comin' nearby. They had to move quickly, Uncle Jay, had to pull the building down fast. Said any moment, she could've caved in. And Aunt Rose, the school is right there too, you know.

"That's why, like you said, you saw the cleared lot between the school and the rectory. They saved the rectory . . . 'course it'll need more repairs and the school, old as she is, was untouched 'cept for the smell of smoke throughout."

Thomas' emotions began to erode.

"I still can't believe that church is gone.

"These past two weeks have been tough, real tough on me. Wait 'til you see the pictures we took . . . pretty much shows it all."

His grief was so overwhelming that his eyes welled up. Hiding his tears, he left the room and searched for photos.

Mary Kathleen took Rose upstairs on a pretense. Her aunt could feel the uneasiness and apprehension, even as they slipped away and climbed the stairs. Both of them sat down on the bed as Mary

Kathleen thanked Rose for coming down for a visit so quickly. The tension began to dissipate as she poured out her concerns.

"Thomas has been so down-in-the-dumps, not at all like himself. Hasn't been eating or sleeping. Actually, last night right after he talked to Jay, I saw him take his first plateful since the fire at Saint John's. I tell ya' Aunt Rose, it was like his best friend died."

"The boys noticed the change. Michael said Thomas seemed depressed, and he was worried about him too.

"I knew he needed to talk to someone who loved that old church as much as he did so I coaxed him into writin' the letter he sent to Jay, explainin' all about it. But this is so much better. Can ya' feel Thomas lettin' it all out, much like the steam backin' up on a pressure cooker and the little knocker a startin' to rock?

"Rose, I was afraid he was gonna blow, I'm tellin' ya' . . . thought he was gonna blow!" Rose patted her on the back.

"When I got the call, you sounded upset and I was concerned about you, Mary Kathleen. We would have come sooner, but Jay had somebody working on some new idea of his, that he wanted to bring along, so we had to pick it up before we came. That's what's in those big 'ol boxes on the truck. I'm hoping whatever we brought, whatever he's got up his sleeve, will help."

Mary Kathleen smiled, hugged Rose and said once more,

"I'm just so glad you're here."

"I'm sure after dinner they'll be getting into all of that—whatever it is on the truck," said Rose.

"Guess we'd better get started, although I put a chicken in the oven earlier with some carrots, celery, potatoes and onions and they're all still cookin' right now. Won't take long to get it all together. I made a cherry pie this mornin'. Sound good? Food always seems to make things a little easier to live with, don't 'ya think?"

Aunt Rose nodded and licked her lips.

# CHAPTER TWENTY-FIVE

𖠚𖠚𖠚𖠚

When Rose and Mary Kathleen came down the stairs and walked through the hall and into the parlor, they saw both of their men looking at the loose pictures and joined them. Rose was anxious to catch up and see what had been photographed. She was shocked as she heard the details of the story unfold, photo by photo. Jay still couldn't believe it, but the visual proof of the damaged church explained what he had found so hard to comprehend.

They all shared the sadness and concern for Saint John's Parish, which they loved, and which had been so much a part of their past.

"So that's why you brought some of the religious articles to your barn, Thomas, like you wrote about in your letter?"

"Yeah, Aunt Rose, the Nativity set is boxed up and put away. I know it'll be safe here. I'll cherish it and watch over it 'til they put it in the new church that we'll have to build. Got the votive stand and all of its glass cups stored—'course it's all pulled apart and layin' out flat.

"I offered to put as many pieces as I could fit into the barn. So, three days ago, a bunch of us crated up more of the things that went to the rectory basement temporarily, right after the fire. We wrapped 'em up pretty sturdy before bringin' 'em here in our trucks. Used little them wood shavings—curlicues they call 'em—as a cushion. In fact, one of the men brought 'em from his packin' and delivery business, plus I've got all of the excelsior from packagin' that you've brought here from time to time.

"The men piled the boxes in one, whole corner. The marble angel statues were delivered by the tombstone company, Mathias Monuments, that afternoon. See, they used their machines to transport them angels. When they got 'em here and pulled 'em off their trucks, I thanked the men, shook their hands and they were gone.

"Can't tell you how anxious I was to use my own system to lift 'em up and fit 'em just where I wanted 'em . . . one on each side of the barn, hands folded and facing each other, just like they were on the altar at the 'ol church.

"But yesterday was the best day of all. The Stations of the Cross, all fourteen of 'em, came to my barn. Cully, Lester, Charlie, and me took care to wrap each one with burlap from old potato sacks and laid 'em just so on our trucks and in our cars. Made a bunch of trips, not wantin' 'em to slam against each other and maybe crack, should we hafta' stop real sudden.

"Except for the men who brought 'em, Uncle Jay, Aunt Rose, nobody knows they're here. Haven't even told the boys anythin' yet, figured today would be a good day. Don't wanna' tell 'em too much about the boxed up pieces, you know how boys their age love to snoop around. I'll just be tellin' 'em to leave those boxes alone, leave 'em be, and that Monsignor asked me to hang onto a couple of things for a few months, is all."

Thomas continued.

"I was surprised, that those Stations came ready to be hung by twisted wires at the rear of their frame. They were huge, but because the statues and their backs were hollow, not too heavy. Been playin' with 'em before you got here today. Unwrappin' 'em, lookin' at 'em real close, impressed me even more. Tilted 'em back against the walls in the smaller barn 'til I get ready to hang 'em all up.

"Had to be careful how I handled 'em 'cause those statues on 'em stick out and the standing characters are about two feet tall. The ones crouching down or bending over are twelve to eighteen inches tall. Bigger than I realized, each figure was. Two and a half feet, I guess that's about right. Yeah, the whole scene must take up about two and a half feet."

Aunt Rose asked, "Just how big are they, I mean with all of the trims and toppers? It's been quite a while since I've seen them. Now I know they're mighty big but I just can't remember."

Thomas said, "Just about the size of a front door, only three quarters as long, but . . ."

She frowned and shook her head from side to side, questioning, not quite able to visualize them.

"Well I'll just have to show you all of 'em later, out there in the lower barn . . . but well, look here in the scrapbook, Aunt Rose, at the photos of Saint John's at Christmastime.

"Now I know you've been there for Midnight Mass, remember us all goin' together, what maybe ten years ago?" said Mary Kathleen. Well yeah, I guess it has been quite a while since you've seen it all, now that I think about it."

Thomas said,

"First, look at those evergreen trees—huge! I always cut down six of the fullest Scotch Pines that I had grown each year, some smaller ones too, to fill in, and medium sized ones at the sides.

His excitement grew as he pointed it all out to her,

"Yes sir, up there on that altar, what a backdrop against all that white marble!

"Oh yeah, and them marble prayin' angels flankin' each side! Look at those swags, Aunt Rose—twenty-five feet, each one!

"I remember them ladies in the decoration group, wirin' up the fir and the spruce . . . kept addin' more and more greens so the swags were full and real sturdy. Now they were the hardest to put up, especially goin' all the way up in the eaves—Saint John's was pretty tall.

"Now does that strike a bell?

"Had red bows attached and red poinsettias—Dutterer's Flower Shop donated 'em, grouped 'em in clusters, here and there, settin' everythin' off . . . that red, ya' know."

Rose nodded in agreement, the photos and his description jarring her memory.

Thomas added,

"Oh yeah and don't forget the candles. How could anybody forget the candles?

"Why, there were so many candles to be lit on that altar for Christmas that two altar boys had to start lightin' 'em a full half-hour before Mass started!

"Sure was beautiful . . . a magnificent sight!

"Okay, now, back to the Stations. The box, you might say, that encases the scene, measures six feet high by four feet wide, and then there's the point of the inverted V at the top.

"See, see, right there," he pointed. "Brings the center up to a point, like an A-Frame on a roof. Well, that adds another twelve inches, I guess.

"Then all the way around the top and bottom is what looks like hand-carved gingerbread, kinda' to the Gothic side. Each top corner has a finial and the whole thing is finished off by a beautiful cross at the very center top of that A-frame.

"Course the finials and the crosses are separate pieces and each has an extended rod on its tip that fits into a carved hole at each side. They're a pretty tight fit, but I'm keepin' 'em boxed up . . . not gonna' attach 'em to the Stations when I hang 'em in the barn . . . no need to take a chance on breakin' 'em.

"After all, shouldn't be too long a'fore they'll be needin' 'em back, once we build a new church.

"We've got the plannin' meetin' later this week. They're sendin' decision makers up from the Archdiocese. Should be very productive. Heard the Archbishop himself will be there.

"Oops, got off the subject a bit, I was describin' 'em . . . sorry 'bout that, Aunt Rose.

"The base, the part all the characters stand on, is very thick with the corners squared off before the trim was done. They all look like they are on a platform within the box of the tableau, as some people call 'em. Made of horsehair and wood paste, don't ya' know.

"Used in the eighteen hundreds . . . the wood paste was pliable, molded easily and that horsehair must've been twined in and out and around and through to make it strong just like ya' use wire mesh before pourin' cement.

"Good thing they did—make 'em strong, that is—'cause when that eleven hundred pound bell and the steeple fell, just the vibration alone could've cracked 'em if they were only plaster, I bet.

"Glad I have them pulleys and levers to attach each one. Should say, glad you put in that gambrel roof, Uncle Jay, squared off like that, which gave me a good, flat surface to attach 'em to. Yes sir, you and my father, a great team."

Jay's ego was stroked and he puffed out his chest, hearing his nephew's praise.

"Hey, Uncle Jay, Aunt Rose, will ya' listen to me, I've been running on and on at the mouth . . . sorry."

Both were mesmerized by his descriptions and agreed that they wanted Thomas to continue.

"Well, okay. Where was I? Okay, okay.

"I decided to put seven on one side and seven on the other. Only way they should be hung, accordin' to my way of thinkin'. Drawback is . . . it is gonna' be dark up there in them rafters, and although I won't be able to see each crisp detail once they're hung, I'll have to light the space with as many lanterns as I've got. And my memory will just have to serve me well, especially if I hold 'em in my hands up close, just before I hang 'em." Thomas nodded in agreement to his voice.

"Told the bunch of 'em that brought 'em . . . oh, I know they're okay, can trust the whole lot of them guys. I told 'em, 'Let's not spread the word that all of the artifacts are here. Don't want anybody snoopin' around out there . . . don't need any trouble.'"

Uncle Jay spoke up and his face brightened like a little child's.

"Boy! You are gonna' be so happy if what I brought works out. Just wait 'til you see . . . after supper . . . after supper!"

He raised his hand as if to stop himself, while he giggled a bit.

"It can wait 'til after supper, but just you wait and see!"

# CHAPTER TWENTY-SIX

ॐॐॐॐ

Both of the men walked to the barn after they ate, while their wives did the dishes.

"We'll be out there chewin' the fat, checkin' out my new idea," Jay said.

He could hardly contain himself as he rambled on ahead, disappearing inside the barn and swinging open its doors wide. Then he stopped himself and Thomas by holding up his hand.

"Hey Thomas, first turn on the radio so we can get a weather report. That could be a problem tomorrow," he said as he frowned in deep concern, realizing he hadn't checked that.

The old transistor radio crackled as it was switched on.

"Weather coming up at the top of the hour," said the D.J. But first, Don and Phil, The Everly Brothers, and their latest hit, 'All I Have To Do Is Dream'.

While the background filled with easy sounds, Uncle Jay was ready and eager to surprise his nephew.

Earlier, Thomas had been bursting at the seams with the news, with *his* news, about Saint John's and couldn't wait to get it off his chest to relieve some built up uneasiness and despair. But now he actually focused in on the large boxes which earlier had only caught his eye. Seeing them definitely aroused his curiosity.

Thomas took one look at Uncle Jay's grinning face and knew it had to be good. He said with a hitch of humor,

"Okay Uncle Jay, whatcha' got there? Wait a minute and I'll pull the old tractor out and make some room for the truck."

Thomas yanked at the tarp covering the 1934 Farmall F-20 tractor.

"See ya' still got her after all these years and she looks brand new," Uncle Jay said, "and I'll betcha' she purrs like a kitten—ya' always did have a way with engines. Go on, pull her out and we'll play with her later, if we git time. We'll be needin' the room for this project of mine."

The ladies walked down to the barn and Mary Kathleen put her arm around Aunt Rose, who was anxious to see the items Thomas had discussed earlier. They surveyed the men and their new toys—the old tractor, huge boxes and their big smiles—shook their heads and left for the farmhouse.

"I'll bet their leavin' to go make us some lemonade for later," Uncle Jay said, winking.

"We'll be back, we'll be back," their wives said, smiling as they interlocked arms and stepped in unison.

# CHAPTER TWENTY-SEVEN

❧❧❧❧

$\mathcal{I}$t wasn't until he had the room to pull his truck in and then close the barn doors that Uncle Jay finally said,

"When you told me in your letter that the stations were gonna' be up inside the roof, I got an idea that I wanted to test out on your barn. Knew it would be kinda' dark up there, like you said. Now, if it works, we can sell them and make a fortune. Maybe not quite as fancy as these I'm proposin', but I saw stained glass panels in the stairwell of the Heinz Company in Pittsburgh and it hit me.

"Got in touch with a glazier who does stained glass and asked him to make up panels for me. They seem pretty strong, the way he put 'em together with lead and wire. Like I said, if it works, you're gonna' have extra light comin' in through the cupola, ya' won't need as many lanterns when you're workin' in here and that'll surely make it much safer. Now here, hold this ladder so I can get up there and measure out the space."

Thomas looked at his uncle with apprehension and said,

"Say, Uncle Jay. I can climb up that ladder and check out the exact dimensions for us."

Uncle Jay cocked his head back and looked at Thomas crossly,

"What's goin' on, Thomas? Don't cha' think I can climb up a ladder? I'm only seventy-seven, ya' know . . . not like I'm ninety-seven or anythin'. I still got it in me and can probably run rings around you or any of those nephews of yours."

"Okay, okay, Uncle Jay, it's your call," said Thomas, backing off.

"Now, that's more like it. Let's use the longest ladders, the ones your father and I made, and shimmy up there to see what we'll have to do, Thomas. Those pulleys and levers you installed sure will come in handy for this project, don't cha' think?"

Uncle Jay knew exactly what the dimensions needed to be, but had dropped it down one inch for the glazier, just to be safe. He eyeballed the space and surmised it would be close as he marked the spot, centered just below the peak of the roof. He saw that the panels would fit if they reinforced the edges with a track of molding to make up the small amount of difference.

As he was climbing higher, Uncle Jay yelled back,

"Barns are always so dark. If this works it could change the design of their roofs forever.

"Tomorrow we'll start," he said assuming that Thomas would want the changes to the barn roof without question. However, Thomas couldn't quite envision what the master plan was to be or how the concept could work so he had to trust his uncle's idea, just as he always did.

When they unpacked the stained glass pieces, Thomas was very pleased. He saw the prototype sketch and some notes.

Uncle Jay said,

"I had the glazier make these designs. Don't know exactly why . . . just liked 'em. Here he wrote down a description of just what we are seein'. It says . . .

"They will be consisting of a five point star surrounded by beaded bevels and clusters mimicking prisms in shades of red, blue, green, purple and yellow in a variety of textures being held by a series of triangles, all multiplied by two."

"Thomas, I hope you're gonna' like this shape. Wanted somethin' fairly simple, somethin' that made sense up there, right in the middle of the roof. It was either a star or the sun and when I told my friend all about you and me he said, 'Sounds to me like you've got your *son* already.'"

Once he said it, Jay started to act shy and even blushed a little.

"Hey, Thomas, don't take that the wrong way," he said.

He put his arm around his uncle's shoulder and said,

"Uncle Jay, that's one thing I would have been proud to admit to."

They actually froze eye contact for a few seconds and then, unsure of what they should do next, broke the connection and awkwardly walked away in opposite directions.

֎֎֎֎

Andrew and Jonathon came home before William, anxious to see Aunt Rose and Uncle Jay. All met between the farmhouse and the barn with a joyous reunion, hugs going all around.

After the normal play punches to the gut and the latest "knock-knock" jokes, Aunt Mary Kathleen sent them in for the homework ritual.

After dinner they played some card games, and Uncle Jay showed them some new magic tricks. In fact, his idea that night was to hide some candy in their house and make them follow riddles to find it.

The time flew and all settled in early for the night, Thomas and Jay knowing the next day held a full load of work in the barn.

જે⊸ક⊸જે⊸ક

Later the next afternoon, support system in place, they summoned William, Andrew and Jonathon, who had returned from school to help them lift and guide the stained glass panels.

When the fourth section was secured, it was necessary to use a leading iron to create a firm bead, sealing and waterproofing the seams for the skylight.

They continued into the night, incorporating as many lanterns as Thomas owned, although working in the eaves proved to be very challenging.

"There, finally finished. Now tomorrow we'll use the hose outside the barn to squirt water on the panels to see if there's any leakage," Uncle Jay said.

Thomas looked up at the panels against the night sky and saw only black. Even though he didn't normally question his uncle, this time he wondered if it was all worth the fourteen hour effort.

Exhausted, the men and the boys headed for their firm mattresses and soft pillows.

# CHAPTER TWENTY-EIGHT

❧✦❧✦

As the morning sun shone, it was clear that Uncle Jay had a wonderful idea, at least for Thomas. Beams of light came in at ninety degree angles, highlighting the space in the rafters where the artifacts that had been saved from the old gothic church would be attached. As time passed throughout the morning and the sunlight angles changed, more and more of the barn was lit, sending beautiful streams of blue, green, red, yellow and purple throughout, which spotlighted onto the barn floor like an actor's stage. The bevels and clusters were diffused into smaller, more delicate hues, almost like rainbows.

Thomas was amazed at the difference throughout the entire structure. Suddenly the rafters seemed more open, the barn siding looked less dreary, and his private loft was catching a few tinted rays as well.

He always liked the look of stained glass and respected the workmanship that each piece had required.

"Now, how'd you get the idea for this, Uncle Jay?" he asked as he looked up to admire the intricate design, now ready to fully digest the concept.

Uncle Jay relayed it all.

"I was studying Mr. Tiffany's work in the alcove at the H.J. Heinz Company and I just couldn't stop lookin' at it. Must've' been the start of my idea. That's the way my ideas get a hold of me, just seep into my brain without me even knowin' it.

"The very next day I was meetin' with some people at the 'ol train depot, Station Square—you know it's the one that sits below Mount Washington near the cable car, back home in Pittsburgh. It's not the station you came in on when you came to visit me; it's on the other side of the bridge. Don't know if I took you there as a boy. Yeah, sure I did, but you woulda' been too young to appreciate it. Anyway, that 'ol station has stained glass panel's both in the sides and the roof, and it's a tall, a very tall building.

"I'm sittin' there and at that point I'm tunin' out the gibber-gabber—you know me—and I'm sippin' on my last coffee. Then lo and behold, I could see it all . . . the light, the colors, the changin' effects.

"I thought if it worked here in the ceiling', why couldn't it work in the roof of that old barn back in Maryland?

"Got my creativity goin' and began plannin' just how it could work. I, err, rather we could maneuver the panels with the ladders and the pulleys. It'd be tough but I knew we could do it. I felt the dimensions were indelibly etched in my brain from so many years ago when me and your father raised that barn in Westminster. I took the chance and went with my idea to a friend of mine, a glazier.

"Told him the sizes I needed. Loved to watch how he drew out a pattern, then using a diamond cutter, scored and tapped each glass piece with intense precision. Yep, precision, cause you know how glass needs to be just so.

"It took him days to finish each part of the project, but he completed his work with pure artistry.

"Had him workin' on it long before the fire at St. John's, but last week I had to nudge him so's I could bring it along on this trip."

Jay really became visibly excited.

"You know, Thomas, this could be the big one . . . *the* big one!"

 ❧❦❧❦

His mind could see it all—he, himself, as one of the entrepreneurs that filled Pittsburgh's rich history. Mellon, Carnegie, and of course, the man he admired most, H.J.Heinz, who not only built a huge company, but treasured the workers who helped him build it. Jay also liked the fact that H.J. treated the women workers as good as the men.

Now that was the kind of man he hoped to become, a philanthropist with a good heart. All he needed was a major breakthrough of one of his creative ideas.

But now that the pet project was finished, Jay began to tally up the hours of labor and the cost of the materials. He realized his idea of the distinction of glass barn roofs was a pipe dream, much like the others.

He stood staring, hands on hips as he started to remember . . . There was my invention, seven years ago, of a bottle so inexpensive that it could be tossed away. Friends told me it would never work. So then I tried creating a plastic bottle, and they laughed at me. Gosh, my own brother, Thomas' father, invested what little money he managed to save from the farm over the years for that project, but that idea fizzled out. Instead of doubling or tripling his money, as I had promised, he lost it all. And what about other friends that were drawn into my ventures who were told that *positively* it would be a sure thing, but little or nothing happened?

Then there was that vision of mine—a unique bottle cap that could initially be pried off, then screwed back on the bottle, sealing the contents within.

Man! I must have been crazy! No wonder those Pittsburgh capitalists just weren't ready to invest in what I called creative genius.

I remember how I knocked on a number of their doors, so sure that one of my ideas would work; but logic made them skeptical, afraid to invest. Now I can understand why. However, I was not a man who gave up.

He anchored his legs and continued focusing on his latest project, not saying a word, just shaking his head and puckering up his face and his lips into a snarl rubbing them over and over and over.

Jay thought about his background . . . a young man starting in Baltimore, working with blue glass in a factory and later, at twenty-one, apprenticing at the Corning Glass Company in New York, where the first automatic bottling machine was created.

He remembered how he had gotten some of his best ideas there.

I was about twenty-five when I relocated to Pittsburgh and have been inventing there ever since. A few small contraptions worked, and financially things aren't bad. Actually I'm comfortable . . . made a good life for Rose and me. Just got to get that big, winning idea to explode! He turned, looked at the ground and sighed and began walking away.

Thomas was watching him and saw him acting dejected. He has been so close, so often, he thought. He felt he had an idea that could make his uncle feel like a success.

"Hey Uncle Jay," he said, "I need some help over here."

Thomas pointed to the first and the second Stations of the Cross.

Into the larger barn they carried them. Number three through fourteen followed, were unpacked and lined up just below where they were to be raised and attached. It was obvious that Jay enjoyed just holding them and looking deep into the faces before him. He could see how his stained glass project had brought illumination to the area.

Thomas could see his uncle's facial expression changing.

"Uncle Jay, I'm really gonna' like your idea. Just look how much bigger and brighter the barn is. Once we get these hung it'll be just great!"

# CHAPTER TWENTY-NINE

❧❧❧❧

They were hustling toward the barn after they stopped by the house to drop off their book bags. The day before had been quite an adventure—climbing ladders to help hoist the stained glass panels and maneuvering the levers and pulleys with Uncle Jay as they had done so often with their Uncle Thomas. Both Andrew and Jonathon were giddy with laughter and anticipation until they saw what was before them. They stopped as if their sneakers had hydraulic brakes.

"Hi boys . . . sure glad you're here," said Uncle Thomas.

Then he cupped his hand as he whispered to Jay,

"I told Mary Kathleen to tell 'em to come on out but not to tell 'em why. They didn't know anythin' about what me and the guys stashed in the lower barn. Wanted 'em to be surprised when they saw the things from Saint John's. Both of 'em bein' altar boys, they musta' loved lookin' at all of them religious items, much as me.

"And now, they'll get a chance to see the Stations of the Cross every time they come into this barn, seein's how I'm gonna' attach 'em up high, but keep 'em right out in the open for everyone to see."

Thomas smiled. "Well, looks like you boys are mighty surprised, all right. Want you both to know how lucky you are to be a part of the family, blessed to be the caretakers after that horrible fire."

Andrew was a little more shaken by the whole scene as he stood lock-legged just at the entrance. He glanced around the barn and saw many of the things that had surrounded him in the body of the church every time he assisted the priests at Mass before . . . he thought . . . before . . . oh God, before . . .

His stomach churned; his jaw tightened.

Thomas didn't recognize it as Andrew's apprehension, but thought it was just excited anticipation.

"I'll be needin' a little help from you boys, makin' sure not a one of them people on the tablets get a broken arm or a chipped nose as I'm hoistin' 'em up. Have to be sure those ten-penny nails will be strong enough to hold 'em as we attach 'em before lettin' 'em hang on their own. Andrew, let's give it a try. Guide the first one over toward me and hoist it up usin' the pulleys."

Thomas looked down at him from the ladder. He was white as a ghost.

"You okay, boy?

"You'd better hightail it out of here—get Aunt Mary Kathleen to fix you somethin' to eat and then come on back out later to help."

He sniffled a bit and Thomas noticed that Jonathon, bein' the good, younger brother that he was, went right on over to Andrew and took his arm, standing face-to-face with him. He thought that Jonathon probably told him to go lay down, to take it easy and he'd help instead.

Thomas and Jay watched as Andrew ran out of the barn. Jay said,

"He sure is runnin' faster than a fox being chased by the hounds."

Jonathon showed off a little attitude, saying to his uncle,

"Why don't you just stack 'em over in the corn crib and cover 'em over with a tarp? You can get to 'em easier. Why do we have to hang 'em?"

Uncle Thomas shot him a look.

"What? Don't like that idea at all and I'm tellin' you so. You just be my helper, my extra set of hands, and let me tell *you* how it is. And if I were you, I'd change that flip attitude of yours, mister!"

Jonathon quietly began to assist his uncles, seething all the while as they hung all fourteen of them.

# CHAPTER THIRTY

❧❧❧❧

$\mathcal{M}$ary Kathleen and Rose did it again. The piece of beef which they had prepared had all of their mouths' watering and with the vegetables looked like a magazine advertisement.

Thomas called out.

"Andrew, Jonathon, get in here, right now. We're not gonna' be waitin' for you after these two special ladies worked over a hot stove all mornin'."

Michael and William were already seated at the table when their brothers walked into the room. They heard the conversation and Jonathon thought, what else—they're talkin' about Saint John's again.

Both of them took their regular seats at the table and looked at each other when they heard Uncle Thomas.

"Had to put the stained glass windows somewhere after the fire. Laid 'em all out in Lester's barn, flat and straight, between layers and layers of straw 'til we'll be needin' 'em for the new church walls."

Jonathon kept his head down, swirling peas on his plate, and eked out a sideways glance to Andrew who was staring at Uncle Thomas like a deer caught in headlights. He could see that the guilt was whirling around inside him, ready to spill out everything. As Andrew pursed his lips, Jonathon just knew he was ready to blurt out exactly what he didn't want anyone to hear.

"Uncle Thomas, I've got something . . ."

Over went the glass of milk at Jonathon's fingertips. He purposely shifted the focus on the accidental puddle, as he yelped. While Aunt Mary Kathleen sopped it up, Jonathon went to Andrew, faced him eyeball-to-eyeball and said with coercive enthusiasm,

"Come on Andrew, sit next to me tonight."

He knew that would mean that William would have to shift out of his nightly spot over to the opposite side of the table, but Jonathon didn't ask him for the favor.

"Can he, can he please? He doesn't feel well." He pleaded to his aunt, who in turn, questioned a glance to William, who knew it meant—change sides, now!

As Andrew sat down, Jonathon smiled his biggest broad-faced smile while reaching under the table with talon-like claws. He gripped Andrew's leg inflicting steady pressure as if to freeze him with a strong reminder of his bullying techniques.

"Were you about to say something?" his aunt asked.

The talons tightened.

"No, no, never mind," Andrew said, faking a smile.

# CHAPTER THIRTY-ONE

❧❧❧❧

Before Uncle Jay and Aunt Rose left the next day, he and Thomas walked out to the barn once more. While he told Thomas that this was not the big one as he had hoped, he reached down into his pocket and pulled out a wad of bills, all twenties, with a tight rubber band securing it.

"Take this, Thomas. Put it safely away and let's call it a down payment on a new church. For something like the old church, tall and imposin', full of statues, stained glass windows, marble and those Stations of the Cross ya' got hangin' up there.

"It's not much right now, but it's a start. Someday, I'm hopin', it'll be plenty. I just feel like God will be helpin' me secure that money somehow, and if I'm right, I swear I'll do my part to make it happen."

❧❧❧❧

After Jay and Rose left, Thomas stayed out in the barn while Mary Kathleen was in the farmhouse preparing for bed. She looked out through their upstairs window and could see the beautiful colors of the stained glass warming the night sky, illuminated by Thomas' lanterns within.

Looks like Jay had a good idea puttin' that colored glass in there, she thought. The various hues reminded her of their wedding day at Saint John's, many years before, when she gazed into Thomas' eyes and said her vows. From behind and surrounding his head was the most beautiful biblical scene depicted on a very large stained glass window. It featured rays emanating from the sun. As she walked toward him on the altar that day, she couldn't help but notice how that sun and its rays fanned out as if Thomas had a halo. She always remembered that vision and all of the beautiful colors within the scene, and now it was replaying as one of her most treasured moments with him.

Mary Kathleen returned to the present and looked at the barn door, which remained closed, sealing her husband inside and continued to fantasize about the rest of the night.

# CHAPTER THIRTY-TWO

❧✦❧✦

$\mathcal{T}$he rubber band zinged into the air as Thomas unrolled the wad of bills Uncle Jay had given to him.

"Where am I gonna put this?" he asked himself out loud, then decided, heading for his loft and mattress to tuck away the twenty-five, twenty dollar bills. He refused to use a traditional bank to house most of his money. Thomas remembered the Great Depression of the 1930's again and the lesson he learned from his Father, when the banks failed. And, in his mind, he just knew he could be a better protector of his hard earned cash and now Uncle Jay's. He found his bedroom loft, there in the barn, to be a safe haven for his bills.

Lifting the mattress revealed pieces of burlap that encased some fives and tens that he had stashed away. All in all, he had accumulated six-hundred and seven dollars, counting Uncle Jay's money. He divided up the parcels and enlarged the area spreading them from head to toe trying to eliminate any lumps, so as to cushion his body more smoothly. More and more layers of burlap finished the make-shift box spring, and he lifted the pad onto it to cover the bounty.

As his body touched the mattress, he couldn't help but smile as he wiggled his back, knowing it was elevated by so much cash. Thomas liked the idea that this was his private information, his personal spot for such a worthwhile goal.

While he leaned into it further, against his head he felt the down pillow that Mary Kathleen has gotten him recently, which he had immediately marched out to the barn, to her surprise.

All of the lanterns had been extinguished, but for the one next to him on an old wooden keg, which he then blew out.

When Mary Kathleen saw the stained glass glow darken, she tried to quiet her inner resentment of that huge monstrosity before her. She'd had three full days with Aunt Rose and Uncle Jay who now were driving home sitting next to each other in the truck while she, filled with sadness and despair, sat alone on the window seat in her room.

# CHAPTER THIRTY-THREE

❧❧❧❧

When Thomas walked into the school cafeteria, he was anxious to see several representatives from the Archdiocese of Baltimore, including the Archbishop.

He could smell the heavy residue of smoke lingering in the air from the church that had been next door. It triggered in his mind a replay of the recent events of the fire and its devastation. Lately, it had been hard to think about anything else and he couldn't seem to get a full night's sleep.

His friends looked at him rather strangely, he thought, and then Cully Anderson put his hand on his shoulder.

"Lookin' kinda' the way I feel, Thomas, like somethin' the cat dragged-in."

"I know, I know. Can't seem to shake this one, Cully." "Hard walkin' in here tonight, lookin' next door, expectin' her to be there, projectin' into the sky."

Some of the elders, including Charlie and Lester, shook their heads in agreement.

Monsignor Bollinger took a visual scan and saw basically two groups, including many of the people always active in parish activities and several younger, newer parishioners from Baltimore City, that were recent transplants to Carroll County. He said,

"Your Eminence, we are all present and accounted for, so whenever you would like to begin . . ."

The Archbishop nodded and waved to his delegate as a sign.

After all of the formalities of introduction were completed, the chairperson from the financial committee spoke,

"We've had an emergency meeting downtown. I'm sorry to inform you that we cannot offer substantial funds to build a church, in a short period of time, to equal the magnitude of the former church of St. John's Parish—time, being one of the crucial factors, because we will have no facility large enough to house all of the people who had been attending Sunday Masses here. Now, Baker Chapel, over at Western Maryland College has been offered, and we will accept, but we don't want to take advantage and overstay our welcome.

"We know the former church was truly a masterpiece created by parishioners who emigrated from the Old Country, their respective homelands, including Italy, Spain, Poland, England, Ireland and Germany, and of course many, many others. In fact, some have referred to it as a mini-cathedral.

"And, the precision with which those masters of their trade were willing to put forth their talent was truly a gift, one which we cannot begin to subsidize with the craftsmen's fees of today.

"Therefore, I am at liberty to tell you that we would like the new St. John's Church to be streamlined, very modern in design. By building it in this way, it will be less costly to construct and run, because the maintenance will be lower, as well.

"Land has been purchased overlooking, Route 140, and the plans I have brought along tonight would allow us to begin work on the new church as soon as possible.

"If we decided to raise the funds for a larger, traditional church, however, the additional difference for that type of design would be well over two million dollars, and all of it would have to come through donations. On the other hand, if the ceilings are low and the internal spaces kept simple, the builder said that besides his crew, many of the nails could be hammered by the volunteer church members and the costs kept down.

"The old benches were spared from the fire's tongue and can be used for the first few pews, and more will be ordered in a similar style. And the altar and baptismal font that are being stored in the rectory basement . . . is that correct, Monsignor Bollinger, in the rectory basement?"

The Monsignor nodded.

He continued.

"Both of those items can stay there 'til needed. After the building shell is in progress, wiring and electrification for the structure will be completed . . . oh, and that we do have covered by our electrical staff kept on retainer at the Basilica. It'll be done at a fraction of what it could cost otherwise."

Blueprints were then spread out on the long tables, by his request, and all were invited to peruse them.

He finished with, "Of course, there are details we will have to continue to discuss, but these renderings are the ones we recommend."

Thomas was shocked by the simplistic design, low and round, more like a bunker from World War II, he thought, as he snorted to himself.

Many of the others, including Cully Anderson and Charlie, who scanned the blueprints at the table, were equally overwhelmed. Cully dropped his sheet and took a few steps back in disbelief when he saw the design.

They had to do something . . . say something . . . to keep this design off the drawing board.

Some of their first suggestions were unrealistic—bake sales, spaghetti dinners, carnivals and bingo—any kind of fundraiser, any way to get the money started.

"Pledges, that's what we'll do, get pledges from every family in the parish," said one of the elders.

"I'll start with a strong pledge," said Thomas, remembering Uncle Jay's wad of bills. Let's just hold off for a little while. Use the chapel at the college for a longer amount of time while we jump on this. Monsignor, you said we were welcome there."

Monsignor Bollinger, somewhat intimidated, didn't answer.

There was a buzz throughout the crowd while Cully again began to study the blueprints laying them out full and wide on the table at the hall, giving them another once-over.

"Look here, Thomas," Cully said. "There's not one statue proposed to be in this new building, except the Corpus on the Cross, the Blessed Mother and Saint Joseph. I don't see the spaces allotted for most of the beautiful pieces from Main Street."

Thomas agreed with Cully Anderson and couldn't contain himself. His words huffed out.

"Sir, the kind of buildin' that your committee is proposin' is too modern . . . ceilin's too low . . . seems more like a meetin' room than a church."

Then his voice rose.

"A church should have high ceilings, a choir loft, paintings of angels, and statues . . . why, we'll need more room to use the statues. And, what about the Stations of the Cross? There's no wall space for them either. And, the traditional stained-glass windows, you'd have to chop 'em all up to use . . ."

The same member of the financial committee spoke up, cutting Thomas off in mid-sentence,

"We just don't have the money to build the kind of church we had before, with those high ceilings you are speaking of. Back then in the 1860's when St. John's was built, not only were many of the items donated, but as I said, there were stone masons, painters and carpenters who donated their time to build the old church. You know how difficult it has been in recent years to pull a team together just for the carnival stands, much less to consider building a traditional church. We'll be lucky if we can cut expenses by using some muscle from the parishioners here in your parish, like it was just said.

"As for the statues, we all know who the saints are and the stations we will get will be smaller, more tailored, too."

Thomas was furious at that statement and retorted,

"What'dya mean we all know who the saints are? What about my nephews and their children, and their children's children? How are they supposed to learn?

"And the Stations of the Cross!

"What could be more heart-wrenchin' than seein' in full color what Christ must have gone through, since the statues are so lifelike in every detail, includin' drops of blood . . . and the sky? Did 'ya look at the sky that the artist painted on 'em? Why, it is so realistic you can almost hear the rumble of the clouds behind the Crucifixion scene. Now, you're tellin' me we're gonna' just forget about 'em and go with some modern sculpture or wooden pieces, like a little chapel might have, that probably don't even have a realistic lookin' person on 'em?

"What you're proposin' is not for a church, and a Catholic church at that. Why, when you look around and see all of those things, it just makes ya' strive to be more holy."

Thomas continued to be persuasive to some of the listeners, as the debate continued, but when the vote was cast that night, St. John's Church was to be low, round and modernized.

The committee leader shook his head.

"I'm sorry, but that's the way it is. The new church will be started within the next few weeks. We will be using identical blueprints

from another church, recently built in Illinois, like those which you
see on the table before you."

Thomas was beside himself with frustration, but knew he was
waging a losing battle. His only hope was to persuade Monsignor
Bollinger the next time he and Cully got together with him to pitch
horseshoes and then hope that he would dissuade the Archdiocesan
committee from pursuing their plan.

As he left the meeting he stopped at the open space where St.
John's once stood and walked onto it until he reached the spot where
he felt the tabernacle had been.

He knelt down, looked up into the sky, and said a special prayer,
like he had on the day the inspectors took him into the site of the
destruction for one last look before it was razed.

Thomas pledged his continued support for all of the artifacts that
were now in his care, back at the farm. He prayed to understand why
these beautiful items were no longer wanted. After all, both he and
his wife had been baptized and made their First Holy Communion
while all these pieces were in the church. They had been confirmed
by the Bishop under the shadows of them, as well.

He remembered Michael, William, Andrew and Jonathon, as
infants in his brother and sister-law's arms, being taken to Saint
John's baptismal font, surrounded by the rich beauty of the religious
items detailing the walls.

Then he visualized thoughts of Christmas in all of its
magnificence. Stately evergreens he always donated for the altar,
thirty feet tall, would tower into the expanse of the sanctuary and
gradually taper down to six or eight feet. The garland draped around
the entire ceiling, each loop twenty-five feet long.

And the candles, so many candles that the Deacon and the altar
boys had to start at eleven-thirty, thirty minutes earlier than midnight
Mass, lending a flame to each one.

On Good Friday, the church was packed, all of the people
participating in the Way of the Cross services. The Stations were
there, creating a pictorial essay portraying the events leading up to
the Crucifixion of Christ.

The stained glass windows, each a painting of a Biblical scene,
proving the old adage that *a picture paints a thousand words*.
Colors—ruby reds, blues, gold, rich purples and cooling greens, all

within a design that Thomas always felt was guided by the hand of God.

How could these things suddenly be outdated?

He thought about his grandfather baking all the bricks on his farm and methodically bringing every one of them to Main Street. As he rubbed his forehead and could feel the tension within, he solemnly closed his eyes for the moment.

A strong breeze came from out of nowhere, touching Thomas from behind and causing the hairs on the back of his neck to stand on end. As a chill began to encompass his body, he raised his right hand to God once more, and swore his oath again.

"Someday, God, if you give me the power and the ability and the fortitude, I will build a new church as magnificent as the one was where I stand today.

"It'll be a church like our forefathers built out of their sweat and blood, a church that will withstand the test of time through the wind, rain and snow, and be a testament to your goodness and love for all of us.

"Somehow, someway, I swear I'll do it—so help me God!"

He made the Sign of the Cross on himself, turned and left.

# CHAPTER THIRTY-FOUR

❧❧❧❧

*A*rriving home, Thomas immediately went to the barn and began sorting out everything.

Having been up half the night rehashing the results of the meeting and then thinking, planning and maneuvering the money Uncle Jay had given to him, Thomas felt physically exhausted and depressed yet, at the same time, emotionally exhilarated.

In the back of his mind he kept trying to decide how his uncle accumulated this *down payment* on a church, as Uncle Jay called it. He thought about asking him, but didn't . . . private, none of my business, he thought.

Now the adrenalin had subsided and his eyes began to feel heavy as a series of yawns overtook him.

Thomas climbed the ladder his father and Uncle Jay had made to enter his private getaway, the loft.

Many years ago he had set up the simple cot but tonight it felt like a full sized mattress. The makeshift table he had fashioned held an oil lamp, two carpenter pencils he'd whittled points onto, and a pad of paper.

As he rolled over, his vantage point allowed him to gaze directly across the barn and view the magnificent stations that he had attached to the inner walls of the gambrel roof.

Some were covered with straw and burlap to keep them clean, but he had left at least two of the fourteen exposed. Sometimes he would stop whatever he was doing to stare at them, while forming a little prayer, but now all he wanted was sleep.

He felt the movement on his back, over and over. After climbing the ladder as he always did, Torpedo was cuddling up to him and nudging while meowing louder and louder.

"You're not gonna' give it up, are ya?" Thomas said.

"All right, all right, I'm gittin' up, Torpedo," he said reluctantly, as the meowing became incessant.

"I know, you're hungry. Shoulda' fed ya' while I was down below. Had a lot on my mind, and I didn't see ya' anywhere. Out doin' your duty, I 'spect.

"Guess it's a good thing that you're here helpin' to keep my thoughts on somethin' else, 'specially while we wait to see what's gonna' happen with St. John's."

Torpedo meowed louder.

"Okay, okay, I'm comin'," he said.

Stretching and yawning again and again until he squeezed the sleep out of his eyes, he backed himself down the tall ladder. Torpedo followed, twisting and turning on its flat rungs.

Thomas opened an old Esskay Sausage tin he kept on a wall shelf, then reached inside for the measuring cup and bowl he needed for his barn companion.

"Now I know you'll eat just about anything, but Mary Kathleen swears by this blend of nuggets. Now we'll get you some fresh water and . . ."

Torpedo was ready to eat the crisp particles in the bowl when, like the bullet he was named for, he sped across the barn and disappeared through a hole just big enough for his body to fit through. He was back in a flash.

"Saw somethin' that interested you, eh, Torpedo? Goin' after it later, I suspect. You're the best."

There must have been American Short Hair lineage in Torpedo's history, mixed with Westminster city alley cat and typical mixed mouser, for at different times each seemed apparent.

While Torpedo ate, Thomas watched his tail swish back and forth and up and down in a complete circle.

It always amazed him and he thought how much he enjoyed the personality of his cat, who as soon as he finished eating, rubbed his body up against Thomas' legs completing his ritual.

He picked up Torpedo, who didn't flinch, and held him up with one hand under his chest, looked him in the eyes and said,

"I remember when you first came to live here, 'twas strictly by the skin of your teeth. Good thing Mary Kathleen's friend was walkin' by that ol' metal mailbox back then.

"She heard ya' meowin' inside, ever so softly," he continued, holding him closer now, while stroking his head, neck and ears.

"Why, what kinda' sick mind woulda' put you into a metal mailbox out there in the blazin' sun on a hot, summer day?

"Soon as she opened 'er up and put her hand inside, you grabbed onto her fingers with all the strength you had left to muster. And that weren't much."

He held Torpedo up higher than his own head, looking up at him while the cat peered down into Thomas' eyes.

"You must've been all dried out, 'cause that lady told us she immediately took you to a nearby stream to give ya' a drink and you let her put your whole body right down into the runnin' water."

He cradled Torpedo and continued to stroke him.

"Now, I know how you hate even getting' your paws wet, so I'm pretty sure you were a mighty sick, little guy.

"When that lady told Mary Kathleen and me that story, why, she became furious to think a human being could be so cruel, so inhumane, to a defenseless animal.

"She said, 'Thomas, now you know how I feel about people who mistreat animals. Always felt that they will get their just desserts. Why I'm bettin' that fate will deliver a horrible sentence to that creep, that would-be murderer.'

"Man, she was hot!" he told Torpedo, who meowed as if he agreed.

Thomas stroked his back now and the cat arched in unison with the placement of his hand.

"'Course, you still didn't come to us yet, oh no. That lady took you home and ya' still had a problem to overcome. Seems she had a new puppy, a St. Bernard weighin' thirty pounds and growin' by the minute. He thought you was his toy and kept battin' you around with a whack and a thud.

"I gotta' give it to her—that lady certainly protected you.

"Why, I'll never forget it. She pulled up in her car and, in a little basket with a lid on it—there you were.

"Hey, nobody's listening right?" he said quietly, looking around the barn.

Suddenly his whole demeanor changed and his voice went up three octaves.

"You were grey, actually darker than you are now, with black stripes and against all of that, the palest green eyes I ever did see—such a cutie of a kitten."

His voice reverted back.

"As soon as she opened the little basket and put you down you were in your domain and ya' seemed to know it right away. Walked around the property with a regal attitude as if to say, 'ya' can relax now, I'm here and I'll prove myself to be very worthwhile. I'll take care of everythin'.'

"And, by golly, you did! Why you nestled right into the scheme of things on that very day. So, of course, we knew you had to stay.

"Ridded the smaller barn of vermin first and then took on this huge barn where I spend most of my private time.

"And, your name came to me, like none other. It had to be *Torpedo*. I watched you stalk prey like no other cat we had on the farm. You'd find a strong vantage point and just wait.

"Unsuspectin' critters would scamper through the barn lookin' for tiny specks of grain that fell from the sheaths of wheat and oats we were carryin' in for storin'.

"Torpedo, your body was quiet but you kept crouchin' lower and lower, hunchin' your backside and pullin' down your tail as well. I looked into your eyes, but they was sorta' like you were in a trance—starin' di-rectly at your prey.

"That's when I cinched your name . . . Torpedo.

"It was obvious you were preparing for a launch, just like in the World War II John Wayne movie, *Operation Pacific*, made in fifty-one, when I bought my old truck. I took Mary Kathleen to see it at the State on Main Street, just the night before you got your name.

"When the torpedoes swished out with great speed and strength, they exploded with tremendous force on the enemy . . . bam . . . bam . . . bam!

"Just like you. You'd be waitin' for that perfect moment and then jump . . . no, actually you'd leap across the room and then zap, like a bolt of lightnin' straight ahead.

"Them little critters were no match for you. You'd be after 'em and next thing ya' know, in a flash you'd be prancin' back, mouse in tow, and drop it at my feet.

"Then, it 'tweren't long before you'd be climbin' up that ladder and findin' a soft spot on my cot—why, sometimes you'd even let me use it," he laughed.

Both of them were now climbing up the ladder again.

As Torpedo eased onto the cot next to Thomas, he tucked his paws underneath his body. Then he wrapped his tail around his head and tucked it low, creating a circle resembling an embryo.

On that night, just as Torpedo began to nod off, swallows soared into the barn through a small space in the air vent that was near the stained-glass panels that Uncle Jay, Thomas and his nephews had installed. Thomas looked at the birds against the beautiful colors that were slowly appearing—the morning sun rising behind their project.

He nodded off, but not Torpedo. Instead, the cat lifted his head and followed the birds with his peridot green eyes and marked where they went. When he would see a bird perch on the frame of the stations or on one of the statue heads that protruded forward, he didn't budge because he knew it was impossible to catch them or get nearer to them.

There was no bridge to get him from the loft across the expanse of the barn to the birds atop the figurines. They sensed it and didn't fly off.

It didn't, however, keep him from his pre-attack ritual, gnashing his teeth, an ongoing chatter-type succession, while his eyes became fixated, gradually enlarging as he stared.

And if only a cat could, he would have wished and hoped for a magic carpet to appear between the loft and the opposite wall of the barn, upon which he could have zoomed.

# CHAPTER THIRTY-FIVE

❧❧❧❧

## EIGHT YEARS LATER

## 1966

𝔍he new Church had been built—sleek, round and streamlined, and although Thomas continued to be very active in parish activities, his heart pined for the tradition he felt was missing. Eight years had passed, but it all seemed like it had happened yesterday. He remained an usher at the Masses and watchdog over the collections, helping count the weekly donations.

Uncle Jay continued to send in his white envelopes, with no markings on them, through Thomas. He would discreetly drop the envelope into the collection basket, and it would show up when all the money got counted by the financial committee. Their eyes would pop each time they opened one of these mysterious envelopes and see five, one-hundred dollar bills, drop out.

Each of them tried their best to see who could possibly be the generous donor as they passed the basket down each pew, and it tickled Thomas, who kept a poker face through it all.

The Monsignor would raise his hands and say,

"God bless them, whoever they are," and end the discussion. Thomas couldn't wait for his next visit to Pittsburgh. He would report back and share a good laugh with Uncle Jay, who could visualize a certain usher rubber-necking, looking for that white envelope.

"Sure wish it could be more," Jay would say, "to build a new church, someday, much like the old one . . . tall, wide . . . one that could take all of those pieces you've got stored in the barn."

"Do ya' think it'll happen someday, Uncle Jay?"

"I dunno', Thomas, guess that's in the Lord's hands. But I'd like to do my share," Jay said as he handed Thomas a small paper bag.

When Thomas looked inside, this time he found twelve one-hundred dollar bills rolled and wrapped with a rubber band.

"Put these with the others, Thomas. I know they'll be safe with you."

"Uncle Jay, how . . . when?"

"Thomas, God's been good to me. Strong back, nimble fingers and a creative mind, many talents . . . the rest was up to me. Sometimes I'd get ideas crazier than usual and fall flat on my face, but then again . . . been talkin' to the manager over at the Heinz Company, now and again, and maybe, just maybe, I've got somethin' he can use. Fair man, good businessman, certainly has made some of the right decisions. Only hope, in the future, I can be part of the company that H.J. started in the past."

Later in the day, as Thomas drove home with the sun setting behind him, he played it all over in his mind, just as he had done so often. It was as if a cancer was tearing away at his skin—the fire, the devastation, the tragedy—how could it all have happened?

He was constantly fighting it all, back and forth in his mind, over and over again. And Uncle Jay, especially now . . . he should be able to reap the benefits of his hard work, but instead he keeps puttin' aside more and more money for St. John's. He certainly isn't livin' like a king—same old house, same furniture, as always.

God, why did you let this happen, he thought. His anger grew as he said aloud now,

"God you could have kept this from happening. How could you put all of us through such pain when we were trying to do Your work in Your house?" his voice raising as he hit the steering wheel with the palm of his hand, rebuking the Almighty.

He had a hard time giving the road his full attention. Ahead, he saw the rest stop, pulled into it and decided to close his eyes.

When he started to doze a feeling came over him haunting, eerie—almost seductive. Sounds surrounded him—light and melodic—almost as if the wind was blowing through the trees, but none stirred!

He thought he saw movement . . . heard a voice, quiet yet powerful . . . *build that new church, Thomas, just as you dreamed it should be. Build it big, just as big as the money will allow. Bide your time, Thomas. There is a plan.*

As he opened his eyes, he looked around. Did I really hear someone or something . . . just now?

His watch showed an hour had passed. It only seemed like he shut his eyes for ten minutes. There was nothing there but his ever-ready pickup truck and the trees before him.

He played it back in his mind, rubbing his eyes in disbelief, emulsifying sweat into their sockets.

His surroundings blurred as he tried to wipe away the problem, only to intensify it with his salty perspiration. Finally he used the inside edge of his shirttail, sliding it out of his Levi's and wiping from corner to corner.

"Did I really hear a voice?" he asked himself again, blinking over and over.

"Was it a dream?"

But he remembered the voice . . . so powerful . . . and there was light.

Probably a headlight from a car bearin' down the highway, he thought. But the voice . . . the voice was right at his ear, tellin' him. It had said, *build that new church.*

But we've only been in the modern one such a short time, he thought.

*Build it big, just as big as the money will allow.*

He thought, what money? The collections were just makin' expenses, even with Uncle Jay's generosity.

*Bide your time. There is a plan.*

"What plan?"

The doubts were real, but he was not sure if everything else was.

He started the engine and headed for home again, now wide awake, pondering each and every detail of that day and trying to sort it all out in his mind.

❧❧❧❧

After two days of intense prayer, Thomas decided to broach the subject to the new Monsignor, who had replaced Monsignor Bollinger, about building a larger church. The bounty was continuing to grow thanks to Uncle Jay's generosity, although that was a secret kept just between the two of them. That night Thomas would be attending a parish meeting and he decided to press the issue.

He waited to get Monsignor Gerard, with whom he had little history, alone.

"Just how much would we need to start building a new church, Monsignor?"

"New church, now why would we want to do that, Thomas?" he asked.

"Well, Father, I've always thought that someday we would build a new church, one that was more traditional, more like the old church that was on Main Street over where the Davis Library is today. You know, like the one my grandfather helped to build with bricks he baked himself on his farm, back in the 1860's.

"Now I know she was torn down, before your time here and everythin' but . . ."

Monsignor Gerard broke in.

"Thomas, there's not a thing wrong with the church we're in now. There are benches still available on Sunday mornings for all the Masses and I can think of a hundred places I can use any loose money I can find. Oh no, no, no . . . there's no new church on *our* horizon!"

"Okay . . . okay . . . I see, Monsignor," said Thomas with a heavy heart.

# CHAPTER THIRTY-SIX

৵৽৵৽

## 1966

Andrew walked into the room and scanned it, searching for the tan jacket he needed for work the next day. It was nowhere in sight, but the pile of books on the coffee table and the large one that was opened did catch his eye.

"Boy, I haven't seen these old books for years and years," he said aloud, his lips curving into a smile as he saw his ancestors looking so prim and proper in their photos.

He spied the brown Naugahyde cover, remembering it from his youth. Sinking into the sofa cushions he pulled the album to his thighs and scanned the rough-textured pages that held photos of him and his brothers.

There he was when he made his First Holy Communion, dressed in his navy blue suit, hands folded with a rosary draped over them and looking so angelic. Another photo showed him a few weeks later on Easter Sunday, basket in hand, in the same suit. His brothers were in the picture too, but only he had been in a suit; the others, only a white shirt, tie and dark pants. He remembered, the family couldn't afford a suit for all four boys and, unless there were hand-me-downs that fit, you didn't get one again 'til graduation.

Some of those old shots had him grinning from ear to ear as he kept turning the pages.

"Wow!" he said aloud when he saw it.

There she was, tucked under the next page on the front cover of a brochure from the auto dealer highlighting a 1961 Pontiac Catalina Sport Coupe, just like his first car in midnight blue.

"Yes sir, two-hundred ten inches of pure power—she had it all. Man, I loved that car—fastest thing on the road back then."

His mind drifted back five years when he was seventeen to one of the experiences with that car and with his brother Jonathon that which he would never forget—its first race and all of the turmoil that it brought to him.

Only five years ago, he thought again. But it seemed like an eternity after what he had been through recently . . . his buddies, the war, death and destruction.

Andrew shook his head in an effort to rid his mind of those thoughts and all of the others that were sure to follow if he would let them.

No, not now, he thought, not right now.

Glancing back to the brochure made him smile . . . made him feel happy again.

As he started to think more about it and Jonathon, he decided to play it all over again in his mind. Perhaps he could resolve some unanswered questions that had continued to haunt him.

He began to see it all, like it had happened yesterday, could hear their conversation, bouncing back and forth as it all started.

I remember . . . I remember just how it happened . . .

*Shhhh, don't wake them up,* Jonathon had said quietly to me as we tiptoed from our bedroom, then down the hall and onto the steps leading downstairs.

We had straddled the middle of the stair treads, carefully pressing each foot as if a slower motion would prevent any squeak as the wood raised and lowered—so stupid, as I look back on it.

Once downstairs, we eased outside. Jonathon shifted his eyes to look at me while he held onto the 'ol screen door, gradually lettin' it shut quietly.

*It would spoil everything if they woke up,* he whispered to me and I can see him then, cocking his head toward the door of our aunt and uncle's house.

As we walked away, Jonathon had said in a low voice, *do you know how much money will probably be bet on tonight's race? Ten guys, at least twenty bucks apiece for each of the three races, that's two-hundred per race. Sounds like a decent number to me. So what dya' think, Andrew? Are you in?*

I remember I'd whispered back, *I dunno'. Where's it gonna' be? And, don't push it, Jonathon. I told you, I gotta' check it out first!*

That made Jonathon ease off a bit, but not too much. He'd kept on pesterin' me, whisperin' in my ear like some pesky, old moth bug flyin' around.

Jonathon said, *on Bachman Valley Road, headin' towards Route 30—it's the best straightaway in the whole county. We just checked it out the other day.*

He knew I loved that road . . . said to me, *your speedo, Catalina, will be against Richie's Impala! You know you got him worried. Doesn't seem like much of a contest 'cause even though the Chevys are pretty fast startin' out, I know your Pontiac would be tough to beat. Pure power, once the weight of her gets the momentum goin'. What did ya' say, yesterday? She's got a one-by-four carburetion?*

I swear, that brother of mine knew just how to tantalize and I fell right into his trap . . . every time.

Andrew dumbed down his voice as he said,

"Dummy me said, *yeah, and she's got a 10.25 Compression Ratio and 348 horses under the hood.*"

It sure made me excited back then when I thought about all of that power. Can't believe I can still remember his every word and all of her statistics. Why, it's like I have a photographic memory about that night.

He laughed to himself. Then it was my turn to mess with him. Jonathon had almost flipped when I shook my head from side to side and said something like, *nah, I'm not in. All I have to do is get caught and Uncle Thomas will skin me alive and worse—take my license and keys away. I can't chance it. He made me promise . . .*

And now, as I look back on it all, I should have kept that promise—what a close call and what humiliation—oh well, water over the bridge now.

I can still see Jonathon when I said that I couldn't chance it. He'd held back his voice into a whisper while his body language screamed as he flailed his arms up and down like a chicken flappin' its wings.

Through clenched teeth he said, *you're not gonna' get caught. What! Are you crazy? Did you hear what I just said? Ten guys, twenty apiece, for three races. Get it? Six-hundred bucks, just like that.* He'd snapped his fingers quietly, while his eyes were buggin' out. *Andrew . . . six-hundred smackaroos!!!*

"He just never gave up," Andrew said aloud.

Then Jonathon had started in on another angle while whispering through his teeth all the while. *Do you know how many car payments*

*that is? I don't wanna' hear it. You're in. Your car's a speed demon.*
*I told the guys you'd race—you can't let me down.*

"Let *him* down—now that's a joke," Andrew said with a sarcastic edge.

Good ol' Jonathon kept on proddin' me, *it's an easy six hundred.*
*You and me, we'll split it—easy money. You just told me how great*
*she is—210 of this and compression that, and skatty-eight horses of*
*power. Prove it!*

Now, that bugged me and I had to pipe up. I remember I looked at him and said, *you're unbelievable, Jonathon. Hey, and anyway, what's all this about— we'll split it? Split it? I take all the chances, use my car and we'll split it?*

I couldn't believe him, but did I say no, did I back down—hell no. Just went along' as usual, he thought, hitting his forehead with his open palm in a self-deprecating gesture.

And then, like a big shot, Jonathon said, *hey, don't forget, I'm the promoter. Without me, you wouldn't be havin' this race. The guys are comin' because I told 'em it would be worth their while to show up. Told 'em how I cleared it with the cops.*

*You did—with the cops?* I asked, so full of belief . . . yeah, sure he did.

Then, lyin' through his teeth, he said, *oh yeah— sure, sure—all taken care of.*

I was so gullible as I listened to him sayin', *we'll be hittin' Bachman Valley Road on that straightaway, fast and furious. The only road that cuts through is John Owings Road, and I told Joey to be on the lookout for the traffic; that is, for ten bucks. We should be fine.*

"Yeah . . . fine," Andrew said aloud caustically.

He relived how Jonathon had really turned on the charm, actually more guilt than charm. He mimicked Jonathon's voice,

"Gee, Andy, if I can't count on my own big brother . . ."

And he said it just like that in that poor me, poor little brother voice that always worked on me.

I was always such a sucker for Jonathon . . . his techniques and his lies, he thought while shaking his head. Part of it though, was my own fault. When I think about past experiences, whenever I listened to Jonathon I always got into trouble. I could have said, *no way.*

But, this time I really wanted the chance to show off my new toy and I didn't care about anything but that. 'Course, I wanted to show Jonathon, first and foremost, just how important I was and that I could top out as a winner.

I'll bet it wasn't five minutes before Jonathon and I were in my shiny new two-door Pontiac that was loaded and ready to roll . . . thinkin' how we really were pretty slick to sneak out of the farmhouse and not get caught. Had a mighty cool way and it worked every time—like a charm. When I'd park that car, I remember, I always backed into a space far enough from the house so I could release the emergency brake and let her simply glide down that slight incline, there in the lane.

That night it was so quiet, or maybe I just thought it was extra quiet, 'cause I knew we were sneakin' around and the guilt was gettin' to me.

Can picture' it though, how we were driftin' with each of our doors open and could hear what seemed like each and every pebble underneath the tires crushing deeper into the gravel as we rode. Couldn't slam the doors shut. We knew if we did, Aunt Mary Kathleen and Uncle Thomas would have been on us, and then . . . deep trouble.

"So instead, look what happened," he said with that touch of sarcasm and irony in his voice as he snapped his hands together.

Yeah, I remember, we'd continued movin' until the weight of my heavy car created more and more glide. Finally we decided we were far enough from the two people who would have stopped us to start the engine. I turned the key and we shut the doors. When my foot touched the throttle—he sighed—the sheer power of that car gave me a sense of infallibility.

It was pure heaven. Thought I was such a big wheel, he analyzed.

Once out of earshot of the farm, I gave it more fuel and could feel and hear the hum of the motor.

Yeah, that's just the way it was happenin' that night, like so many others when we cruised around with the radio blarin'. 'Course we kept the windows up so only *we* could hear it so loud. Pressed in my favorite station, last button on the right—1470, WTTR. I'd heard 'em say—*The Voice of Carroll County*—as they always announced, and I can still hear what they played. It was Ray Charles wailin' out 'Hit The Road, Jack,' just as if it's in my brain right now.

When we'd heard that music come on, we both laughed and I said, *is that just too much,* and Jonathon said, *it is sooo cool.*

We both sang right along with Ray. Then to top that one off . . . it was perfect . . . 'Runaway,' by Del Shannon, was broadcast on the station next. Jonathon was strummin' an air guitar, while we both kept right-on singin'.

Andrew started singing quietly in the living room and then he remembered . . . We were bouncin' up and down in the seats and shakin' our bodies to the beat . . .

"It was like *the-e-e-e* best!" he said.

Actually that part was great, he thought and paused. Can't believe I'm rememberin' all of this!

The music blasted as we skimmed along fast, but not too fast; wouldn't want to let the cat out of the bag as to how fast my car was if the other cars pulled up, I was thinkin'.

But it wasn't until we turned onto Bachman Valley Road that I couldn't resist any longer—didn't care who saw—I just had to give Jonathon a sneak preview.

He'd continued to ride shotgun while I downshifted into a lower gear, popped the clutch, and threw her into second, forcin' both of our bodies to sink deep into the seats.

"I have to admit, we really were havin' a ball," he said.

Jonathon giggled, his stupid internal giggle, like a girl, while saying, *she's a pistol, Andy, a real pistol. This thing is fast, just like Jake's horse he raced last week. He beat out that filly from Manchester. I won twenty-five bucks on that one.* He patted and slid his palms back and forth as he continued. *This race tonight is gonna' be like takin' candy from a baby.*

We pulled off the road in an alcove, near a driveway under some trees, and waited with our lights off. I decided to turn the radio volume lower so I could roll my window down. Jonathon rolled his down too.

The air was cool as it breezed through the car and we could smell unpolluted country air that blew over from the borderin' Bachman Valley Road. Once in a while we smelled cow flop and I shoved Jonathon's shoulder and I told him to stop fartin'.

We cracked up at that one, he thought and chuckled out loud.

As we'd sat there for what seemed an eternity, we didn't say another word, but we were both gettin' antsy, and I was thinkin', like when are we gonna' get this show on the road.

# CHAPTER THIRTY-SEVEN

❧ ❧ ❧ ❧

We heard 'em first before we saw 'em, Andrew remembered. The first car pulled up, dual carburetors noisily rumblin', the pistons creatin' sounds that an auto mechanic dreams about.

They tried to get me to back down by revving up their engines, but I thought, no way, ain't gonna' happen. He whispered,

"I was cool."

Kept wonderin' though—just how many of them were there? Kept thinkin', got to show all of 'em that I've got the fastest car goin'. Not gonna' let 'em intimidate me. I know I've got power on my side!

But as I look back, I really had been shakin' in my boots.

Man, oh man, it's like a slide-show of that night, all of the details are dancin' around in my head!

Then nobody said nothin'. Jonathon and I just got out of the car and stared at 'em as three guys filed out of the first car. I heard sounds from another vehicle gettin' closer. It pulled up and three more guys got out and the driver pulled onto the old Baugher's orchard property, then got out and joined 'em.

I had seen those guys around town and I knew that they didn't go to Westminster High.

*Where's Mookie . . . and Wilson?* Jonathon had asked.

The tallest guy answered like he was mad at the world. *Ain't comin!*

And I thought, well, that ended that.

Jonathon walked over toward me and I could see his wheels turnin' as he calculated the numbers. He spoke under his breath. *Crap, both of those guys were always good for a card game and I know if they were here, they would want to get in on this action. Humph, only one hundred and eighty for the night. It could be a lot better. A side bet or two could make up the difference.*

That's when he really went into action, tauntin' the driver and his buddies. I'm thinkin'—what is he doin' *that* for?

He started in on 'em, insultin' 'em with his cutting remarks. *So, you think ya' got a real winner here, huh? Somethin' that can beat that heavy Pontiac? Oh, it's that car,* he said pointin' to their car, the Impala, like it was a piece of junk. He continued sarcastically. *That's the car? What, is that the car you rebuilt in Wood Workin' shop, I mean eh, Auto Mechanics at the Vo-Tech? Are you sure it's got enough under the hood?*

The guy Jonathon was talkin' to was really gettin' hot and real protective and it seemed to me he was stretchin' out quite a bit taller than his six-foot-three frame. He had seven inches on him and a meatier frame compared to Jonathon's wiry build. Man, I thought my brother was a dead man and I'd be next.

And then he started forward toward Jonathon, using one flat hand to push against his chest, forcing him to flounder backwards on his feet and started shoutin' at him. *Look you creep, I don't need you to tell me what I got or ain't got. Get it?*

Then he flat handed him again. His eyes were poppin' out of his head and he was yellin'. *It's a 409. Have you got that? A 4-0-9. Look, do ya' wanna' get this race goin' or not?*

I was ready to jump in and help Jonathon when he motioned with his hands for me to stop and wait. *Sure, sure. Prove how ya' feel about what ya' got. I'll give you two to one odds that my brother and his Pontiac can beat ya'. What d'ya' say? Put your money where your mouth is.*

With that, the guy whipped three twenties out and whacked 'em into Jonathon's hand while his blood boiled up into his face and his neck as he shot a threatenin' look directly into Jonathon's eyes.

Gutsy, I thought, very gutsy.

Jonathon didn't care. He was countin' on the fact that he could tantalize that guy beyond a twenty-dollar bill and that's just what he did. Then he started in on the others and I thought, man he is gonna' get his teeth knocked out. But not Mr. Lucky, oh no.

He mouthed off again. *Okay, you guys gonna' let him stand alone? He only gave me sixty bucks, but I haven't heard from the peanut gallery. He's such a good friend of yours—prove it. Cough it up and let's get this show on the road, if you really think he's even got a chance.*

He knew what he was doin'. Got 'em all angry, ready to show off, prove what a big man each of them was by toppin' off each other's bets, higher and higher.

It was like watchin' a pro in action.

The crew started diggin' deep—tens, twenties, fives and another twenty. It kept rollin' in and Jonathon held the bundle in his pocket, two hundred and fifty, or so he told me.

Before the race, the guy I was gonna' be racin', Richie, drove his car the full length of the road to check it out. 'Course, I knew that road by heart, every bump and dip. That's why Jonathon set it up there, since we'd been zoomin' on that road lately to practice. And being a perfect straightaway, Richie's buddies could see his bright red tail lights as the car disappeared into a gully of the deep hill, the only hill on that road for about three-quarters of a mile. Then it climbed up and out, revealin' his tail lights again.

Andrew said,

"What a road! About seven miles long, banked by farms for its entire length; it was . . . the . . . perfect . . . track."

Remember how we waited for Richie's car to come back after checking out the road for its glitches. Joey, our lookout, pulled up with his brother Eddie and got his instructions as to the exact location of his spot and how much he was gonna' be paid.

Jonathon had him positioned, what, maybe two miles ahead to the left on John Owings Road, and I heard him tell Joey that his job was to warn us by blowin' his horn three times in a row if the cops came.

Joey was at the crossroads. Our guy, Eddie, and one of their guys were stationed with watches, at the startin' line. Jonathon and the rest of their gang were at the finish line.

"Whew. This is scary how this is all so clear to me, like it was yesterday!" he said in an unbelieving voice, while shaking his head, side-to-side. "Just can't get over how all the details are popping up in my head like its happenin' right here, right now!"

Let me think, what was next? Oh yeah, after the first race we were supposed to return to the starting point for the next two heats.

And then he said mockingly while hitching a breath out loud, knowing what happened next,

"Yeah, sure."

Jonathon liked the heats back-to-back because he knew he would get the wad of money to grow as the guys got more and more excited. I was petrified, and my heart was in my throat . . . even thought I would have to take a leak before the race.

It was Pontiac against Chevy. We both made our way to the start, revvin' up our engines like jet planes as we left. When I looked through the rear view mirror I could see a glow from my tail lights each time I hit the brakes in the darkness, and that was it. I knew it was our D-Day.

# CHAPTER THIRTY-EIGHT

❧❧❧❧

$\mathcal{M}$y heart was beatin' so loud, I could hear each pulse of it while waitin' and waitin'. It seemed to take forever.

Suddenly, in the headlights, I saw Eddie and their guy drop their arms in succession, and we were off.

My engine sounded strong as she began on that straightaway. Then I hit second, and she began to roar. I popped her from second into third, but at that point Richie's Chevy was nosin' me out. I felt like I could catch him and I knew I was gainin' ground. We were headin' towards the finish line and then, from out of nowhere, I heard the sirens. Then I knew we were dead in the water. We both skidded to a stop and almost hit each other.

"Can see it all again! Can feel that feeling in the pit of my stomach and can even smell the air once more!" Andrew said.

I remember lights were flashin' from the cop cars, all over the place, like the first night at the Firemen's Carnival.

One pulled up next to me, and the officer grinned at me, as if to say, *You've had it, chump—gotcha!* He motioned to me with his fingers to pull ahead and over, where his buddies had the rest of the guys rounded up.

They followed both of us, and I was sweatin' bullets, not knowin' what would happen, but knowin' for sure Uncle Thomas was gonna' skin me alive.

The cops took over and made each guy stand spread-eagle against a broad oak tree by the road while being searched. 'Course, none of us had any weapons or beer.

I remember how the policemen talked back and forth to each other as they whispered and shook their heads. Meanwhile we were all tremblin' like scared dogs walkin' into the vet's waitin' room.

Then, the cops were talkin' louder, discussin' how each of us guys could be hauled in, fingerprinted, charged and held in jail for our involvement.

"They knew what they were doin', teachin' us one, valuable lesson," he said.

It seemed like I stood there for about an hour, sweatin' the outcome. Then they had us turn around while keepin' our hands above our heads. I'm sure they were havin' a lotta' fun, seein' the look of fear on our faces especially when they said to each other, *So, what dya' think? Should we take 'em in? Call their parents? Fingerprint 'em?*

My hopes fell into the pit of my stomach, 'til they said, *Nah, let 'em go. I think they learned their lesson. Is that right, boys?*

All of us, in unison, said, *Yes, sir! Yes, sir! Thank you, sir!*

Some big shots, he thought now, as he grinned.

The cop finished it off when he said, *Now get outta' here.*

I remember how we all got into our cars, the cops, too. But before the teenagers left, the squad cars pulled off and were gone.

Man, I thought that was the end of it; how wrong I was because it was then that it all started to explode!

Just as I began to back up to clear my car and get it onto the road, two of the guys stopped me.

Andrew shook his head as he continued to play it over. I thought they were gonna' break my neck when they reached in and yanked on me, tryin' to pull me out through the open window. When that didn't work, they opened my door and jerked me out, lettin' me bash my knees to the ground. Then my car stalled, and I was all alone. Eddie and Joey had disappeared when the cops came as did my little brother, Jonathon.

I have always wondered why he didn't hang out in the distance to watch what was happenin'. Normally, that's what I think Jonathon would've done . . . would've wanted to take it all in and be on top of things.

He always had the scoop—yeah, the scoop—except this time.

"Why *not* this time?" he wondered aloud.

The guys were really rough on me, pushin' me around. They were furious and yelled in my face somethin' like, *Your brother said he fixed it with the cops. We gave him ten bucks apiece when he set-up this race to buy protection. And, you owe back our money, plus your end of the payoff, since Richie's Chevy was way ahead of you when the cops came. That means, you lost at two-to-one odds and with the insurance money, I figure, altogether, it's about, six-hundred bucks. So, pay up!*

Yep, that's pretty close to what they said, and I knew I couldn't argue with 'em about who won, even though we didn't finish the race. I didn't have a leg to stand on, but I didn't have the money either, so I said back, *Pay up? I don't have the money. Jonathon's got it. He made it outta' here when the cops came.*

I started to get up on my feet and I told 'em, *When I get home, I'll get your money from Jonathon and have it by tomorrow, after school.*

Richie said, *No way—now, or else.*

And that's when it really hit the fan. All of them were coming towards me; then one guy punched me, and another guy pushed me down again. Two others were bangin' me around, really roughin' me up.

Then, the worst. When I think about it, I still can't believe it . . . just can't believe it really happened!

The ringleader, that tall skinny guy, Richie, said, M*aybe he's got the money hidden in those pants he's wearin'. Take 'em off.*

I was floored. I said to the jerk, *Take my pants off! You've gotta' be kiddin'.*

*Do I look like I'm kiddin'? Get 'em off or we'll rip 'em off,* he said.

Even now, as I think back, I have to ask myself, I had no choice, did I? Get the pants off or get totally whipped while they ripped 'em off; some choice.

I don't know which was worse—my fear or my humiliation; but at the time my fear took over as I untied my Jack Purcells, yanked 'em off and then stripped off my dungarees.

They grabbed 'em from me and searched every pocket, comin' up empty.

Then, finally, they said, *let's go guys. We'll be lookin for you later today after school, outside the Hole in the Wall, and you'd better have our money. Tell your brother Jonathon to be there at the pool hall or he's finished.*

That was it, word for word! Man, I remember that same creep walked over to my car, opened the door and rolled up my window. Andrew said,

"I dunno' why I'm rehashin' this stuff that hurt me! It's like its possessing me. All I know is I can see it so clearly, and I gotta' play it all out!"

Andrew began to perspire as he relived it.

That creep came over, grabbed my keys and pants and tossed the pants in my car, then locked and slammed the door. Held up the keys and shook 'em for me to see and then took 'em with him!

He got in his car, started it and sped away. The others left too!

My mouth must have been wide open in total shock.

There I was, standing all alone in the cold, morning air, almost buck-naked, lookin' at my brand new, 1961 Catalina Sport Coupe, the one I saved for, worked so hard for—locked and just sittin' half-on and half-off the road.

At first, I didn't know what to do, but my only recourse was to walk home in my skivvies, right? What could I do, break the window? No way, he assured himself.

I couldn't try to flag anybody down to hitch a ride, if they came by. There were no phone booths out there, and even if there were, who would I call—Uncle Thomas?

I'd broken my promise to Unks never to race my Pontiac, and that promise was the only reason he let me get that car. No way would he understand—no way. I'd 'a been grounded forever.

And so, havin' no choice I put my tennis shoes back on and put one foot in front of the other, sadly walkin' toward home, keepin' close to the side to duck out of sight if a car came by.

When I get into familiar territory, I thought, I'll cut across some fields. But then, I thought, what if one of the farmers sees me in my drawers? What could I say or do then? Man, I sure was thankin' God that I didn't have to pass through anywhere except those country roads.

And it was just about then I started to fall after takin' a step on a big rock, slippery from the mornin' dew, when I heard what I thought was a giggle. I caught myself and turned around, and as I looked behind me and all around, I saw nothin'. I said, *Jonathon . . . Joey . . . Eddie?*

I waited and listened. Then as I turned and started walkin', I heard it again, and I could've sworn it was Jonathon and his internal giggle, that only he could do so well.

I turned around again and said his name but got no answer.

Then, I heard a car comin' and scrunched down behind a bush 'til it passed.

I got up, looked once more, listened but didn't hear anything, and started walkin' again towards home.

The more I think about it now, the more I wonder . . .

He paused for a full minute flipping all of it over in his brain.

It must've taken me about an hour or more to walk home. I had to keep cuttin' in and out of the fields, waitin' for the clouds to move and uncover the moon so I could see where I was goin'. And when I snuck-in back at home, there he was, snickerin' and pointin' at me, 'cause of me bein' in my underwear. He was keepin' it quiet though, and doin' that inward giggle thing, so's nobody would wake up.

I threw on a pair of pants, grabbed Jonathon's arm, pullin' him outside so's we could talk. I made him walk down by the barn, and he started actin' so different then, like he was sympathetic to me—not laughin' or anything. Wanted to know what happened.

As I kept tellin' him, especially the parts that happened after the cops left, he seemed to be really listenin'. Kept sayin', *Really? . . . Well, I'll be! . . . Ya' don't say'* and stuff like that.

I remember tellin' him, *The guys want their money back, after school today, and they'll be meetin' me and you outside the ol' pool hall for their dough.*

Jonathon said, *Don't have it. The cops stopped me further down the road and took it all—every cent.*

I said, *Look you'd better help me find some money to give 'em. They already told me I was dead meat, and I don't wanna' be. Came close enough last night, got punched, pretty bad.*

Now that I think about it, what exactly did he say when I told him about gettin' punched? Humph, he didn't say anything about me gettin' punched. Didn't ask how or who, or want any of the details. Knowin' him, he would have reveled in me gettin' slapped around. But, he didn't push for the details. Humph.

I just remember him tossin' me five twenties and sayin', *Here, take this hundred I've been savin' and tell 'em that's all ya' got right now. You'll pay 'em a little each week or,* and then he giggled again, *they can take it out of your hide and get nothin'—their choice.*

I remember how I screamed at him, *Their choice . . . my hide, their choice? Where are you gettin' these ideas brother? It's my butt on the line. You'd better go talk to 'em, Jonathon.*

He kept proddin' me to go with his hundred and to promise them that we'd repay.

So I did. I gave 'em the money, and, whew, I felt lucky they didn't rough me up. Probably 'cause it was in broad daylight and right in the heart of town. Guess the hundred slowed 'em down, too.

Then there was the problem with my car. I had to make sure I got it home so's Unks wouldn't be the wiser. Hustled out of the house extra early, and it's a good thing one of my buddies helped me out, snatchin' the keys outta' that guy Richie's pants while he was takin' a shower after gym at his school. Had to hike on out to snatch up my car, sittin' half-on and half-off of the road.

"And, there inside were my duds remindin' me of the night before," Andrew said.

Did Jonathon go to bat for me? No. He even made me pay him back fifty of the first hundred for the gang. He skirted any of the guys from that gang, too. He told me so. I met 'em once a week payin' 'em, twenty bucks—half from me and half from Jonathon. He kept tellin' me, very convincingly, *Since we were in it together, and were gonna' split the profit, we should split the responsibilities, too.*

"Him, talkin' about responsibilities, is that a joke, or what?" He mused, shaking his head in his thoughts, as they spun 'round and 'round.

While Andrew sat there in the living room going over the race, he stared straight ahead; but now he wasn't smiling. His mind had been processing so much lately, so much had happened to him to make him see things so differently.

He was back at home now, safe at home with his family. Vietnam was so far away. Deep in his mind, he remembered his buddies that stood by him in the very worst situations, life and death situations, and that they always came through for him.

Now, as he relived his first car race, the incident that seemed like a rite of passage led him to remember other instances involving Jonathon. He recalled his first bike or the one that should have been his and how his brother shiftily maneuvered it away from him. He also thought of Jonathon's attitude and how he smirked as he spit-shined the chrome, basking in his ability to have outsmarted Andrew.

Then, there was the fire—the horrible fire at St. John's that he and his brother were responsible for and how they had hidden the truth. It was there, now, blazing up in front of him as it had so often when he was away and faced with all of the turmoil of war. He was seeing himself hypocritically saying his prayers to keep himself safe on the battlefield while knowing how he'd disappointed God by not confessing to his uncle.

Now here he was, rehashing an incident where Jonathon let him fend for himself. He should have been there for him, his own brother, his own flesh and blood.

Whenever he rewound memories, it always came out the same. Michael and William were there for him. His fellow Marines were his brothers, blood or not. Jonathon was only out for himself and didn't care who got in his way.

Andrew knew he had made his own decisions back then, but now he saw it all and how it should have been. He promised himself at that very moment that he would never let Jonathon get away with more dishonesty and that he would never be used by him again.

Then Andrew promised God to make amends for what he had been part of so many years before. He knew he couldn't turn back the clock, but from this day forward he was going to make things different, make his moves count.

# CHAPTER THIRTY-NINE

🙟❦🙟❦

𝒯he old screen door was about to slam shut, but Jonathon grabbed it in the nick of time. The card gods had been with him tonight, well for most of the night anyway, until the last hand.

It was all-in, and he was eased out of his two-pair hold by a full house.

Won all night and lost it all at the end, he thought. Oh well—some ya' win and some ya' lose.

As he walked into the hallway, Andrew was leaving the parlor and brushed past Jonathon, giving him a dirty look and a grunt for a hello.

Wonder what's with him, Jonathon thought as he watched him go upstairs and heard his bedroom door shut. Oh well, he thought, and shrugged.

He grabbed some cookies and a glass of milk, set both on the coffee table and plopped onto the sofa to watch a little TV. When he spied the scrapbooks that were still sitting there since he last saw them, his curiosity was aroused.

In one of the closed photo albums he saw a colorful paper sticking out, holding a place in the book.

After flipping pages throughout, his eyes lit up as he opened it to the marker.

I can't believe they saved this old brochure with a car like Andrew's Pontiac on the cover and stuck it in here with all these pictures, Jonathon thought.

How many years ago was that, four? No. Five, yeah five in fact . . . still in school yet pulled off one of my most ingenious schemes, if I do say so myself.

I could talk anybody into anything, maneuvering a zig and then a zag. And the beauty of it all . . . never got caught.

Still got the gift, but back then, that's when I was learnin' the ropes, just gettin' started.

He chuckled.

"Once we snuck out of the house that night, I just kept talkin' my way through it all. Gotta' see how much of this I can re-create in this memory of mine."

I remember layin' the groundwork after school at the Vo-Tech to Richie, with his souped-up Impala. The guy was a cinch, had most of his lights on, but nobody was home. And that car, he was so in love with it, he probably kissed its back fins every night, heh, heh.

I got him to agree with me—a race—his car against my brother Andrew's Pontiac.

*Make some easy money,* I told him, *if ya got anything decent under the hood. I know what my brother's got, and it's probably no contest. He could whip you with no problem and before he hits third gear.*

Man, I could feel his eyes burnin' a hole in me when I said that, but did I back down—no way!

I started to push him, like only I can do. *Bring your buddies to back you up and maybe they can push you to the finish line first.*

*You're lucky there are teachers standin' around here or you'd be flattened out, hear me, flattened out. I'd kick your butt,* he said to me mufflin' his voice so they didn't hear him.

*I'll show you, just let me know . . . where . . . when. And bring your cash 'cause you're gonna' be needin' it,* Richie said.

"That did it. Magic words! Cash! Now he was talkin!" Jonathon said, rubbing his hands together.

I piped up, *How about Bachman Valley Road—straight, long and out in no man's land?*

I knew Andy and me just checked that spot out the week before.

After settin' it up, Andy floored me when he almost backed out of the race, but I knew I could talk him back into it.

"Gift of gab—some got it, and I got it—Mr. Persuasion!" he said.

And, of course, Andy wanted to show off, especially to me, show me how that car of his could fly like the wind. Seldom did he get a chance to outshine *me* . . . and he knew it.

Tellin' him a little, white lie about the cops and how I cleared it with them, cinched it, 'cause he didn't think he could get into any trouble. Feed it to him, and he'll believe anything, I always say.

I kept thinkin' I just wish Andrew would relax, take some chances, kick up his heels a little and stop being such a wimp. So if ya' get into trouble ya' just talk your way out of it, right? What's the big deal?

"He sure got his taste of trouble that night, though, but did he get himself out of it? No way," he said.

It was like a movie on the silver screen at the State. Those guys drove up, dual carburetors rumblin', pistons firing. Why, I thought Andy was gonna' pee his pants, standin' there with his mouth hangin' wide open.

And man, when I was eggin' them on to up the ante, he looked like a scared, little boy about to cry.

He didn't think about how I was paddin' the wad of bills into better than five hundred of 'em, nestled deep in my pocket, safe and sound. Just a scared rabbit, that's all.

First, I was lookin' for Mookie and Wilson, but they didn't show, I remember I wasn't too happy about that. They were always good for some action, but I started calculatin' numbers without 'em and knew for sure it would be a little light in the take.

Now I knew I had to light a fire under 'em . . . hit 'em with a couple of side bets, get 'em all worked up so they'd drop more cash.

"I let Andy watch the Master in action," Jonathon said as he cracked his knuckles backward.

Boy, when I think about it, this is so cool how I can still re-live it and remember how much fun it was gettin' 'em hot under the collar.

I looked right into Richie's eyes that night and said, *so ya' think ya gotta a real winner here, huh? Somethin' that can beat that heavy Pontiac? Oh, it's that car?* I said it like it was a piece of trash—I can be ever so sarcastic—and I kept goin' with it.

I said in my ever so-cool way, *That's the car? What? The one you rebuilt in Wood Workin', I mean, eh, Auto Mechanics over at the Vo-Tech? Are ya' sure she's got it under the hood? What are ya' carryin', anyway?*

Man, oh man, now, he was gettin' hotter than before and real defensive. I remember how he got up into my face, bendin' down to do it. I think he stood about six-three. Bean pole!

Andy told me later he thought I was gonna' get sent to the moon when that happened.

Actually, that's when I thought I was in for it, too, 'specially when that guy started flat-handin' me on my chest. Started fallin' backward, and he kept comin', pretty much knockin' me off my feet.

The worm was yellin' at me. He couldn't handle it. His eyes were blazin', said, *look, I don't need you to tell me what I got or ain't got. You got it!*

Man, he kept on pushin' me down. I didn't like that, but I knew he was bluffin'.

*It's a 409—you gotta' problem with that?*

Hit me even harder, and I thought, whoa, I'm in trouble.

Richie said again, *A 409. Hey creep, are you ready to get this race goin' or not?*

His teeth were clenched so tight I thought they'd fall out. They looked like little Chicklet gum that we always got in the vending machine at the movies.

Andrew started in to help me, but I didn't want a full-blown fist fight—was just gettin' 'em shook up a bit, that's all. I gave him the stop-wait sign.

I told 'em, *sure, sure. Hey no hard feelin's'! You can prove how ya' feel about what ya' got. I'll give you, two-to-one odds that my brother, and his heavy car can beat ya'. What'dya' say? Put your money where your mouth is.*

Ah ha, now that got him goin'.

He whipped three twenties and whacked it into my out-stretched hand, while shootin' daggers into my eyes.

Did I care? No way. I just wanted to juice him up a bit, have him dig deeper than a measly, ol' twenty, and he did—he followed the plan.

I had to prime up the others, too, told 'em, *Okay, you guys gonna' let him stand alone? He only gave me sixty bucks, but I haven't heard from anybody else. He's such a good friend of yours? Prove it. Cough it up, and let's get this show on the road if you think he's even got a chance.*

I knew they had to prove how cocky each of 'em were. Money started rollin' in—fives, tens, twenties and other bets they brought from their buddies at school. Now, that was a surprise. I marked it down quickly and held the wad in my pocket.

Not bad at all, almost six hundred includin' insurance. Sure kicked it up from that measly one-sixty I calculated as a base.

Remember watchin' Richie in his Chevy, checkin' out the road, the perfect track. The whole road was about seven miles long, but—that's right—we didn't use all of it. It was a straight shot, farms on both sides for its entire length.

I could see his car's bright, red tail lights as it disappeared into a gully of a deep hill, the only hill on that road for about three quarters of a mile.

Joey, the lookout, walked up to me and got his instructions as to the exact location of his post and, of course, his agreed upon payment. I tried to hold him off for his money, but he wouldn't budge. I had to pay him right-on-the-spot.

"Can't blame a guy for trying," he giggled.

I told him, *Two miles ahead to the left, on John Owings Road. Hit the horn to warn us, three times in a row, if the cops come.* He nodded and was out of there in a flash.

"It was a great set up, if I do say so myself."

Let's see . . . I had Joey at the crossroad and his brother, Eddie with one of their guys stationed with synchronized watches at the startin' line and the rest of their gang standin' with me at the finish line.

After the first race, Andrew and Richie were gonna' return to the startin' point for the next two heats.

I would be all set to elevate the money from a wad to a heap, especially with the guys' adrenalin pumpin'. I just knew Andy was gonna' beat out Richie, and I would throw some double or nothins' their way.

Oh yeah, then I could hear the bugler in my mind, like I saw on TV once, before the Kentucky Derby, 'cause it was time to start the race. What a cool sight—Pontiac against Chevy—both of 'em made their way to the start, while we watched their tail lights against the dark sky.

Waitin', I could feel my blood bubblin' up, gettin' all excited.

"I loved it! I loved it! What a rush!" he said.

As I listened, I heard the squeal of wheels diggin' into the asphalt as the cars were headin' toward us and the finish line, and after that, they had one-half mile to stop.

Those engines were roarin' on that quiet country road. Second into third—they reached the point just before the gully where the road dipped, and at that moment the lights proved that the Chevy was nosin' out Andy's car.

Better not do it now, but I remember, man, I remember yellin' as loud as I could to him, *C'mon, give it everything you've got, Andy,* but the jerk couldn't hear me.

I kept squeezin' that wad of bills in my pocket as tight as I could, 'cause I started seein' it growin' wings, if he lost that race.

I couldn't believe' it! When their cars came up on the other side of the gully, Andrew was really behind.

I was so mad at him that I yelled out, *Why don't you floor it, meathead?*

Those guys were lovin' every minute of it, lookin' at me, starin' at me. And then they started that laughin' and pointin', yeah, just laughin' and pointin'. I hated it!

"Thought they were gonna' win the cash from me, that's what," he said.

"They just kept laughin' and pointin'—I hated it!"

I couldn't even watch the race anymore. Had to stop 'em from makin' a fool outta' me.

His mind played it all out again—laughin' and pointin'—I'd show 'em. With all my might I started for 'em. Would've taken 'em all-on at once, kicked their butts, but good.

Were they nuts? Here I am comin' at 'em, and they just kept doin' it—laughin' and pointin'!

"Ha, Haaaa," he laughed sensing retribution, "But boy, did they get theirs, and I didn't even have to lift a finger."

I was just about to cream 'em, when the cops came. Sirens blared loud enough to wake up the dead. Lights were flashin' all over 'em—red, yellow and orange—glaring into the sky as dark as the ace of spades.

I remember thinkin', where in the world are they comin' from and how come Joey didn't blow his horn.

Then I realized the cops were waitin' for this race. Somebody tipped 'em off, probably sittin' in somebody's driveway with their lights off.

All hell broke lose. Everybody started to scramble, but most of the guys were headin' in the same direction.

I took off the other way.

Cops went for the numbers, ran after the bigger group; nabbed some by the shirt tails or collars. To the others, they ordered, *Halt*! All of 'em stopped dead in their tracks.

They rounded up everybody, 'cept me, and marched 'em back to the police cars.

Why I just perched myself up in a big ol' willow tree with lots of branches, high enough not to be seen, yet low enough to have a great vantage point. I'm nobody's fool.

I saw two of the cop cars that had cornered both of the racing cars, and they had to follow Andrew and Richie in their squad cars back to the finish line where the rest were gathered.

"Oh, man!" he said aloud, and then Jonathon started laughing so hard he grabbed his stomach and covered his lips with his other hand to stifle the noise and started giggling deep in his throat.

"What happened next was . . . hysterical!!

"I have a mental picture of it all, and it is in living color, right in front of me!"

I saw the cops and how they made each guy stand spread-eagle against a thick oak tree over near the road while being searched. They didn't find anything just a bunch of very, cool kids, scared-stiff, 'bout ready to throw-up or worse.

Andrew was up against one of the oaks, right in the middle of it all, lookin' like Casper the Friendly Ghost, pale as could be.

I remember how the cops were talkin' amongst themselves, whisperin' and noddin' their heads. Then they started talkin' louder 'bout how each of the guys could be hauled-in, fingerprinted, charged and held in jail—and just for bein' there.

Had 'em stand there stretched out for about, what, an hour?

My butt was startin' to hurt, but I didn't dare to move.

Wasn't much goin' on at three in the mornin' so the cops were bidin' their time and lovin' every minute of it. Heard one of 'em say, *We'll have some fun with 'em and teach 'em a lesson.*

Another one said, *Okay boys, turn around, but keep your hands over your head.*

They were sweatin' bullets, their faces were pale, and I swear I could hear their hearts poundin', even from the tree.

Jonathon said,

"Man, I had to bite my lip. I was crackin' up, especially when they said to each other, *so, what d'ya' think? Should we take 'em in? Call their parents? Fingerprint 'em?"*

All of 'em turned grey and the cops waited for . . . like . . . a full five minutes before they said, *Nah, let 'em go. I think they learned their lesson. Is that right, boys?*

And, in unison, like jackasses, bobbing their heads, they said, *Yes sir, oh, yes sir!*

*Now get outta' here,* one of the cops said.

All the guys got into their cars and the cops did too. But, before anybody else left, the squad cars peeled off and were gone. I always thought they musta gotten a radio call, zippin' outta' there like that.

I almost busted a gut then 'cause, just as Andrew was backin' up into the road, two of the guys stopped him by reachin' in to pull him through his open window. Then I saw that they released him, opened his door and yanked him out, lettin' him fall to the ground on his knees.

They started talkin' about me and were they really hot under the collar. One guy said, *Your brother said he fixed it with the cops. We gave him ten bucks apiece when he set this race up to buy that protection. And you owe back our money, plus your end of the payoff since you lost at two-to-one odds, and with the insurance money, I figure altogether, it's about six hundred bucks. So pay up."*

Andrew said, *Pay up? I don't have that money. Jonathon is holding it. He's got it. I don't. I scrambled when the cops came, like we all did, only he made it outta' here.*

Sarcastically he said,

"Oh, boo hoo!

"I watched it all, heard it all, but just listened from my hideaway."

Andrew got to his feet, man, was he shakin'.

He said, *When I get home, I'll get your money from him and have it by tomorrow after school, at the Vo-Tech, near the football field.*

They said, *No way, now or else . . .*

The whole gang was comin' down on him, their veins were poppin' in their necks, and their fists were raised. One guy punched him and another one pushed him down again. Two of 'em were equally tough, roughin' him up.

Finally, the ringleader said, *Maybe he's got the money hidden in those pants. Take 'em off!*

"That was the one! Yep, that was the one!" he said aloud, giggling inside and holding his stomach as he pushed his body deep into the sofa.

"Yep, yep, that was it! That was it!"

Andrew said, *Take my pants off! You've gotta be kiddin'.*

Richie said, do I look like I'm kiddin'? Get 'em off or we'll *all* rip 'em off.

"Now, *that* was rich! And, off they came. I can still see it all."

He chortled,

"His big 'ol shoes . . . dungarees . . . stripped . . . drawers, his skinny 'old hiney!

"Ha, ha, those jerks grabbed 'em and searched every pocket coming up empty, of course," he said, patting his own pocket as if it still held the money.

I heard 'em say, *Let's go guys. We'll be lookin' for you later today, after school, outside The Hole in the Wall. You'd better have our money. And tell your brother, Jonathon, he's dead meat if he doesn't come through!*

The tallest boy walked over to Andrew's car, opened the door and rolled up the window, tossed Andy's pants in and locked and slammed the door. He took Andrew's keys into his own car, which he started and sped away. Everybody else left, too.

"It was hysterical! Hysterical!" Jonathon giggled as he remembered how Andrew stood alone in the cold, early morning air.

"At first, I could see Andy didn't know what to do, but his only choice was to walk home in his underwear, right? He couldn't try to flag anybody down to hitch a ride, right?"

Jonathon very sarcastically said,

"Poor Andrew, he looked *so* sad as he walked towards home, keepin' close to the side to duck out of sight if a car came by.

"Man, I giggled and almost let the cat out of the bag, but he looked so pathetic.

"I held in my laughter and it was . . . not . . . easy!

"Saw Andy stop and turn around, even heard him say my name. I thought he found me out. I had to be extra quiet, but it was too funny for words. I wish I had a camera, but I can see it all just like it happened back then."

I kept watchin' from the tree and had to almost bust a gut holdin' in my laughter. Andy looked so stupid walkin' down the road in his skivvies. I had never seen anything like it and was splittin my sides."

Once Andrew was out of sight, I had to speedo out of there and beat him home.

When Andrew came home, there I was, waitin' for him and actin' like I cared, listenin' to his each and every word as if I knew nothin'.

Andy said, *The guys want their money back after school today . . . meetin' me outside The Hole in the Wall for their dough.*

I said, *Don't have it.* The cops stopped me further down the road and took it all, every cent.

"Eh, what's a little white lie, right?" Jonathon said.

Andrew said, *Well, you'd better help me find some money to give 'em. They already told me that you're dead meat, and I don't wanna' be. Came close enough last night . . . got punched, pretty bad.*

I remember word for word, I said, *Aw, you did? Well, here take this hundred I've been savin' and tell 'em that's all you've got right now. You'll pay 'em a little each week or they can take it out of your hide and get nothing. It's their choice.*

Andrew screamed at me. He was furious, *Their choice? My hide? Their choice?*

*Where are you gettin' these ideas, brother?*

*It's my butt on the line. You better go talk to them, Jonathon!*

We argued about it, and I told Andrew I wouldn't, so he met with them and forked over one-hundred dollars and the promise to repay. They didn't rough Andy up though, not in broad daylight and right in the heart of town.

He told me how he got his keys back. Pretty cool!

I skirted any of the guys from that gang for a while and had Andrew meet them once a week to pay them twenty bucks, half from him and half from me. I convinced Andrew that since we were in it together and would split the profits, we should split the responsibilities, too. But, of course, what Andrew didn't know was that the cops didn't take the money from me. I didn't even see them again on my way home.

I actually made money on that brother of mine, pocketing all the money from the race and sixty dollars from hypothetical police insurance that came from Richie's gang.

I let Andrew carry the burden of it all, after all, *I,* was the promoter.

I kept thinkin' just how shifty I was to come out smellin' like a rose.

I want to go upstairs, right now, to rub Andrew's face in the fact that I put another one over on him. Instead, I'll just keep laughing to myself over and over again, just waiting for the moment to tell it all to him.

He giggled,

"It *will* be rich! Andrew's day will come!"

# CHAPTER FORTY

అల్⁊ఆల్⁊

# THE FOLLOWING DAY

Jonathon grabbed a bacon and egg sandwich that his Aunt had prepared for him like he did every other morning, then wrapped it in waxed paper and hustled out of the door, leaving for work.

She yelled out, "And don't let the door . . ." but before she could finish, it slammed behind him.

Every day it's the same, she thought, shaking her head as she watched him toss up gravel on the driveway, his truck full of produce moving further away.

He always left early to get a jump on the other farmers who also sent produce to the city. Even though Jonathon had verbal agreements with many of the restaurant cooks to buy his wares, he was afraid that if someone else showed them juicy, plump tomatoes and crisp beans and beat him to the punch, they would likely buy from them.

Baltimore had some great restaurants dotted throughout the city. It seemed that each nationality took great pride in presenting their native cuisine, and especially on Thursday, Friday and Saturday, when people lined up to sample the best.

Haussners, known for an extensive menu including delicious soups to incredible main dishes like sauerbraten and wiener schnitzel, was one of Jonathon's best customers.

They would accept only the finest produce, and he always went there first, selling a large portion of his truckload.

Not too far from there was another fine restaurant in East Baltimore.

Karl, the head chef at Winterlings, was always pleased to see Jonathon and liked the way he could joke around with him.

"Go ahead Jonathon," Karl said, "Let's see who can stack the most cherry tomatoes on a dinner plate before one falls onto the table. I'll bet you a twenty I can top your number."

After four or five games and eighty to one hundred dollars later with both intent on beating the other, Jonathon would try to entice his friend to double or nothing. A wager like that got his adrenaline pumping, and he loved the rush that he got from betting.

"Oh no, one hundred is enough. Not betting anymore than that—you win," Karl said and changed gears.

"Now, you know I'll take all you can carry in here, Jon. And only the best! What's fresh today?"

He dropped off asparagus, spinach and leaf lettuce, emptying his load between his first and second kitchens.

"Six eighty-five, six ninety and ten makes seven hundred," Jonathon counted out loud. "Plus, I've got the hundred I won from Karl. Finished early! Not a bad day!"

After he grabbed a newspaper, he decided to have lunch where some of his customers had great delis. Lombard Street, not far from the Baltimore harbor, was *the* place to get a great corned beef sandwich on rye and a juicy, crisp, dill pickle that was made from the cucumbers he had previously sold to them. He always made sure he brought them the freshest cucumbers and of just the right size to create uniformity.

The owners enjoyed buying from Jonathon; he was always joking with them and he won them over. None of them got to see his other side, the side that was exposed to his family. He knew they wouldn't accept it and that they would just buy from someone else.

When he walked into the store, Jerry shot him a big grin and said,

"Such a surprise . . . such a surprise! Today, you want to buy, not sell? Grab a crème soda and the table in the back. Lunch—I'm gonna' take lunch. We'll talk, and then I gotta' run."

Jonathon nodded. Jerry brought back two sandwiches piled high with steaming corned beef.

"I added horseradish and mustard just for you. Taste that dill pickle—it's from the last batch of cucumbers you brought. That's what I like—six, maybe seven inches. Crisp and fresh. Makes the best . . . with just the right amount of dill, vinegar and spices—the perfect brine.

"There was a lady from New York in here last week. Bought six gallons of pickles. Takin' 'em back to her family. I guess we're makin' it big now. A rival to the New York delis?

"Look out Nathan!" he reported, while shaking his finger into the air. "Just a Baltimore boy, but I'm on your tail!"

Jerry reached out his hand and said,

"Let me see your paper. Sports. Whose running in the feature race at Pimlico today?

"Oh, for crap sake! He didn't tell me he was gonna' run that filly today. Crap, I can't get outta' here! I know that baby's gonna' win! If I wasn't runnin' this place by myself later, I'd hit the track. Crap!"

Although Jonathon had never been to Pimlico the desire to check it out was pretty strong.

"So you can't go, Jerry? I'm finished for the day. I can take a bet out for you."

"What? I should let you take out a bet for me? I should let you have all the fun? I should let you rake in the big bucks, hookin' her up in the Exacta?"

He hesitated, shrugged, and then said,

"Okay, okay what can I say? My hands are tied!"

&#x6047;&#x6043;&#x6047;&#x6043;

As Jonathon pulled into one of the side roads with the empty produce truck, he looked up in awe at the huge old clubhouse he had heard so much about. He saw barns, quite a few horses being led toward the paddock, and some of the jockeys who were walking through. When he got closer he could begin to see the odds board in the infield, so he walked a quick pace to get inside.

"And, they're off!" He heard the announcer's voice on the loudspeaker so he began to run to catch a glimpse of the race. As he ran faster and faster the adrenalin began to pump, and he could feel the rush he had come to love whenever he gambled. He didn't have a bet on the race, and he started cursing himself for wasting time talking to Jerry and laughing with him because he missed this chance to wager.

"How could I be so stupid, wasting time with that old guy," he said.

Each race that followed produced exhilaration like none he had known before.

He bet on the sixth race and went outside by the rail to see the strength of the animals as they leapt from the starting gate. Jonathon was swept up in it all—the power of those horses, muscles tightened in sinewy legs, chests sculpted and defined, manes and tails free and flying in the wind behind them, and thunderous hoofs pounding the unyielding earth. The incredible energy of it all gave him an unbelievable feeling in his whole body, rising to a new high.

He lost after betting ten dollars to win. What's ten dollars, he thought. After all, I won a hundred from Karl today. That last show, alone, was worth ten dollars, he said to himself, alluding to the race.

Jonathon bought a racing card, looked at it briefly and on a hunch picked a gelding for race seven. He bet twenty dollars. Got to get my money back, he thought.

"And, they're off" blared from the speaker.

Seven furlongs later, he had lost.

The adrenaline was really pumping now. The eighth race was the feature, the race Jerry needed him to bet on.

He put one hundred dollars to Win and fifty to Place on the number seven horse, *Shoes to Run, for Jerry.* He thought, if Jerry really liked that horse, I'm gonna' go with it, too. I'll bet fifty to Win and twenty to Place, yeah, that's what I'll do. I'll shoot the works.

The race began and Jonathon was at the rail. He started to chant . . .

"Come on . . . come on, baby, come on! Come on . . . come on baby, come on!"

As if that horse and jockey could hear him, he started screaming it louder and louder.

His heart was in his throat. It was pumping with such intensity, he could feel himself shaking.

As the horses rounded the clubhouse turn, he saw it . . . number seven was out in front. He was blinded by some people in front of him for just a few seconds, but when he could see again, he couldn't believe it.

The number five horse had jumped ahead. How did that other horse pull to the front so fast?

"And what is *that*?" Jonathon said out loud, "Number eight is comin' on strong!"

The seven horse was fading fast. How could that be, he thought.

"Come on, baby . . . kick it in again. Give him the boot. What's wrong with that stupid jockey?

"Kick him in the sides. Whip that baby. Oh no, it can't be," he screamed. "What's that jockey doin, pullin' him up?"

The five horse was now out in front, the eight horse was neck-in-neck with Jerry and Jonathon's pick, number seven. If only he can hold on from the sixteenth pole for a place finish, he hoped.

As they hit the finish line, it was 5-8-7, flashing in front of him.

"I swear! What luck! I swear! Never thought he'd finish third.

"I swear! He said it over and over, as he walked out of the track, ripping up his tickets and throwing them into the air.

"That stupid Jerry. Sure thing, humph. Sure loser, if you ask me. What kind of a tip did that jerk get from his tout?

"Really wanted me to lose my money. Thanks a hellava' lot for nothin' . . . What a jerk!"

# CHAPTER FORTY-ONE

❧❦❧❦

## A FEW WEEKS LATER

𝒮he phone rang at the farmhouse, and Thomas was on it by the third bell.

"Uncle Jay? Is that you? Our connection's not good. I can hardly hear you. You what? Want me to come up soon? *Soon* is that what you said?"

Thomas wasn't sure if the connection was poor or if Uncle Jay sounded frail and weak.

"Well sure . . . I'll try. Tomorrow?

"But I have to get the boys to cover for me, and now they're all doin' the Baltimore routes.

"You know I'll do my best to get up there. Is everythin' alright?

"Are you feelin' okay?"

"Sure, sure, I'm fine. I just wanna' . . . gotta' see ya', that's all," said Jay, with a quaver in his voice.

Thomas' sixth sense was kicking in, and he knew something was wrong with his uncle. He was always right on target whenever he was concerned, and it just wasn't like him to say, "I gotta' see you," with such urgency.

Within the hour Thomas called two of his older friends who had sold their farms. They had covered for him in the past when he visited Uncle Jay; in fact, they relished being back-in-the-saddle on the tractors and combines.

Mary Kathleen packed some sandwiches, popped Thomas' clothes in a suitcase and waved goodbye half-heartedly, smiling as he drove away.

She knew he had been summoned by Uncle Jay, but in the back of her mind she couldn't help but think how she would miss Thomas. Whenever he left, her thoughts wandered back to the times they had shared when it was just the two of them.

Reaching for her box of treasures, she began to read each little scribbled note that Thomas had written to her so many years before.

Some were smudged, some crumbled then straightened out, and some obviously had been rubber banded . . .

*Thanks for a great lunch*

*My, you sure are lookin' pretty today*

*Gee, you smelled good today*

*Can't get you off my mind*

*Nobody sings Stardust like you do*

*Glad you're my wife*

*You're a beauty, all right*

*Honey, I'll always love you*

Now that's the one, that last one, that I cherish the most, she thought as she heaved a heavy sigh.

She clutched the batch of them to her chest as she closed her eyes, making sure none would fall from her hands.

If I only had one new one a month to add to these . . . if he would take me in his arms, his big strong arms, and gently squeeze me close to him . . . if only he would look into my eyes, smile that smile of his and say, *Honey, I'll always love you* like he did so often before . . . before . . . before . . .

Her thoughts trailed off into her what was, what she considered perfect, and what could never be the same again.

# CHAPTER FORTY-TWO

## THE NEXT DAY

When Thomas pulled up outside Uncle Jay's house on Mount Washington in Pittsburgh, he wasn't standing at his door as usual.

He used his key to enter and found his uncle sitting in his favorite chair in a darkened room with the shades drawn.

"You don't know how happy I am to see you, Thomas," he began. "I need to talk to you, straighten a few things out."

"Uncle Jay, are you okay?"

"Just listen. Yesterday I contacted Mr. Codday, my lawyer, and we went over my paperwork. Some of it, you don't need to worry yourself with now, but . . .

"Grab a pad in that desk over there. You an' me, we gotta' get our heads together and make a plan, a plan that only works when specific things are done.

"You know I love my Maryland roots, love St. John's Church, and I wanna' do somethin' special if they ever get around to buildin' a bigger church; and Mr. Codday, he knows my wishes.

"But ya' know me, I can't just hand 'em over a check toward it. Got to keep 'em guessin', right to the end."

"End? End?" Thomas began before Uncle Jay interrupted.

"You know that money I've been giving to you, well that's just the beginnin'. Here, take this."

Thomas was surprised to see an even bigger wad of twenties wrapped with criss-crossed rubber bands.

"Where, uh . . . how did you," he sputtered as Uncle Jay handed it to him.

"Never you mind. Let's just say if things keep on going like they have recently, our dream just might come true. I've been talkin' to some people, some very influential people, and they're supposed to get back to me . . . seem to like my idea. I'm not one to sit back and wait it out.

"Now let's get to plannin'. It's got to be a humdinger as I go out."

"Go out! Whatdya' mean? How *are* you feelin'?"

"I'm okay, but I can't live forever, you know. Now, let's get to it. Think, Thomas, think!"

# CHAPTER FORTY-THREE

ॐ∽ॐ∽ॐ∽ॐ

"I guess she wants to ask you a few more questions about St. John's Church, Thomas. I don't really know. She wouldn't say that much to me, wanted to talk to you. Wanted to know when you would be available. Told her, you set up your own schedule," said Mary Kathleen.

"Well, I did see Cully Anderson again, in town, and he did ask me if I met with Maggie Fischer. I told him 'bout Uncle Jay not feelin' well and that I had to cut our meeting short. So, I guess I'll get it over with and give her a call."

ॐ∽ॐ∽ॐ∽ॐ

As Maggie walked from the drive to the porch, she saw the flowers and shrubs bogged down by weeds and began to visualize how they once looked. She could work in there, save the best and tidy up the lay of the land.

It was just a thought . . .

Her creative juices were always stimulated when she saw something disheveled. She liked building something from nothing, then standing back and appreciating the more pleasing picture.

Must be in my personality, she said to herself, 'cause I did that every time a new client sat in my chair in the salon.

I would look for their positives, then snip, color and design to make them look and feel great.

'Course I won't mention my idea of tidying-up their place to these people—wouldn't want to offend. But if I knew them better, I'd offer, she thought and then knocked twice on the front door.

"Sorry we had to cut it short last time, but my Uncle's health has been up and down lately. By the way, I want to thank you for stoppin' by with the cake and coffee, 'twas very good."

Thomas became shy and slightly uneasy as he noticed her looking straight into his eyes.

"Err, uh, thanks again. Your thermos is in the kitchen, and I don't want you to forget it."

Maggie spoke up,

"I'm so glad you liked it. The recipe is my mother-in-law's—very easy, very quick. I'll make a copy for Mary Kathleen."

"Now about St. John's and your key . . . did ya' bring it again? Can I see it once more?" he asked.

Maggie dug it out of her purse, opened the cloth it was in, and handed it over. Thomas held it like he was cradling a small animal, gently rocking it in both hands while he closed his eyes for the moment.

"Mr. Frank, I did find an article about the church from an old Carroll County Times newspaper at the Historical Society of Carroll County archives, although you may have it in your collection.

"Here it is. It describes the old church back then and how beautiful it was."

He began to read most of the article to himself, until he read aloud—

> *"The church is topped off by a magnificent tower and spire, surmounted by a lofty cross on whose summit the first rays of the morning love to play, and, the last beams of the evening sun delight to linger.*

"Sure is a fancy way to say how special that old church was," he remarked.

"Maggie, if you were gonna' create a church for a Christmas garden, and you could choose any shape or size, St. John's would've been the one you'd pick.

"Still can't believe she's gone," he said sadly as he shook his head side to side.

Mary Kathleen broke in with a sarcastic tone while walking from the kitchen.

"'Course you've got just about the *whole* church recreated in your barn."

She caught a frown from Thomas, became quiet and then said,

"Lemonade, anyone?"

After carrying two glasses with napkins for coasters she sat them off to the side of the photo albums, then flipped a few pages to their wedding photo, leaving that page exposed.

Maggie saw the interaction and, although initially puzzled, caught the clue,

"My, what a lovely couple you made . . . and still do. The two of you seem to fit together so well."

That remark made Mary Kathleen smile.

"And, you have four sons," she mentioned, after looking over her shoulder toward the pictures on the drum table of both of them, at a much younger age, surrounded by two and holding two other boys.

Thomas and Mary Kathleen interrupted together.

"They are our nephews," they said.

"But just like our own boys," she said.

They proceeded to tell her the whole story of how the boys came to them when their parents were in the accident.

She offered her condolences.

"Can't believe that was in 1947, nineteen years ago, this year," Mary Kathleen said.

She and Thomas were reminiscing side by side on the sofa, and Maggie could feel the love between them as they showed her their family history through the photos they saw in the books.

At times he was very open, yet if Maggie questioned him, he seemed to become withdrawn and secretive. She felt lost on some of the explanations, but hung in there.

They were now coming closer to present day, and Mary Kathleen pointed out Aunt Rose's photo with her husband, Uncle Jay, with the stained glass panels that they had installed in the barn. It had been taken on the day they came from Pittsburgh. They agreed that one photo was from 1958 after the fire at St. John's and the relocation of its items. Thomas didn't seem to want to talk more about those things or about the panels in the barn, but Maggie continued to piece together their family background, layer by layer.

"Special lady . . . that's my Aunt Rose's picture; she died in 1961. Uncle Jay's been alone ever since, and, Maggie, he's the one that got sick . . . that I went to visit last time we got together," he said.

She showed empathy in her face as she nodded, seeing both of them become moved by the photo of their Aunt Rose.

Thomas flipped back a few pages, and there was Westminster High School in the background. Maggie mentioned that her daughter,

Gretchen, had graduated from that school before she went off to college, and all three of them were enjoying one another's company, discussing how their nephews might know her.

They found out that Maggie was a retired hairdresser and now helped her daughter in the dog-grooming salon, which was becoming a local success.

As they talked, Thomas skimmed through his ancestors and stopped at a photo.

There they were again, as Maggie remembered seeing them so vividly weeks before, dangling from the ring attached at the waist of Thomas Frank's great uncle, Thaddeus.

Those keys became etched in her mind as soon as Thomas had first turned the page of the tattered scrapbook, exposing the railroad station, the train and that man in his crisp uniform. And, although she liked following the general history of the Frank family, this was the part of it that had intrigued her.

Now perhaps, without interruption, she could dig into the story of this uncle and his keys and the answers to her questions.

"Now, where did we leave off?" asked Thomas.

"You were starting to tell me about your Uncle Thaddeus and how he bought his way out of the Civil War, something I had never heard of before."

"I did tell you then that he saw all of his buddies marchin' off to places like Antietam and Gettysburg? That they were involved in all that bloodshed and that none of his close friends made it back? So, I did tell you that?"

"Not really, but please go on. I'm finding it all very interesting."

"Yeah, well, when he realized what happened to his friends and that he was the only one of those guys alive—and only because he paid money to get outta' goin'—it just about killed him.

"He felt like a coward and that he had brought dishonor to his family name.

"To tell ya' the truth, even though what he did was *by the book* as they say—signin' up for a deferment, back then called conscription, for three hundred dollars—I think he did bring on terrible shame."

"That's a part of Civil War history that escaped me. Conscription, you called it?" asked Maggie.

"Yep," said Thomas. "Got shot in the leg durin' a tussle when some guy called him a coward. So now he couldn't join up, though now he's changed his mind, wantin' to be part of the Union Troops—the U.S. Army.

"Maggie, right here in Westminster, seein's how we are on the Mason-Dixon Line, you had people from the same family fightin' that Civil War. Some were for the North and some for the South; cousin against cousin, even brother against brother.

"But, now wait, the story of Thaddeus ain't over, not by a long shot!

"Ya' see, he fought with himself over his decision and finally made up his mind to serve in another way. Know what he did? Got a job with the railroad, that's what. Figured if he could help get troops and ammo to the front lines, just maybe he could make a difference, could help Mr. Lincoln bring an end to that melee.

"Worked fourteen to sixteen hour days, throwin' himself into his work. Went all over, accordin' to his journals—Washington, Pennsylvania, every tip of Maryland and even into Virginia—seems like everywhere the trains went.

"Sometimes his brother, my Great-grandfather Jed, who had the farm where all of the bricks were baked for Saint John's Church, worked together with Thaddeus. Grandpa Jed wrote somethin' about the rectory when he was gettin' it built, and it sounded like Thaddeus had to put his two-cents into that project.

"Seemed like he finally started to feel better about the conscription and all, and accordin' to his notes, he seemed to be lighter. And then . . . Oh, my Lord . . . President Lincoln was assassinated. Why, accordin' to his letters to his mother that just about did him in. He cried like he knowed 'im personally.

"I guess he felt like he just didn't repay his debt to Mr. Lincoln like he wanted to, in not joinin' up.

"Why, when he found out that the funeral procession of Mr. Lincoln was travelin' by train through Maryland, on its way to Pennsylvania, New York, and then onto Ohio before Chicago and Springfield, Illinois, for his final restin' place, he was determined to somehow be a part of it.

"And ya' know what, even though President Lincoln was dead, some people still hated that great man. There were threats against the funeral train, threats to blow it up! Do you believe that?"

He didn't wait for her to answer.

"Uncle Thaddeus saw his chance to clear his name, bring honor back to his family. Tell ya' what he did. He took the Western Maryland line into the Relay Station, near Lake Roland, where he transferred onto the Northern Central Line. Easy for him, ya' see, wearin' his railroad uniform includin' his flat topped cap and a' course his pocket watch on a chain . . . all lookin' very official. That there was the way they dressed back then, and his ol' suits, still today, are all tucked away in moth balls up in our attic.

"Now eventually, he made his way into Baltimore and then Washington. He talked his way onto the pilot engine, he knowed the General that was in charge of the railroads, along with the Pinkerton guards, which preceded Mr. Lincoln's train, by runnin' the track—checking it out for explosives, that is—about twenty minutes ahead of the special Baltimore and Ohio."

Thomas pulled out an old history book from a bookshelf in the parlor and skimmed its pages.

"Here's a picture of one of the trains, all draped in black, American flags aflyin' off of it and the number three and a one just above the cow catcher on the front of the engine. I can't see the other number. Not sure, but I think it was snapped in Philadelphia.

"They say it was amazin' how people traveled to that train line where they stood and just waited to get a glimpse of that great man's coffin. Farmers in their fields removed their hats, and they knelt down bowin' their heads in reverence as it passed whilst Mr. Lincoln lay within the train. Tears flowed freely. Neither men nor women could believe it really happened, as they watched until the funeral train became a speck of smoke on the horizon, I read.

"See, when President Lincoln's body was leavin' Washington, they used the Baltimore and Ohio Railroad. Had a locomotive and tender, eight passenger cars, the funeral car and baggage cars, all beginning' its seventeen hundred mile journey from that point.

"His body was in a private, sixteen-wheel railroad coach, ironically one that had been built for the President's official travel but never used until his death.

"Mrs. Lincoln remained sequestered with her youngest son Tad. Read that she was in complete shock. Why, you can just imagine, 'specially diggin' up her son to send him along to be buried with his father. But her eldest son Robert, representin' the family, rode in the special funeral train of the U.S. Military Railroads.

"At ten o'clock it pulled into the Camden Street Station in Baltimore, preceded a few minutes by that pilot engine."

He flipped all the pages in the scrapbook and pulled out an old parchment that had been tucked in the back of the book.

"Look here, Miss Maggie, in his own words. You go on and read it out loud."

Maggie gently held the actual paper from Thaddeus and with reverence began . . .

*"While his remains were taken to the rotunda of the Exchange Building in Baltimore, where tens of thousands viewed him, my only goal was to keep secured a spot to be on that pilot locomotive. It mattered not to me that one crazed maniac might bury powder and explosives to destroy Mr. Lincoln and his entourage by exploding track, train and all of it—in its entirety, also destroying my body. But, that I could give my life to prevent such a travesty would but be a minuscule repayment for my cowardice. I now realize, although only one body am I, courage to fight for that which I believe in did not come to me, and for that I shall always repent.*

*Dear Mother, I prayed to the Almighty before I left—Let my soul be sacrificed if it is necessary to allow my dear President Lincoln to find his final resting place in his own Springfield, Illinois. Let my body be torn to shreds to spare one more eruption of violence to this great man. My tears flow freely and my eyes do not fully close at night since the horrible event at the Ford's. Let me do my best, dear God, my very best . . .*

She paused as Thomas handed her another script and said, "And see here in his notes . . . he goes on . . ."

Maggie feeling very privileged, again began to speak the words of Thaddeus . . .

*"As Harrisburg was the next destination, his body was then taken to Baltimore's Howard Street Station of the Northern Central Railway, where a new locomotive had been readied. Our engine left at twenty minutes to three, but later I was told, a few minutes after three o'clock chimed, and I shall never forget the date, Friday, April the 21st 1865, that the funeral train slowly steamed away.*

*And by accounts, as it traveled through the Maryland boroughs of Ruxton and on upward, passing Lutherville,*

Monkton and into Parkton, crepe-hung evergreens lined both sides of the tracks and mourners, hands over hearts, sadly stood in disbelief of the events, watching soldiers salute their passing Commander-in-Chief.

In the tally of citizens, I figure, more than seven million shared in an emotional good-bye, from our Washington D.C. to Illinois, a distance of seventeen-hundred miles. Once you counted all the cities, including Philadelphia, New York, Albany, Buffalo, Columbus and Indianapolis, you could understand that he traveled on eight railroads to cover them miles. Thursday, May the 4th was the date of his final resting place in his beloved Springfield. It was hot as blazes, that day, yet silence overtook them all. The coffin was taken to a finely appointed hearse laden with gold, silver and crystal. I hear told it was borrowed from the city of St. Louis, for only this occasion. Sadly, walking behind it was Old Robin--President Lincoln's horse wearing a mourning blanket finished off with tassels. I thank God that I was able to assist and hope you approve, my dear Mother.

Thomas continued,

"After Thaddeus returned from the Illinois funeral, he wrote again to his mother—quite a writer he was—seems he was always doin' that. Guess I got that from him—seems I'm always writin' everythin' down too."

He handed those papers to Maggie. She noted the warm greeting to his mother and then picked up the paragraph about the late President.

"Only with permission through Brigadier General McCallum of the Military Railroads was I able to fulfill my objective-to pray at his feet. Within President Lincoln's railroad coach, I gazed through tears and shall never forget seeing his flag-covered casket, and his twelve-year old son Willie's coffin, nor, reading the silver plaque identifying the man-

Abraham Lincoln
16th President of the United States.
Born, the twelfth day of February, 1809.
Died, the fifteenth day of April, 1865

I can still see the black, walnut woodwork, the combination of dark green plush upholstery and curtains of light green. A ceiling, paneled with crimson silk and gathered into a rosette in the center of each, will always be emblazoned in my mind.

How can I not remember the exterior
of it all, with American Eagles and
national colors appearing in a large
medallion on each of its sides, flanked
by flags of the United States flapping
even as they waited for the procession
to begin?

And the elaborately draped black
cloth with silver bullion fringe, silver
spangled stars and large silver
tassels of about nine inches in length
and three inches in diameter.

There were also many black tassels
used about the biers on which rested
both coffins, that of the President
and his son Willie, who had died
three years before.
You see dear Mother, Mrs. Lincoln
ordered the boy's body be exhumed
and returned to rest in Springfield
with his father.

These funeral trappings' of which
I speak were removed on the return
of the railroad car to Alexandria,
Virginia, and divided up as relics.

I treasure, now, one of the tassels
and a key to one of the custom made
cabinets built within the sides of the
railroad car, originally to be used as
a safe.

*Oh Mother, if I only knew . . .*
*when I think of the many travels*
*I completed in and around*
*Washington, to courier the*
*secrets . . . yet never did I touch*
*the hand of the great President*
*Lincoln, therefore sadness fills my*
*days and shall forevermore."*

Maggie was stunned as she finished reading, her eyes wide as saucers and her mouth agape.

Could Thaddeus have a key from President Lincoln's funeral car?

Now, she was convinced. It had to be one of the keys she saw on that ring he was carrying in his photo. After all, he was in his railroad uniform and . . . wait a minute . . .

She quickly asked Thomas Frank to turn back a few pages to Thaddeus' picture in the scrapbook.

And there it was. He was standing in front of a train draped in black cloths, flags fluttering on each side of an engine whose number, or part of the number that she could see was #3 on the left and #1 on the right. She looked among the history pages, and there was an almost identical photo of the train. And, as she looked more closely, she could see a side view of a man, same clothes and standing off to the right.

It had to be Mr. Lincoln's funeral engine, Thaddeus and the key!

"Look, Mr. Frank, do you think that is your great Uncle?"

"Yup, I'd say it is. 'Tis why I've got this here old book that I keep handy."

"Mr. Frank, er, Thomas, do you, or have you ever seen one of these keys from Thaddeus' belongings?"

"Oh sure, I remember having an old key with his things; can't tell ya' where it might be, though. My father wanted me to have all of Thaddeus' notes and the odds and ends that were his, so he gave 'em to me before he died."

"Well, if you ever find it, please think of me. I'll buy it from you for my collection."

Thomas didn't answer, but continued,

"One of them old trunks up in the attic has the tassel, some pieces of black ribbon, just about shredded to bits, originally from the black crepe rosettes that the train had worn at the funeral rites and probably the key."

Thomas didn't commit himself, nor did he tell her about the other Civil War artifacts he had housed up there besides Thaddeus' railroad clothes and his hats.

She was gettin' a little too friendly, asking him to sell her one of his treasures. Why, if she knew he had a Confederate sword inscribed with an artillery scene and the name Johnson on it, that was captured at Gettysburg, or a Bowie knife, sheath and belt, not to mention the Belt Plate with the initials, C.S. on it and all the others—well, she just might be wantin' them, too. Just better change the subject, he thought.

As he got up from the table, she hoped he would head toward the stairs, but instead he turned and said,

"How about a cup of coffee?" and he walked into the kitchen.

Over the years, Maggie had honed her ability to read people's feelings and Thomas Frank would be harder than most to persuade. He seemed so suspicious of her question, unlike Cully Anderson, who answered all of her inquiries so freely.

Mary Kathleen was asked more questions by Maggie about the stained-glass panels and items from St. John's that were mentioned to have been hanging in the barn. She started to answer, but Thomas shot a look to his wife, and she clammed up.

Maggie respected his decision not to discuss those things, but she had to win him over . . . had to come up with an idea to get him to search for that old key, even if only to hold it in her hand while knowing it was part of the Lincoln legacy.

Then and there, Maggie decided, if not today, then soon, very soon.

# CHAPTER FORTY-FOUR

೪೨೬೪೨೬

$\mathcal{M}$ary Kathleen intercepted the call from Pittsburgh and handed the phone to Thomas.

He knew he was eighty-five.

He knew he was becoming frail.

He knew he couldn't live forever.

Yet, when Mr. Codday's words told Thomas the news, a chill spread throughout his entire body.

Tears spilled down his cheeks as he looked into Mary Kathleen's eyes, handed her the receiver and said,

"My best friend is dead."

# CHAPTER FORTY-FIVE

৯৯৯৯৯

*W*hen word came that Uncle Jay had died, Thomas was full of remorse.

Why hadn't he said to him more of the things that were on his mind . . . more personal things, like explaining how much he meant to him, how important his teachings were, both to him and his nephews, Michael, William, Andrew and Jonathon.

But instead they talked about Thomas' old farm and his mortgage, the restaurant deliveries and the business and the secret plan both of them had started creating for St. John's legacy—yes, especially that.

Now, as he searched his memory, he could feel the urgency about that conversation. Usually they would joke and banter, each feeding off the other's tease and play, but that day—their last day together—Uncle Jay had serious questions that he posed to Thomas.

They had worked together planning through the entire day.

He now remembered saying, *Uncle Jay, the next time we get together, we'll write out the final chapter,* and now he recalled not even the faintest smile crossed his uncle's lips.

Thomas analyzed, he must have known . . . he must have known . . .

How Thomas wished he had given a stronger notice to his intuition or that he had caught the subtle clues that he now pieced together in hindsight.

৯৯৯৯৯

Mr. Codday met the train at Union Station in downtown Pittsburgh and watched Mr. and Mrs. Thomas Frank, Michael, William, Andrew and Jonathon all disembark, while wishing their first meeting could have been on happier terms.

He had hired two full-sized cars to transport them and was glad that he had after seeing the substantial men that the great-nephews had grown to be, compared to the photo he'd noticed on Jay's mantle.

There was a definite resemblance to his client, in each of them, but especially in Jonathon, the youngest, and in Michael, the oldest.

They would all stay at Uncle Jay's old Victorian, kept in tip-top condition, thanks to the foreman that Jay had hired while convalescing. He had seen that which was inevitable and knew he needed someone to oversee his care and that of his home.

When they arrived, Thomas broke down and cried, looking at the front door, knowing Uncle Jay would never appear there again. He felt the hugs and pats on the back that his nephews were giving and welcomed Mary Kathleen's open arms of sympathy.

The plans were solidified and flowers were ordered. The wait began until the viewing the next day.

❧❦❧❦

It was a crisp, clear morning and Thomas asked the drivers to take them to the West End overlook before going to the viewing. Once there, they all piled out, and Thomas began reminiscing about he and Uncle Jay's many visits to the top of the western edge of Pittsburgh. They could see the three rivers below and the skyline of the industrial city, often hidden in years past because of the smoke from the Bessemer converters at the steel mills.

Memories surfaced of Aunt Rose, now gone too, taking a sweeper to the floor, and then wiping the window sills and kitchen table before breakfast each morning to remove the layer of soot accumulated from the settling airborn particles.

He also thought of how she'd packed Uncle Jay an extra shirt on special meeting days for the afternoon. His own shirt would be dirty and dusty by noon, even though he didn't work in the steel mills.

Thomas liked using the soot on his hands to smudge stripes on his face to pretend he was an Indian or a coal miner or a steel worker. He could almost smell the heavy air the mills created as he closed his eyes, remembering, although the air he breathed in was now clean and clear.

His thoughts drifted further back, and he relayed his memories to all of them about Kennywood, the Amusement Park, the Duquesne funicular they rode to climb up to the top of Mount Washington and the Indian Trail Steps they used on the way down.

"We would float on the barges that Uncle Jay's friends worked on. Many a day we would be drifting on the Monongahela, Allegheny and Ohio Rivers, pretending to be pirates. Uncle Jay seemed to know everyone, and they would play along. Just like it was yesterday, I can hear the guys sayin', *What are yins guys doin' today?* Sometimes we would ride the trolleys all day making sure we always went to South Hill Junction to pass through the nearby tunnel that went to the far side of Mount Washington. Sometimes, we would grab hold of a sandwich at Primanti's Restaurant, bite into it and keep on goin' . . . just keep on goin'.

"Ya' know Uncle Jay had to almost bribe my father to let me come to visit him and Aunt Rose. He'd write to my mother and father saying he needed help and wondered if I could visit for two weeks at a time. I'd ride up on the train, and he would meet me at Union Station, usually with a new toy or a balloon; and off we'd go. It was new and different on every visit.

"Sure liked to joke around, especially with those guys he worked with at the glass factory. He was always catchin' 'em in a practical joke—never hurt anybody, mind ya—just had great timing and would catch 'em off guard."

"Now we know where you got your sense of humor, Unks. Sounds like it was from Uncle Jay," William said.

"Yeah, I can count on both of my hands and feet, the number of times you put one over on each of us. Remember Michael and the disappearing ink, Jonathon and the soap that turned your hands black when you used it, Andrew, and of course me. I remember . . . hey, do you still have that box containin' the furry tail attached to a spring? I'll never forget it. Remember, it was a little square box, and there was a screen on one end and a little door with a latch on top. You could see a fluffy tail of some type of animal inside? Said you didn't know what kind of animal it was.

"You said I could peek into the screened end, and when I did you released a hidden latch which sprang a tight spring openin' the lid and catapulting the fake critter onto me.

"I thought it was real and alive, just about scared the livin'
daylights outta' me. We screamed with laughter for half the day,
playing with it and shockin' our buddies," William detailed.

Then, after the laughter, quiet moments overtook them all.

Each of them stared out into the open expanse of a metropolis
where cars, busses, trains and water craft all moved at varying
speeds—alive—bringing to them the realization of the reason for
their being there.

# CHAPTER FORTY-SIX

❧❧❧❧

## FOUR WEEKS LATER

𝒯he drive to Pittsburgh seemed longer that usual. Thomas felt it would be difficult to face the city without his uncle and their normal banter.

As Thomas walked into the William Penn Hotel his mouth dropped open in amazement. Only in movies with Fred Astaire and Ginger Rogers had he seen such opulence.

Huge crystal chandeliers hung from the center of the room. Walnut pillars held up the ceiling and rose to what seemed like two-hundred feet in the air.

Floors were made of green Italian marble, and elegant chairs and tables filled the room with guests holding cups of tea and coffee and nibbling on finger sandwiches or petit-fours.

He saw a huge dining room to his left decorated with gilt-edged mirrors as he walked forward searching for the check-in desk.

"May I help you, sir?" asked an employee in a crisp uniform, the William Penn crest on his breast pocket.

"Thomas Frank, here," he said, shaking hands with the man.

"Supposed to check in, I guess they say. Mr. Codday, the lawyer, set it all up."

"Mr. Codday? Oh, yes *sir*, right this way. We were expecting you, Mr. Frank. Only the best for you, *sir*," and he escorted him to the immense desk, telling the captain it was, Mr. Frank, Mr. Codday's client. The bellman took him directly to the bank of six elevators. One whisked him to the top floor by use of a special key. When the door opened, he walked directly into a huge suite full of the same finely detailed furniture as was in the lobby.

"No, there must be some mistake," Thomas said, knowing he wouldn't be able to afford this extravagance.

"It is your suite, sir. Mr. Codday arranged for it for the next two nights and paid for it in advance. May I offer you some coffee or tea, sir, or, perhaps a glass of sherry?"

As he looked over, he saw that coffee had been perked and tea steeped and a full bar was there, ready and waiting for him. There were sandwiches, cookies and cakes under glass and chocolates—big, beautiful chocolates in little lace cups.

"We were told, sir, just when you would be arriving and—yes sir—right on time, sir," the bellman said as he plumped up the pillows on the sofa and rearranged the cut flowers at the bar.

"Are we havin' a party here?" Thomas asked while scratching his head.

"No, sir, this is here just for you. And what may I offer to you, sir?

Thomas remembered an old movie he saw.

"That will be all, young man. You're excused." And he pulled a tip from his pocket.

"Oh no, sir, please. Mr. Codday took care of everything."

When the bellman left, Thomas looked out his window and had a great view of downtown Pittsburgh. The people below hustled back and forth, in and out of the buildings, and they looked so small. He could see traffic backed up at one of the intersections and a cop waving it on.

In the distance, he could see the cliffs surrounding part of the city and the wire cable suspensions at the tops of several bridges.

The phone rang and Mr. Codday welcomed Thomas back to Pittsburgh exactly one month after Jay Frank's death and asked if he liked his room.

"Like it? It's beautiful, but I could use the rest of the family to fill 'er up. How much is this place costin' me?"

"Not at all, sir . . . not at all. Our company is taking care of everything, Mr. Frank."

"Hey, just call me Thomas and thank you, but I don't expect that."

"Okay, Thomas, but it is our pleasure, and please call me Alex. I took the liberty to arrange breakfast tomorrow, and then I'll take you on a V.I.P. tour of the city."

"But, I've seen it before."

"Your Uncle Jedidiah, er Uncle Jay, as you called him, left instructions and asked me to be sure you would see it one more time. He said in his last meeting with me that he wanted that for you because, after he died, you probably wouldn't be driving to Pittsburgh anymore. All future dealings can be through the banks."

"Have ta' say, I always liked his style, all except his ideas about the banks. No, I didn't agree with that. Did you know we were workin' on a special plan for St. John's Church back home in Maryland? The two of us got our heads together and started plannin' out quite a scheme.

"Don't know now if it will work or not, but he told me he had set some plans into motion with you, Mr. Codday, er, Alex."

"Yes sir, Thomas, yes sir, that he has. And tomorrow we will begin."

☙◦❧◦☙◦❧

After sharing breakfast in the lavish hotel dining room, both men were driven around the city of Pittsburgh, as if Thomas had never seen it before—as were his uncle's wishes.

They were dropped off at a corner grocery store to purchase gum for Thomas and then walked one block to Mr. Codday's office.

It would take two days to unravel and initially start a plan regarding Uncle Jay's estate, including his assets and liabilities. And until he received a clear understanding of Jay's estate and Thomas got to know Alex Codday better, they agreed he would drive to Pittsburgh monthly, while settling the paperwork.

As Uncle Jay's lawyer, trustee and executor, he felt compelled to inquire, but he hoped he would be received favorably.

"Thomas, now I know it is none of my business, but being aware of your uncle's devotion to you all his life, I feel compelled to inquire . . . what type of investments will you be making with your inheritance?"

He didn't take offense to the inquiry. After all, he knew Uncle Jay believed in and trusted this man with his business dealings from the very beginning.

"No offense taken," Thomas said.

As Jay's business continued to expand, the firm of Codday and Dawson, Attorneys Chartered, grew in direct proportion. Mr. Codday recommended the best accountants, bankers and financial advisors to counsel his client. Since Uncle Jay had left a trust, he was trying to insure that Thomas would also invest wisely. He likewise hoped his firm would be contracted by Thomas to care for the legal aspect of his investments, while his associates from the St. Francis Corporation could handle Thomas' financial queries.

"Alex, I do appreciate your concern and your forthright way of asking, and I know you took good care of my uncle's affairs. But I've decided what I'm gonna' do with my gift, my trust I think you call it, from my Uncle Jay. First, I'm gonna' continue payin' the notes that I owe. There were some good people who helped me out when I had dry spells, and I plan to treat 'em real good. Now the second thing I'm gonna' do is surprise my wife and nephews with some special treats. The third, and to me *the* most important thing I'm gonna' do with Uncle Jay's gift, is to make sure it feeds back to the church."

Thomas had no idea of the scope or the size of his uncle's estate.

Mr. Codday replied,

"An admirable idea, Thomas."

They began to set up the paperwork until the close of the day, and then Mr. Codday surprised Thomas with plans for dinner.

ॐ᪥ॐ᪥

"I'd like to be workin' on our basic plan we started yesterday, and as I go, I'll work out the details. Hashed out some questions last night, back in my room, but to be honest I think the bubbles from that champagne kept me from thinkin' straight. Gotta' get it all in order in my mind first 'til it all makes sense to me, and then you and me will put our heads together and make it all work out, a little each month."

They continued as they entered Mr. Codday's business office and sat at the conference table, the paperwork before them.

"If you don't want to drive here each month, Thomas, I can transfer the amount Jay designated to your bank in Maryland and add it to your account. That way you won't . . ."

"Hold it right there," Thomas said heatedly.

"I don't want to hear nothin' about tranferrin' money through some electronic mumbo-jumbo to some bank."

He continued sharply.

"I want it in my hand, in cash, and ready each month. I'll be doin' the transferrin', and if you want to continue advisin' me, you can; but just 'cause you do, don't expect me to change my mind about that. I saw my father and mother lose all of their savings when the banks failed, years ago.

"It was there one minute and then *whoosh*—gone the next!

"I was young, but I remember *sooo* well. My daddy almost lost his mind, and if it wasn't for some good people they knew who raised cattle, we could've starved to death.

"They came through for us, and I have never forgotten!

"So, you can expect to see me on that first Monday of every month at 9:00 a.m. when your doors open."

Thomas continued to be annoyed and said,

"We'll have our little get-together, but you have the cash ready. We'll count it, and I'll be gone. And it won't be goin' into some bank, I can tell you that. No sir, no banks for me!"

Mr. Codday realized he was on thin ice with Thomas and didn't want to provoke him any further, but felt he must have a clear picture of their impending monthly meeting.

"Thomas, you want cash . . . *all* in cash? Do you really want to transport the money yourself? What if someone finds out that you're carrying that much cash, why they . . ."

Thomas had cooled down, feeling in control again.

"I know you're concerned. I'll just have to leave it up to you to cover your end and make sure that no one finds out that I am carryin' that money out of here. Once I leave, then it's up to me. I'll be fine. Who would expect someone like me in an old pick-up truck to have pockets full of cash?"

Although Mr. Codday thought it reckless and advised Thomas of the impending danger that he could be subjecting upon himself, he promised to prepare the trust payment to be ready by 9:00 a.m. on the first Monday of the next month.

He decided to let things cool a bit.

"What do you say, Thomas, let's get back to planning your ideas for the church."

On and on, the day progressed as they brainstormed, setting up various proposals that Thomas and his uncle had discussed before his death. Mr. Codday could only shake his head and smile at times, in total disbelief of their ingenuity, their originality.

When evening came upon them, Mr. Codday was in awe of Thomas Frank's keen mind as much as he was inspired by the genius of the inventor, Thomas' uncle, Jedidiah (Jay) Frank.

"Tomorrow, we will have to go over a few more things, and then we'll be finished for this month's meeting. I can always call you long distance if I need to ask you something. But for tonight, Thomas, considering all that we have accomplished, we have a lot to celebrate. Please, be my guest at one of the finest restaurants in the area."

❧❦❧❦

After that initial meeting, Mr. Codday was confident that Thomas would reconsider and allow him to start the electronic transfers to a Maryland account. He reassured himself that once he saw he could walk into the bank and withdraw at his whim, he'd appreciate the convenience. And, as time went on, he'd see that banks were safe. Between him and his associates at the St. Francis Corporation, they'd begin an investment portfolio for Thomas. It would be much like the one now in force for the future of St. John's Parish that he, Jay, and Bill O'Reilly, St. Francis Corporation's owner, had created when Jay's business took off.

❧❦❧❦

As a farmer, it was quite a treat for Thomas to sleep-in the next morning. After he met with Mr. Codday and set up the next date, he was ready to say good-bye.

Mr. Codday surprised Thomas, handing him a large paper bag. He looked inside to see packets of paper money, stacked, one on top of the other. His eyes widened and Mr. Codday saw his bewildered look.

"Now don't say a word, Thomas, just think of this as a first installment. It'll just make it a little easier on you, especially with all of the things you said you wanted to do for your family. I feel that Jay would have wanted it this way."

"Well thank you Alex . . . I guess I wasn't expectin' this much. Really can't thank you enough for all your help. It's been a pleasure workin' with ya', and I know we will continue settin' up a special gift for the church, just like Uncle Jay wanted. May God bless you in all that you do!"

కాఠ్ కాఠ్

Before Thomas started for home, he felt compelled to visit some of the places he and his uncle had enjoyed together.

But now, here he was, alone in the city. Uncle Jay was gone, and Aunt Rose had died a few years before. He was overwhelmed by sadness, even more sadness than he had experienced when he lost his own father, or his brother.

Most of the trolleys were gone, but the inclines were still in operation, although he wouldn't leave his truck unattended to ride them. Then he remembered . . . Grandview Avenue . . . he could ride the old pick-up to the summit!

# CHAPTER FORTY-SEVEN

❧❧❧❧

𝔉rom the street below he could see the huge homes on the cliff that were built in the eighteen hundreds. They were nestled on lots that were considered *the* prime residential real estate. Each one had that breathtaking view of the entire city of Pittsburgh, including the vista that the rivers created, now that the smog and smoke from the mills was gone.

His truck had wound its way to the top of Mount Washington. Thomas pulled up to the curb and forced on the emergency brake. He looked around to be sure that no one was watching, then ripped up the floor mat and stuffed some of the bills under it. He put some in a compartment in the dashboard and hid the rest under his suitcase.

I'll have to create a false floor space for the next time, he thought. It shouldn't be hard to do. I think I can do it using blocks of wood to fill in empty spaces. It will be easy to pull back the mat, remove the wood and replace it with cash. I'll get a new rug to cover it all, and when I leave Codday's office, I'll find a deserted lot and stuff the bills under the floor mat of the truck.

No one would ever expect an old pick-up truck to be full of such a bounty, he reassured himself again.

❧❧❧❧

As his eyes scanned the city he saw the place across the Monongahela River where Uncle Jay had taught him how individual parts were custom-created by tool and die makers. In the distance he could see the bottling company they had visited every time they got together, where he had explained the technique to develop tempered glass of various thicknesses.

To the west was his all-time favorite—the machine shop with the pulleys, wheels and tracks in the ceiling. That was where his fondest memories of his uncle transpired.

He was about to relive them.

As he reminisced, he remembered that all of the workers were happy to see *little Thomas,* as they had called him, whose wide-eyed curiosity had given them a chance to show off while explaining to him just how the elaborate system worked. Jay would lift him up and sit him on his shoulders, giving him a closer view of the apparatus.

In his mind, he could hear Uncle Jay . . . *This here is my boy, Thomas, er, I mean, my nephew, Thomas. Teach him what we do here, men. Someday he'll probably be working with us.*

Thomas shuddered and gulped hard, keeping his emotions in check.

If only his father would have let him move to Pittsburgh. He could have worked into Uncle Jay's business. But his father made him promise he would continue farming the land that he was developing, which had been his father's and his grandfather's before him. When Thomas even began to broach the subject of Uncle Jay's business his father would become furious, and he swore to Thomas that he would stop his visits to Pittsburgh if the foolish talk didn't stop. Thomas relented, made his vow to his father to farm, and being a man of his word, he kept his promise.

He began to mull over his previous decisions.

*I'm happy in my life, right? I love Mary Kathleen and our nephews that we're raisin'.* Farmin' has been tough though, so very hard to get ahead. Sometimes nature stepped in and threw me a curve—too much or too little rain or an early frost coverin' the crops. Another problem would be if and when a major piece of machinery needed to be replaced. And I thank God that Uncle Jay had really helped me climb out of the debt that had been growin' over the years. Besides inheritin' the farm from my parents, I got the unpaid bills as well.

The boys, men really, had some needs that I just couldn't afford to take on before.

As he sat on that high elevation, he first rehashed the idea that Michael had wanted to go to Agricultural School in Ohio.

*My Michael and his ideas*—he wanted to eventually use some sort of an electronic gadgetry, a computon or somethin' like that, to help him figure out what he needed as he farmed.

I remember when I told him, *Michael, ya' can't figure out farmin' on a machine. You get out there, check your soil, plant, fertilize, and pray for rain and a good harvest. If the good Lord is willin' it all works out. You get a few dollars in your pocket and then ya' start plantin' your winter crop.*

But Michael sure didn't see it my way. After joinin' the Future Farmers of America, he told me he learned that more plannin' was producin' results that my generation only dreamed about. Michael was sure that if we could afford that machine and the *software*, as he called it, that he would show me how it could be done more scientifically, producin' a stronger crop with more yield per acre.

"Humph. Don't know about that, I'd hafta' see it to believe it!" he said.

His thoughts turned to William, who was interested in becoming a veterinarian.

I'm thinkin', after regular college, William would have to go to one of them special schools for animal study. Heard of a real good one in Ohio and one in Virginia, my friend from Grange meetings told me about. Altogether it would mean six or more years of studyin'. I'll have to check out the cost of that idea, if William still wants to go for it.

Then there's my Andrew . . . loves music. Now that he's back from Vietnam, thank God, I wonder if he's still thinkin' on it. Was talkin' about gettin' a guitar, an electrical one—not sure of the cost and then there's the lessons. Wonder just how many lessons most people need before they can read music and play pretty good. Hate to think of him goin' off travelin' with some band. But, then again, his head's on straight. Maybe now, I can make it happen.

What'll I do for Mary Kathleen? I know. I'll have to tell her that she can visit her friend Molly and maybe take a trip with her for a week or two. With the farm, I'm pretty locked in, tough to get away. It's hard enough to find good coverage to come up here to Pittsburgh every month to visit Uncle Jay and . . .

He caught himself as his eyes started to fill, but he controlled the urge and shook it off.

Yep, she'll be surprised when I tell her she can go away without me. Why, I bet she jumps for joy when she hears the news.

Thomas' thoughts zeroed in as he unwrapped two wads of bubble gum and began to chaw away.

Jonathon, he's the one I'm broodin' over. He can't seem to stay focused on any one thing long enough to make up his mind. He's mostly always in trouble, it seems. I've bailed him out of mistakes he's made in the past, always hearing a promise that he would never do it again.

Thomas' thoughts about Jonathon vacillated.

Sometimes Jonathon didn't repeat his mistakes, well not exactly. He did try to do better about his lack of responsibility, or at least sometimes. And I'm not catchin' him in any lies, well not too many, like before.

I know I should've been stern with Jonathon, early on, but I just couldn't. But why? Maybe it was because he was the youngest, the one who didn't get a chance to know his own mother and father at all. That really bothered me, and I know it kept eatin' away at him, especially as he grew older. It was as if he thought his parents purposely left him, abandoned him, like they didn't want him. Mary Kathleen and I explained, again and again, that they were goin' on a weekend trip to Ocean City when they were in the accident. They were plannin' to come back to 'em—back to *him*.

I'll never forget it—why it's emblazoned on my mind like somebody used a brandin' iron on it. What a horrible accident! The driver of the eighteen-wheeler fell asleep while at the wheel, crossed over the grassy median on Route 50, near Easton, and hit their car head on. Mary Kathleen and I decided not to go into details with the boys while they were so young. Jonathon was almost one year old and, of course, he didn't establish any memory of either of 'em.

How he hated that fact!

Whenever his brothers brought up little things as they talked about their parents, especially their mother, he just couldn't handle it. Once, specifically, I remember when Michael, William and Andrew were talkin' about rememberin' her holdin' 'em and comfortin' 'em, and, my God, Jonathon threw a fit!

Well, it was like *up jumped the devil!* He almost got green with envy. And anger, I never did see him so angry before.

Always thought he should listen to his brothers and learn about his mother. Even Mary Kathleen and I couldn't bring her up without him gittin' all flustered—givin' us, kinda,' the evil eye—like her death was our fault or somethin'.

Every time I saw him like that I would feel guilty, somehow, and Mary Kathleen would feel the same way. And I guess we shouldn't have let 'em have his way, quite so much, in spite of it.

I don't think I was so easy with the other three boys. Oh they were favored at times, but I was firm with each of 'em and kept 'em in line. I know they weren't too happy about it at the time—that's for sure.

By golly, sure wish I could've had that tightness with all of 'em like I had with my Uncle Jay—special, mighty special.

He heaved a deep sigh as he made up his mind—*Jonathon is my last chance.*

As he sat on that hill, spinning ideas and thoughts, he dragged out more and more people who were in the recesses of his memory. Time was not part of the equation; he needed to clear his mind.

One person in particular that flashed into his head always made him feel especially good, so strong and smart.

Thomas said out loud, "Yessiree I'm gonna surprise 'em."

He started the truck, made his U-turn, and started down Grandview Avenue.

# CHAPTER FORTY-EIGHT

ﾞﾞﾞﾞﾞ

ℳary Kathleen watched the clock as she did whenever Thomas went to Pittsburgh. It seemed to creep along, hour by hour, even though on those days she tried to keep busier than normal.

Why couldn't she put these doubts out of her mind? Surely, Thomas was just meeting with Mr. Codday—but for three days? And why was he going to meet with him every thirty days? Wouldn't they be saying the same things over and over again?

She began to calculate. When he called me yesterday, he said he'd be leaving in the morning after a short meeting. The drive takes five hours, and if he left at ten a.m.—meeting probably took one or two hours. After that—lunch, five hours to drive back, should be home by maybe six p.m. at the latest.

Constantly peering at the clock, she counted off the time—six, seven, eight p.m.

Whenever Thomas had a long drive, she couldn't help worrying. Losing her in-laws, who had been killed driving to the beach years before, had changed her life so drastically.

Soon, she thought, soon, he'll be back home safe and sound.

So where is he? Where could he have stopped?

He has been acting so strange lately.

Her mind wandered back to Uncle Jay's caretakers, especially to the nurse, Laura, the slim one that laughed so loud at Thomas' jokes that he managed to sputter out at Uncle Jay's wake, before breaking down to tears. She remembered how the woman put her hand on Thomas' shoulder, squeezed it and said, *If you ever need a shoulder to lean on mine's available, Thomas.* Then she turned to see Mary Kathleen glaring at her with an angry stare. The woman blushed when she saw her; no actually, she became nervous. Why, she thought, why, if it was just an innocent gesture of kindness, then why would she become genuinely flustered?

Ping . . . bing . . . the last two notes on her little mantle clock that was about ready to be retired because of its inability to keep perfect time, had chimed off-key as usual. Numbers ten, eleven and twelve marked the hours that brought the problem to an auditory awareness and continually warranted the decision—wind it or make it a decoration? Now it was ten o'clock; her watch verified it. She said,

"Tonight, dang it, tonight it's on time."

She thought about anything she could think of, other than *that* woman, that Florence Nightingale with a flirting eye. Why, next time he goes to Pittsburgh I might just go along with him. I'll sit real close to Thomas and wear that cute, shorter dress I've had for a while . . . might even put my arm around him while he's drivin'.

Hurriedly, she went to the closet and pulled just that one out to try on—that sassy, rayon print dress that zippered under the arm through the waist and hips.

*It'll be easier to put on with that zipper, and it will hug your figure,* said the saleslady at Mather's Department Store when she had bought it.

She undressed. Mary Kathleen felt the soft rayon material slip over her head and begin traveling down her arms. Then, it stopped.

"I know what's wrong, I forgot to open the zipper," she said as she managed to reach her right hand over to the metal threads. But, it *was* open, and as she turned her head to the left, she was staring at her reflection in the narrow mirror straight ahead. Her eyes peered through the open space the zipper would have closed, had it fit. She could see the bulges at her midriff and at her inner and outer thighs. Some of her weight gain was hidden throughout the arm and shoulder area by the skirt of the dress, which was all around her neck at this point.

She couldn't deny it any longer. She had gotten fat. Pounds had been added, not ounces, but pounds. When she bought the dress she was now trying on, it just skimmed over her lean body and the metal teeth that the interlock fastened had connected effortlessly.

Then her mind traced back to *that* woman, that svelte hussy who laughed at her husband's jokes.

She barely heard the truck that night. Her mind was inundated with details that intensified and expanded with every replay of the intimate squeezed shoulder incident, Thomas and the *bimbo*.

While scrambling to remove the dress, she ripped part of the shoulder area that was stuck and grabbed a pink, chenille bathrobe to cover her underwear while shimmying into her red, fuzzy slippers. On the way out to meet Thomas at the truck, she threw on one of their nephew's army surplus jacket, a camouflage print. Her slipper caught on a sharp edged stone and partially tore, which then created a flap at the heel. Dust swirled into a cyclone with each step as she followed the dirt road to the barn.

As she rushed over to meet him, she had forgotten about looking sassy or cute. Her only thought was that he was home safe and sound until he got out of the truck to open the barn doors. He looked rumpled, but wouldn't anyone who had been on the road all day?

Thomas had a very funny smile on his face that night.

He kissed her with a quick peck, halfway missing her lips.

"Got to stay out in the barn tonight . . . got a lot of thinkin' to do. You go ahead into the house and get some sleep," he said gingerly.

"But, how did it go today? What happened? Was it a successful trip?" she questioned.

"Let's just say it turned out much better than I planned," Thomas said.

He pulled the truck inside the barn. As he closed the huge, barn doors she stared straight ahead at him and saw on him a strange look that started as a smirk and wound up as a twisted smile. It was as if he was hiding something and she couldn't help but think that a wry smile like that would also be found on *the cat that ate the canary*!

# CHAPTER FORTY-NINE

❧❧❧❧

𝒜s he walked into the kitchen, having stayed all night in the barn, she looked at him apprehensively.

While pouring out the coffee into his favorite mug, she could see he was not tired, but exhilarated, bubbling over. He remarked,

"Well, you shoulda' seen it, Mary Kathleen, things shinin' like I never did see before. Crystal chandeliers everywhere and one hangin' right in the middle of the lobby as big as my tractor. Why, marble so clean you could eat off the floors. And everybody all dressed up, all the time! The kinda' chairs you always liked, with them little flower do-dads in the material, and with feet!

"Mr. Codday's office was just up the street . . . guess that's why he put me up at the William Penn Hotel.

"You shoulda seen my room. Room? I mean rooms! I had a suite! Even had little samwiches with all of the crust cut away, and all of 'em just for me!"

He proceeded to clue her in on all of the amenities, including a blow by blow description of the feather bed and the modern toilet fixtures that he was sure were solid gold.

"One of the bellmen said he thought it was the same room Jackie Gleason stayed in once when he came there to perform with Art Carney and the June Taylor Dancers.

"Breakfast, the next day—*Benedict eggs*, never had 'em before! Sauce, swimmin' all over 'em. A little combo, includin' a piano player and a violin strummer, played music—right there while I drank my orange juice!

"Also had dinner there and then they pulled out all the stops! The thickest pork chops I ever saw, split and laid back; looked like a butterfly with sauerkraut oozin' out of the middle with some special sauce I never did have before—brown sugar in it—that I know. And champagne—I had champagne and I gotta' tell ya, it was good!

"In fact they had a full piece orchestra there by the name of the "Champagne Music Makers" and the people were dancin'," he said as he held out his arms and spun around.

"This orchestra leader named Lawrence Welk was smilin', and he started off his band by sayin', *and a one and a two*, and you won't believe it . . . they had bubbles floatin' up behind the band while they was playin'!

"Not like the little bands we went dancin' to at Beard's on Main Street, or over at Frock's Sunnybrook Farm, here in Westminster, but a full-piece orchestra like at a symphony or somethin'.

"They were playin' songs like, 'Dancin in the Dark,' and waltzin' to it.

"Benny Goodman's old song, oh, what the heck is the name of it? Anyway, they were doin' some swing to that one.

"The next night they took me to another great restaurant, La Monte, over on Mt. Washington, known for their Steak Diane, a special steak so tender you could almost cut it with a fork—that's what the menu said about it. Cooked it right at the table—sizzlin', smokin', right at the table! Two guys, one called a head chef . . . each one shakin' a pan, heatin' the burner, doin' all kinds of things. I saw one table get cherries with a wine poured over 'em, and the chef guy lit a match and caught it on fire. Then they poured the whole thing over vanilla ice cream. I guess they wanted to melt it pretty quick.

"They had a band, too. Played one of our songs, 'It Had to Be You,' and I danced with Mr. Codday's secretary. But honey, I thought of you the whole time. Wasn't that great?

Mary Kathleen lost it.

"Great? I'm supposed to think that's great. I'm here, you're there, dancin' with some woman and I'm supposed to think it's great? Thomas, I thought you went to Pittsburgh to settle Uncle Jay's affairs. Just what kind of an affair was there?" she screamed and stormed up the stairs slamming the bedroom door.

"Humph! Only gone three days, and she acts like I did somethin' wrong. Women! I guess she's goin' through somethin' in her monthly. Best let her be to work it out. Sure, she'll come to me when she wants to talk about it," he said out loud, while scratching his head and backside as he walked outside.

As the door slammed shut, Mary Kathleen lifted her head from her pillow. While tears streamed down her face, she looked through the window to see her husband walking toward the barn.

"The barn," she said. "That cursed barn. Every time he needs to escape he goes off to that barn and plays with his toys, his machinery and those pulleys and levers.

"When the boys were small and needed reprimandin', he'd say, *now stop it boys,* but did he stay and carry through? No, instead, off he'd go to the barn. When the homework needed to be heard, it was Thomas walkin' out to go to the barn, and when the dishes needed doin' or the clothes needed washin' or foldin'—for four growin' boys—off he'd go to that playhouse of his, and every dag'on time he came back from Pittsburgh, he stayed out there late into the night while I'd be layin' here all alone.

"I never get half the attention that old dilapidated barn gets. I wish it would fall over!" she sobbed burying her tears deeper into her pillow.

# CHAPTER FIFTY

∂∾∾∂∾∾∂∾∾∂∾

$\mathcal{W}$hispering, Thomas Frank felt like a schoolboy again as he called Maggie Fischer early the next morning. He kept turning his head from side to side, watching, making sure no one was seeing his giddiness.

"Maggie, Maggie, it's Thomas Frank. Yes, I know it's early, but I had to talk to you. I can't speak up—don't want to. Tryin' to keep this on the Q.T.; got back late last night.

"Can we get together? I've got to see you real soon and . . ."

Before he could finish his sentence, Mary Kathleen came through the basement door with a basket of clothes in hand.

"Who do you have to see real soon?"

Thomas put the earpiece into its cradle without saying another word.

He grinned a wide-toothed grin toward Mary Kathleen, his eyes dancing everywhere but into hers, as he said,

"Good mornin', honey, er, what's for breakfast?"

He turned his back to her and sheepishly said,

"Never mind, don't worry about breakfast. I've got to go into town. Got a few things to pick up, but I'll see you later today."

She did a double take and stared at him, thinking—Thomas, not wanting me to fix his breakfast?

Something must be wrong.

Before she could ask him, out he went, the screen door slamming just the way it always did.

But today, something was very different.

Mary Kathleen was beside herself.

What could he be so secretive about? Did I hear him say, Maggie? No, couldn't be. Lately he's actin' so strange. Hope he's not goin' through his second childhood.

She wondered where he could be going without his breakfast?

I was all a'flutter about, Laura, the nurse, and now here he is callin' someone and actin' all mysterious. Throughout the day she played it over and over, but just couldn't put her finger on it.

Although Thomas always used Bowman's store for his seeds for the farm, he had not ventured into their garden area. But today was different. He saw the manager of the store and said,

"I've got to have some help, plannin' this, ya' see, it's got to be really special. Ya' know how some of those bigger houses up near the college have flowers a bloomin' throughout the seasons, but 'specially in the spring? Well, that's what I gotta' get together for my wife.

"Haven't had much time for each other, or the money—not that we got that much money now—but, I came into a few dollars, and I wanna' do somethin' I know she'll like.

"So, what da' ya' think?" he asked the manager.

"Thomas, we can send out somebody to lay out a complete plan for you. That's what you'll need. Here are the prices for some of our shrubs and perennials. Once you set up a good base planting, the colors come and go into the next flower, week after week."

"But, I want a . . . what did she call it? Oh, I remember, she was talkin' to her friend a while ago and told her how she wished she had her house lookin' like a springtime bouquet. That was it, a springtime bouquet.

"I know she loves all the shades of pink, so's we could start there. But, *I'll* draw ya' a scale measurement of the yard, front and back surrounding the house. Don't want anybody ruinin' my surprise by comin' out to measure. I'll come in, we'll make the final decisions and then I want 'em to show up one day and just start diggin'. Deal?"

"Deal," said the manager.

Thomas stopped at a pay phone and dialed, Maggie Fischer's home. He was so bubbly, she thought, not at all like he was the last time they were together.

They began to scheme and plan, giggling to each other over the phone, while she jotted everything down.

He told her to keep a look out and buy only the best. After they summarized their ideas, he shared his newly formed plans for the springtime bouquet.

"Dropping off the measurements and sketchin' out the layout is the way to go and, by tomorrow, I'll make sure they'll have all they need.

ଛ∕ଉଛ∕ଉ

Thomas called Maggie again the next day.

"In one week it will all be done—azaleas, rhododendron, flowering trees and impatiens, all in pink, purple and white.

"When autumn rolls around, they'll be back to plant hundreds of tulips and daffodils and top 'em off with fall flowers—called chrysanthemums—all in shades of yellow, burnished orange, they said, and deeper bronze, kinda' like a copper penny. The impatiens will be dyin' off as the mums take over.

"They explained it to me at the garden center."

They said exactly this,

"That way, all year long you'll have a beautiful show of color.

"Now, do ya' think that oughta' make Mary Kathleen happy?" He asked Maggie.

"Sure thing," she said, "and our surprise will just be the icing on the cake."

# CHAPTER FIFTY-ONE

*ঔ৵ঔ৵ঔ৵*

$\mathcal{A}$s she scurried in and out of the kitchen, Mary Kathleen thought something was strange. Whenever she stepped into the dining room, everyone stopped talking, looked at her, and grinned. When she went back into the kitchen she could hear the buzz of voices whispering. Something was up, but she had no time to worry about it now. She remembered how the last time Thomas was so secretive she wound up with a beautiful garden. What a surprise compared to what I had been thinkin', but today Thomas and one of his riddles or games would just have to wait. It's Thanksgiving, and the turkey comes first.

"Eh, Andrew and William, I sure could use a couple of good helpers in here," she yelled through the open archway that led from the kitchen to the dining room.

"And I could use you too, Michael, to set the table and put out extra hot plate holders."

"You got it," they said, almost in unison.

All four nephews were taught to pitch-in to help, but today Jonathon hadn't shown up at the designated time. They wondered why, although many times he had kept them waiting only to show up after all of the work was completed and just in the nick of time.

Each of them surveyed what needed to be done and started in on their appropriate duties just as they had learned as small boys.

*ঔ৵ঔ৵ঔ৵ঔ৵*

Mary Kathleen had insisted that they all become self-sufficient. She had taught them to peel potatoes, snap green beans, husk corn on the cob, prepare roast beef and then pull it all together for a nutritious meal.

"Some woman's gonna' be pretty lucky someday to marry anyone of you," she had said to them previously.

Sometimes, she would let them bake, but that was usually her domain, although once on their Uncle Thomas' birthday she waited until he had gone into the fields. All four boys joined in to master a plan to puzzle him for a change. He was the one who had always pulled one over on them, hiding Easter baskets in the most unlikely places or creating riddles for them to complete.

On that occasion they started making cupcakes. Mary Kathleen pulled chairs over to the table for Jonathon and Andrew, the two smallest boys, to stand upon so they could see into the mixing bowl. William pulled all the ingredients the recipe card listed, while Michael went downstairs to the unfinished basement to prepare that area for their party.

Aunt Mary Kathleen preheated the oven to 375 degrees.

She oversaw each step, guiding their little hands.

One cup of softened butter was first put into the bowl. Two cups of sugar were added, which Andrew stirred until nice and creamy.

She had cracked four eggs and separated the whites from the yolks, letting Andrew put only the yolks into the mixing concoction, which he again stirred.

A sheet of waxed paper to cover the kitchen table was torn and onto it Jonathon measured and sifted together three cups of flour and two teaspoons of baking powder with one-quarter teaspoon of salt. He lifted the edges of the waxed paper and heard the paper crackle while he guided the dry ingredients into the liquid all at once. He'd stirred it gently to blend it all.

One of the boys added one cup of milk at room temperature and two teaspoons of vanilla followed by a gentle beat. Finally the egg whites that their aunt beat separately were added by folding them lightly, a technique that was a little tricky for the boys.

The batter was ready to go.

After the two younger boys, Andrew and Jonathon measured and mixed, William and Michael, using two tablespoons, scooped up the batter and delivered it into pastel multicolored papers that were inserted into a tin pan with twelve compartments in it. Their Aunt popped them into the oven and noted the time, which they watched for the next twenty-five minutes.

The aroma throughout the kitchen of vanilla and sugar made the boys lick their lips in anticipation. Each of the chefs checked his cupcakes for doneness by inserting a toothpick into one of them to watch for a clean stick, free of gooey batter.

Once baked and cooled, all four of them iced the rounded tops using delicious chocolate frosting that Aunt Mary Kathleen whipped up.

Telltale signs of fun were everywhere—smeared on the table, on the floor, but most of the signs showed up on the faces of the four boys who licked spoons, beaters and bowls.

Aunt Mary Kathleen baked the roast that day, but she'd let the older boys make the gravy and prepare the vegetables and take all of it to the table. After the delicious meal each boy excused himself—one by one—to quietly tiptoe down the basement steps, followed by Auntie. When Uncle Thomas was finally alone and wondering where everyone was, Michael beckoned Unks in a quavering voice to come downstairs.

Uncle Thomas slowly descended the stairs to a dimly lit area illuminated only by the candles on the cupcakes that each boy held up for him to see, as they yelled surprise.

To his amazement the dull basement had been transformed into a party room. Balloons and streamers of bright reds, blues and yellows filled the space matching the crayon decorated paper tablecloth that each boy artistically designed.

They had put one over on him, or so they thought that they had in their own juvenile way.

ॐॐॐॐॐॐ

The final rush was about to begin to put everything onto the table, hot and all at once. It was time to test out all that they had learned as young boys, and though always a challenge, with everyone's help it would be completed like a choreographed symphony.

Aunt Mary Kathleen was the Maestro, her arms and voice moving in syncopated rhythm while the men staggered around one another as if in a special type of dance.

"Michael, pull the sweet potatoes out of the oven and the gravy, too . . . hot . . . be careful!

"Corn—add a dollop of butter to the corn, William, and salt and pepper, too.

"Michael, check the sauerkraut while you're at the oven. Green beans are in there too, stayin' hot. Make sure they're not burnin'.

"Thomas, how's that turkey comin'? Keep slicin', we've got lots of hungry mouths to feed. You're done? Okay, great!

"Let's see, cranberry sauce, with and without nuts. We also need milk and extra butter . . . Andrew, there, in the refrigerator.

"Michael, dressing is ready to go onto the table too, but cover it.

"Mashed potatoes, oh my, I gotta' start my mashed potatoes! Where's my spatula?

"Bread, rye and white are in the basket, William—check it."

The orchestration of the meal preparation and serving it to the table was finished, and all of it was hot or cold, as needed.

"Okay . . . now let's eat. Where is that Jonathon?" Uncle Thomas asked aloud. As he did, the door opened, Jonathon stepped in and it slammed behind him.

Michael and William looked at each other, shook their heads and William, cupping his hand, said softly,

"Of course, Jonathon shows up now—the work is done, and the meal's ready."

"Hurry up, wash your hands, Jonathon, and sit down. I can't have my dinner served cold, and especially after all this work your brothers, Uncle Thomas and I have done."

Jonathon wrinkled his face in disapproval, curling up his lip as he thought sarcastically, *there she goes, always with the guilt trip.*

Uncle Thomas was determined Jonathon would not ruin his happy surprise. He said,

"Okay, let's begin by bringing a little love to this table. We're all here now, and that's what matters."

When they all sat down he began,

"In the Name of the Father and of the Son and of the Holy Ghost . . . Amen."

As they were finishing the blessing before the Thanksgiving feast, Aunt Mary Kathleen thought she saw her husband smile and wink to Michael as he added his personal ending,

"And, dear God, we give thanks for all the future gifts that are sent our way. Amen."

The boys looked at each other and held back the grins they were trying to hide, then, as they did throughout the meal. One or the other kept glancing toward the windows that faced the lane leading to the house instead of concentrating on the mealtime conversation; that is, except for Jonathon, who spied their actions but felt lost as to what was taking place. It did seem a bit unusual to Mary Kathleen, but she was so busy watching for and listening for positive responses to her hours of cooking and baking, that the *yums* and *ahhs* were more captivating.

Mary Kathleen and five men devoured the main course.

She gathered up the dinner plates and left the table to fetch dessert in the kitchen.

William tried to quickly tell Jonathon what was about to happen.

Jonathon became angry that he hadn't been told and that his brothers knew all about it. He sulked and pursed his lips, never once admitting that he, too, would have known if he had come earlier.

"Well you did it again, Auntie," William said loud enough for her to hear while patting his stomach as he rose from the table.

"I'd give you a blue ribbon for this one. Everything was great. Someday, if I can only find somebody who can cook like you, I'll . . ."

His conversation was interrupted by the sound of spinning wheels coming to a sudden halt, a car squealing—obviously needing a brake job—and gravel scattering onto the porch several feet away.

All of the attention became focused through the windows, their necks straining to see who was making such an entrance. Then they quickly looked toward the kitchen.

They heard the familiar sounds of shifting dinnerware as the sink captured used plates before the dessert ritual began.

As was customary on Thanksgiving, Aunt Mary Kathleen was scooping out vanilla ice-cream on warm pumpkin pie slices and squirting Reddi-Whip down into chocolate pudding, creating a pillow of whipped delight which pushed the chocolate up from the base of the narrow-necked, holiday, cut glassware. The brown and white concoction was a family favorite, light and airy, like puffed, white clouds tumbling in a sea of cocoa.

She hadn't heard the noisy brakes outside. After answering William's compliment with a lilting thank you, she began to sing, 'Over the River and Through the Woods'.

Although its words presented more of a blustery Christmas vision, she had always liked it and, though slightly off-key, today she sang it very loud.

The nephews raced into the kitchen to keep her busy while Uncle Thomas opened the door before the knock. They chimed in on the second verse with uneven harmony, keeping her unaware of the activities in the parlor.

Thomas opened the door.

"Hi . . . Mr. Thomas?

"I'm Gretchen, Maggie Fischer's daughter. She has the flu but didn't want to disappoint you, knowing how much you wanted to surprise your wife and especially on the holiday.

"So . . . I brought her," she said as she exposed the cutest little white puppy with beige-tipped fur from the soft blanket she was carrying.

"Is your mother, okay? Come on in," he said, and then he smiled at the puppy.

He looked over his shoulder and whispered while motioning her to a hassock across from Mary Kathleen's favorite chair,

"My wife is in the kitchen, and I don't think she heard us."

"Okay, and my Mom will be fine—she just needs rest, that's all," Gretchen said.

Thomas called out his nephew's names, and out they came, one behind the other, each halting his own warble as he noticed the beautiful stranger.

She definitely noticed each and every one of them and thought how lucky she was to see such a parade.

Each one cocked his head, winked or smiled broadly to her and sat or stood opposite a delicate-looking chair, most likely, Gretchen thought, one from which their aunt would soon hold court.

Then he called Mary Kathleen, and out she came with a tray full of desserts, hitting a very long *O* on the word, *snow*, in the song.

She slowed her gait when she saw the stranger sitting there, stopped singing and glanced toward Thomas who was grinning from ear to ear. The nephews started to giggle, just as they did when they were little boys. Although puzzled, she felt that something wonderful was about to happen.

"Honey, come over here and meet Maggie Fischer's daughter, Gretchen."

She set the tray down on the coffee table and walked over to Thomas, who picked up the bundle from Gretchen and handed it to her.

"Why, what's this?" she exclaimed, while smiling as she felt movement in the blanket and gently sat onto the chair that Andrew had positioned adjacent to the audience.

She began opening the layers of cloth and exposed the puppy, while they all yelled,

"Surprise!"

Mary Kathleen didn't know what to make of it all.

"Why . . . what? Whose puppy is this?

"Mine . . . it's mine? Really?"

Thomas said,

"You've always wanted your own special house dog. One you can train, like Lassie, you always said. But one that's all soft and cuddly that you could brush every day, right?

"Well . . . Maggie Fischer helped me and was gonna' bring the puppy here today but she has the flu. So that's why Gretchen's here instead. Maggie suggested a poodle 'cause they train so well. *They love to please,* she said. Hair can grow as long as you want it to. Can even dress her up with one of them frou-frou hairdos I've seen 'em in . . . pom-poms and everything. So what d'ya think?

"Do ya' like her?"

While taking her out of the blanket and lifting her up for all to see, Mary Kathleen became misty-eyed. She thanked Gretchen and said,

"Oh, I can't believe it. Yes, I like her, and I bet by tonight I'll love her."

While eyes were fixed on the puppy, two sets of eyes were focused on the lovely dark-haired beauty sitting forward on the ottoman. The mind behind one set of eyes thought how sweet she seemed, and he noted she was obviously so happy to see the rapture she brought to his aunt by delivering the puppy, and on Thanksgiving, too!

He noticed how her bright, blue eyes sparkled almost with glee as she watched Mrs. Frank cuddle the eight-week old puppy.

Skin like velvet, Michael thought.

Two other eyes kept glancing back and forth between his aunt and Gretchen, but with questioning familiarity.

Gosh, she's so pretty, and I think I . . . he stopped his thoughts and then suddenly said,

"Are you the same Gretchen that went to Westminster High and graduated in 1961?"

She nodded.

"I went to school with you. You played ball, basketball . . . varsity, right? I was on the varsity squad, too . . . er, boy's varsity, that is. Well, you certainly have . . . ah, changed. Ah, er, did you go off to college?" William said, stumbling all over his words.

"University of Delaware," she said smiling, proud of her Alma Mater and happy to be remembered by such a cute guy.

"Been home long? Haven't seen you around town," he said.

"Actually, I was out of state and had been working to get my certification in dog grooming. My mom and I have opened up a shop over on Anchor Street, at our house.

"We've added a new entrance and a couple of rooms for the equipment like the grooming tables, shampoo tubs and drying cages. So far it's really turning out great. I'm so lucky to be doing something I truly love.

"You'll have to spread the word for me. Here, I have these cards," she continued as she handed them out to each person in the room.

When she got to Michael she fumbled them, and they fluttered to the floor in front of him. As she reached for them, he did too. Their heads cracked against each other rather hard.

"Ouch," they both said in unison and laughed at the irony of both instances.

"Owe me a Coke," she said and reached out her hand to secure the promise by hooking his pinkie finger into hers, slightly squeezing them together.

"You're on," he said.

# CHAPTER FIFTY-TWO

❧❦❧❦

"Ally-oop," Gretchen said to Maggie as they lifted, Sherlock, the Old English sheepdog, onto the grooming table.

"Look at this guy. Don't think I can even get my fingers—much less a brush—through his dense coat that's so matted. Feel this, Mom—he's a hair factory," she said incredulously.

Maggie agreed as she reached into his tangled hair and felt the thickness.

In her heart, Gretchen knew he would be a challenge and told his owner that Sherlock would be with her all day—that in fact, she would save him for last.

Usually she had the bigger dogs use a ramp to reach the table, but he was so traumatized that she thought their joint heave-ho would be better for him.

"I thought I could brush him out and save some of his coat, especially for this time of the year with Thanksgiving just behind us, but, it's not gonna' happen," she said in frustration.

"I just can't do it. They're gonna' be forced to put a sweater on him if it's chilly, or he'll catch his death; and to protect his eyes, not too much sunlight for this guy once I clip off the mats. He's not familiar with too much light of day, so I'll try to keep a fringe over his eyes."

Before she could touch one drop of water to his back, Gretchen proceeded to clip his coat down to an inch or two, lifting the snarled hair with one hand while she glided her older pair of electric clippers under each section and watched the buzzers magically trim hair-upon-hair.

Maggie went to answer the phone.

As the gnarled coat fell away, it did so in one continuous layer, dropping to the floor in a pile resembling a large animal sleeping. She kicked sections into place with her foot to carve out two ears, four legs and a tail and dropped three black licorice gum drops onto the piles that looked like eyes and a nose.

When Maggie returned, she had to laugh at Gretchen's humor. "Should we take *its* picture for our before photo wall, too?" she joked.

At this point, Sherlock was their only customer, and Maggie started to close out the books.

Gretchen yelled over the noise of the clipper.

"Mom, did you charge Pat for Jimmy's nails? You know, the Yellow Lab that got a bath, too? Is he lovable, or what?"

"Yep, sure did," said Maggie and continued, "And the Buckleys picked up Abbey while you were clipping away in there—said they loved the lamb clip and the precise way you trimmed around her pads and toenails. They left you a hefty tip."

"JoAnn and Don were here earlier asking for you, Mom, while you went for the lunch. They are entering their Welsh Corgi, Keegan, at the Fifth Regiment Armory in Baltimore for the dog show this year. He'll be coming in tomorrow morning . . . just needs a bath, nails and his undercoat removed. He's accumulating quite a few points—can't remember just how many. She told me; I just can't remember."

Maggie said,

"We'll find out tomorrow. Gretchen, how much did that Irish wolfhound weigh? I'm sorry I wasn't here."

"Oh, you mean, Christian, Katey's dog?

"I can tell you right now, if I didn't have that wedge that the dogs use to walk up and into the bath, I couldn't have lifted him. He weighs one-hundred and ten pounds!"

"Actually, he weighs more than all the little dogs you did altogether, both yesterday and today."

"Right, but even though he is enormous, he didn't offer a challenge like this guy. Mrs. Pictor needs to have him groomed more often, especially if she's not gonna' brush him. I'll do it for her if she wants me to. His undercoat alone needs to be sheared out occasionally," Gretchen said, the sound of obvious annoyance in her voice, not really wanting to cut off his hair that short.

The phone rang. Maggie hung up and told Gretchen she just booked an appointment for Bella, a Yorkshire terrier who needed her monthly bath and, of course, a new slide pin for her hair.

Gretchen spoke up. "Now see, Mom, that little dog is never matted. Terri keeps her coat wrapped in curling papers, so she'll be a pleasure to do.

After she snipped the last section of matted fur, which fell on top of the accumulating pile of "dog," Sherlock looked his body over, investigating parts of it he hadn't seen for quite a while.

"Yep, they're all there," Gretchen laughingly said, as she and Maggie switched him to the tub. She turned on the water to hose him down, and the warm water must have felt unfamiliar, but appealing, to the English sheepdog. His tail was wagging from side to side with great fervor while he affectionately licked Gretchen's face, arms, and even her neck with great intensity.

"Oh, you're such a good boy, Sherlock, but just who is giving whom a bath?" Gretchen asked while lathering up the almost hairless body and messaging the shampoo onto him.

"I'll bet he feels better now," Maggie said.

"I'm so glad *you're* feeling better, Mom, and thanks for the hand with Sherlock and the others. He must weigh ninety-five pounds."

"No problem. And it was only a little cold, barely anything," Maggie said.

"But enough to keep you home and me there, right in the midst of it all," she said, referring to her recent adventure at the Frank's house on Thanksgiving.

While the bubbles increased with the friction, she picked up the conversation that they had begun earlier, one that Maggie had wondered if Gretchen would initiate a second time.

"Mom, I don't know if I told you the whole story or not, so I'd better go over it again," she said.

As Gretchen continued relating the events of Thanksgiving afternoon, Maggie began to sense some electricity between her daughter and Thomas Frank's nephews. Until now the men her daughter had dated had all become friends, rather than romantic partners. Gretchen had always told her mother, *If they just don't have the qualities I'm looking for in a husband, I'm not going to lead them on.* And she didn't. They pursued, but she kept them wishing and hoping, that is perhaps until now.

Gretchen delivered a blow-by-blow description to Maggie about William and Michael. Not only had she noticed their looks, but also how they pitched in to help their aunt, how they enjoyed seeing her excitement and happiness with the surprise of the new puppy, and, of course, how they engaged in competition to walk her to her car.

"Both of them tried to give the other one something to do to clear the way to talk to me alone, Mom. William, the one I went to high school with, tantalized his brother by saying, *Michael don't you need to take the extra pots downstairs for Auntie? I heard her calling you,* knowing that as soon as Michael disappeared in the stairwell, he would offer to walk me to my wagon.

"Their aunt, Mrs. Frank, heard William and said, *Oh yes, Michael, I would appreciate that.*

"Of course she was unaware of the master plan each of the guys had in mind.

"Michael grabbed the pots and lids and ran down the stairs and William and I went outside.

"When Michael came up from the cellar and saw that both of us were missing, the front door flew open and cracked against the house, while Michael froze. We heard the noise and both of us jumped. The door swung back and clipped Michael hard, although he was oblivious to it while watching William and me.

"As he crashed the scene, he mumbled something about saying good-bye, embarrassed and blushing, knowing I was seeing right through his actions."

Gretchen thoroughly enjoyed the attention, as well as the boyish uneasiness she had seen in both of her suitors. She couldn't wait to continue telling her mother how they fumbled all over each other to win her favor as they stood near her car.

Maggie watched her expression change. Gretchen giggled, remembering the head-butting incident as it played itself over in her mind, and she told her mother why she was laughing. She also wondered if Michael would call her after locking their pinkie fingers together as a promise to pay up on the—*Coke that he owed her.*

Although she had heard most of this story earlier, Maggie listened again, realizing that Gretchen was savoring every moment.

# CHAPTER FIFTY-THREE

❧❧❧❧

## DECEMBER 1966

ℛopes were cut, allowing the short and long-needled pine trees to roll off the sides of the flat bed that hauled them into Baltimore.

The day before, William and Andrew dropped a load at three street corners in Highlandtown—Eastern Avenue and Conkling Streets, at S. & N. Katz Jewelers; Eastern and East Avenues, at the Patterson Theater; and Eastern and Linwood Avenues outside of the Ma and Pa grocery store. But today, Jonathon and Michael were supplying the shopping centers, and Eastpoint was first on the list with Cedonia Mall, a close second.

Michael was outside the truck unloading, lifting and stacking four, five, six and seven foot evergreens, while watching for his brother to give him a hand. When is he gonna' finish with the paperwork tallies and get out here to help, he thought, but kept right on lifting and stacking for their customers.

Jonathon spied her getting out of a yellow 1963 Chevy with a black vinyl top and then saw her reach back-in for a couple of bags.

Gretchen sure looks good from this angle, he thought as he studied her closely.

She stood up and turned toward him, not seeing the truck or the men attached to it.

"Mmmm, she looks good from this angle too," he said under his breath as he giggled nervously.

"Yep, I see ya' lookin' over here at me, Gretchen. Just can't take your eyes off me, can ya'?" he whispered.

He pulled down the rear view mirror and admired what he saw as he cocked his face from side to side and grinned to his reflection.

When he looked back, she and her mother, Maggie, were walking into a department store, laughing.

Annoyed, Jonathon said quietly,

"Where does she think she's going', leavin' me here all alone. She ought to know better than to walk away from me.

"Can't stand it! I think I might just have to follow her in there and give her a piece of my mind.

"Yeah, that's what I'm gonna' do. Walk right on in there and . . ."

Michael roared,

"Jonathon . . . Jonathon, what are you doin'? Where are you? Git your butt out here and start pitchin' in. What are you doin', talkin' to yourself again?"

With that, he snapped out of his mind set and giggled to Michael,

"Hey, don't be such a killjoy. I'm in here workin', just like you. Give me a break, will ya'?"

He opened his door and slowly slid out, scratching his head, stretching his arms over it and then, out in front as he repeated the ritual again and again.

He looked like an old Art Carney TV gag as Norton the Plumber on Jackie Gleason's *The Honeymooners.*

Finally he started lifting the trees and then saw one of the young teen helpers who had been working there.

"Hey Bud, gimme' a hand over here. Hurt my back and need to take it easy," he said, out of earshot of Michael.

The kid nodded and pitched right in. Jonathon told him he needed to figure the tally and would be right back and climbed inside again.

Michael was on the one side of the truck and saw movement and action coming from the other side, but didn't know it was not his brother.

Jonathon leered. There she was again, leaving the store, but this time she crossed to the driver's side and stood watching for Maggie to catch up.

She faced toward the truck.

"Lookin' at me . . . she's lookin' at me . . . again," he said in a very low, emphatic voice.

Gretchen spied the truck and Michael working.

"Look at that man, will you," she hummed, and then waved towards Michael. He missed it all.

Jonathon saw the wave, "Humph, just like I thought. Can't take her eyes off me."

Michael went inside a building, and Gretchen didn't want to seem anxious and wait for him, so she and Maggie jumped into the yellow Chevy and were gone.

# CHAPTER FIFTY-FOUR

࿇࿇࿇࿇

"Sure, sure, bring her on in." said Maggie. "Later today will be fine."

As she hung up the phone, she harmoniously called to Gretchen,

"Oh, Gretch, honey, you know that little puppy we got for Mary Kathleen Frank? Well, the puppy's uncle—Michael—seems to think it may need to be clipped before Christmas! He's bringing her right over."

Gretchen stuck her neck out, dropped her mouth open, and grinned from ear to ear.

"Are you kidding me?" she asked, knowing her mother wouldn't tease her like that.

"Mother, watch this little guy. I need some lipstick, and I've got to put my eyes on." She grabbed her make-up kit from the purse and headed for the bathroom.

Not even ten minutes elapsed when Michael walked in cuddling Flurry.

His eyes sparkled and his smile widened, fumbling the puppy as she jumped out of his arms, remembering Gretchen and covering her with kisses.

He drifted and quietly said,

"What a lucky dog," and sighed, catching himself being too obvious, as fire spread through his cheeks when he realized that Maggie had heard him.

Their conversation was easy and their attitude light and amusing as Maggie continued grooming Gretchen's former client discretely disappearing with him.

Both of them seemed to lose track of time as Michael continued to stroke Flurry while Gretchen held her—the puppy being the conduit of the emotion flowing between them.

"I waved to you the other day, down at Eastpoint Mall, when you were unpacking Christmas trees," she said.

"Didn't see ya', and what in the world were you doin' all the way down in the city, you livin' up here in Westminster and all?"

She spelled out, very deliberately,

"S-H-O-P-P-I-N-G and that can take me just about anywhere my little heart desires, or my Mom's. The two of us are a tag team. She tags, and I gotta' go. It's in the rules. You'll find us at early birds, and midnight madness sales, it doesn't matter."

She spun around, opened her waterproof smock and said,

"Got this little outfit at a buy-one-get-one-free sale. Actually, got the extra one for my Mom. Tag team, see?"

She was adorable, he thought, cute as a button, and he hoped to learn a lot more about her and her family.

And thinking of her family, he thought her mother, Maggie, was pretty smart to back out of the picture, take the dog outside and leave them alone to talk.

Michael said, "Guess I gotta' let you get back to work. Please tell your Mom I said good-bye and it was good seein' her again.

"I'd tell her myself, but I don't see . . ."

He walked forward as he spoke, taking in each room, not really in a hurry to leave.

"Hey, this here's a pretty nice business ya' got. Now, there's a neat idea—keys of every shape, size and metal. Take that back, 'cause I see a glass one, one outta' wood and what . . . even a little rhinestone key? What's that, a Las Vegas special? A key to Liberace's closet?"

After that, he clammed up and thought, Now here I go, talkin' too much about stupid things. She's probably gonna' think I'm nuts or somethin'. But, wait, she's laughin' . . . thinks I'm funny. Well . . . thank you . . . Lord! He said to himself, while flashing a grin.

His courage bounced back. He needed to set up another meeting—a date—and said,

"Ya' know, ya' never did buy me that Coke you owe me for us lockin' horns on Thanksgiving."

In a playful manner and with a gleam in her eye, she said, "*I* never did . . . *I* never did? You owe *me,* Mr. Frank, and I expect you to pay up. I'm going to hold you for it."

Michael heard that slight alteration in the phrase and began some wishful thinking.

Gretchen looked directly into his eyes and blushed a little, seeming to get lost in some wishful thinking of her own.

# CHAPTER FIFTY-FIVE

ॐॐॐॐ

## SUMMER 1967

𝒜pprehensively, Jonathon pulled his truck onto the dirt lot that was partially covered with straw. The lot was located deep in Baltimore City, about six blocks east of the Washington Monument. It was early in the day, about six a.m., but by the noise and excitement he had heard and felt, it could have been high noon.

He saw twelve wagons parked right next to one another. Some had canopies made of canvas or wood, but all were obviously homemade. Each had a horse, attached to a highly ornamental harness, to lead the way through the city streets or alleys between rows and rows of Baltimore dwellings.

The horses were beautiful, each in its own way, although most had seen thousands of sunsets. All had those sorrowful, round eyes in diverse shades of brown, varying from amber to red to a golden-walnut hue. Many of them sported makeshift hats with brightly colored plastic flowers attached. Their ears protruded through sliced holes to allow erect vertical movements to either side as their keen hearing dictated that the openings were necessary.

Their manes were braided and sometimes beaded, with interspersed colorful balls, creating a uniform design of plait-upon-plait. Usually the beads matched the colors in their hats, and more plastic flowers decorated the wagon.

Wooden wheels were smaller than on some of the carriages of yesteryear, and the brake consisted of a wooden shoe that pressed on the outer portion of the wheel to halt any motion. It was controlled from a thick, long, wooden stick that the driver grabbed with his hand and pressed to that shoe.

Of course, those trusty, old horses were so well trained that the slightest touch of the reins on their back prompted their movements or lack of. As they followed the same routes each week, the animals became accustomed to stopping at the same houses time and time again. Therefore, when they reached certain spots, the driver dropped the reins, and the horse automatically paused, allowing him to jump off and meet his customers.

Many of the housewives who didn't drive a car would buy from the arabber, whom they trusted to bring to their door the finest fruits and vegetables.

He was the *man of the hour* so that they could start planning the evening meal for their families.

One could hear him almost sing as he came through the alleys and streets, *'maters, sweet and juicy . . . 'maters, red and sweet . . . drawberries, beans, get your drawberries.*

Over and over, in his own special arabber language, the tomatoes became, 'maters or 'matos, and drawberries were actually strawberries. But everybody knew exactly what he was saying. It was part *Balmorese*, the language of the streets of Baltimore, and arabber lingo. After all, this colorful tradition was over one-hundred years old starting after the Civil War.

Wooden boxes would be stacked inside the wagon, and the produce was displayed with such care so the colors of the red strawberries would sit adjacent to the grass green beans. The yellow squash might be next, followed by bright orange carrots, or light green husks encasing corn on the cob with pale, golden silk softly protruding from each ear—like a child's blond hair.

Each man took great pride in his business. Although most had no formal education, they were street savvy, could deal out the exact change, and subdivide bushels into pecks and quarts into pints and in a split-second. These early entrepreneurs created the concept, *customer service.*

At one stop there might be three or four women rushing from both sides of the alley between the rows of brick houses in places like Highlandtown, Canton and Fells Point, to be the first to pick from his wares.

He knew them all by name . . .

*Nice day ta'day, Mrs. Pickford. Got some real nice cherry 'maters for ya. Them green beans snap real crisp—fresh, very fresh.*

*How's about some for you, Mrs. Neukum? Sure do know Mr. Joe likes his green beans, like ya' told me last week. Got corn right from the field, too—yellow and white.*

*Now don't you be a'worrin', Mrs. Carol and Mrs. Janice. I'ze gots plenty to go around. Maters and green beans— two pounds each?*

*Lo, Mrs. Myers, got some small onions, like you like. Red 'pataters too and not too many eyes in dese' ones today. Plump, juicy 'maters—just the right size to fit on a soft crab sam'wich.*

*Mrs. Hutson, youse makin' crab soup? And you too Mrs. Peeling? Heard youse two talkin' 'bout it. Got all the vegebulls youse are gonna' need—carrots, lima beans, green beans, and of course, 'em maters, I just told your neighbors 'bout. Corn, don't forgit corn! Them husbands of yours are real lucky, ya know . . .*

*Plenty here,* he'd say, *got plenty to go around and only the best for every one of ya'.*

*Only bananars, grapes and drawberries for you Mrs. Voelcker? Gotcha' covered.*

He'd bag it all up, and for the ladies who had trouble walking, he would carry the bags right to their door. Always left them with a *thank ya' kindly ma'am,* or *you have a nice day,* or *see ya' next week.*

If any of the homemakers had a complaint about the previous week's purchase, there would be no questioning her. He would give her the same amount, plus a little more to satisfy, and apologize as well.

*Almost missed ya' Mrs. Rajotte, how many pounds of grapes did you say? Sure are sweet. You sure two pounds gonna' be e'nuff? Very sweet.* This time he was piling the grapes into a metal scale with a spinning dial, which bounced from zero to five pounds over and over when it was empty and the wagon moving. But now it was stationary, gradually lowering as the metal tray held and weighed the green and burgundy grapes.

*Oh, alright, gimme' three pounds,* she might say, *and I want two pounds of tomatoes and green beans and three quarts of strawberries. Makin' two strawberry shortcakes tonight, and they are the reddest berries, think I've ever seen.*

After each sale and his friendly close, off he would go throughout his route.

During the day many of the ladies and children who otherwise had never seen a mare would buy carrots or apples and feed the nag.

At times the arabber would ask to fill a galvanized aluminum bucket full of water for her at the garden hose. The kids loved to see how she'd put her head into the bucket and slosh away.

Sometimes while standing and waiting, she'd clop her hooves on the city blacktop as if she were counting off her daily time clock. The mare knew when her workday was over, and when the day was done it was time to get out of her way!

The arabber would plop the reins on her back and make a noise with his tongue. Her hooves clickity-clacked at top speed, sending the scale a'rockin' and the plastic flowers blowing in the breeze down the streets of Baltimore while heading for the stable and the feedbag of oats.

Mr. Frank had established an account with these hard working arabbers. He had won their trust and he always said, *When they liked ya', they liked ya'.*

When Jonathon was old enough to drive, they became part of his delivery domain. In the beginning, he always brought them the best and only sold to the men who wanted the best. But, as he started skimming to tuck away money to gamble, he looked for ways to make that quick buck. He began to bring them the produce cast-offs from the restaurant chefs. He would save up what they had refused all week and what normally his uncle would have tossed out, only to fill his truck to take these seconds or thirds to the stables so he could pocket the money.

"Smitty" Calvin Smith, senior arabber, met him that day when he pulled in and said,

"Don't you be bringin' me no over-ripe 'maters like ya' done last week!

"Why, by the time the sun set on that same day, them 'maters were splittin' open. 'Dem ladies ain't gonna' buy 'dem 'maters like dat. I be losin' money; you hear me, losin' it—big time!"

"Hey Smitty, hold your horses, ha, ha," laughed Jonathon.

"I brought you the best. Go ahead—you unload from my truck first, today. Yeah, givin' you first pick. How's that? Better? Here, take an extra coupl'a quarts of strawberries. No charge."

Jonathon knew he had stacked beautiful, fresh strawberries on the top layer of the quarts he had not sold earlier that week. Their shelf life was limited, one day at best, but he acted like he was really giving Smitty a great deal.

It seemed to pacify Smitty, at least on this day busy as he was, and as for Jonathon, he only lived for the day.

After Jonathon finished unloading his truck, one of the younger arabbers, Zeke, came over and whispered in his ear,

"They is a craps game tonight, down on South Clinton Street near 'da docks. 'Der is a ship in from South America, and 'dem sailor's gots money to blow. Last night me and some of 'da guys got into a whopper and Bill Jackson won seven hundred."

"Yeah! Wow! Sure I wanna' go!"

Jonathon was hooked.

Zeke was also a numbers-runner. He "sold" numbers to Jonathon to bet on whenever he stopped by, so he felt he could trust him.

He would pick three numbers and bet an amount, two, maybe three dollars. Odds were determined and the winning number chosen using actual races at a legitimate race track. If that number tallied up and he had a bet on it, he won a tidy sum.

One of his best customers was Jonathon.

He said,

"Hey Zeke, I got nothin' ridin' right now. Tell ya' what, here's ten bucks. Put five of it on 1-5-0—straight and the other five—box it. Man, when that comes in, I'll be celebratin', alright!"

Smitty couldn't hold it in any longer. He pulled Zeke on the side and said,

"Now Zeke, what you be doin,' tryin' to get Thomas Frank's kin deeper inta' the pitfalls of gamblin'?

"His uncle ain't gonna' take kindly to it.

"If I told you once, I told you a thousand times—gamble all your money away, and you'll be doin' a back-brakin' job for the resta' your life.

"See this back?" he asked, tapping himself on his shoulders. "Back-brakin' work, I'm tellin' 'ya, so's I wanna' put somethin' away—just a little at a time, mind ya'—and I might be able to git myself outta' this, if I do. 'Course, shoulda' started when I was younger.

"You're young—brains, young too—use 'em. Keep yourself on the straight and narrow.

"Like I said, puttin' somethin' away. I'm savin' the money for my kids—high school now, and college in three years and they'll be makin' me proud. Then four more, and when they graduate, it'll be like I made it too.

"I swear if I gotta' hock the horse, dem kids will have it better'n me.

"Education, yep education—that's the key!

"If you'd be takin' some learnin', 'stead of tossin' dem snake-eyes and runnin' dem numbers, you'd be inta' somethin' better, for you—for da' whole family. What about your kids?"

Zeke shook his head and said,

"Listen 'ol man, I'm gonna' hit the *big one*. You just worry 'bout yourself, and don't you be tellin' me how to live my life."

He shot Smitty an aggravated glance as he walked back over to Jonathon.

Before he pulled out, Zeke told him to come down to Clinton Street to the spot where the coal cars dump their load into the ships.

"You won't miss it, Johnny. It looks like a railroad with tracks 'dat run from 'da ground to a high spot where a full boxcar is flipped over, by some contraption, and unloads the coal into little cars.

"Then, 'dem little coal cars roll right across 'da track—it's set up high too, over 'da street, and they roll on and on 'til they dump their whole load into the ships to go out to some foreign place across da water.

"We'll meet under 'dem overhead tracks in a little out-of-'da-way place. We already knocked out 'da street lamp with a brick we throwed at it last night, so nobody would expect a craps game back 'der. We'll have a coupl'a lanterns. Don't you be worryin' 'bout nothin'. Just you bring 'da bucks."

Jonathon left. He had his number he bet on with Zeke and would watch for the outcome, in about an hour. His brothers would expect him home. The tallies had to be calculated from the day's receipts, and the truck needed to be cleaned and stocked for the next day's deliveries, but he'd come up with some excuse.

It was mid-afternoon, and he had to kill some time before the crap game.

*And, they're off . . .* played in his brain and he was off to Pimlico, the daily cash receipts in hand. He thought that if he hurried, he could catch a couple of races and be at the dice rolls tonight.

He began mimicking the trumpeter at the track, with the traditional music played before every race. As he tried to create a horn sound by blowing air through his pursed lips, he quickly sped away, catching the ramp near the Maryland State Prison onto the new Jones Falls Expressway to exit at Northern Parkway leading to Old Hilltop.

# CHAPTER FIFTY-SIX

❧❧❧❧

$\mathcal{T}$here must be hundreds of train tracks in this eastern area of Baltimore, Jonathon thought, as he felt his truck waggle from side-to-side as he made his way closer to South Clinton Street at the Canton waterfront. The lights on Boston Street were dim from overhead bulbs, left over from the 1930's, that hadn't yet been replaced with more modern, brighter lighting.

Whistles blew from cargo trains that had been filled with freight earlier in the day and unloaded onto the massive ships that were docked ahead and to the right. Some were pulling out for various ports after traveling under the Chesapeake Bay Bridge and heading for the Atlantic Ocean or using the C&D Canal connecting the Chesapeake and Delaware bays.

Jonathon said aloud as he took it all in,

"Will ya' look at this place. Things are buzzin' down here. Never knew about this part of Baltimore—it's on the move!"

Through the breaks between the warehouses to his right and across the water, he could see lights gently illuminating Fort McHenry where the 'Star Spangled Banner' was written by Francis Scott Key during the War of 1812. The old cannons surrounded the abutment, and the American flag fluttered in the night breeze illuminated by a huge spotlight. Only saw pictures of that, he thought.

He passed Tindeco Wharf, where many years before, specialty tins with promotional designs for candy, chocolate powders or teas had been made into banks or containers for various businesses.

Passing by the former canneries which now were empty, he remembered seeing in a Baltimore history book at school, photos of thousands of baskets of tomatoes and the young workers preparing to peel and pack the fruit in various sized cans for grocery stores. If it were in my time, I could have dropped the entire load from my truck at once, he thought as he continued on Boston Street, turning right onto South Clinton Street.

There was a lighthouse, smaller than most, its light now extinguished, almost hidden on his side of the harbor. When he saw it he thought, man that looks really old. I'll bet that broken down lighthouse and some of these warehouses were built back then, around the time of that war. Should I go check it out? Na', time for some real excitement, here and now; can't wait!

He saw sailors walking into weather-beaten, shanty-type bars—formerly two-story brick row houses—displaying lighted National Bohemian, Gunther and Hamm's beer signs in their windows. One of these brews was being made that very night just a few blocks away at the National Brewing Company, over on Conkling and O'Donnell Streets. As Jonathon drove, large clusters of loose bubbles came drifting down from the sky, residue from the brewery. He could smell the hops in the air and wondered how it tasted as it covered his truck. The bubbles quickly dissipated from the wind, popping furiously. He licked his lips in anticipation of a beer.

More train tracks were ahead. Slowly he maneuvered his truck over the original cobblestone street which had been covered over with asphalt. Intense truck traffic from the industrial area had worn away parts of the blacktop leaving irregular depressions.

As he slowed for a large pot hole, he looked to his right and again saw the point of Fort McHenry and the Baltimore Harbor. Clouds blocked the moon from full illumination in the night sky, but there was enough light to see choppy water lapping against the huge ships docked in the massive slips.

But the coal cars lay ahead, and to those he would give his full attention. He was two or three blocks away when he first spotted the coal car brigade. The late shift was in full swing, and waiting ships needed to be filled with black ore from Pennsylvania, Western Maryland and West Virginia.

Just like Zeke had said, there were perhaps thirty or forty little bucket-type cars on tracks, spaced twenty feet apart, rolling back and forth across the road on an overhead bridge.

Jonathon checked the time. He was early and was curious to see how it all worked. He got a little closer and pulled over.

On his left, a boxcar heaped with coal was uncoupled from a train allowing it to roll to a specific spot where it was captured, lifted and dumped by a huge crane, sending the contents into a chute. The empty boxcar rolled out, and a full one was prepared to be moved in. Each of the empty bucket-cars was pulled along a track—conveyor belt style—automatically stopping at the chute to receive a specific amount of coal. Once loaded, the cars crossed the road on a bridge tall enough for eighteen-wheelers to haul under. As the full bucket-car passed over the ship's hull on temporarily installed track, its bottom opened and released the ore into the hold of the ship, for eventual distribution all over the world.

These little bucket-type cars and the tracks leading from the railroad cars to the ship, brought back a memory—the diamond mine, being worked by the seven little men in Walt Disney's, *Snow White and the Seven Dwarfs* ®.

He had seen it as a child and loved it, but he was very young and that old witch scared him so much. Jonathon had cried that night, cried out in his sleep for his mother, and dreamed she came to him, consoled him and rocked him. When he awoke, he was angry—again, she wasn't there, nor would she ever be. So he kicked the dog out of his bed and rolled over, hiding his head under the covers.

He slowly drove his truck which rocked over more tracks on the street. As he got closer to the coal cars, he stopped and listened. He could hear the sound of steel wheels running over connections in the track.

"Almost there," he said.

Grease and oil odor permeated the air from the lubricant used to prevent sparks and friction in this heavily used industrial area full of machinery.

Jonathon had been told to flash his headlights on and off, twice, a block away from the coal cars. When he did, he saw a lantern sway up and down and then side to side, like a cross. He knew he was in the right place and parked.

He hustled toward them, his adrenaline pumping faster.

There were six of them—Zeke, the arabber, Jonathon and four other men, three of whom were sailors who spoke very little English. But craps are universal, and dots would add up to mean the same in any language.

Some broken glass was on the ground. Two of the men used heavy cardboard to clear the debris, leaving a safer spot to kneel and throw dice.

After about forty-five minutes of play—ten of it on one continuous pass—money flowed into the growing pile.

Somebody spied the police, who were coming by on a routine drive-through.

Everybody started to scramble. All hands went to the pot to pull out their contribution from the bet. Nobody wanted to leave their money behind. As Jonathon reached in, one of the sailors across from him started to run. His heavy boot came down directly on Jonathon's hand. Pain shot through his finger and thumb as he cursed the guy and pushed him down. As the guy staggered and tried to get up while grabbing for Zeke, Jonathon pushed both of them down together and then ran away.

Thank God I parked the truck only a block away, he thought, as he ran for it and hopped in. He shimmed down low inside the cab and waited, acting as if he were asleep. If the cops come over, I'll just tell 'em I was too tired to drive after my last delivery, and I was lookin' for a quiet place to take a nap.

The cops did come by and shined their bright lights into the cab. The stream brightened the roof of the interior, but when they saw no head exposed they drove-on to continue their rounds.

He waited until they were gone.

"Whew! Get me outta' here," he said, as if the truck could hear and the key could carry out his wishes.

When he turned the key he felt the pain in his fingers. The truck engine started, he maneuvered the pot holes and the railroad tracks repeatedly, and started the long drive through the city of Baltimore heading west toward Carroll County.

# CHAPTER FIFTY-SEVEN

✍✍✍✍

$\mathcal{P}$imlico was beckoning Jonathon. He stood at the track rail on Northern Parkway watching the jockeys exercise their horses while his produce truck idled.

His eyes surveyed the area looking for a tout, hoping for some inside information before the scratch sheets hit the pavement.

On his way to his first drop, Jonathon stopped off at Jerry's Deli to talk about that day's racing card before dropping a wad of tens with a bookie on Fayette Street.

A few miles away, he parked, sauntered into a restaurant kitchen and was verbally assaulted.

Tony was really hot under the collar and while flailing his hands and arms, yelled furiously,

"How many times do I have to tell you, Jonathon? Stop in here after ten a.m., and you can keep your produce!

"The lunch crowd will be starting at any minute, and the kitchen is crazy. You think I should just let you dump your onions, boxes of tomatoes and cases of lettuce! Where'm I gonna' put 'em, on the customers' laps?"

Jonathon opened his mouth about to say, *So what's the big deal,* feeling the delivery time to be inconsequential!

He was about to play with fire, but by Jonathon's pure luck, Tony got the upper hand and said,

"Now get outta' here! And if you don't get your crap together, I'll have you blackballed from Little Italy! Ya know we're tight down here, and it'll only take a coupla' words from me. You're not the only huckster comin' in here ya know."

Angelo, the restaurant manager, chimed in.

"I told you we have very close quarters here in the kitchen and to bring all deliveries in before eight a.m. I want the produce here early for my workers. Get it?"

✍✍✍✍

The prep staff, consisting of several High Street and Stiles Street residents, worked there early in the day to be home in time for St. Leo's school lunch-time dismissal. A good, solid lunch for their youngsters, whisk them back to afternoon class, and then they returned to cut the pasta that had been drying all morning.

These homemakers/kitchen staff gave their jobs as mothers first priority, but to make a few bucks they would peel and chop the tomatoes, onions and peppers needed to start the numerous sauces. Marinara, pizza, and meat sauce all started from the plum tomatoes Uncle Thomas had grown after the restaurateurs requested a certain variety.

*That Carroll County soil seemed to be most like the soil in Italy,* two of the guys had said, *not too much acid, not too much alkalinity.*

Tony, the owner of Milano's had brought some seeds back from a recent trip abroad. He had met with Thomas Frank and said, *These are from my grandfather's prize, Cannellini tomatoes. His farm, south of Rome, in the Campagnia region gets about the same amount of sunny days and close to the rainfall we get around here in Maryland. How 'bout it—you grow 'em and we'll buy from you, exclusively? It'll be like Grandpapa was helpin' us at the restaurant. And if it does real good maybe we go inta' tomatoes together. Make a business, eh, we'll see.*

Thomas wanted the seeds, but not the proposition to go into a partnership and had said, *Okay, I'll try the seeds, but when my nephews grow up they'll be the only partners for me—nothin' personal, Tony.*

He wanted to make it clear from the beginning where he stood. Thomas compromised and gave him a great deal, selling two bushels for the price of one. But only to this owner, the man with the seeds and the "in" to all the other businessmen who wanted the plum transplants, direct from Italy, by way of Carroll County, Maryland.

Seven years had passed, and their relationship continued to grow with mutual respect. Now Jonathon was jeopardizing this business relationship. It, in turn, would affect all the other Italian-owned restaurant accounts, of which there were fifteen within a three-block square area and a nice chunk of the East Baltimore businesses that Thomas had secured.

❧❧❧❧

Jonathon grabbed his notebook and pencil and scrambled out of there, feeling them staring at his back. He was incensed, and he said as he gritted his teeth,

"I'll show 'em."

Near the rear of his business vehicle stood a young woman with dark hair and beautiful olive skin. She had a cigarette in her hand, keeping it close to her body as she kept looking back and forth toward the two restaurant entrances.

"Who you expectin', Sinatra, or maybe Al Martino?" he asked as she spun around to see who had said that.

"No, but Dean Martin would be nice, in fact, just the coolest, ever," she smiled dreamily as she answered. "Yes, if Dean Martin walked up to me, I'd plant a big kiss right on him, and he'd take me to see the new movie that's coming to the Patterson tomorrow."

"So, Dino, my man's not here, but we are," he motioned his hand back and forth between them, she with her wide smile and Jonathon with his boyish grin.

She flirtingly gave him a peck on the cheek, but just then Jonathon looked over toward the restaurant, then grabbed her and planted a kiss, full on the mouth, surprising her. Before she could respond by pulling back, her father, Angelo, the manager of Milano's was coming out the back door and saw him pull her to him and execute the kiss.

He was raging!

Through clenched teeth, he screamed,

"Git outta' here, git outta here! You got it, you little creep? I said git outta' here, right now. If I get my hands on you . . ."

He reached for Jonathon's shirt, but Angelo missed as Jonathon turned and then ran for the door of the truck. Angelo grabbed Angela and pulled her to the sidewalk as he heard the truck engine rev-up.

Jonathon blew her a kiss and winked, and as he drove off he cracked a sly smile to her father, infuriating him even more.

Angelo decided he would teach this punk a little respect. But first, his daughter had to be dealt with immediately.

"Get inside!" he commanded, and by the look on his face she knew she would be getting the lecture of her life.

After he yelled at her for being so free with her affection, he grounded her. She'd be home the whole weekend, no movies and no friends over to her house, which was just around the corner from the restaurant amid the other row houses in Little Italy.

She expected it, knowing he would make her life miserable.

ം∽ം∽

Angelo finished the lunch rush, smoldering over the incident between Angela and Jonathon, yet never letting on to his customers how angry he was inside.

That boy, blowin' her a kiss and winking, knowing—yeah knowing, I was watchin' him, he thought. And that smug grin, why that no-good . . .

He began to seethe.

"Why doesn't that Thomas Frank teach him some respect," he said out loud while reaching for the phone.

"He did what?

"And then what?

"And he showed up when?

"Angelo, I'm sorry. Jonathon really put you through it this morning. I'll talk to him about your daughter. And, as for the produce, it will be delivered *early* just like Tony and I agreed years ago. I can't understand. He left very early, at the crack of dawn this morning, and you were his first stop. Let me work it out. Okay?

"I will pull him off your delivery, yes sir. I'll send one of the other boys tomorrow—early, very early. Again, I'm sorry. I'll take care of it. Good-bye.

"Why, I'll wring his neck," was all Thomas could say out loud.

Michael was coming into the room and heard him muttering angrily, although his uncle didn't see him at first, and then, Unks proceeded to tell him the whole story . . .

"And he blew her a kiss and even winked as he drove off, right in front of her father, Angelo, Milano's manager! Shot him a twisted grin, to boot! What's he crazy? In front of her father!

His voice raised higher in disbelief as he repeated . . .

"After gettin' caught, he then blew her a kiss in front of her father . . . and then gloated!

"He's lucky Angelo didn't reach into his cab and yank him outta' there."

"Unks, I'll take Andrew with me, and we'll smooth down Tony and Angelo's feathers and keep the account working," said Michael who took Jonathon's actions very seriously.

And knowing how hard Unks slaved to secure those accounts and that this could wipe out an entire segment, he decided to grab his brother and try to knock some sense into him as soon as he showed his face.

The next day Michael and Andrew made the delivery.

"Mike, Andy, thanks for comin' in early. After yesterday, I am outta' everything, and I got da' ladies scheduled in a little while," Tony said while reading what Unks had written on the invoice.

"What, the whole order, write off the whole order?" Tony said in disbelief.

"Hey Angelo, listen to this," he said as he called him over repeating the message written on the invoice.

"Yes, my uncle says please accept this as a token of our apology. Now, where can we unload?" asked Michael as his eyes searched for an open spot in the kitchen to pile the boxes, hoping to slide past this problem and move on.

Tony seemed satisfied with the gift and the change of drivers from Jonathon to Andrew, but the incident with Angelo's daughter was not yet settled.

They apologized to Angelo, but they could see he was not satisfied with this personal affront to Angela and the disrespect shown him. He told them he expected Thomas Frank to keep his nephew far, far away from his daughter.

After all, he told them—*Angela is only fifteen.*

# CHAPTER FIFTY-EIGHT

❧❧❧❧

$\mathcal{B}$efore Thomas Frank could grab hold of him to discuss the Milano's incident involving Tony, Angelo and his daughter Angela's kiss, Jonathon had loaded up his truck earlier than usual and was headed into Baltimore. His sixth sense was kicking in, like it always did when he was close to being caught. He knew just when to disappear.

Today was the day he would make the Haussners, Winterlings and Eastern House restaurant stops on the southeast end. He'd drive west later to deliver to the Broadway Market, the Waterfront Hotel and Admiral Fell Inn on Fells Point.

He liked that Fells Point run. There always seemed to be people milling about, especially in the market grabbing a hamburger or a bowl of chili.

He remembered that when he was a kid, Uncle Thomas would bring him into Baltimore to buy seed at Meyers' store. They would walk the few blocks and stop at a restaurant whose countertop jutted outside the market building bordering Fleet Street. Both of them would sit on a round stool, one of a bank of ten which were built low to the ground. Just before they ordered lunch, they would spin around on those stools. While looking north on Broadway, his uncle would point out St. Patrick's Church, Polish Home, nearby and Johns Hopkins' cupola, about eight blocks away. After lunch they would walk to Ostrowski's, and he would pick up kielbasa sausage to take home.

Today, at his first stop, he remembered it all while he drank a coffee with one of the Haussner's chefs, but then started the conversation rollin' about cards, the track and how many cars would come by the restaurant window within the next ten minutes.

There's always a game around, Jonathon thought.

When he finished the Highlandtown drops, he continued to reminisce and headed west on Eastern Avenue, toward Fells Point. He crossed Conkling Street and Highland Avenue and drove down the hill, seeing part of the downtown skyline that sat beyond Broadway and Little Italy. He decided to recreate a memory—spinning a stool while munching on a sandwich at the Broadway Market. But before he got very far . . .

The fact that it was a clear day made no difference; he would have spied Angela even if the fog had rolled in. Call it internal radar—his eyes zoomed right toward her as he watched her pull the glass entrance door open and quickly take the seven stairs to the dining room of Matthew's Pizzeria near East Avenue.

He tried to glance inside as he drove by, but couldn't see her. Around the block twice he drove, finally finding a space for his Chevy truck about a half a block away.

When he walked in and didn't see her, he immediately headed for the kitchen.

Boldly he passed the small square tables and chairs lined up in a row—four on each side—with a slim walkway right through the center. He stopped at the navy blue Pepsi-Cola machine and dropped his coins in the slot, pulled out a bottle, opened it and took a long swig.

These new twist-off lids are great, he thought, and kept going, although, no one got into Mr. Matthew's kitchen unless invited.

As he rounded the glass case he stared at Angela while he watched her cover the steaming pizzas with a heavy paper plate and then wrap white craft paper around them, sealing the encasement with three inch wide masking tape for each takeout pie.

Suddenly, while staring at him, she asked crossly,

"What are you doing here? Are you following me?

"You got me into a heap of trouble with my father yesterday. Now I'm grounded for the weekend and talking to you is only gonna' extend my punishment. She stomped her foot and said, "Besides that, now you're gonna' get me into trouble with my boss who just walked out the back door to get a pack of cigarettes!"

"Hey, don't be upset with me. C'mon . . . why . . . you're so pretty even when you're mad. Look across the street. There's the Patterson Theater and they're showin' *The Silencers* . . . with your favorite . . . Dean Martin! Let me make it up to you."

Jonathon smiled his boyish smile, though he was now twenty-one, and charmingly nudged Angela with his elbow causing her to sway and said,

"C'mon . . . you know you want to see 'ol Dino. You said so, yesterday."

She broke her scowling face into a coy smile and crooned,

"I'm working here 'til nine and then . . ."

"Perfect, the last show starts at nine-fifteen. I'll wait for you outside, and I don't want to hear a no—understand?"

She had never had a boy be so forceful with her, and she thought she liked it. Angela decided she would call home and talk to her mother, who wasn't there earlier to find out about the grounding punishment from her father. He had dropped her at her job at Matthew's and then went out for the night to play cards. Once she got her mother on the phone, she would ask her if she could go to the movies after work with a girlfriend who would drive her home after the feature.

"Suppose I don't like the movie?" she flirtingly teased.

"Oh, you'll like it all right. I'll guarantee it," he said, with the sound of an innuendo, and then he watched her blush, enjoying it.

At fifteen, she was really innocent. Her father constantly protected her. She was his princess, and he wanted to keep it that way.

She was enjoying tantalizing Jonathon, just like she saw in the movies. And he was reacting to her exactly like the heroes she had watched as they *fell in love* on the silver screen. While mimicking the fictional heroines, she fantasized that it would be a fairytale romance with this Jonathon character, whom she had only met the day before while she sneaked a smoke outside the restaurant.

Angela kept the call short and sweet. Her mother agreed to let her go and said she would see her at home later.

Just before closing, she took her purse into the tiny bathroom at Matthew's Pizzeria and teased her chocolate-brown hair, loaded on the Aqua Net hair spray, then added pale lipstick and blusher. To accentuate her brown eyes, flecked with gold and amber, she applied the darkest liquid eyeliner and loaded on the black mascara.

As she checked herself over in the bathroom mirror, her spit curls on either side of her face were lifting up off her skin. She licked her thumb and pointer finger and smoothed a curl on each cheek.

Her boss said she could leave a few minutes early. She wrote her name on the sign-out sheet and started for the door.

Al Martino records that had been ordered up by the couples eating the crunchy delicacy were playing In fact, almost all the records on the jukebox were by Al Martino, with an occasional 'Volaré,' by Dominico Modugno or 'Al di la,' by Jerry Vale, all for five cents per play or six for a quarter.

Straight ahead, she saw the frozen smile of the ceramic chef, highlighted with red checks, who stood about three feet tall and always held court in the front window near the stairs of the restaurant. His billowy chef's hat was half as tall as he was, and he was eternally holding a pizza pie, also designed in plaster. He matched the red and white plastic tablecloths.

Narrow mirrors that butted next to each other and started at four and one-half feet off the floor to the ceiling, surrounded the room and Angela checked her top half.

She spied those three-inch long, spit curls again, in front of her ears, blowing in the breeze as she walked.

Her Dippity-Do gel didn't—hold that is. She went back to the closet-sized bathroom, and reaching deep into her huge pocketbook, she finally found the clear nail polish type glue called Guice. It would replace the hair gel that didn't hold with enough stickum to keep the curls close and against her face.

Opening the clear, alcohol-rich tack, she used the brush like a nail polish and marked her face exactly where she wanted to stick the hair. When she pressed the strand taut against her face, the glue that she had applied to the last half inch of hair at the end of the curl continued to adhere while the alcohol in the lacquer dried.

Angela pursed her lips, studied her reflection and thought she looked sultry, like Elizabeth Taylor.

There, now that's a good hold, she thought of her hair.

But when she smiled, the air of sophistication she had tried to create dissipated. The tip of the glued hair was held tightly to her cheek while the middle of the hair, which was never secured, opened up to expose a half-moon space on either side of her face, like large dark brown hoop earrings.

She decided to pout to keep the hair in place, plopped all of her accessories into her satchel and flew out the door to meet her *man.*

Jonathon had parked his truck on Potomac, a safe, residential street that sat across, but perpendicular, to Patterson Park. He had ideas about that park and planned to use the fact that his truck was parked there to walk Angela next to the grassy expanse. As she opened the door she saw him leaning against the Formstone wall, waiting for her. They crossed the street after he watched for a break in the traffic, and he touched the back of her waist ever so gently as they walked.

After purchasing tickets, Jonathon had bought her popcorn with lots of butter on it and chocolate covered mints. He gently cupped her elbow as he motioned which aisle to use to find a seat. She remembered in *The Sound of Music*, how delicately Captain von Trapp had treated Maria as he coaxed her by a gentle touch or a cock of his head which she then, followed obediently. During the movie, Jonathon put his arm around her but made sure his fingers carefully touched only the chair.

He's such a gentleman, she thought, or at least she surmised that is what a gentleman would do. Having never been out with a boy, she didn't know. She only knew what she had learned from the movies, and her parents guarded what she saw.

Tony Curtis had impressed her in *The Great Race*, which she sneaked out to see last year. She sighed as she dreamily imagined whether her date paralleled the movie star—he was so cute and had that sparkle in his eyes just like Jonathon has tonight.

Her innocence failed to recognize the parody of the screen character even to the point of a faux-twinkle emanating from his teeth as he smiled again and again in the show, suggesting his handsomeness, incredible good looks and captivating charm.

At the end of the film, after a gentle squeeze around her shoulders, Jonathon looked into her eyes as the lights came on.

He felt compelled to possess her.

As they walked toward the door, Jonathon reached out and held the door open for Angela to walk through.

"My truck's down the hill and across from the park," he said.

Turning right onto Eastern Avenue, they walked toward Patterson Park, and Jonathon quickly walked around her to be on her left side, the traffic side of the pavement. Just like my Dad always does with Mom when they walk down the street; and now he is watching out for me, she thought.

She was impressed.

Angela's idea of what the perfect date would always be revolved around the movies. *Photoplay* and *Silver Screen* were the magazines she bought and read cover to cover, fantasizing about the most current movie star, Elvis or Fabian. In her mind they would come into her life and sweep her off her feet, always acting like a gentleman, yet a little rough around the edges, perhaps stealing a kiss or two. They would act just like her date, Jonathon, had acted outside the restaurant in Little Italy.

"Hey Angela, let's walk into the park and talk a little while," he said, as he led her by the arm through the stone-walled entry amidst the oak and maple trees. He squeezed her arm as a motion to stop near the lower part of the wall and turned to face her. He started to kiss her, and she pulled away like Sandra Dee did in the movie—*A Summer Place*—rather coy and yet flirty.

He told her she was the prettiest girl he had ever seen, prettier than, Sophia Loren, Gina Lollobrigida, or even Annette and was built like them, too. Now, that was the magic name—Annette. She had been told over and over again that she looked like Annette Funicello but never by a boy, er ah, a man. And never that she was prettier than or that she had a great figure.

She leaned into him and melted into his arms. As he kissed her, she kissed back. He kissed her again, but with more force, and squeezed her tight—so tight that he hurt her. As she pulled away, he grabbed her blouse at the throat and started to fumble for the buttons.

"Hey, what is this? What are you doing? Don't do that! I'm not that kind of girl. Stop it, Jonathon!"

She started pushing away harder as she yelled at him to stop,

"Stop, leave me alone . . . Leave me alone!"

It triggered his emotional baggage.

The harder she pushed, the harder he pulled. He tugged at her blouse aggressively, popping pearlized dots through their buttonholes and off the fabric. As they escaped, they went rolling down the black-topped path.

She realized she was not in a movie, and he was no leading man. Tears rolled down her cheeks. Her thoughts raced—I've got to make a run for it.

Angela stomped on his instep and took off running out of the park and onto Eastern Avenue. She was crying and screaming as she ran zigzagged, not knowing where to go or what to do next.

Jonathon was furious. He couldn't believe she would deny his advances . . . thought she led him on—teasing and flirting.

He thought, how could she leave me, abandon me? Nobody was gonna' do that to me again, but there she is, running hysterically toward Linwood Avenue. I'll stop her.

And off he ran, limping slightly from her delivered blow, but definitely gaining on her.

"Angela, Angela, get outta' the street," he yelled. "Hey baby, come back here."

"Get away from me," she screamed and almost got hit by a passing truck.

From two blocks away Angelo, Angela's father, saw part of the scenario, but at that moment he didn't realize it was his daughter.

Earlier, when Angelo and his wife had compared notes, he had been furious and told her that he was going to wait outside the movie theater to pick up Angela and give her a piece of his mind.

Now, suddenly he saw it was Angela being chased out of the park by a man. As he neared he slammed on his brakes and leapt out of the car, running toward the figure.

Jonathon saw the car stop, heard Angela begin to yell to her father, and skidded to a halt. He started running backwards, then turned to give his escape his full energy.

I'd better get lost fast, he said to himself, and hustled double time to be out of the scope of Angelo's vision.

"Angela!"

"Poppa, help me!" she screamed and ran into his arms.

He saw the open blouse, the tears streaming down, mixed with black mascara smudge and felt her shaking.

"Get inna' car," he commanded, as he dug his feet into the ground and began the chase.

As he ran he saw the jacket insignia on the body, far in front of him. It had been indelibly etched in his mind. He had seen it the day before at the restaurant on Jonathon Frank from Westminster.

# CHAPTER FIFTY-NINE

❧✧❧✧

"Do you believe it?

"Well, I can't believe it!

"He's pulled some fast ones in the past, but this time it's just too much," said Michael as he paced back and forth, shaking his head and grunting as he looked at Andrew.

"Michael, you know how he is. We've always had to cover for him," said Andrew.

His pacing intensified like a lion's in a cage.

"But he looked me straight in the eye and lied, lied about it all. Told me how the case of tomatoes fell on his hand.

"Laid it on so thick—tellin' me how tired he was, gettin' in here so late the other night and blamin' it on the restaurant accounts.

"And how that full case of tomatoes crushed his fingers!

"'The pain, the agony,' he said. Lies, all lies. Everybody else had to cover for him on the routes. All the while, out shootin' craps in Baltimore on Clinton Street with those Longshoremen.

"Ya know, Andrew, I couldn't believe what I heard. Zeke told me how that guy had stepped on Jonathon's fingers when the cops came and how he had cursed him and pushed him down, almost knocked him out. And then as the guy got up he pushed him *and* Zeke down and ran for the produce truck.

"I mean it, Andrew. I couldn't believe it. Zeke helped the guy up, practically carried him off, and they got away just in the nick of time. Of course Jonathon was long gone, the gutless creep!"

Michael's legs stopped but his upper torso picked up the tempo as he pounded his right fist into his left hand over and over. He continued storming to Andrew, while his neck muscles tightened and his veins pulsated.

"Where's he gettin' that kinda' money anyway?

"Where? I'll tell you where, right off the top. Jonathon takes his cut, adjusts the numbers on the receipt tally, tells us some of the produce fell off the truck or was stolen and then gambles away our hard earned profits. I've been checking lately, keepin' a closer watch, and I know I'm right."

While he finished his statement he charged over to the ringing phone.

"Hello, yeah this is Michael Frank. Whoa . . . Angelo, is that you? What's wrong? Yeah, I can hear you're furious. What in the world happened?"

Angelo proceeded to tell Michael what he actually witnessed after Jonathon attacked his daughter and how she ran into the street and almost got hit by a car.

And the rest of the story . . . as he looked down at her ripped blouse and saw that boy, running away like a coward.

"I know it was Jonathon," Angelo said. "Doesn't he have a dark blue jacket with a picture of a white shark sewn on the back?"

Michael's face turned beet red, and he had no doubt now.

He remembered going with Jonathon to drop off clothing to be altered for their aunt to Mrs. Nash, who made their clothes as little boys. Jonathon kept making a big deal about his being like a great, white shark after spying one on a patch lying in her sewing box, and he pleaded with her to please sew it on for him—centered on the back of his jacket.

*That's just like me,* Jonathon had said, *cunning, fast and able to wriggle out of anything with the speed of light.*

Now, that was even more proof that he was there, that he was the one, Michael thought.

Angelo screamed through clenched teeth and violently verbalized his feelings at the same time to his boss, Tony, at the restaurant and to Michael on the telephone,

"No one will compromise my daughter and get away with it. NO ONE! He is gonna pay! I'll handle it.

"I don't care what kinda' relationship we've had in the past wit' da' family.

"The business dealings . . . they're not up to me.

"I'm tellin' you both, he is not gonna make a fool outa' me and treat my daughter like that. No way. I'll teach him how to show a little respect!"

After raging on the phone, Angelo silently vowed to himself that Jonathon would pay to avenge Angela's honor, and he thought of someone who would be able to make it happen.

As he hung up the phone, Andrew saw the muscles in Michael's face tighten. He said exasperated,

"I'll . . . I'll . . . I don't know what I'm gonna' do to him. He's continuing to fool around with Angelo's daughter even after the other day when he caught Jonathon kissing her outside the restaurant and chased him off.

"But, now it's worse. Ripped some of her clothes off, and . . ." while pointing his finger into the air, said, "I'll tell you right now, if I don't strangle him, he'll probably get shot."

Uncle Thomas walked in and heard Michael ranting, who then brought him up to date.

After verbalizing his disbelief—especially the part about Angelo's daughter and then trying to wish it away—he realized he had to face facts. He pulled out a black leather journal from his hip pocket and began to research dates, times and amounts.

He said,

"I hate to admit it, but I can see by the tallies, Michael, that what you say is true—Jonathon was at the very places on the dates that all of this happened.

Michael's anger escalated.

"How dare he attack that young girl, ripping her clothes, treating her so disrespectfully. I can hardly believe it!

"And I can see another fact as well . . . Jonathon is stealing from the business, from the family and from each and every one of us!

# CHAPTER SIXTY

❧❧❧❧

$\mathcal{A}$bout an hour later, Jonathon walked into the farmhouse only to find Uncle Thomas, Michael, Andrew and William—all waiting for him.

Michael had brought all of them up to the minute, and now they were going to confront Jonathon.

"Get your butt in here and sit down," said Michael.

Jonathon looked surprised to see all of them there.

He thought, They're staring at me. They're all lookin' at me as if daggers could come shootin' out of their pupils and all of them standing there with their teeth and jaws clenched shut.

Slowly, he sauntered into the room and locked his legs, looking at them, side-to-side, out of the corners of his eyes.

They all hate me, he thought. But, what did I do?

Before he could analyze his thoughts further, Michael, normally the peacemaker, cocked his fist back and lunged forward, his strength delivering a blow directly onto Jonathon's jaw, and knocking him backward onto a cushioned chair.

"Michael!" Uncle Thomas shouted as he jumped up from his chair, grabbing Michael's other arm to stop a second blow. "That won't solve anything!"

Jonathon sunk deeper into the seat as he grabbed his jaw. His mouth dropped open as he rubbed skin and teeth, feeling the pain. He shot a hateful glance at Michael who noticed the hand that Jonathon used to make this maneuver of rubbing and rubbing his chin was the one the tomato case had supposedly smashed.

Michael's emotions churned up even more. William and Andrew held him back. Michael screamed,

"What do you think you're doin'!

"Tryin' to ruin the family business and our good name?

"What did you do to Mr. Angelo's daughter, Angela, last night?

"She ran to him cryin', her clothes half torn off. You're lucky she got away and that he didn't call the cops 'cause you'd be in jail for a long time. She's fifteen years old! He'd have you for assaultin' a minor!

"But come to think of it, maybe you're not so lucky after all. I'd watch my back if I were you, 'cause nobody's gonna' hurt his daughter like that and get away with it, are my thoughts.

"And, by God, for that, you'll get just what you deserve!

"Curse it all, Jonathon. So help me, if you ruin all that we've worked for, all the accounts that all of us," he said, motioning to include his Uncle, William and Andrew, "gave our time and sweat to build—I'll break your neck!"

Jonathon sarcastically spoke up,

"What'a ya gettin' so ruffled-up about Michael? It was only a coupla' kisses. So she's a little young and, so-called, innocent . . . sure I'm not the first. Stop blowin' up.

"So, what's the big deal?"

William and Andrew had to use all their strength to subdue their older brother as Michael's body tensed, his biceps trembling, as he continued,

"Look Jonathon, it's bad enough that you don't pull your share of the workload—plowin', fertilizin' and the like, but now I know what you've been doin' with the books, too. How much have you stolen? How much have you gambled away? Ya' know there's not a magic place that money comes from. You're stealing from Uncle Thomas and Aunt Mary Kathleen and Andrew and William . . . from all of us!"

Almost boasting, Jonathon said,

"Is it my fault you didn't think of it first. Pretty good scheme! 'Bin doin' it for years . . . and it looks like I put one over on ya!"

They all just looked at each other, unable to believe their ears. He was boasting about it to the very people he had hurt by his actions.

He began to grin 'til he turned it into a sneer, his eyes dancing around the room, finally landing on Andrew.

"Actually, I've been puttin' one over on each of you for as long as I can remember.

"Remember, Andrew, how I bought that bike right out from under you. Thought your face would drop off when you saw me polishing it up. Oh, boo hoo!

"And remember that drag race when I got to hold all the money. You thought the cops took it, but I was up in a tree watchin' those guys makin' a chump out of you. Them takin' away your keys and lockin' up your pants . . . and inside your own car!!!

"Man, did you look like a bumblin' idiot walkin' down the road in your drawers, or what?"

Uncle Thomas, William and Michael were puzzled while Andrew's eyes grew wider as he played out the old scene in his brain. His suspicion was correct as he realized that Jonathon didn't try to help him, acted like he wasn't there and let him fend for himself from the gang of teenagers up on Bachman Valley Road when they roughed him up and pushed him around.

He tuned out Jonathon's babble while he began to seethe. He considered how many times he had fallen to Jonathon's hurtful personality—all the while, as a child, wondering what he had done to provoke him each time.

Now, as an adult, the realization had set in that he did nothing wrong to Jonathon and that all of the times that he covered for him, all of the times he wished for his acceptance was just that—mere wishful thinking.

And now, after the worldly experiences he had just lived through, he understood that Jonathon's childlike tantrums had grown into a monster that could destroy their family.

Andrew focused in again.

"I never laughed as hard as I did when I watched you walkin' home in your underwear, Andrew," Jonathon smirked, while his internal giggle took over.

When Andrew heard it, it cinched it for him; there was no doubt.

"And then I raced home to beat you."

In an emphatically caustic voice, he said,

"Acted like I couldn't believe what happened when you got there and told me all about it. And, then for the payoff, you had to come up with half the cash to settle up with Ritchie and the guys. I banked quite a bundle, thanks to you and outta' your own pocket, no doubt. And I had to hold it all in, back then . . .

Jonathon bubbled into laughter through the pain in his jaw as he said,

"What a performance! Pretty easy though, you were such a chump!"

Andrew clenched his fists but controlled himself. He never forgot the utter humiliation he felt and the danger Jonathon had put him through—seeing the guys that the money was owed to and hearing their threats on a daily basis; and finally, paying off the debt, mostly from his own money.

Andrew was jolted as he heard Jonathon switch gears.

"And you, William, I purposely trashed your room so many times after you left for school. Didn't you think it was funny that Aunt Mary Kathleen kept after you to keep your room straightened?"

Sarcastically he continued,

"She told you you'd better keep your model airplanes put away and all of your other special collections in their boxes under your bed which you always did, always left them tidied up.

"I'd go in there sometimes after you left for school and pull the stuff apart, knock over the top few in your comic stack—just for fun, heh, heh. It drove her crazy! She'd go in and blow her stack, but she always put things away for ya'.

"But boy, little did I know she'd go through with her threats and wind up tossin' out your comic books. When I found out that happened—I almost wet myself, I laughed so hard."

Uncle Thomas heard Jonathon's vindictiveness towards his wife, and William and cringed in disbelief.

William wanted to square off with Jonathon but decided to stand his ground.

Jonathon continued,

"And now try this on for size, William. You know that one and only comic book that you were able to save . . . ya' know . . . Archie," he said in a sadistically animated way.

"Good 'ol Archie, tucked up there in your closet oh so neat, protected by the rocks, the badges and that piece of string layin' across it all. Ya' know, the one you wrapped with white butcher paper, just so.

"The one that," he blew into his clasped, almost praying hands, as he rubbed them back and forth and then blew into them again, opening them to show empty palms, "abracadabra, poof . . . disappeared a few years later."

"You, *you* took it," William screamed at Jonathon. Then he looked over toward Michael, his roommate back then, whom he had blamed over and over while Michael had sworn on a "stack of bibles" that he didn't know anything about it and that he hadn't touched it. William never believed him. He always thought he had taken it, but couldn't bring it up to anyone.

"Yah . . . not only did I take it," Jonathon said arrogantly, as he looked at William, "but I sold it, heh, heh."

"You, did what?" William screamed and seized Jonathon, grabbing him out of the chair and lifting him up by his shirt collar, which tightened at his neck as he rose. His eyes were bulging and his color reddening.

"Who gave you the right, you little ferret. I'm gonna' knock some sense into you and teach you a lesson you'll *never* forget!"

Michael and Andrew pulled William off and had to use all of their might to prevent him from blasting Jonathon with both fists.

Jonathon grabbed his throat, coughed a little and sank back down into the chair, but it didn't stop him. He seemed to babble on, his eyes slanting tighter and tighter, his teeth sometimes clutched in an evil grip of anger. His words were like a vulture's talons ripping and shredding the hearts of each of his brothers, for his goal was not to confess or admit a wrong in hopes of rectifying it, but to release object hatred meant to destroy each of them.

Andrew wondered what would be next to come up in Jonathon's barrage of psychotic, verbal vomit.

Uncle Thomas pushed his body deeper and deeper into his chair with each new story he heard Jonathon tell. It was as if this person he was seeing was not the nephew he had raised but some diabolical creature, ready to instill harm at his every whim.

And every time he verbally attacked, each of the men had to hold himself back from jumping on Jonathon with full strength as he rounded the room with his spiteful tales.

"Ya' know, I knew which buttons to push to get to each of you.

"You, Michael, the receipts and the money—you William, the comic books and your room—and you, Andrew, you were the easiest of all!

"All I had to do to get to you was threaten to have you sent away from the family. Just like I did over by the railroad tracks after we started the fire in old St. John's, remember, Kemosabe?"

Jonathon was ridiculing Andrew and crowing as he did it.

Uncle Thomas was not sure he had heard that correctly, yet he saw Andrew's face ashen as his eyes widened.

Andrew realized Jonathon was truly letting *the cat out of the bag,* but before he was ready to face it all and confess to his uncle.

"Jonathon, what do you mean—started the fire? Andrew, what is he talking about?" asked their uncle, wishing and hoping he had heard it wrong while facing Andrew head on.

"It was all a mistake, an accident," started Andrew. "I know we shouldn't have been smokin' up in the steeple, but we heard somebody comin' after flippin' our cigarette butts out of the louvers. I don't know if a butt caused it or the candles we used to light the cigarettes caught on fire, but . . . oh God, I'm sorry . . . so sorry!"

Andrew was sobbing as he brought it all out into the open.

"I've . . . I've been holding it all in, for all of these years. I told the Chaplain while I was in Vietnam the whole story. How sorry I was to cause that beautiful old church to be destroyed. He told me I had absolution, and just then, a bullet skimmed by my head. I actually heard it pass my ear, and it got him instead . . . killed him instantly."

He sobbed.

"I know it was meant for me . . .

"God, why did it pass by me, and my God, why did he have to get my bullet?

"I promised God that day, that if I got out alive I'd set the record straight, and I've been tryin' to get up the nerve to tell you, Uncle Thomas; but couldn't because I knew it would hurt you, and you'd probably hate me and send me away."

The tears continued to trail down his face as he went on, his jaw pulsating as he looked at his brother, eyeball to eyeball, and said,

"I told you, Jonathon, that we should've gone back, should've told Monsignor Bollinger when we first saw the flames. You frightened me, swore to me that I'd have to leave the family, and I couldn't bear it.

"You were right. After losin' Mommy and Daddy, I couldn't bear to be by myself—ever again. When I went away to 'Nam it was the hardest thing I ever did. I hated being away from my family.

"I shouldn't have listened to you, but I did—like I always did. I trusted you. Always wanted your approval, I guess, your love.

"But, I can see now that you are incapable of lovin' anyone except yourself, Jonathon."

He turned back toward his uncle and pleaded,

"Uncle Thomas, will you ever forgive me?

"I know how much that old church meant to you, and I know this must be a shock to you—to realize two of your nephews caused it. I'll do whatever it takes to make it up to you."

Uncle Thomas was shocked, and stared in frozen disbelief. Michael and William couldn't believe their ears as Andrew stood there dejected, full of shame and contrition.

Jonathon, on the other hand, showed no remorse. In fact, he said contemptuously,

"Hey, so what's the big deal—it was only a building."

Only a building . . .

Only a building . . .

Only a building . . .

The words resonated in Uncle Thomas' head . . .

He visualized his grandfather sweating profusely, baking five hundred thousand bricks on his farm and repeatedly loading the wagon and hitching up the mule team. And then he saw him slowly making his way to the Main Street location to empty each load. The masons were laboring to build that beautiful church, meticulously detailing each nook and cranny.

The Stations of the Cross were being hung, and the stained glass windows were being installed after hours and hours of devotional toil.

In his mind's eye, he saw the dedication and pictured the black drapes over the doors of the church following President Lincoln's assassination and Uncle Thaddeus in his railroad uniform inside, kneeling at Mass.

He imagined that he could hear the bells that had rung from the steeple three times a day for the Angelus and envisioned the townspeople who stopped to honor God with a bow or bended knee.

Over the years, radiant brides and handsome grooms had rice thrown on them by hordes of people as they left from the vestibule. Once, it was him and Mary Kathleen.

Thomas remembered a casket that had being carried out, his father's casket, and the crowds of parishioners paying their respects.

Things were flashing fast . . .

He saw his brother and sister-in-law, almost a year before their death, carrying Jonathon after his Baptism and remembering each of the boys at their own ceremony—Michael, William, Andrew—and the friends who came.

And then he saw the destruction. He smelled the stench after the fire, recoiled as he touched the smoldering ashes and envisioned the smashed pews inside the doors as he opened them in his imagination.

On the floor lay the bronze plaque—now shattered pieces scattered through the rubble. It had listed the names of Westminster's war heroes including the Civil War, World War I, World War II and the Korean War, honoring men and women who had worshiped at St. John's and given their lives for them. Now their memory was desecrated, all busted and broken like they had been while defending us, our country and our freedom.

There, straight ahead, he formed a mental image of what was left of the massive steeple that had marked the Westminster skyline since the 1860's—now lying on its side—charred and blackened and carved through the crushed walls of that English Gothic masterpiece.

Only a building . . . only a building . . . only a building . . .

Uncle Thomas stood. His body began shaking profusely. Veins in his neck protruded as if ready to pop. Never had he experienced such emotional turmoil.

He walked over to Jonathon and looked him straight in the eye.

Words danced in his head, words he wanted to say to him, words he wanted to use to ask why . . . but, then he realized it had all been said by Jonathon's cold, calculating responses.

Uncle Thomas spoke slowly and with resolution,

"Just leave, and don't ever set foot on this property again. You have broken my heart, and I will never forgive you."

Jonathon, who seemed shocked by his uncle's statement, grabbed his jacket, turned and ran.

All that remained was silence, broken only by the old screen door as it slammed shut behind him.

# CHAPTER SIXTY-ONE

❧❧❧❧

$\mathcal{T}$homas emotionally and heatedly repeated the entire story to Mary Kathleen, who was deeply overwhelmed.

She responded,

"What's gotten into him? I can't believe Jonathon did all those things. And the church, well that's the most unbelievable of all and keepin' it a secret all these years!

"And our Andrew, part of the whole thing. You know how gentle he is. Now I know he had to be a' bustin' at the seams over all of it, carryin' it around with him!

"And the part about him not ever wantin' to be away from the family, well I can see that. Ever since he came home from the service he has been keepin' real tight, real close to home. Why he almost doesn't want to let me out of his sight after he's home from work. Always checks on me too. If I tell him I'll be back home at a certain time, like if I go to town, he gets real upset if I'm later than I said I'd be. It's like he's afraid somethin' is gonna happen to me. He never did that before."

Thomas shook his head and said,

"I just never expected anythin' like that could possibly be the cause of that old church bein' taken down!"

"Are you sure, Thomas, really sure?"

His pitch escalated.

"Mary Kathleen it came right from the horses' mouths, and also Jonathon boasted about it!

"I hate to say it, but it was like I was lookin' into the eyes of the devil himself as he was talkin'. Told him to leave—can't have that kind of evil hurtin' our family!"

She grabbed his arm to settle him.

"All right now, Thomas, calm down . . . calm down!"

He pulled away and tramped back and forth trying to release some of his excitability.

"I can't, Mary Kathleen, I just can't!

"Hard to believe he's our blood. Didn't show one bit of remorse. Somethin' must've snapped way-back-when, is all I get out of it.

"He even talked about how he conned his way into gettin' that old bike that Andy wanted so badly and how he sold the only comic book that William had saved and treasured. Boys do spiteful things, but do they brag on it years later and take a chance on gettin' their heads knocked off?

"He just wanted to hurt everyone, the whole family!"

Mary Kathleen didn't answer.

As her mind reflected back on her own shortcomings, remembering how she trashed and burned William's comic collection, a wave of shame came over her like a cloud shades the sun.

"Took on Michael alright and us, too, stealin' out of the dailies. Who knows how much he skimmed. Don't matter much though. It could've been two dollars or two thousand, he stole, and that's that!

"Now that I think about it, there were other times when I was missin' money . . . I just wonder . . .

"Can't believe that he thought it was okay, that he deserved it—like we didn't!"

Thomas' emotions escalated further, and he could barely contain himself when he began discussing St. John's and the fire. He slowed as his voice broke,

"And that beautiful old church . . ."

Swallowing hard, he choked back the tears,

"Said it was only . . . only . . . a building. Showed not one ounce of sorrow."

Anger stirred.

"Said it was *only* a building!

"Only a building that wove its strength through each and every member of this family, for generations is all!

"My grandfather must've rolled over in his grave three times when he heard that! Uncle Thaddeus too!"

He softened. "True, I thank the Lord nobody got hurt, but when I think what could've happened—the boys, the Monsignor, and even Cully.

"Yeah, Cully, 'cause he was inside. I remember him tellin' me so—to fix the squeaky Communion railin' that day. And the firemen and Monsignor's mother, the list goes on. How 'bout the kids gettin' outta' school . . . forgot about them. Oh my God, if all those kids had been hurt . . . !"

His voice trailed off as his eyes welled up.

Mary Kathleen saw him having a tough time and went to him, wrapped him with her arms and held on tight. At first, he just stood there, feeling her concern, while his body continued to heave.

She kissed him and touched her finger to his tears. He let loose and started to sob, and she just held on tighter, letting him release his tension in her arms for several minutes.

It felt so good to have him in her grasp. She sighed, suddenly realizing how much he must truly love her to have let down his guard.

Emotions rose in her that had lain dormant.

Fear . . . fear that her Thomas had been unfaithful no longer existed. She knew now, deep in her heart, that he could love only her.

Somehow, she started to realize how the time away from her, the time she had grown jealous of, was filled with hard work and think-time to plan a better life for all of them.

It was the farm, the produce business, and the restaurant accounts, all heavy responsibilities that grabbed her husband and pulled him into their clutches.

Through the hold of the moment, she looked up into his face and used the apron of her skirt to dab the last drop. She saw the lines that had been etched during their many years together, furrowed at the brow, vertical at the mouth and jaw, and a chin that sagged.

Yet, even though his eyelids were drooping, within them were still the most honest and sincere blue eyes that she had ever looked into—the very color of an early morning sky.

He must have felt the moment, too.

As he looked down he saw Mary Kathleen, not as she was, but as his young bride of so many years ago. His mind drifted to one of their very special times out in the cornfield, when he flapped the blanket and let it fall.

He visualized the thermos and felt her dab the warm water on his face, much like she dabbed his tears today.

Hands, now old yet still strong, caressed her shoulders. As he looked at his hands holding her, he remembered feeling the hot towels she had placed on both of them as she washed off the dirt from the fields.

Her tenderness . . . it all came back to him. How much he missed receiving it. As he looked down into her eyes, he realized he hadn't been very tender to her lately. Everything else seemed to take a part of him, but now he was going to give all of his love and attention to her.

Thomas motioned toward the stairs, and she complied, feeling a very special joy within.

He stopped her, grabbing her arm gently, and as she turned, he looked longingly into her eyes and said,

"Honey, there's something I have to tell you."

She cringed apprehensively, but somehow with her recent revelation she knew his statement wouldn't hurt her.

"Yes, Thomas, what is it?" she asked, all the while looking up into his eyes.

Their emotions continued to stir, each needing the other.

He took her into his arms, looked deeply into her eyes . . . her soul and said,

"Honey, I'll always love you!"

# CHAPTER SIXTY-TWO

ๆ๛ฬ๛ฬ๛ฬ๛ฬ

$\mathcal{T}$homas barked, "I'm fine, I said. Just let me work this out myself, Mary Kathleen. Just gotta' catch my breath."

"But Thomas you look so pale."

"It's just indigestion. I shouldn't have eaten that fried food—too greasy. Make a cup of hot tea for me. I'm sure I'll be fine."

Mary Kathleen dialed zero on the phone in the kitchen and quietly asked for an ambulance. She proceeded to begin heating water in the kettle for Thomas' cup of tea.

"Come quickly, your uncle is very ill, and yes, I did call the hospital," she stated when she reached Michael on the phone before the bubbles caused the tea kettle to whistle.

"And Michael, please call your brothers. I need all of you here as soon as possible."

Quietly she hung up the phone, quickly made the drink, and went back to the living room where Thomas now lay on the sofa.

He looked pasty and very drawn. As she set the cup next to him, he peered up at her with glassy, hollow eyes. It was a frightening look. She was relieved that she had placed the emergency call and hoped help would arrive soon.

Within ten minutes an ambulance reached the front door, and two attendants were inside in a flash, immediately attending to Thomas' needs.

About one minute later, Andrew pulled up abruptly, followed by William and Michael. Each had seen the flashing lights of the empty ambulance sitting at the farmhouse. All three ran for the door, and as they rushed inside, Flurry, their aunt's puppy, scurried past them and ran out into the night.

"Hey! Wait a minute. Get back here," said William, who kept on going.

He knew she never went out alone, but his only thoughts were to get inside to see his uncle.

The medics were working quickly. They had started immediately and were adjusting the oxygen tubes, something they had done hundreds of times before, knowing that speed was crucial.

Aunt Mary Kathleen was overcome with emotion and started to cry when she saw her nephews. Michael put his arms around her and held her close consoling her as she sobbed. William and Andrew patted her back, but their attention was held by the men working on Uncle Thomas.

His eyes were closed, and he seemed to be unconscious, his breathing labored. They rolled the stretcher to the door. Within the minute, Thomas was inside the ambulance, but they didn't leave immediately.

Andrew and William agreed that it seemed odd. Normally the ambulance would have sped away, but both of the attendants were working on him as they shut the back doors.

The nephews quickly closed the door to the house after securing Aunt Mary Kathleen into Michael's car. She was no longer crying, but she was shaking, filled with apprehension and fear.

Michael slid into the car, and the door slammed behind him, startling his aunt whose eyes were fixed on the emergency vehicle.

"Why aren't they speeding away to the hospital, Michael? What is goin' on? Maybe I should be there with Thomas. Yes, that's what I'll do," and she started to open her door.

But before the latch began to open, Michael had grabbed her hand firmly and said,

"No, gotta' give 'em room to work. They're securin' all of the important machines to give him oxygen, watch his blood pressure—things like that.

"You'll go with me. We'll be right behind 'em."

His voice was firm, very controlled, but inside he was quivering, afraid for his uncle's well being. He knew they should be zooming away, knew the ambulance team was working on him, and he felt that their delay was not a good sign.

William hopped into Andrew's truck where they sat helplessly waiting, hoping and, of course, praying.

Andrew thought, Uncle Thomas was strong as an ox, he had never been sick and suddenly, here he was in an ambulance with a probable heart attack.

Andrew spoke to William,

"He's been through so much lately, a constant strain. First, Uncle Jay died, and you know how close they were, like father and son."

William said,

"Yeah, you're right, and then Jonathon and all of his problems. I still can't believe how he treated Mr. Angelo's daughter. I'll tell ya' somethin'—he's real lucky he's still alive. Ya' don't go messin' with a man's daughter and not expect retaliation. No woman should be treated like that!"

"Just who does he think he is?" Andrew said, his voice growing enraged and his emotions of the moment overflowing into his conversation about the past.

William said,

"I know if I were her father, I'd probably skin 'em alive, and that's probably too good for him."

"What's takin' 'em so long? That ambulance should be screamin' outta' here by now," Andrew said, straining his neck as if that could make him see through the closed ambulance doors.

William continued,

"And thanks to him we probably lost a good many of the restaurant accounts in that area of town. Ya' know it's like an unwritten law—mess with one, and you're takin' 'em all on.

"Word spreads. He's foolin' with our reputation. You and me and Michael and Unks, workin' so hard to build it up, and he comes along and beats it into the ground."

Andrew said,

"True, true. And, we've gotta' find another delivery person, 'cause now we realize Jonathon was only doin' a half-way job. Michael said he's had to bend over backward for some of Jonathon's accounts that he's taken over, and I know some of mine seemed relieved that he's not coverin' 'em. Some told me he was too unreliable with his delivery times.

"I wonder just how many more surprises are out there in store for us, once we really start checkin' everythin' out?"

"I'll tell ya' what I think," said William. "About the worst thing Unks had to deal with, more than anythin' else, was our family fight. Yep, I'd say that was the final blow. In all our years, not once did all of us git into it like that.

"I don't think Unks could believe what he was hearin'—all that about St. John's and the fire and all."

Suddenly, William caught his words running faster than his brain. He looked over at Andrew, who had closed his eyes while he shook his head gently, sighing again and again.

"Eh, ah, Andrew, you okay? Sorry I brought up that stuff about the church. After all, it was an accident. You said you had wanted to report it . . . had good intentions. It just sorta' got away from ya', that's all. And Jonathon kinda' pulled you up on it."

William started to reach over to knuckle-punch his brother's shoulder as a gesture of apology and understanding, then thought otherwise. He brought his outstretched arm into a half yawn stretch instead and then quickly changed the subject.

"Thank God, Auntie called the hospital," he said.

Andrew popped his eyes open and came back to the moment.

"But shouldn't they get goin'? It seems like it's takin' forever," he said as he fidgeted with his seat belt, pulling it away from his chest to relieve the hold it had over him.

He repeated impatiently,

"They should get goin'. Why is it takin' so long?

"And Will, you really should put your seat belt on, ya' know."

William ignored his suggestion, but tried to calm his brother. He was thinking the same thing about the ambulance.

So they sat, engines rolling and exhaust billowing from the truck at one a.m. They looked over to see Michael and their aunt, waiting, while neither spoke.

The silence seemed deafening.

Five minutes later, the vehicle began to pull away with its red lights flashing. Sirens weren't needed until they pulled onto the main road, about five miles away. There was no traffic on the country roads, leading to Route 140, but as soon as they neared that highway they turned on the volume.

Just hearing that blast begin shook all four of those that were following close behind, as both vehicles continued to hold the speed of the ambulance.

"Only a few more miles . . . hold on Uncle Thomas," said Andrew as he wiped one lone tear away from his eye. Got to be strong for him, he thought.

Andrew said, quite surprisingly,

"Jonathon, we've got to call Jonathon. Forget about the past. He'll wanna' be there. We'll need him there. All four of us together will bring special prayers that I know God will answer. It'll be just like it was when we were growin' up. We would all be together and the prayers would be led by Uncle . . ."

More tears fell. They couldn't be held back this time, and he grabbed some napkins from the dashboard.

He thought, control . . . gotta' get control before I walk into the hospital and before I see Aunt Mary Kathleen.

William knew Andrew must be thinking strictly for Unks to initiate a call to Jonathon after all that he had said and done to him.

He looked over and saw him falling apart, and he knew he wouldn't be much better at it, but said,

"Eh, Andy, want me to drive?"

Hearing William say that helped Andrew gather up his feelings, and he kept his vehicle even closer to them than before. Finally the hospital appeared, and the emergency crew came outside to assist.

When the ambulance doors flew open, they all rallied into their positions. They had him inside in a flash and had secured him into one of the coronary units before the family stepped foot into the hospital. The medics had used their C B radio to call ahead and alert the emergency team.

A nurse met them, firmly grasped the arm of Mrs. Frank and escorted her to the admitting cubicle to ascertain Thomas' medical history. Andrew borrowed her phone knowing that his uncle would approve as he called St. John's Rectory to ask for a priest to come to pray at his uncle's bedside. While she rifled through her purse for the necessary cards, she kept looking over her shoulder towards doors marked, Emergency, for some sign.

It wasn't long before a critical care nurse came to meet her and her nephews and said,

"There's not a lot I can tell you right now except that Mr. Frank had gone into cardiac arrest when he was initially put into the ambulance. The medics worked on him to encourage his heart to start pumping again. They succeeded, and we are working to stabilize him. The critical care doctor and several nurses are with him. He is very ill, but be assured we will do our best and will get back to you as soon as we have something else to report."

They all breathed a sigh of relief, at least a temporary one, hearing that he was still alive.

William, Michael and Andrew were a great solace to their aunt. She would need their strength and wisdom to help her make serious decisions for their uncle. At this point, she knew nothing of his condition, only that she was glad he was there. Together all of them would meet with the doctors to hear the prognosis and their plan of action.

Andrew approached Michael and William questioning whether to call Jonathon. Even though he had been ostracized from the family three months before, this was a vital development that he would want to know about. Other problems between them could be put on hold.

All of them were sure he would be at their side as soon as he received word of his uncle's health problem. After all Uncle Thomas was in critical condition, and at this point no one was sure if he would live through the night.

They swallowed their own emotions, trying to think what Uncle Thomas might want them to do, and all half-heartedly agreed. As he dialed Jonathon's phone, Andrew bit his lip waiting for him to answer.

Someone picked up the phone, but said nothing.

Andrew said,

"Hello, Jonathon? Jonathon are ya' there?"

"Hello, Johnny F. here," Jonathon started with an upbeat tone after recognizing Andrew's voice.

"Jonathon, is that you?" Andrew wasn't sure, but continued, "Jonathon, it's Andrew."

"Oh sure, hey Andy, how you be—longtime no see—been hidin' out after a spree? . . . Get it?

"Hey are we supposed to be talkin' to each other, or are we gonna' let the past be the past and bygones be bygones?"

Andrew said,

"Forget it. Listen, Jonathon, listen. Something's happened— Uncle Thomas was rushed to Northwestern General around one a.m. He went into cardiac arrest and is in Coronary Intensive Care.

His condition is critical, and they aren't sure if he will regain consciousness.

His eyes began to well as he shook it off and continued.

"We're all here at the hospital—Michael, William, Aunt Mary Kathleen and me—and I knew you would want to know, would want to come."

"Oh yeah, sure, sure—whoa, what a heavy thing—cardiac arrest, huh? Rushed him there, sirens blarin' and everything? Can't believe it . . . ol' Uncle Thomas . . . he's healthy as a horse.

"Yeah, sure, I'm glad you called me. I'll definitely be there.

"Northwestern General? . . . Got some great docs there. Bet he'll be fine.

"You're all stayin' there tonight, all night? Kind of, keepin' a vigil?"

"Yes, we'll be here. Come as soon as you can." said Andrew.

"Yeah, thanks for callin'. You don't know what this means to me."

As Andrew walked back to the waiting area, he felt relieved to tell the others that Jonathon was coming, and they agreed in unison. Aunt Mary Kathleen actually smiled.

They were putting all of the recent problems with him aside to deal with later.

Andrew thought about how they would be together again, all four brothers sharing their strength, their love and their devotion—surely that would make a difference. Yet, in his heart he knew that a whole army of men really wouldn't make a difference. It was all in God's hands now, and prayer was the most important thing any of them could offer to help Uncle Thomas.

⊱⊰⊱⊰

"Flurry!" William said suddenly remembering in all of the excitement she had run out of the house, just past him, as he and his brothers were going inside.

His aunt heard him mention Flurry and realized she hadn't secured the little dog in her cubby, a small, hard, plastic carrier made warm and cozy with lots of soft area rugs. Whenever she went into town, Flurry was kept there.

"I can't help but worry about her, William. She never stays outside alone. Flurry always sleeps at the foot of the bed between me and Uncle Thom . . ."

Before she could finish, her eyes began to flood with tears.

William saw the tears coming and tried to break the ice, to make her laugh . . .

"Guess Flurry will just have to sleep out in the barn with Torpedo."

That was quite a joke. Torpedo, didn't get along with Flurry. She didn't think very much of him either. He would hiss at her, and she would bark at him, both stating their cases to the other. Nothing became of their vocal retorts, but it was comical to watch.

They would face each other and start. Both of them would circle, staring eye to eye across from each other. They looked like they were dancing. You could tell both wanted to be in charge, but neither was aggressive beyond "words". Eventually, they would both utter one last remark and almost lift their heads in complete assurance of their victory and walk away. Never did they actually scrap with each other. Everyone that got to see them remarked that they had never seen anything like it.

Torpedo came by his name honestly. He would run so fast he almost flew across the barn chasing field mice, sometimes banging into the wall like the head of a torpedo ready to explode. He would then shake his head and stalk again.

William remembered one of his funniest moves. It happened when Torpedo perched himself on the four foot high divider that Uncle Thomas had built just inside the barn door. He spied two tiny unsuspecting mice nibbling on the grain just below him. He shot down to them, then chased them into the hay at full speed. The only thing left to see was the tip of Torpedo's tail sticking out of the tunnel he had created, going round and round like a propeller. Somehow, he captured both specimens and proudly pranced over to William and dropped them at his feet.

` He recounted that incident to Auntie, and she had to laugh a little at the very thought that Flurry and Torpedo would be together, and that little bit of humor was needed just now to ease the tension.

William approached Michael.

"Do you think I should call Maggie Fischer or Gretchen?

"Maybe one of them could go over to the farm and try to find Flurry and take her to their kennel, and then Auntie can relax, knowing she is being cared for.

"She could put out fresh water and food for Torpedo—she'll never catch him. Later today I'll call the Hundley's to go and check on the livestock. I think Flurry will go with Gretchen since she's been groomin' her these past few months."

Michael said, "Great idea, but let me call. I'll ask her."

He hadn't told William that he had been calling Gretchen regularly so Michael caught him off guard by his insistence to make the call.

William had agreed, only to wish later he had made the call himself. Gretchen Fischer had been an acquaintance of his since high school, and he could certainly use her empathy right now.

# CHAPTER SIXTY-THREE

ھۇمئاھۇمئا

*The* phone only rang three times when Gretchen reached for the receiver.

"Hello. Michael, is that you?" She heard his voice, but it didn't sound like the friend who had been calling her recently. Instead, it had a sense of urgency and a certain sadness about it.

"What's wrong? I can hear something in the sound of . . ."

"Gretchen, I need your help. Uncle Thomas is in the Critical Cardiac Unit at Northwestern General. Not sure of his condition—they said something about a cardiac arrest, but we haven't gotten the whole story. Doctors are trying to stabilize him. My aunt, William, and Andrew—they're all here. We'll be meeting with the docs as soon as they know something else."

"Oh, Michael, I'm so sorry. Sure you can count on me. What can I do to help?

"Should I come there?" Gretchen asked with concern and empathy.

"No, got a problem, Gretch. When we were rushing into the farmhouse, Flurry flashed past us into the night. She probably was scared, most likely got a whiff of the paramedic's gear they carried in—alcohol, stuff like that.

"Anyway, after we all reached the hospital somebody remembered that she was loose and that she's never had the run of the farm, her bein' just a puppy and all.

"Can you go over there and try to find her?

"Aunt Mary Kathleen is crazy-worried about Uncle Thomas. Then when she found out that Flurry was loose, she got even more upset.

"I know she'd be so relieved, and I'd be very grateful if . . . if it's not too much trouble."

"Michael, of course I'll go right over. In fact, when I find her I'll take her to my house in the travel crate. You know she's familiar with me since I've been grooming her. And I know she'll come when I call her.

"I'll love her like she's mine . . . give her lots of kisses and hugs.

"Tell your aunt, that Flurry can go to work with me tomorrow. She'll have lots of company at the grooming salon. She'll be fine . . . just fine!"

"Gretchen, you're a life saver. Thanks so much.

"Wait, I just remembered Torpedo, the cat. He should be in the barn. Usually he's okay out there, but since Uncle Thomas won't be around for awhile, he's gonna' need to be fed and watered. He doesn't warm up to strangers, so you might not see him when ya' go in. He'll usually hide out in there and then come out after you've gone.

"But his food—you'll see the container on the shelf to the left as you go in. I've been up in the loft, and I've watched him eat. He always reacts the same way, like a phantom."

"Consider it done. After I finish I'll be waiting at home. *Please* call me, let me know your uncle's prognosis. I'm concerned about him—and about you—and I can tell you how it all works out at the farm."

"I'll call you as soon as I hear somethin' and . . . and thanks again, Gretchen. I really appreciate your help. Bye."

Michael was relieved that Flurry would go with Gretchen, and Torpedo would be cared for, as well. Later, he would call her to verify that all went okay, but for now, he could tell his aunt that everything was going to be under control.

As he walked backed into the waiting room, he didn't like the look on William's face.

He's heard some bad news, he thought, and his instincts were right.

"They want to discuss in detail, Unk's condition, but we were waiting for you. Everyone is in that room, down the hall, second door on the right. So far, what I've heard doesn't sound good, Michael."

William hung his head and slowly shook it side-to-side, in total disbelief of the events that were unfolding.

As they entered the room, the cardiac care doctor walked toward them and began,

"I am Doctor Jensen, chief resident on Mr. Frank's case. He went into cardiac arrest when he was put into the ambulance at his home, as you were told. The medics worked on him to administer oxygen and medication to keep him alive. Their fast action kept him going and allowed them to get him here as quickly as possible. We have begun to deliver stronger medication to regulate his heartbeat. Right now it is very weak, but he seems to be a fighter.

"Mrs. Frank, does your husband have a history of heart problems?"

"No, Doctor Jensen, never. Why, he's always been healthy as can be, not a chest pain or anythin' like that."

"Well, we think he may have had an infection which caused fluid to build in his lungs, which stopped his heart."

Some of them looked at him, questioning his statement.

"To put it into other words, it works a lot like your car engine . . . too much liquid, and the carburetor floods, stopping the engine. But, we're doing our best to keep that from happening again.

"Was he complaining? Did he seem to have any problems?"

"Ya' know, he did have a problem goin' to the bathroom all this week," she said as she remembered that Thomas seemed to be fine as he held her close. Even after, he wasn't complaining, seemed to be very relaxed. But then, he wanted pillow after pillow to prop himself up in bed, and that was just a couple of hours before he told her he felt so bad.

She relayed the need for the pillows, but not the private events and continued,

"Why he just kept on feelin' worse as it got closer to midnight. Ya' know, he did say he needed to catch his breath, once or twice. I wanted to get the boys, our nephews, over there sooner, but he wouldn't let me call to tell anyone that he was feelin' bad—can be stubborn sometimes. Sure glad I called 'em after I called the hospital.

"When can I see him, Doc? When can we all see him?" she asked, motioning inclusion of her nephews.

"Well, right now Mrs. Frank, my colleague, a cardiologist, is there with him. Let me see if he is finished the procedure he was doing. Now you know, if you go in to see your husband, he is going to have various things attached to him—things to help him.

"He has an oxygen mask covering part of his face, medicine in a bottle dripping through a tube that is going into his arm, and special machines, which may be beeping sporadically, that help to tell us his vital signs on an ongoing basis. Do you think you can handle seeing him like that?

"You must act strong if I let you go in there. And, Mrs. Frank, one more thing. Even though his eyes may be closed, he might be able to hear what you'll be saying. Be careful not to discuss how bad he looks—keep it positive."

"Doctor, I understand. I'll be strong for Thomas. My nephews will go in there with me, and together he will feel our strength. We'll pray over him so he'll be able to make it through this. We need him. He's always been the rock for us, now we'll be there for him."

Doctor Jensen escorted them to the Coronary Care Unit entrance and gently released her into the room.

She breathed deeply as she closed her eyes, gaining composure.

The husband and uncle they saw was a frail specimen of the person they knew, his eyes were closed, his face pale and drawn.

Before they gathered around him as a group, all three men watched as she walked over to Thomas, picked up his right hand and kissed each of his five fingers gently as she replaced his limp hand back on the bed.

Mary Kathleen summoned all of her strength, squeezing back tears and closely whispered in her husband's ear,

"Honey, I'll always love you," and somehow, began to hum their favorite song, *Stardust*, while she watched his eyelids for some sign of understanding or movement, some sign of life.

The three of them were moved by her gestures and felt their hearts ache.

As Michael looked at his watch, he thought how so much could change, so drastically, in only a few hours.

It was three a.m., and time seemed to stand still while all of them waited at the hospital.

The medical team had to work on him so the family had to relocate in a small room, not far from Thomas.

When no news had come for almost an hour, they inquired with the professionals in the coronary unit and were told, *As soon as we know anything more, we will let you know.*

Michael decided to go to the farm. On one hand, he felt Gretchen would find Flurry, feed Torpedo, and head home, puppy in tow. But, something told him, she might have trouble finding her, and he knew she wouldn't give up and just leave.

Gretchen just might need my help, he thought, and besides, he really wanted to see her.

As he looked at the clock, it read four a.m.

His aunt was sitting on a sofa, flanked by William and Andrew, all of whom stared into the space directly ahead. He knelt before her, took her hands into his and told her where he was going and why, and that he'd be right back.

"Go Michael. I'll be relieved that you are checking on the animals, since everybody is here at the hospital. Thank Gretchen for me, when you see her."

As he stood to leave, Doctor Meyerson, the Chief Cardiologist walked over to them and said,

"You can all go into his room again, if you promise to remain calm and quiet. There's not any change, he is still in a coma, but I thought you would want to be by him and, Mrs. Frank, please know that we are doing everything we can to help him. Right now we just need to wait and pray."

When Michael heard him say that, he decided not to leave at that very moment.

He said to his aunt,

"I'll visit with him for a little while, and then I'll go."

She nodded in agreement and released a sigh.

Together they huddled in his cubicle, watching the monitors. The electrocardiograph showed a pattern that was anything but stable. From his experience in Vietnam, Andrew knew it to be abnormal, but said nothing. Off to the side, the spirometer continued to measure the rate and volume of air being inhaled and exhaled and a defibrillator with its paddles sat, waiting should it be needed to restore normal heart rhythm.

"Uncle Thomas has a lot that he's hooked up to," said William apprehensively. "Guess I gotta' just be glad he's here."

"Aunt Mary Kathleen, did Uncle Thomas complain lately about feeling strange?" asked Michael.

She shook her head, side to side.

He continued.

"Two weeks ago, I spied Unks out in the field and rushed over to tell him about two new restaurant accounts we had just landed in Baltimore.

"Day was comfortable, slight breeze cooled the air, but when I came up to him, he was sweatin' like it was a hundred and two degrees outside. Face and neck were drippin', clothes wet enough to wring out!

"Said to him, *Unks are you okay? What's wrong? How come you're so wet, even though it's pretty cool out here?*

"Unks said, *Ah, I've been pullin' and pushin' them bales of hay around and worked up a sweat, is all. You know me, I'm fine, be fine in a coupla' minutes. So, Michael, whatcha' got to tell me?*

"So I told him, 'bout the restaurants, Bo Brooks and Hutzlers. Both of us were standin' there for a while, so he sits down . . . Uncle Thomas sits down, right in the dirt!!!

"I said to him, *Hey, you alright?*

"Just wasn't like him to plop down on the ground like that. Keep rememberin' now how he looked at me, especially when I said, *Unks are you alright?*"

"Yeah," sounded the groan from the bed, just barely audible.

Michael, William and Andrew all nudged their aunt, who didn't hear him. They all stood up and went closer to his bedside. His eyes were glassy, he did flutter his lids, and a moan could be heard.

"Doctor! Nurse!" William called out as he left the room.

Doctor Jensen and a nurse came in and saw the change in him. All of the monitors kept the same pace; the numbers had only changed slightly.

Thomas reached up to his mouth and throat, touching the intubation system, crooking his finger around part of it. They stopped him before he could pull out the tube.

"I think he wants 'em out," said William. "Is that right Unks, you want 'em out?"

Thomas fluttered his eyelids up and down and forced a slight nod.

"Doc, can ya' get 'em out? I think he wants to say somethin," said Michael.

The professionals could see that he was no longer in a coma, and they proceeded cautiously to remove only the tube that would allow him to speak. They checked his vitals manually as they watched the patterns on the screens above him.

The family was overjoyed; they'd take any sign as a good sign!

Thomas' eyelids fluttered irregularly, occasionally opening and glancing toward each of them.

Mary Kathleen commanded to the doctor,

"He's gonna' be okay now!

"Ain't that right, Doc? Well . . . ain't it?"

Thomas' eyes were closed, and Doctor Jensen motioned to all of them to leave the room.

Outside he said,

"Mrs. Frank, please don't ask me questions like that one in front of Mr. Frank. I don't want to discuss his prognosis with him, unless he is stronger. Earlier, I explained to you that if he pulls through, it will be a miracle. After a cardiac arrest, only about twenty in a thousand regain consciousness again."

"But Doctor, he has already opened his eyes, and I just know it means he's gonna' be okay"

"Mrs. Frank, this is only the start, and sometimes it is a false start . . . so please . . . be patient," he said with little empathy and less tactfulness as he walked away.

Now, that made her hot. Nobody was gonna' talk to her about Thomas like that. She waited until the doctor was out of earshot and marched back into his room, the nephews following.

Thomas' eyes were closed. She took his hand and said to him,

"Thomas now look here, I expect you to be alright. You gotta' get better. Do ya' hear me?"

He actually opened his eyes, even surprising her, and looked around at each of them and said in a trembling voice,

"Somethin' ya gotta' know . . . and ya' gotta' promise me . . .

"I wanna' keep 'em there until they come for 'em.

"No matter what happens . . . no matter what . . . I wanna' keep 'em there until they come for 'em and mark my words . . . someday they will!"

Michael, William and Andrew nodded although at that moment they didn't understand what he was referring to. Mary Kathleen was losing her patience, but agreed.

"Everybody's here," he said weakly, "except Jonathon."

"Yes, Thomas," she said, "He's on his way. We called him."
His voice was low, his breathing labored,
"Tell him I love him."
"You'll tell him yourself," she said emphatically.
Barely able to nod, he motioned to Michael and said,
"Take care of her . . .
"I love you, Michael."
Michael's throat closed as his eyes teared. He could scarcely talk. In a hush, he said,
"I will. Love you too, Unks."
To William he said,
"Love you . . . watch over her."
"I will, I will, and I love you too," was all he could say.
Andrew knew he was next. He went over to the bed, put his head down and began to cry, while he grasped his Uncle's weak hand. Uncle Thomas squeezed it ever so gently and said to him,
"Forgive you . . . and . . . love you, Andrew."
Although she was standing right next to the bed as he said his good-byes to his nephews, she would not admit it could be his last time with them.
Quickly, she moistened a towel with hot water at the sink.
Andrew stood to move from the bedside to give her room to be near Thomas.
She lovingly wiped Thomas' forehead, face and neck, especially his lips, so parched and dry. Next, she took his hand, the one free of the apparatus, wiped it too, and then kissed each and every finger very tenderly.
Kissing her finger, she transferred it to his lips and said,
"I love you, Thomas."
He gently opened his eyes, looked at her and said quietly,
"Honey, I'll always love you."
As he closed his eyes, Doctor Jensen stepped back in and said,
"The priest is here from St. John's Church to be with Mr. Frank. Father said he came directly from another parishioner's call at a nursing home as soon as he could. When he is through, Mr. Frank must rest. Please take a seat outside, be very quiet and let him get some sleep. Later you can come in again.

Out in the hall, their emotions exploded as they held onto each other and shared the compassion that each of them needed.

Even with Thomas' good-byes, they still were unable to admit what the doctor had continued to reiterate. Instead they saw this happening as a breakthrough to take him on the road to recovery.

In their minds, these past few hours had been like a Hershey Park roller coaster kind of ride, but, always thinking positively, they felt the highest hill had been scaled, and the rest would be clear sailing until Thomas beat all of the odds and walked out of there.

And now that the Priest was here they were sure his prayers for Thomas would be heard. They chose not to admit that Thomas might be receiving his very last Sacrament.

# CHAPTER SIXTY-FOUR

࿊࿊࿊࿊

He opened the door gingerly, peeking out of the corners of his eyes, shifting them side-to-side, scanning the parking lot of Jerry's apartment which sat above the deli in Baltimore. The word was out. Angelo had someone looking for Jonathon, and the past few days he had been especially cautious.

Sonny Krepnic, a loan shark, had also lost his patience after hearing about Jonathon's split from the family and thought his investment needed an immediate pay-off.

Wasting no time, Jonathon quietly closed the car door, suspiciously glancing in all directions. He flipped the key to start the engine, shifted gears, and was off.

He headed northwest from the city using Route 140, as he traveled toward Westminster, and passed the Hannah Moore Academy, which marked the halfway point and thirty-five minutes of drive time.

This place sure is far from the action, always was, he thought.

Yeah, love that action . . . more time for it now since I'm not drivin' the produce into Baltimore.

Baltimore, now that's where there's some fun to be had. Many a day, found a juicy poker game in one of the restaurant kitchens and the craps games, tucked away in somebody's basement or in some out-of-towner's hotel room.

Where else could I find three race tracks? It's like I had my own gambling circuit by just sittin' my butt down at either, Laurel's flats or the sulkies or Pimlico, depending on which one had their card goin'.

Man, what an adrenalin rush—love it.

Only problem now is my money source dried up. It was so easy before, collectin' money from the restaurant managers and pullin' my take off the top. Unks could live with a lesser total, and I always came up with a brainstorm of an idea to cover my tracks.

I can remember tellin' Unks and Michael. He distorted his voice.

"It was so hot that some of the tomatoes were soft when I got into Baltimore, so I had to give the buyers a better deal or some of them rolled off the truck as I made a wide turn, heh, heh."

Remember how, one time I used the excuse that somebody stole baskets of produce from the truck, but I'd sold 'em to some of the housewives down in Canton, 'specially Miss Sue on Potomac Street. She didn't know what I was doin'. Just gave her a good deal and asked her to spread the word fast that the produce was on sale. Boy, if she found out, she'd wanna' kick my butt, as honest as she was!

Emptied almost the whole truck that day, and I needed to 'cause the guys told me about the sure thing runnin' in the feature race at ol' Hilltop. Couldn't just bet that one race, now could I?

That money sure came in handy for the Exacta and the rest of the card at Pimlico.

Michael said he knew I was skimmin' money.

"Bull," he said out loud. "He found out at the end, but I was doin' it for years."

Luck was pretty good 'til the family cut me off.

Good thing I met Sonny. He's been helpin' me out, makin' it real easy for me to get what I need.

Jonathon's thoughts shifted. True, he's a little agitated with me right now maybe, but only temporarily.

He flipped back.

Now, *he* was actin' like a real brother. After my slow start in the game a few months ago, he walked over to me and patted me on the back. I remember him sayin', he exaggerated Sonny's voice,

"Hey, Johnny, ya' need a little extra cash?

"How'z about three hundred? Is zat gonna' do it for ya'? You can pay me later . . . a little interest, it's true, but . . . I know you'll be a good pay. Right?

"After all, you're a part owner of 'dat fruit and veggie company. Ya' gots no problem pullin' in cash. I see bills flashin' in your hand alla' time.

"Heh, heh . . . I just love that accent of his."

Hey, that's right, he recalled. That's when he called me Johnny, and I really liked it. I thought, Man I could latch onto that name. Now, he boasted out loud,

"In all the right circles that's what they call me—Johnny!"

He lent me three hundred dollars that night. Ah . . . that's right, I pulled in trips to that guy's aces and won four hundred, he thought, as he hit the steering wheel with his palm.

What a great guy, even when I tried to pay him back his three hundred, he had said, *Ah, no sense payin' me back just yet. Keep the three hundred, invest it, and make it pay off. We gotta' coupla' games, comin' up soon. I'll let ya' know where and when on 'dat day, so the cops don't git wind of it. Gimme' your phone number, and I'll call ya'. Bring a buddy, too, if ya' want.*

*If I don't get ya', I'll leave a message that I need a delivery. The number of bushels of tomatoes will be the date, beans, the time, and the delivery address will be the location where we'll have da' game.*

Jonathon said to the air, "Now was that a cool guy or what?"

I had five hundred in my pocket that night headin' home to Westminster—three from Sonny, the hundred I won and a hundred from Uncle Thomas' vegetable fund—heh, heh.

Got the word, just like Sonny said, on the answering machine, but I told Michael I called the guy, and he changed his mind about the delivery and off I went to the deli.

As I rounded the corner, I saw him and thought, There's Jerry, fatter and balder than ever! And I said to him, *Jerry, my good man, wanna' go to a crap game today? It's gonna' be a big one. Was supposed to be at some guy's store but they just changed it.*

When I told him it was gonna' be on Recreation Pier in Fells Point, cattycorner from the Admiral Fell Inn, he told me how he had played up on that pier as a kid.

*Alright, alright,* I told him, *enough about you. Later today, at six o'clock. I'll come by. If you can get away from this place, I'll drive.*

Jerry was always ready for a craps shoot. At five forty-five, when I drove by, there he was waitin' and pacin' near his door.

*Take Fayette Street up to Broadway,* he'd said to me, and I said, *like I don't know how to get there?*

I told him that I heard the cops in the area were bein' kept busy with a ploy on the opposite end of Patterson Park, over by Block's Pharmacy.

And how right I was too when I told him it wasn't gonna' be a penny-ante game. Man, money was flyin'. I got the fever for sure, seein' those big bets; after all I didn't want to be a slouch.

I laid out three hundred on the next roll of the dice and won, like a champ, I must say. I had plenty now and bet even higher. I couldn't lose. The stakes grew, and I kept makin' bigger bets.

Jerry got cold feet, and backed out. He looked at me and said, *Too rich for my blood.*

But not for my blood, it couldn't get rich enough for me. I'll never forget that high I got, winnin' over and over again. Wow!

He began to analyze. And then, things changed. And now that I think back on it, I'm sure it was because Jerry backed out, 'cause as soon as he did—after a few more passes—I started to crap out.

Lost the shirt off my back.

But then Sonny showed up behind me, patted me and said, *Hey, Johnny, need a loan? How much? Say, five hundred? Sure, Johnny*

I felt lucky again.

After just a few passes, Sonny lent me two hundred more.

My luck was about to change, I could just feel it.

Jerry grabbed me by the arm and said he had to go. So, I got up, but I bet if I had stayed I would have gotten more cash from Sonny and turned things around.

I remember tellin' Jerry, I lost one-thousand dollars, but, eh, it's only money. I'm pretty lucky, next time I'll clobber 'em good.

Just wrote it off to a bad day, but Jerry almost flipped. Tried to preach to me to cool it on the big bets, what, now he's my Pastor?

❧⧽❧⧽

Jonathon was digging a hole for himself that could swallow him alive.

Sonny was not the kind soul he led Jonathon to believe.

His nickname was Sonny Twotime. Owe him, and he would give you a day or two to pay up but renege a second time and . . .

Sonny had his thugs who would intimidate and had the muscle to follow through. They would deliver several blows, and as the guy was getting up, a second barrage with a warning—*Twenty-four hours, that's all 'ya got. All of it in Sonny's hands within twenty-four hours or else!*

But lately, Sonny had been baiting Jonathon by pulling him in, easin' him onto the hook.

He had told his brass, *No boys, leave him alone. I got the feelin'* *I gotta big payoff with this one. He's got easy access to cash and I* *want it.*

&#x6bd;&#x223;&#x6bd;&#x223;

Jonathon shook his head and thought, Yeah that was a bad day. Been havin' my share of 'em lately, just bad luck.

Humph, even back at the farm, I guess, I really have to admit that I was havin' a run of bad luck, too.

I covered my tracks pretty well, but I was surprised last time we all got together. Man, Michael, William and even Andrew—Andrew of all people—the guy I taught the ropes to. All of 'em jumpin' all over me, sayin' how each of 'em knew I was connin' 'em into doin' my share of the plowin', fertilizin' and harvestin'.

He said,

"Well, for five years, I got away with it, heh, heh. Not bad, not bad at all. Sure saved my back."

As far as me pocketing money off the top, well, I saw it like this . . . I did the work that day, and I needed to have some fun. So, besides gettin' paid by Michael each week, I took out my fun-money, my little extra. What's a coupla' hundreds once or twice a week and, okay, sometimes more if I could sell the seconds.

"But, what . . . they thought I'd admit it to them? What'd they think, I'm crazy. So, I lied. So what's the big deal?"

Andrew had said to me, *You know you did it, and yet you lied, just* *like you always lie to cover your butt. You always blame everything* *on somebody else.*

I have to ask myself, is that really true?

"Hell, no," he said aloud. "I guess I showed 'em."

And, how stupid they were . . . how I got all that over on 'em—Michael, the leader, William, the collector, Andrew, the . . . how should I say it, the wimp, Aunt Mary Kathleen, the pushover and Uncle Thomas, the . . . he paused in his thoughts and then said,

"Yeah, just how stupid they were.

"Just had to do it," he laughed aloud thinking of their ineptitude.

"And, the look on their faces . . . unbelievable!"

Jonathon's demeanor became serious, and in anger he thought, they only got one thing up on me, and I hate it . . . they all remember my mother . . . what she looked like . . . sounded like, even what she felt like.

Was her skin soft and pink? Were her eyes blue, real blue?

"That's what they said."

He drifted in thought for a bit, and then his mind tried to shuffle the subject like a deck of cards, and it just couldn't.

It hurt too much to think that they all were able to remember her, especially Andrew, who was three when she died. He said he didn't remember much, but still, he remembers! How could she go without stayin' long enough for *me* to remember? How could she?

At night, I close my eyes so tight and squeeze myself inside tryin' . . . I keep tryin'.

Jonathon switched gears.

And there are two things that are hard to fathom . . . Michael poppin' me straight on and Unks tellin' me to leave.

I never thought Unks would turn on me like he did, tellin' me, *Don't come back.*

I can't believe he wants me away from him, and Aunt Mary Kathleen. He said aloud,

"No! Now I get it. They want to leave *me*. They want to leave me high and dry, all alone. Alone, like I was, once before, a long time ago when *she* left . . . a long time ago," he repeated as his mind locked—staring at his thoughts.

The light changed to green, and he continued on.

"Ah, so, do I care?" He said in a whisper, trying to brush his feelings off. Now, I get to call my own shots. So, I owe a little money. Thirty thousand ain't quite chump change, but I got it all figured out. The angels must've been lookin' over my shoulders when I got that call.

He said empathically, "Now . . . I've got it *all* figured out!"

# CHAPTER SIXTY-FIVE

⮜⮜⮜⮜

When Jonathon reached the cut-off heading toward the hospital, he ignored it. Instead, he continued to go straight for a few more miles before turning right toward Pleasure Valley.

As he drove up, he spied William's vehicle. There were lights on in the farmhouse, here and there, and the door was unlocked. He walked in and started up the stairs toward his aunt and uncle's bedroom, opened their door and said aloud,

"Now there's got to be some money hidden in here. The old fart had to stash it away somewhere."

He began rifling through the metal boxes that Uncle Thomas had kept under his bed and in his closet. He couldn't find anything, but then he remembered that his uncle had stored farm-oriented paperwork in boxes in the basement.

As he came down the stairs and entered the kitchen he stopped at the refrigerator for a beer, popped the cap off and guzzled it while spying another one. After using the bottle opener again he put it away and set the empty bottle and its cap near the door, reminding himself to take them along later. He speculated that this was evidence that he was there, and he certainly didn't want anyone to know that. But, he asked himself, who would miss two beers?

Jonathon chug-a-lugged number two and methodically lined up the bottle and its cap next to the other one.

Flicking on the basement light, he hustled down the steps, two at a time, like he did when he was a young boy in that house.

First, he saw boxes of papers and said,

"Where do I start? Gotta' think like him. Where would he hide some money?

He shifted the boxes around and saw only invoices. But there, behind and below the others was a different box—a wooden box from Great Uncle Jay's house in Pittsburgh. It was etched in his memory because it was branded with large Z's on both sides of the box. Jonathon had always liked that box and had wanted it for his marble and toy soldier collection, but Uncle Thomas said that he couldn't have it, had said that *he* needed it.

After prying the make-shift clasps open, he removed the rolled up papers that were secured with a rubber band. He flipped them backwards, then perpendicular, smoothing them out. Looking them over he thought they were old farm papers, and as he was just about to give up he focused in on one of the pages upon which his uncle had written a note that had concealed several printed sheets. The listing read—

*The Attorneys are Codday & Dawson and Bill O'Reilly of the St. Francis Corporation is the Financial Advisor. D. Hull's Company would be the Certified Public Accountants for Uncle Jay's Accounts*

Their Pittsburgh addresses were listed too. The next sheet caused Jonathon's blood to surge.

> Thirty-thousand dollars delivered in cash on this day, the second of January of the year nineteen hundred and sixty-six, through and including the thirty-first of January of the year nineteen hundred and sixty-six, and is formulated from the trust prepared for Thomas Stefan Frank, Jr. from the estate of Jedidiah Thomas Frank, Jr. through William O'Reilly of the investment management firm of the St. Francis Corporation. Rendered and certified, D. Hull, Certified Public Accountants.

It was signed by his Uncle Thomas.

Another letter read the same, except it had February's dates.

Still another and another, month by month tucked under the first one that he read. There were at least twelve of them, all neatly placed in order still trying to roll up. Each of the copies that he saw had the same amount listed—thirty-thousand dollars. There had been payment in cash from each of these. It said so, there, in black and white. Jonathon said vehemently,

"Holy crap! Where is it now?

"Uncle Thomas must have hidden it somewhere, but where?

"He hated banks, would never deposit the money in one, but where? Where would he hide that much money? Holy crap!"

Jonathon continued to search in the basement, but nothing turned up. After looking under the steps in some old tins, a light bulb went off in his head. He yelped,

"The barn!"

He started analyzing—of course it would be in the barn. After all he had spent so much time in there. He had probably hid the money in those large wooden boxes stacked on top of each other that he moved around with his block and tackle apparatus. Yeah . . . sure . . . the ones he told us never to open!

Jonathon grabbed all of the papers out of the box to verify that he would find everything that was listed on them. He said,

"Don't want to miss a single dollar. I'll make one big hit, pay off Sonny and the rest of my gamblin' debts and have plenty left over to head out to Atlantic City or maybe even Vegas. Yeah, gotta' check-out Vegas.

"Wonder if Angela ever went to Vegas?"

On the way out through the front door, he grabbed both bottles and caps. The screen door snapped out of his hand and slammed shut. He went back inside to pull two more beers to drink while he searched the huge barn.

Who would know, he thought.

His butt smacked at the refrigerator door to try to close it, and a few steps later the screen door smacked him as he left before the door hit the jamb.

He tossed the empties into his truck, slammed the trunk shut, drove to the barn and parked where his car would be partially hidden by a tree. Inside the glove box was a bottle opener that he would need. He pocketed it, then opened the smaller door within the bigger barn doors.

As Jonathon went inside and closed the door, he looked at his watch.

It was two a.m.

# CHAPTER SIXTY-SIX

ちゃちゃ

$\mathcal{I}$nside the barn there was no light streaming in through the stained glass that he had helped his uncle and great-uncle install years before, only total darkness. He struck a match to light an oil lantern and set it upon a dividing shelf to the immediate left of the entrance. The flickering fire of the lantern produced mediocre light, but he tried to survey the place.

He said,

"Unks kept those wooden crates to the right side near the back wall, past the marble angel statues."

He pried one open, and there was nothing he needed, just old religious calendars dating back to the year nineteen hundred. It was the first year this old barn had been erected, or so his uncle told him a million times, he thought.

Thomas' father had started the collection. A local bakery produced them as an advertising piece with an H and S logo and their name and address printed on the bottom, along with the calendar months listed. The main focus of each thirty-six by twenty-four inch piece was a full color, biblical portrait. All were neatly piled inside the box, with the oldest buried deepest.

He looked between several—only calendars. Jonathon cursed them as he was so sure that the money would be in those old boxes, buried deeply.

As he continued opening them he found red glass votive holders—three inches tall by two and one-half inches wide, all wrapped in newspapers and excelsior as wadding. Under that box was a heavier box which held long twisted pieces of wrought iron, some three and some five feet long, that when assembled would become a pedestal table to hold the votives, candles and an offering box.

Jonathon recognized it all from old St. John's Church, recognized it all, too well.

He looked inside the empty offering box.

"What would anybody want this garbage for?" He said out loud as he tossed it aside.

As his words hit the air, there was movement from behind the remaining boxes which caught him off guard and made him jump, especially after he made his statement.

"Oh, it's just you, Torpedo . . . crazy cat, trying to gimme the heebie-jeebies . . . *git* outta' here," he said as he tossed a wrought iron rod at him, just barely missing the cat's head. It lodged itself into the disarray of cellulose fibers tumbling out of the wooden boxes.

"I'll do better next time. Teach you to sneak up on me," he snarled.

Torpedo ran into a pile of straw while Jonathon continued his trek to find hidden treasure.

He thought how his Uncle Thomas must have sat and counted and counted stacks of bills and then kept all of them from him as some sort of punishment.

"Probably gave Michael, William and Andrew piles of money, but none for me—I was never his favorite, never," he sulked.

He was affected by the beer he had drunk, feeling sorry for himself and somewhat paranoid.

It didn't seem to matter how kind his aunt and uncle were to him. He just couldn't see it or get a grasp on reality. Thomas tried in every way he knew to teach Jonathon right from wrong, techniques that worked with the other three boys, but he always thought he knew better—had a scheme or a plan. Though a man, he was acting like a spoiled brat, unconcerned about his family or the consequences of his own actions.

He slid the remaining boxes away from the wall and busted the top on the next specimen. Inside he saw shredded wood excelsior, a manger, straw and statues. As he pulled three items out, he saw a donkey, an ox, and a camel. These intrigued him. The remaining pieces included shepherds, three wise men, two lambs and Mary, Joseph, and Jesus as a babe, but no money.

"Humph, humph," he snorted.

One last box sat under the others. He thought Uncle Thomas had surely arranged all of these artifacts from St. John's to protect his pot of gold.

As he was opening the lid all that he saw were crosses—twelve inches high by eight inches at the widest point and carved spires that were fourteen inches by three inches wide—stacked carefully inside.

"Damn, I know where these came from, those Stations of the Cross, hanging up there." He looked up but could barely see them for the dim light.

"That's why I hated to come into this barn—reminded me of church."

He picked up one of the wrought iron rods and used it like a carnival barker would use a baton. Sarcastically he cataloged . . .

"Come one, come all—see the fourteen Roman numerals chiseled on huge pieces of stone that are carved in every lifelike detail of the suffering and death of Christ.

"Crosses, Roman soldiers, a crown of thorns. See pierced hands and feet, bodies falling down, lances, Mary holding Jesus after he died."

Incredulously, he thought, who could believe all that stuff . . . pull up all your guilt, make you suffer. I'm not buying it, never did really. Why, who would believe that Jesus' Mother would let that happen to Him.

My Mother wouldn't let me suffer at all if she were alive, I just know it. She would make my life perfect, just perfect. Why, she'd probably help me get some money together right now, too.

He was exhausted. Four beers were gone, he needed sleep.

The floor was covered with the heavy wooden boxes and the excelsior fiber that had originated from Uncle Jay's in Pittsburgh, previously used for packaging from one of his inventions. Thomas had recycled it all to protect his precious antiques, and now it was everywhere.

Jonathon decided to put it all back together later to hide his tracks.

I would be safe if I stayed right here tonight, or at least for a little while, he reassured himself, while I take twenty winks. Wouldn't have to look over my shoulder, and I could get goin' after I find the money.

Andrew said they'd be keepin' a vigil all night.

Jonathon climbed the ladder to the loft that Uncle Thomas had prepared with a small table and cot for his all-night *brainstorming sessions,* as he had called them. He had a hard time seeing while the lantern flickered behind him, since as he climbed upward his body created a shadow over the area. Once upstairs, and without looking, he stuffed all the papers he had brought with the financial breakdown on them into the tight space between the mattress and rickety box-spring.

"Don't want to lose these," he said out loud, while stuffing them into what he thought was more packaging materials.

"Once I get a coupla' minutes sleep, I'll be able to think straight—straight to the bucks!

"Why, I'll just grab the money and run . . . grab the money and run . . . grab the money and run."

Jonathon kept repeating this chant softer and softer until he began to snore.

# CHAPTER SIXTY-SEVEN

ॐॐॐॐ

$\mathcal{H}$aving compiled a quick list, Gretchen verbally checked off each item as she loaded her station wagon.

"Travel crate, bits of hot dog to entice Flurry, a can of tuna, just in case, for their cat, Torpedo—I think that's his name. Then there's the leash and collar. Hmmm . . . I think I've got it all."

She inventoried one last time as she closed her hatch, jumped in the wagon and left.

When Michael called earlier, she had just finished watching a movie, an old love story, *An Affair to Remember*.

When Cary Grant realizes the fate his love, Deborah Kerr, has had to endure, Gretchen's tears would always come like clockwork. She'd had her cry, removed the mascara residue and nestled into bed.

The phone rang. She must have just begun to doze, and it startled her. At the third ring, she lifted the receiver and was shocked to hear Michael recount the events that were unfolding.

She was glad he called her to ask for help and would have done whatever she could to be of assistance, especially in such a dire emergency.

Lately, he had called several times—*just to talk*. Then he had discussed Flurry, the puppy. Wanted to know where I got her and all the details. Told me how much his Aunt Mary Kathleen was already in love with her. Said he hadn't seen her that happy for a long time.

Michael thought I was kindhearted to make the delivery of the puppy on Thanksgiving, even giving up my holiday, to complete the special event. Said he could see I was genuinely happy to help.

I remember exactly what he said next. *Some of the women I've dated had a bit of a selfish streak, usually lookin' after only their needs to be met. But, you're different, Gretchen, softer and sweeter.*

Well, when he said that, I almost dropped the receiver. Glad I kept my cool, though. He kept hinting around about a date, but only hinted even when I reminded him about the—*owe me a Coke*—head butting incident.

As she drove along she began to reminisce, offering up a giggle now and then . . .

Michael didn't know how long I'd been secretly checking him out. My high school graduation—that's when it all started—and of course his brother, William's graduation, too. When I was up on that stage for commencement and looked out into the audience, his face stood out from all the others. And then afterward, when everybody started milling around, I saw him on ground level—about six feet-two inches of gorgeous man. Funny, I'm usually not attracted to guys with dark hair, but, humph, those baby-blues against his tanned, weathered skin, not a pretty-boy, but all man.

As I watched him shaking hands with people, I noticed his large hands firmly gripping theirs, along with that great big smile. Michael's clothes couldn't hide his rock-hard body, broad at the shoulders and narrow at the hips.

I had a difficult time paying attention to my own family.

"Couldn't take my eyes off him," she said in amazement.

Then, *she*, that skinny as a rail, model type, walked over to him and gave him a hug. She stuck her arm through his and just kept hanging on and hanging on.

My heart was breaking. Just found the one man who could make my toes curl, and from afar, and no doubt he's taken.

I remember later that same day callin' Jean, who knew who was doin' what, with whom, where, when and how—and of course, she had known.

She had asked why I was checking.

*Oh, a friend of mine wants to know*, I had told her, like she really believed that.

*They had been dating seriously,* she had said.

I had to put him out of my mind. So off I went to college, like that was gonna' help . . . yeah, sure.

Breaking her cavalcade of memories Gretchen heard the WTTR announcer say, *from our stack of Golden Oldies from September of 1962, on the charts at number one for twelve weeks, by The Four Seasons. You'll know the title when you hear the song, and it sounds like this . . .*

Rocking in her vehicle to the beat of the music, Gretchen sang along with the song, "Sherry," and for the moment, she became The Fifth Season.

After she sang the words, her mind flipped back to her inward conversation as she relived her recent past . . .

School was important, and I'm so glad I had the opportunity to go to the University of Delaware. Communications was a good start, and after all, I was holding a 3.7 when I got my Associates Degree, but that road just didn't feel right.

I really thought I would be accepted at Ohio State for the Veterinary program, once I got my B.A. degree, but, getting that degree just wasn't in the cards.

I was convinced . . . it was a sign.

For as far back as I can remember, I thought how great it would be to be a Vet helping dogs and cats, especially. But, when that door closed . . .

She smiled her happiest smile as her thoughts continued . . . the best thing I could have ever done was to go to the Conservatory of Animal Grooming in New York. I have never loved school as much as I did while studying there. It was a ball. Tough at times though, 'specially when we had to cover Anatomy and Physiology, but the rest was so creative . . . it was great!

As I look back, I can see a pattern. Every time I get into something, I've got to do it all the way, and I remember feeling so terrific graduating, top of my class.

There is *no* doubt, I made the right choice.

When we had our ceremony, I remember my thoughts drifting back. I'd wished I could have looked out over this crowd and have seen *him* again—smiling up at me and later having taken his arm and then hanging on, and hanging on and hanging on!

And my Mom and Dad, I thought they'd both pop their corks 'cause they were so happy that I was happy. But my mother—just like my mother—being the dreamer that she is, saw my certification on a much grander scale. On that very day she was laying out a plan for me to open my own business. Humph, guess I know where I get it; she has to do it all the way, too.

Well, I guess, having had her own hair salon for seven years, she did know the pitfalls. Secretly, I've always thought it was her way of keeping us close together especially when she offered to expand her own home to house the shop, or as she called it, *The T.L.C. Grooming Salon.* I liked that name, *The T.L.C.,* and it stuck. Offered to lend her managerial energies and even occasionally her design skills which she does sometimes, and boy, am I glad she does that.

The writing was on the wall though when she had worked out all of those details ahead of time . . . she sighed dreamily . . . she had missed me!

'Course, Mom and I are more like good friends anyway, than mother and daughter, so I was thrilled.

I've been so lucky that we got started right away. And renting the house down the street was a good idea. Told Mom, too much togetherness would put a bullet into her scheme, and I've liked being on my own. So far, so good.

I remember, when Dad, almost threw a fit over part of her idea. Those keys Mom had been collecting for over thirty years that were hanging near the original foyer, soon to be the new foyer, had to be moved.

*Bad enough,* he had said, *when they must come down to paint the walls, and Maggie, we just finished that before you got this brainstorm of a new venture in your head!*

He was hot!

But, he lucked out. Before they had even moved one key, my customers began coming in, and they always commented on them. In fact, they became an icebreaker, and a bonding tool—that's what Mom says—after all, everybody owns keys. It was a unique way to get to know each person and find out what attracted their interest to the keys.

Couldn't believe it, here I am ready to talk animals, and grooming, and I find myself talking about those 'ol key's history and the reason for the collection instead. I remember what kept happening—people wanted to give my mother their old keys or find some for her, just to see them included in the mix . . . not that she minded that.

Mom and I talked about it and decided to keep the whole collection exactly where it was.

Everybody was happy, especially Dad. Mom saw it everyday and got to talk about it, and the collection was getting as much publicity as the grooming salon!

Gretchen made a turn and heard some of the items shift in the wagon.

It's funny how things turn out, fate just seems to play a definitive role, she thought as she replayed how often she fantasized, while at school—the two of them—she and Michael as a couple.

"Then those keys opened the door," she giggled as she said it and thought, no pun intended.

Mom told me how that young girl—the sister to Jennifer, my old basketball buddy—just walked in, even before we really opened our doors. She was responsible for Mom getting the key from St. John's Church after meeting her grandfather, Mr. Cully Anderson.

Luckily, Michael's uncle, Thomas Frank figured prominently into that picture. I guess I could say it was fortunate, for me at least, that the Franks' family history intertwined so much so often with that church and that my mother became friends with him and his wife as her research continued.

When Mom told me that story, I had to be sure it was Michael, *my Michael's* family.

And, now, was that just too perfect, that Mr. Frank needed her help!

It was the fastest research that I had ever done to locate just the right puppy, knowing it would be for Michael's aunt.

My Mother's the best. She became a willing participant, letting me deliver that adorable little puppy and on the holiday.

She had seen photos of all the Frank family men and thought all of them were hunks, she told me.

It was like a plot. I know she even faked a sniffle or two, to give me an excuse to go in her place.

My outfit had to be just right, snug where it mattered, and I must have teased and sprayed my hair six times.

After Flurry came, it was great. Mom was getting closer to Michael's Aunt, Mary Kathleen Frank, so she got the scoop on the "boys" as she called them.

What a glowing report. She told me that Mrs. Frank had said, *all hard workers, all pitch in and help me and their uncle . . . and they go to church, too.*

Mom and I agreed they sounded too good to be true, somebody had to have a freckle, somewhere.

I always say—men either pick their toes or pick their nose—but, ya' gotta' forgive 'em and love 'em anyway, nobody's perfect.

The radio played one of her favorite songs, and she chimed in with The Supremes' *Stop in the Name of Love.*

She faked the words . . .

*Da, de, da, da, de, da*

*Think it* . . .

Gretchen sucked in a surprised breath of air and wailed, "Think . . . think!

"I didn't *think* to get the pads for the dog crate," she said emphatically.

"If I don't have them, Flurry will be slidin' all over the place back there in the wagon when I bring her home, and she could really get hurt. And, I just can't hold her. She's a puppy, and it will seem like she has sixteen legs all over me. Darn it, I had a gut feeling something else was missing when I looked into the pile, and that's why I checked it twice, but I couldn't put my finger on it—'til now.

"Thanks, Diana, Flo and Mary.

"It won't take long," she said, forgiving herself.

She turned back to stop at the business in her parents' house and kept the wagon idling while she quickly ran inside.

# CHAPTER SIXTY-EIGHT

❧❧❧❧

$O$h, I'd better jot them a note, she thought.

"Hey, where are they anyway. Kinda' late for them to be out," she joked out loud and thought, Now that's a switcheroo. They'll want to know—in fact, they may rush over to the hospital.

After mentioning Michael's call and what little information she had regarding Mr. Frank's hospitalization, she continued writing—

> Don't be alarmed if you look down the street and miss seeing my wagon. It's 3:30 am and I'm leaving now.
> Michael asked me to go to the farmhouse 'cause Flurry ran out of the house and is still loose and I plan to find her and bring her home with me. Got to take care of their cat—Torpedo—I think is his name. I'll call you around 8 am. We're booked, starting at 10 and hopefully, won't have to cancel.
> Love ya', Gretch

She attached her note with a magnet to the universal message center, the refrigerator, and off she went to fulfill her promise to Michael.

The announcer on the radio news program proclaimed that it was 4 am, as Gretchen pulled up to the door of the Frank's farmhouse. She saw William's truck haphazardly parked, partially on the dirt and partially on the newly arranged flower beds where cracked branches randomly laid about. He just missed the fence.

Gretchen took it all in and knew—just now it didn't matter.

"Oh, that's right," she said aloud, "Michael said William went to the hospital with Andrew."

As soon as Gretchen stopped her car and slid out of the front seat she began preparing for Flurry's capture. She pursed her lips and created a smacking sound as loud as she could and interspersed the sound with her name as sweetly and kindly as she could.

"Flurry, come 'ere girl . . . Flurry, here girl."

She waited . . . the night was eerily quiet.

Looking up at the stars she said,

"I wonder how Mr. Frank is doing. Dear God, please watch over him.

"Flurry, want some . . . mmm this is good, want some?" She tried again.

The little dog came from the distance hearing Gretchen's voice, the sound of her smacking lips and the words "want some."

Although a poodle, she ran as fast as the German Shepherd on TV, *Rin Tin Tin*. Her ears were flowing behind her, and her tail was wagging furiously as Gretchen scooped her up and got lots of doggie kisses. In return, Flurry got a few tiny, chopped pieces of hot dog that she had brought from her parent's refrigerator.

Gretchen could feel the dog's heart pounding, and she was sure that Flurry was happy to be in her safe-hold. Most probably, she was so frightened earlier from all of the commotion that she had run away, like Michael had said. Then suddenly no one was around, and since the puppy was only nine months old, she was not familiar with the lonely night air and had no sense of direction as to how to get back.

When they went inside the house, Gretchen put Flurry down and saw her immediately run to her water bowl, and then she gobbled-up the remaining hot dog pieces.

They proceeded to give the house *the once-over*.

She went upstairs and saw lights still on in the larger bedroom, and she assumed it to be Mr. and Mrs. Frank's quarters.

"I guess they prepared him for the hospital up here and left in such a hurry they forgot to turn off the lights," she said out loud.

Flurry, who had followed her upstairs, tilted her head to the side, as if that was her way of understanding the statement.

Gretchen flicked off the light, surrounding herself in darkness. She felt the wall nearby for a hall light switch, then noticed a stairway leading to a higher level in the house.

"No need to go up there, thank you," she said turning and scurrying down the hall to the stairs. Taking them quickly—two at a time with several squeaks to boot—soon landed her on ground level.

She felt a little uneasy there and didn't know why but she was glad that her little friend followed her every move.

Walking into the kitchen she noticed the door to the refrigerator was slightly ajar, odd, but maybe not under the circumstances. Upon closing it she turned right and passed the door to the basement. There was another light on down there.

"Flurry, let's go down here together," she said, lifting the little dog to take with her as if it would give her protection from the basement unknown.

While going down the stairs, she said,

"What is it about basements that seem so spooky?"

Gingerly, one foot after the other led her to the bottom. She quickly looked around and saw boxes, some tools hanging on a wall and some loose papers strewn about the floor. All seemed okay, and she quickly turned to run up the stairs.

She jolted backward and gasped, seeing a man's topcoat hanging in the area at the side of the steps. Several off-season garments hung there on a pole attached to the rafters. On her way down she didn't see this storage area but as she turned to leave she thought a man was standing there, and it startled her.

Up the stairs she bolted, holding Flurry even closer. She turned off the light at the top and closed the door tightly behind her. Gretchen saw her own reflection flash in partial darkness in the hall mirror and jumped back again.

"I'm gettin' the willies. Let's get out of here, Flurry. We'll take care of Torpedo and go home," she said as she turned off the final light near the entrance and held the screen door as it lightly closed to prevent a slam and then fumbled for her car keys.

She put the soft, little white dog into the crate atop the pads she had brought from the business. Flurry seemed very content to have the temporary den around her and began to nod-off almost instantly.

Gretchen saw a dim light through the stained glass and drove the short distance to the barn. She began to see what she had remembered to be Jonathon's car that was parked there.

Could Jonathon be inside? He must be, she thought.

Michael hadn't mentioned his name when he listed everyone who was there at the hospital. Maybe he couldn't reach Jonathon by phone and, as yet, he didn't know about the emergency.

"I'd better get in there quickly and tell him about it," she thought aloud.

Gretchen didn't know about his recent altercation with the family or that he had been banned from the farm.

She thought that she would be glad if he were there. For some reason, tonight she felt jumpy and could use the company.

Gretchen turned off the key and left Flurry safely sleeping in the crate in her Chevy wagon. She walked to the smaller door within the larger barn door.

She unlatched and slowly opened it, hearing it creak in the quiet of the night.

# CHAPTER SIXTY-NINE

❧✍❧✍

$\mathcal{T}$here to her left burning on the shelf was the oil lamp that Jonathon had lit earlier. That cinched it, she thought, he wouldn't leave with a lamp burning. He must be here, although there was no sign of him.

Instead she saw boxes with their lids partially pried off with sharp uneven edges jutting upward. Crumbled newspaper was strewn about the floor everywhere that she looked. She walked closer to the disarray to investigate, seeing unusual items you wouldn't normally find in a barn.

Excelsior was all over the floor resembling streamers that explode out of New Year's Eve hand-held poppers. Nativity statues were sitting around everywhere resembling a re-creation of a Christmas scene. In addition, there were at least a dozen crosses and some metal spires which lay about the floor.

Suddenly, she felt she was not alone . . .

She turned to see a white marble life-sized statue of an angel kneeling, tucked in the corner behind her and looking directly at her. Gretchen flinched.

Unexpectedly, she heard the rustling of newspaper on the floor and jumped back, alarmed.

"The cat!

"Whew, it's only the cat," she sighed.

When she began to call him, he recoiled, just as Michael had said he would, and scurried away. Her eyes followed him until, unexpectedly, she saw legs and as her eyes followed them she saw that it was another angel, flanking the first with praying hands, its eyes looking straight into hers.

Spooked, she heard a little groan coming from above and to the right. She clutched at her heart . . .

Jonathon, she thought and smiled, relieved.

Gretchen said his name but got no response. She repeated it, but heard nothing. Grasping the ladder she proceeded to climb 'til her eyes reached the loft floor. She peered over to see him asleep on a cot and, hearing him snore, she thought he must be okay. While hating to be the messenger, she felt she had to wake him and tell him.

Grabbing hold of a cross beam, she helped herself off the ladder and onto the floor's edge gently walking toward him.

"Jonathon, wake up. Wake up, it's me, Gretchen," she said softly. "I have to talk to you."

First he growled, and then he barely opened one eye 'til he saw it was her.

He sat up and smiled, his demeanor changed,

"Gretchen, you . . . you want to talk to . . . me. Well, let me just shake the cobwebs out," he said as he ran his fingers through his rumpled hair.

"Here, come over and sit down," and he motioned her to the bed so that she would be sitting next to him.

He thought . . . how interesting that Gretchen would come to me, here, near the bed.

She turned to face him and cocked her left knee onto the mattress, seeing fine down feathers attach to her black pants in the dim light. Dusting off the debris she started hesitantly,

"Have you talked to Michael tonight?"

He shook his head, side to side.

"I . . . don't know how to tell you this exactly, nor do I propose to know everything that has taken place, but your Uncle has had a heart attack and is in Northwestern General Hospital. I think he is in critical condition. Michael called me earlier. The ambulance rushed him there just a few hours ago, around 1:30. I came over to get Flurry, who had run away, and to feed Torpedo.

"It was a surprise, but a relief, to see your car and now you.

"Jonathon, I'm sorry that I had to tell you this news," she told him sincerely as she reached her right hand out to touch his shoulder in a gesture of empathy.

He knew she would offer him solace, and he acted as if he was going to cry and came toward her burying his face in the crook of her neck.

It surprised her, but she was willing to be his supporter and offer her kindness. She patted his back, as a friend might do, and started to pull back. At that moment, she smelled the liquor on his breath and felt his resistance to her withdrawal.

Gretchen tugged sharply to get away.

He started to grope at her, grabbing and squeezing. He was determined and thought—no way is she getting away from me!

She couldn't believe he was acting this way.

"Cut it out, Jonathon. Let me go.

"Hear me *now . . . let me go!*" she shouted at him as she struggled to get away.

She almost fell to the floor and rushed over to the edge of the loft grasping the ladder and fumbling—almost plunging halfway down its rungs. As she got to the bottom, she saw that Jonathon was right behind her. In fact, he jumped from a high point on his descent knowing it was his only way to get her to stop.

He grabbed her arm and pulled her toward him.

Gretchen's other arm flailed out and swung around with centrifugal force. Her fingertips grazed the lantern, which teeter-tottered, just barely righting itself on the shelf.

She landed a blow on Jonathon's left cheek which spun him around.

That challenge only increased his determination.

No, not another woman deserting me, ran through his brain.

He clutched her at the waist as she scrambled to leave and pulled her backward with intense force. His fingers slipped, and he let go, causing her to be off balance. One leg lifted up in front of the other while she was trying to prevent a backward fall.

Gretchen's body weight continued the momentum—just missing the antique tractor by inches—until she came to an abrupt stop, hitting her head with tremendous force on the edge of the wooden manger.

# CHAPTER SEVENTY

✿◦✿◦✿◦✿

ℋer body looked lifeless as she lay there.

He froze, waiting for her to move—any tiny move. Couldn't believe she wasn't stirring.

Was she . . . could she be . . . dead?

Neither foot would move in front of the other. He just stood and stared at her, waiting.

Nothing happened.

The barn was frightfully quiet. The first crack of dawn had produced rays of diffused light that came through the unique skylight that Thomas and Uncle Jay had created in the roof of the huge barn, but Jonathon didn't notice those beams.

He started toward her slowly—watching for a twitch, listening for a groan.

A barn swallow had been frightened from its nest in the eaves during the confrontation. Now, amidst the noiseless scene, it took flight from behind the station marked with the Roman Numeral X with shredded wood packing in its bill. As it took flight some of the plastic and caked mud that the bird had loosened fell abruptly at the feet of Jonathon.

He continued walking toward Gretchen, lying still on the dirt floor.

A piece of paper floated gently from above.

It fell at Jonathon's feet, stopping him in his tracks.

He couldn't believe his eyes.

It was a one-hundred dollar bill!

# CHAPTER SEVENTY-ONE

❧❦❧❦

As Jonathon smoothed the one-hundred dollar bill again and again against his body he shook his head while thinking—I must be dreaming.

He checked it, front and back.

"Yep, it's real," he said and stuffed it into his pocket.

"Where did this come . . ." but before he finished his sentence, like a bomb exploding in his brain, it hit him.

That's where Uncle Thomas has hidden the money. It's in the crockery from the church, from old St. John's. Talk about *manna from heaven* he thought and whacked himself with the palm of his hand, hitting his forehead over and over while walking to the ladder.

Grasping its thick sides, he moved it as fast as he could without toppling it over. It was extra long and very heavy, but with his adrenalin pumping, it seemed light as a feather. He moved it from the edge of the loft to the spot nearest Station X that he felt the money had fallen from.

He started ascending the rungs one at a time, climbing nearer and nearer to his bounty. All he could say was,

"I'll be damned!"

Jonathon knew that Uncle Thomas had manipulated each one of the fourteen stations to be at the highest points of the barn. Using his pulleys and levers to achieve a perfect balance, he had hung each one in Roman Numerical order—I through VII on one side of the gambrel roof and VIII through XIV on the other.

"Could Uncle Thomas have stuffed all of them?" he wondered aloud. As Jonathon climbed higher, he realized number thirteen and fourteen were missing which would have been at the end of the row.

"Doesn't matter," he said, "I'm just gonna go for the one I think the money fell from—one at a time starting with number ten."

Now he wanted to eyeball them, not for their intent, but for their contents. He could easily imagine each of the statues within the stations loaded with tens, twenties or even all hundreds.

Immediately he started his mathematical calculations. Each statue was up to eighteen inches high by about six inches wide, and some tableaus had as many as six to eight people in their scene, not counting the cross and its dimensions, all of which were hollow. He hypothetically filled each character with one thousand dollars and multiplied that by the number of statues within them, times fourteen.

"Wow," he said aloud, "If that's anywhere near the number of bucks up there, I'm really in the money.

"Vegas, here I come," and then vacillating, thought, I wonder if Angela has ever been to Vegas?

Suddenly it hit him and he said,

"That's why he could move 'em around so easily—hollow backs. I remember now seein' three of 'em at a time—lyin' on the work table where Unks usually repaired his engines—each one about waist high.

"Gave me shivers—walkin' in and seein' hands, arms, and other things stickin' up from the stations. He must've been fillin' 'em up, buck by buck.

"Gotta' give it to 'em, he's one sly fox . . . ah, but not as cunning as a great white shark!

"Only a few more steps, I'll knock it off the wall and the rest, too, then pull out the money and be out of here before Gretchen . . .

"Oh . . . Gretchen . . . that's right. I'll check her when I knock 'em off and go down again."

Glancing down, he surmised, she doesn't look too good from here, and I haven't seen her move. He said,

"She'll be okay . . . just knocked out. Ah, she'll be fine, fine!"

He convinced himself into believing it for she was no longer his objective.

Now, he was at the second rung from the top of the old wooden ladder. It was the one his grandfather and Uncle Jay had made, painstakingly fitting each flat-rung by flat-rung—copying the kind they had seen the fire department use, with extra length.

It all makes sense now, he thought. Scrutinizing more closely as he climbed, he could see the wooden fibers, and the cellulose mixed with some sort of dried mud sticking out of the back of Station X and what looked like something partially encased in plastic bags.

As he drew nearer, his eyes locked in on a color he would recognize in any denomination but only tiny edges of the bills were visible.

Closer and closer he came. As he reached his hand out toward Station X a second barn swallow flew directly towards him, startling him and shaking his composure on the ladder.

"Hey get outta' here," he yelled while righting himself.

"I must've loosened up the gunk where you were nestin' in there," he said aloud. "Nestin' but, not for long . . ."

His slight frame normally served him well, allowing him to weasel around and ferret out another way to solve his problems, but this time, his build was working against him.

He strained as he spoke out loud,

"Can't . . . quite . . . reach it!

"I'll go up to the last rung.

"Damn, still can't reach it."

His eyes searched the vista.

"There it is."

Down the ladder he hurried. He had to go near Gretchen to get it, and he barely glanced at her.

He grabbed one of the twisted iron poles, lying on the floor, formerly packaged with the votive glassware and turned to go back to the ladder.

Gretchen lay there motionless, the dirt under her turning into black, cherry-colored clay.

Once more, he started up the ladder with the spiral rod in hand. At the very top, he reached the four-foot high staff to the corner of the tenth station and started to rock it, side to side, by pushing it up and letting its own weight push it back. He expected it to let go from its hold and fall to the ground. Furiously, he reached out and probed it again, although he could barely touch it even with the four-foot extension. The rocking began again, but it held its anchor to the barn siding, always returning to its original spot.

Jonathon was infuriated.

"God damn it," he blasphemed ramming the rod harder this time.

The station shifted, tilting and swinging higher than before while the force of his thrust created unexpected movement to his ladder.

It slid from the wall, and his arms began to flail to catch hold of something—anything—to prevent the forty-foot fall.

As they raised and lowered, the one-hundred dollar bill was siphoned out of his pocket. He saw it drop. Ironically his foot kicked it into the pile of straw where Torpedo had run.

There was nothing nearby, and as the ladder slipped, he gripped the top rung with only one hand trying to bring the other around to re-adjust his weight.

Just managing to hold-on, he started to recover his balance. The ladder slipped further, his arm sliding in between the rungs, as it wedged itself under some machinery.

As he hung there by one arm precariously twisting in space, he looked up directly at Station XII, into the eyes of Christ hanging on the Cross with both thieves flanking him.

"Damn You!" He cursed.

Suddenly, the ladder snapped, and he tossed his handful—the coiled iron rod. His arms flailed about, but there was nothing to grasp, to latch onto or to secure.

Falling faster and faster, his eyes saw the rod traveling before him wedge itself in one of the wooden boxes that he had opened earlier—the same box that held the rod he threw at the cat.

Both twisted spirals became iron battering rams as they lay directly between him and the floor as he sped toward the earth.

There was no way he could change his course of direction. He would meet the poles as he descended, and he knew it.

"Jesus Christ!" he screamed.

Both tips of the four-foot rods traveled through his body and pierced his heart and his side, leaving a limp corpse lying face down, his own blood collecting in a crimson pool.

Eerie quietness filled the expanse.

Not a wing fluttered, nor a paw tiptoed.

Both Gretchen's and Jonathon's bodies lay still in the silence.

It was five a.m.

# CHAPTER SEVENTY-TWO

ই০৯৯ই০৯৯

ℳaggie and James Fischer liked to encounter date night on the same night each week by enjoying dinner out, catching a new movie or possibly sneaking up to the Westminster pond to feed the ducks and geese. Once their bread and crackers were gone and the feathered friends satisfied, they would find a clean spot, shake out a huge blanket, kick off their shoes, and cuddle.

They would catch-up on each other's lives.

It was their way of keeping the romance flourishing in their marriage of thirty years. They liked to watch in astonishment, the faces of the newly-married as they would mention their various rendezvous' and how long they had been a couple.

But today was different. They left at about ten in the morning and reached the five-mile long Chesapeake Bay Bridge about noon. Since the span had been created which connected the eastern and western shores, businesses were popping up all along Route 50.

They sought out their favorite seafood restaurant, The Fisherman's Inn.

After a quick crab cake sandwich and a bowl of cream of crab soup, they were off again.

Following an antique store stop in Easton to shop for a key for Maggie's collection, they took the highway toward St. Michael's, a little, historic seaport town and then continued until they reached the tiny town of Bozman and their friends' home.

Four comrades piled onto the Hambleton's cabin cruiser and gently glided up the creek, its surface tranquil and unruffled under a clear, blue sky. For hours they caught up on old times and planned an upcoming holiday that they all were anticipating.

It was almost set, nine days—two up, leading through New Jersey into Connecticut and New York and then, stopping in Boston and following the road to the tip of Cape Cod. Upon backtracking, they would visit Plymouth and maybe stay there for the night.

Heavy driving—too heavy, they decided. They would stay in Provincetown on the Cape and spend part of the next day there, then go on to Plymouth.

They continued making and adjusting their travel plans which would eventually take them up to the northern most tip of Maine and *lobster heaven,* as they called it, for an array of great meals. In and out of the small villages, they would investigate the nuances that made each one unique. And Maggie was sure to find a key or two and stories to add to her collection. On the map they circled Portsmouth, New Hampshire. In Maine, Ogunquit, Kennebunkport, Portland, Boothbay Harbor, Camden, Brooksville and Bar Harbor were selected; all were nestled along the coast.

Hours continued to pass as they sat in the kitchen cracking the huge, Chesapeake Bay hard crabs—caught earlier that morning by the local watermen—that James had steamed with vinegar and spices from his family recipe.

Laughter abounded, as it usually does when good friends pick up where they left off, then tease and banter in a good-natured way.

Chocolate brownie essence filled the kitchen while the mixture bubbled away in the oven to become a solidified dessert. Maggie and Tamara had quickly whipped them up when all decided they needed a little something, sugary and decadent. Their excuse always conjured up lots of laughs and an—*I know, you just want to get that taste out of your mouth.* It was a perfect solution and a perfect dessert.

When they realized it was 2 am, they said their good-byes knowing that they had the long drive by way of St. Michaels then across the Bay Bridge to Ritchie Highway and beyond to get to Westminster. They left, knowing that their plans would alter again and again, adjusting, until the actual day they would leave.

ର—ର—ର—ର

James was relieved to see their home. The drive was lengthy, but the memories of the day kept him smiling as he drove while Maggie rested, her head lying on the seat beside him in his Pontiac Bonneville.

"We're home, Babe," he said.

She yawned as she answered.

"Thanks for driving us home safely."

They noticed their light over the sink shining as they opened the door separating the grooming business from their domain.

The jot-a-note couldn't be missed, centered on the freezer door atop the refrigerator.

"James, look at this. Gretchen was here.

"Oh God," she exclaimed, "Thomas Frank has had a heart attack and is in bad shape. She's at their farm, but I'm sure Gretch would like to go to the hospital to be with the Frank family. Let's drive over to help out. We'll do whatever we can."

Maggie, who had slept most of the way, was wide awake.

James, who had driven the hour and forty-five minutes to deliver them home, was tired but upon hearing this news abounded with new-found energy.

They left immediately.

Their home was not far from the farmhouse. At five-ten, they were driving the last five miles into Pleasure Valley, and the outbuildings of the Frank farm became visible as the sky showed the light of day.

James drove onto the dirt lane leading to the house and saw the sizable barn to his left that Gretchen had told him about. She had mentioned how immense it was, and now he decided that he had never seen a barn quite so tall. He wondered how functional it could be and if the higher parts were used at all. As he looked further behind it, he saw two other barns with lower and wider dimensions both appearing newer than this one.

A truck was parked near the farmhouse, a little too near. It was actually in the shrubs with broken pieces surrounding the bumper.

Near the barn was Gretchen's station wagon, and they observed another vehicle, virtually hidden, adjacent to it.

As Maggie left her car, she peeped into Gretchen's vehicle and saw Flurry secured in the container. The puppy then saw her and wagged her tail.

Seeing the odd car, she assumed it belonged to Michael's brother and that Gretchen was busy inside the barn caring for the Franks' cat, Torpedo, as was mentioned in her note.

They opened the creaking door and were horrified.

Their eyes focused on their daughter's languid body.

"Oh, my God!" they both screamed as they rushed to her side, quickly feeling for a pulse which was very faint.

Maggie sobbed as she grasped her and wailed,

"Gretchen . . . Gretchen . . . oh my God, Gretchen.

"You'll be okay . . . we'll get some help. Hold on Gretchen, *please,* hold on!

"James, the farmhouse—break down the door if you must do it but call for an ambulance.

"Run, James—run as fast as you can!"

When he stood up to leave, he saw another body in the faint light not too far from them—a man, lying face down, with two metal rods coming through his upper torso.

Maggie saw him quickly feel for a pulse.

James yelled to Maggie as he ran for the door,

"Stay with Gretchen!"

With all of the speed he could muster, he ran for the farmhouse while grabbing another metal rod that he saw lying on the barn floor to use for protection or as a window breaker if necessary.

The door was not locked.

Feverishly, he looked for the phone. He didn't see one in the kitchen, but he found the black table model sitting next to the sofa in the parlor and his finger rounded the dial from the zero. As the operator came on, James trembled as he said,

"Hello operator, this is an emergency . . . please, please help me. I need an ambulance. No, send two ambulances, to the Frank farm, located off of Route 140 in Pleasure Valley. Tell them to take a right on Hughes Shop Road to the fork in the road. Go left at the lane by the big, green mailbox. It's five miles altogether from Route 140.

"Hurry, please, hurry . . . my daughter is dying!"

# CHAPTER SEVENTY-THREE

✥✥✥✥

𝔐ichael was looking for any slight sign of improvement, and he felt a new sense of relief that his uncle was going to make it.

After all, his eyes were open, and he talked to each one of us, squeezed Andrew's hand too, he thought.

Doctor Jensen had warned all of them that they needed to be prepared—just in case. None of them had really heard him.

Aunt Mary Kathleen said to Michael,

"Why don't you go to the farm now—see if Gretchen needs a hand. We'll be alright, we're all here together. By the time you get back, Jonathon will be sitting right here, next to me, I'm sure of it."

Again he told himself that there was a chance that Unks just might be able to beat this, and, although it was against his better judgment, his emotions made him tell his aunt those same positive feelings.

Trusting Michael's intuition, but primarily hearing what she wanted to hear, Mary Kathleen grabbed him, thanked him and gave him a bear hug as he left.

"And thank Gretchen for me, when you talk to her," she said, her voice trailing off.

As he drove down the lane leading to their private road, Michael saw flashing lights through the trees. He sped up, and as he came closer, he saw an ambulance, the Sheriff's car, Maggie and James Fischer's car and Gretchen's station wagon—all near the barn. Driving on, he saw Jonathon's vehicle, way off in the back.

His demeanor became anxious, frightened, as he said,

"Dear God, what is all of this?"

Michael's tires screeched on the gravel, and he leapt out of his vehicle brandishing a puzzled expression. He recognized Mr. Brackney, the Sheriff, who came out to meet him.

"Don't know if you want to go in there, Michael," he said, alluding to the inside of the barn, while holding up his arms as a barrier.

Before he could tell him anything, Michael blurted,

"Where's Gretchen? Where's Jonathon? Where are Mr. and Mrs. Fischer?"

"Gretchen Fischer was rushed to Northwestern General, and her parents were taken there by one of my men. They were just too shook up to drive," the Sheriff told him.

"Is she okay? How is she?" he asked.

"Don't quite know—unconscious, had a faint pulse, and the medics said she lost a good bit of blood."

"What? But what happened? And where's Jonathon . . . I see his car's over there . . . Where is he?"

"Michael, I'm sorry to have to tell you this, but, Jonathon's dead!

"He's inside. It's a pretty gruesome sight. Like I said, don't know if you want to go in there."

"Of course, I want to go in there, he's my brother!" he said angrily, as he pushed the Sheriff aside and flung open the door.

Michael stopped dead in his tracks. He never expected to see such a horrendous sight and was totally shocked as he saw Jonathon's body hanging there with both rods through him.

"Oh, my God . . . Oh, my God!" at first, was all he could say.

"How could this have happened?

"A fall . . . of course . . . but how?

"When can we get him down?" Michael sobbed, while looking around the room for a cover of some sort to wrap over his brother's body.

"No Michael, we can't touch him, not until the investigators finish in here and check out everything. It could have been an attempted robbery or murder."

"But," started Michael.

"I'm sorry, Michael," said the Sheriff.

While he stood near Jonathon's still body he tried to piece together an explanation as to what could have caused his fall, his death and Gretchen's injuries.

Michael's thoughts were spinning as he jolted. He said to the Sheriff,

"What *did* you say? That Gretchen was unconscious and had lost a lot of blood when the medics found her? Oh my God, I wonder how *she's* doin'. I've got to go to her. But what happened here? How was she injured?"

The officer listened and offered a possible scenario.

Michael was beside himself. He didn't know what to do. It all seemed too unreal.

As he looked around the room he saw it was in total disarray. Flurry sat in a crate wagging her tail while watching him. A ladder, the old rung ladder, had snapped in two. The bottom half of it was still wedged and the rest of it had fallen on a marble angel statue and remained there.

The relics that Uncle Thomas had kept in the barn were all over the place. The old calendars saved by his grandfather were pulled out from their packaging and were strewn about near the Crèche' and Nativity figurines.

He tried to analyze what had happened. Somebody was looking for something . . . a scuffle took place . . .

But the only things that were disturbed were religious items from old Saint John's Church that was on Main Street.

Ah, I bet that's it! Whoever did this must have thought there could be chalices, golden chalices, hidden within the old artifacts. Just like Sherriff Brackney had said, an attempted robbery.

Now, that would make sense. They probably ruffed up Gretchen, and then Jonathon would have jumped in, tried to stop them, and was on his way to protect her when he fell from the ladder coming down from . . .

No, it couldn't have been the loft. The ladder would have been around the other side of one of the main support beams for that to work, which would put it at the side of the loft. It didn't make any sense. Why would the ladder be on the side of the loft instead of at the front of it, at the open space, where you went in or out of it?

Near the side of the loft hung the tenth Station of the Cross, but there was no reason for Jonathon, to tinker with that.

Puzzling, just puzzling, he thought as he shook and scratched his head at the same time.

Michael wanted to leave to see Gretchen, wanted to stay to care for Jonathon's body, wanted to be with Uncle Thomas, and his family—actually—he wanted to scream.

This was too much . . . just too much!

He looked up at the Stations of the Cross and remembered his uncle offering up a prayer and created his own,

"Please Lord, help me to know what to do next," was all he said before he went inside the farmhouse and called the emergency nurses station at the hospital.

They rallied Maggie and Jim Fischer to the phone.

"Oh Michael, Gretchen's in bad shape," Maggie cried over the phone.

"She's lost so much blood, and they feel she possibly has several broken bones. What could have happened?

"Michael, we are so sorry about your brother. Oh, it's so terrible!

"We found him like that and called for help, but he was already dead.

"Oh, I'm so sorry, so sorry . . .

"How is your uncle, Michael?"

She rambled, unable to stop to hear any reply.

He caught a pause and quickly proceeded to tell her what little he knew about his uncle.

"Maggie, I've got to see Gretchen," he said.

"The doctors are with her, Michael, and even we can't get in to see her. Why don't you check on your uncle and after that, come and meet us. We're at the same hospital as him, probably on the next floor."

He agreed.

When he looked at his watch it was five-thirty.

$\approx\approx\approx\approx$

As he walked into the Coronary Care Unit, he didn't see any of his family.

"Pardon me nurse—Michael Frank here. My Uncle Thomas, same last name, was brought in here earlier with a heart problem. Mighty sick, they said.

"Can you help me out? Gotta find the rest of my family, quick as I can."

"Mr. Frank, please come with me. She asked him to sit down in a private area and said to him,

"I'm sorry, but I have some very bad news.

"Your uncle died at five o'clock this morning. It was his heart, and Doctor Jensen will explain the details. You have my sincere condolences . . .

"I'll take you to your family. They're waiting for you, and of course, they know, they were told earlier."

*Your uncle died.*

The head nurse's words echoed in his brain like a child's voice projects while standing on a cliff, yelling to the world below, like his words had, in Pittsburgh, before Uncle Jay's funeral when they had all gone to the West End Overlook.

On that day, just before they left, after everyone had gotten back into their cars, he had waited at the edge of the precipice.

While looking towards the Golden Triangle where all three rivers intersect the city of Pittsburgh, the city his Great Uncle had loved, he had heard his voice as it said, *Uncle Jay, I'll really miss you!*

He had never experienced the sadness of his heart aching, like it had done then, until now, when he felt his heart was breaking.

# CHAPTER SEVENTY-FOUR

᷇᷇᷇᷇

*U*ncle Thomas was dead.

The voices around Michael seemed like an echo and were barely audible. He tried to focus in on them in, but to no avail. They were hanging out in mid-air somewhere.

The reality was beginning to set in . . .

Uncle Thomas, the man who became his role model, taught him everything he had learned since the age of thirteen, suddenly . . . was gone. He couldn't believe it. His whole world was falling apart—Uncle Thomas and Jonathon dead . . . Gretchen hanging on by a thread.

How could he find the right words to tell Aunt Mary Kathleen that after having lost her husband, she would have to bury her youngest nephew, as well?

And Gretchen . . .

He started rubbing his hands through his hair as a release, and the tears came. Just then the three remaining members of his family walked into the room. Seeing Michael's demeanor, they put their arms around him and one another and began to sob and pray.

William choked out,

"The Sheriff's Deputy was here—he told us everything, Michael.

"They think that Jonathon died at the same time that Uncle Thomas died.

"Michael, we're so sorry that you had to see him like . . ."

He quickly pulled away from the circle with William in tow.

"Aunt Mary Kathleen doesn't know how they found Jonathon, does she?" asked Michael.

"No, the Deputy talked to Andrew and me, away from her. She thinks it was an accident and doesn't know anymore than that."

"Nobody should tell her how he was found," said Michael.

William said,

"I'll take care of that, and I'll tell Andrew too. She'll never know."

Michael said,

"William, we need to pray. When Gretchen pulls through, she'll explain it all.

"Oh God, I hope she makes it! She's got to make it! I've got to go to her, maybe now, they'll let me see her . . .

"William, I don't know what I'll do if she doesn't make it!"

# CHAPTER SEVENTY-FIVE

❧❧❧❧

## AUTUMN 1967

$\mathscr{I}$t came in the mail, about two weeks after Thomas was buried, addressed to Mrs. Thomas Frank and postmarked Pittsburgh, Pennsylvania.

She had glanced at it while in the kitchen, but there was too much activity. It was somewhat chaotic, her nephews' discussing the business and trying to piece it all back together after Thomas' death.

Stealing away, she climbed the stairs to her bedroom, closed and locked the door.

Many of the cards and letters offering condolences touched her, and she treasured each one, most of them mentioning her Thomas and the positive way he had affected each of their lives.

She sat on the bed, sinking into the coverlet and began to read each word . . .

> **Dear Mrs. Frank,**
> I was sorry to learn of Thomas' death just the other day when I came back from my daughter's home up in Put-In-Bay, Ohio. I was visiting her for two weeks and was shocked as I read old newspapers and in this case the obituary column. Always read the obituary every day and I always say as long as I don't see my name in there, I must be doing pretty good.
> My eyesight's going now. But I can't complain—had a good life. Full of hard work and I can say I'm proud of what I've accomplished. I worked for your husband's uncle, Jay Frank, as foreman of one of his factories, his machine shop.

When your husband was a little boy, his uncle would bring him to see us. Had all of us teach him how to work the lathes, the drills and the grinders, but, best of all he liked the series of levers and pulleys that we used in the shop to move things around.

Jay had me stick by him, teaching him everything I knew. We always had a lot of laughs—Jay and his practical jokes—always setting somebody up to make them smile.

But your husband was just like one of the guys, fairly young too. We all looked forward to having him come around, but especially me. You see I never had any sons either, just like Jay. It seems your husband filled that void for me, too. So we got pretty close, but then I didn't see him for years. Guess he was busy with your lives. Always asked Jay about him though and sent my hellos to Thomas through Jay, whenever I saw him.

Then Jay died while I was in Cleveland, Ohio, staying with my other daughter and I didn't find out until I got back from that trip. Man, I was pretty sad that it happened and that I missed his funeral. Thought I'd never get to see your husband after that. But, he liked to make people happy too, and had some of the little boy in him just like his Uncle Jay did. When your Thomas opened my door and surprised me, I almost fell off my feet. We caught up on old times—relived our first meeting when Jay hoisted him up on his shoulders at the shop—went over the whole nine yards.

He was there with me for hours and he had to pull his truck inside the shop while the two of us hung around it, talking, just chewing the fat. Said he had just come from

**a lawyer meeting and he left rather late to
be driving all the way back to Westminster.
I told him he could stay at my place, but he
said he had to get home to you.**

At that point, Mary Kathleen remembered meeting Thomas
at the barn. She knew because it was his first of several monthly
trips to Pittsburgh after Jay died. She sighed deeply and continued
reading . . .

**Well you can imagine how happy I was
the next month, just about to the day, who
comes popping out of the shadows but
Thomas and he kept coming each month,
and always on the first.**
    **Mrs. Frank, I've got an old heart, and flies
could hide in the wrinkles on my face, but I
have a lot to be thankful for.**
    **I just have to tell you, seeing Thomas for
so many months and sharing glimpses of
our past, of sweet, bygone days, gave me a
treasure chest to re-open for the rest of my
life.**
    **Thank you for giving him the time.**
    **Again, you have my sympathy.**
    **We will all miss him.**

**Sincerely,
T. Jones
(Jonesie)**

Tears rolled down her cheeks as she realized how she had
begrudged Thomas going off to Pittsburgh every month. How could
she have been so full of distrust? Why did she put him through the
once-over each, and every time he came home, instead of wrapping
her arms around him and welcoming him, loving him?

Here was proof that he had filled his free time in Pittsburgh
visiting an old friend. And didn't he deserve to do just that?

He had always been such a good husband, such a good uncle and such a good provider, she thought.

It was me. It was my problem that I couldn't deal with, and Thomas got the brunt of it. Could I have felt differently?

All I knew was that I was here and feeling lonely, and he was there. If I could only take it all back. Oh, how I wish I could change things. I would wrap my arms around Thomas, look into his eyes and tell him how much I appreciated him.

But now, he's gone. The love of my life is gone, and my life will never have the same meaning without him. I never again will be able to look into his eyes and hear him whisper my name, smile that smile of his or hear him say, honey, I'll always love you.

Yet, still, whenever he came home, it was that barn, that dag'on barn, that kept him away from me. Yes, that barn that stole him away into the night and sometimes all night . . .

Yes . . . the barn.

I can understand, now, why he was in Pittsburgh so long . . . but the barn . . . why that dag'on barn?

Can't even bear to look out my window anymore. Whenever I do, I see Thomas walking away from me and disappearing into that building.

She was convinced and steadfast in her focus.

Yes, it really was that old barn . . . that old barn . . . that old barn . . .

Mary Kathleen hadn't heard the house empty out, but it was quiet and she was alone, left to think.

Over and over she had played it all out—the deadly accident investigation and the report that she had read again and again.

It had said that the Police were satisfied that it was caused when the young man, Jonathon Frank, fell from the ladder as he climbed from the loft and the young woman, Gretchen Fischer had fallen, possibly from the same location and had hit her head.

The barn . . .

The barn . . .

It was her arch-enemy.

Mary Kathleen had the almost insurmountable task of accepting it all, and she wasn't doing well.

# CHAPTER SEVENTY-SIX

❧❧❧❧

Burying her husband and youngest nephew within the same week had left her an emotionally crippled woman, full of anger and disbelief that something so dreadful could have happened to her family. She stood alone, staring out of her bedroom window, glaring at the massive wooden building straight ahead.

The color of the sky was murky gray. Thunder clouds loomed off in the distance while clustering shades of steel, slate and pewter were interspersed with cream and ivory pillows. A hushed rumble could be heard, far from where she stood, signaling impending precipitation as the sky whirled about.

An hour or two passed, she wasn't aware of time. Suddenly down the stairs she dashed, taking them two by two, flashing open the screen door with great vengeance. She heard it slam, louder than ever before, while running breathlessly to her car.

Mary Kathleen shivered from head to toe.

Mechanically, she started her car and sped away from the farm. She landed outside the Tractor Supply Company, unaware of the farms, the houses and the other businesses she passed along the way.

Her breath was huffing in and out while she was trying to gain composure of her erratic emotions. In her mind's eye she remembered Thomas, and she driving into town together. He would go to the Tractor Supply Company, while she had window shopped at Mather's Department Store on Main Street.

They'd finish off their trip with a five cent fountain Coca-Cola at the Rexall Pharmacy, and they'd catch up on the latest happenings about the town from Doc Schmidt who saw everybody, every week.

Today, her determination carried her inside the building.

"Yes, that's right, I want the two biggest and the best padlocks you have in here," she told the shopkeeper, seemingly in complete control.

"Sorry to hear about the loss of your husband, Thomas, and the terrible accident over at the farm, Mrs. Frank."

"Thank you," she said, looking away and down, zoning out and missing his specific words.

He kept trying to reconnect . . .

"Mrs. Frank . . . Mrs. Frank."

"Yes, yes, go on," she said, yet totally unaware.

"Now, about those padlocks that you wanted. These here are a set . . . Yale locks, good company, 'round a lotta' years. They have malleable iron cases and self-locking spring shackles with four lever tumblers inside, and they come with two flat, steel keys that fit either one. You take this chain and feed it through your hook or latch and then into the shackle here and snap it closed. If ya' want it tight, you'll use the link that will give ya' the least play."

She heard that and questioned,

"As long as they're the biggest and strongest locks you have. They must be strong. Heavy duty— iron and steel, you say? Then I'll buy 'em . . . thank you, Alan."

On returning home, she slammed the car door with extreme fervor and dug her shoes into the dirt road that was now sprinkled with raindrops creating puffs of immediate dust. As she marched over to the barn she followed the same path she had watched her husband use so often, cursing it all the way.

Sobbing, Mary Kathleen stood at its doors. She forced the eight-link chain through the larger barn door latch, slid the steel-spring shackle through the link closest to the case of the padlock to create the tightest fit and snapped it shut. Then she latched the second, securing the smaller door, the door that had always closed Thomas inside.

At the very second that the lock's cylinder had bolted, the heavens opened up, and the shower quickly became a tempest, drenching Mary Kathleen to the skin. She pulled at the padlock, again and again with great exasperation, using all of her might to be sure it would not unfasten.

Tears were streaming down her cheeks, mixing with the rain, as she cried out,

"Thomas, how could you do this to me? How could you leave me?

"Now, when the boys are grown, and we could finally find the time to hold each other close.

"Our own special . . . our private times . . . like before in the field.

"Oh, Thomas, I need you . . . I love you . . . I just can't let you go.

"Please, God . . . please . . . don't let this be real," she pleaded as she fell to her knees sobbing ever more deeply while constantly seizing the tension on the padlock and chain in one hand and the flat steel keys that were clenched in the other.

# CHAPTER SEVENTY-SEVEN

❧✦❧✦

*M*ost of the next few weeks were a blur.

As Mary Kathleen lay in her bed one night, she remembered her conversation, in detail, with Michael and William, as they approached her for the keys to open the padlocks that had bolted the barn doors.

Both of them were surprised by the locks.

No one had seen her tearful ritual when she locked its doors.

While her pillows surrounded her she rubbed her temples. The boys had said, *We need the combine parked inside, next to the antique tractor, to harvest the crops.*

Yeah, both of 'em were shocked by me, that's for sure, she thought, especially when I said, *no, that barn will never, I say, never again be opened. I don't care if all the farm machinery in the world is in there.*

I told 'em, *you'll just have to borrow pieces from someone else, or buy other ones, I don't care.*

I was never so angry or determined to get my way. Sure, my eyes must've been buggin' out like they do when I get hoppin' mad.

William! He started in on me with his, *but, Aunt Mary Kathleen . . .*

I screamed at 'em, and I told 'em, *No buts about it—the answer is no.*

They both mumbled under their breath and yanked open that confounded screen door and slammed it behind 'em, harder than ever, thought it was comin' off its hinges.

But I yelled after 'em, *And if I get any back talk about it, I'll take a match to it.*

Her mind floated . . .

A match to it . . .

A match to it . . .

The thought lingered and played itself over and over again in her brain.

A match to it . . .

It repeated and repeated, stuck like the needle on one of her old 78 rpm records that has come to the paper, near the turnstile.

Sleep found her, but she tossed about—first to one side and then to the other—until daybreak beckoned her to rise.

It was eating away at her ... Thomas ... Jonathon ... Gretchen ... how could it have happened?

Her mind raced back and forth as she remembered the times that Thomas had escaped to the barn and deserted her with all of the responsibilities of raising four boys—four boys—and now only three.

Once again, as it had happened so many times before, Mary Kathleen was standing at her bedroom window.

Her fixed stare didn't see the acres of jagged corn stalks, remaining after the harvest, nor the hundreds of Canadian geese that migrated yearly to the farm on their way farther south, helping themselves to the lingering fodder.

She didn't see the threatening weather farther off in the distance, lightning teasing the sky or hear the thunder cursing under its breath.

Her only thoughts portrayed how she must have looked. The old fatigue jacket over her shoulders, the bedroom slipper with a ripped back and her hair in disarray meeting Thomas as he had returned from Pittsburgh only to lose him to the smaller door within the huge one that he had closed, sealing her out from him.

Then, another time, she could see him storming out of the house when she had exploded, accusing him of being unfaithful to her with Uncle Jay's nurse—him raging away from her—to go to that barn.

Watching him on that same day peering down at the ground as he walked away, lookin' side-to-side and kickin' at the dirt, and for what, a copy of *her* phone number, I thought.

It was always the same. Night after night she stood at her bedroom window, lonely, watching that flickering light from the lantern within, as it illuminated the stained-glass roof, signifying that he was there—its walls surrounding him, almost caressing him—while they isolated her.

Now she knew ... in her mind there was absolutely, positively, no doubt.

That old wooden building ... *that* was Thomas' mistress!

Mary Kathleen stood there, in a trance.

Her mind played with it . . . old wooden building, take a match to it . . . old wooden building, take a match . . . old building, take match . . . old . . . match . . .

Grabbing a sweater, she flung it over her back as she tromped down the groaning steps. Her hand reached onto a shelf near the sink where she kept the matches.

She hesitated as she stared down at them in her hand, seeing the slide-away lid and the striker, waiting innocently for a potential partner to create a lethal weapon upon impact.

Into her pocket she stuffed them, then grabbed kindling and a section of the newspaper, which she twisted and scrunched into a torch-like baton and used it to force open the screen door, which obediently followed her lead.

Trudging up the lane, she could see it towering into the overcast sky, looming before her—her nemesis—the barn. Mary Kathleen did not care about anything that was encased within. She had one intention—

She lit the first match.

It fizzled.

The second was struck. She watched as the red tip turned into shades of orange and yellow when it burst into flame and died.

Another and another failed.

On the next attempt, the flare fashioned from the paper and the wood intermingled with the flame and was growing into a menacing incendiary device.

As she touched it to the underbrush and dried vines surrounding the two entry doors, the dehydrated weeds resembled flash paper immediately blazing and then fizzling into nothingness.

Her intention to ignite was squelched, as the wind presenting its own fury, smothered each attack, rather than fanning the fire.

Trying again and again, she snapped in and out of her daze as each attempt failed.

Finally, she ignited the torch again.

She heard the wind howl from above and slowly looked up to the roof's highest point, while she inadvertently resembled the Statue of Liberty, her arm raised holding the fiery club above her shoulders.

In a motionless stance, seeing beyond the barn and into the heavens, Mary Kathleen visualized Thomas, standing firm, arms folded and frowning upon her in anger.

The flame was fanned by the wind until a very cold blast of air extinguished the baton and sent it out of her hand, breaking her state of consciousness. She watched it smoke and crackle apart into harmless debris and blow away like tumbleweed in Kansas.

Her mouth agape, she began to cry, as she realized the severity of her actions. Knees hit the gravel, her body curled, as she prayed aloud for his forgiveness, while bemoaning her imminent fate—life without her only love, Thomas.

The torrent of rain washed about her. Nearby, a few rows of unharvested corn tops swayed back and forth, each holding up the other, all willing recipients of the blasts of wet aggression. An end row of maize could not withstand the battering from the sky and surrendered, lying over on its side.

Dried leaves and debris that nestled within the trunks of the oaks and maples were let loose by the wind, creating their own choreography, twisting and dancing, to and fro. As they left their protective cache' and followed a path unknown to each of them, they assaulted her back—the only exposed section of this sobbing woman assuming the fetal position.

Rain continued, and each flower and leaf welcomed the drenching. The dirt, once dust, became moist throughout, sending tiny rivers of water to the root system of annuals and perennials, long overdue for their sustenance.

Bolts of lightning shocked the sky at unsuspecting intervals, the wind slowed while thunder continued to shout its angry voice for all to hear.

The turbulence dissipated, the trees calmed, stripped of their unnecessary baggage, lighter for the wind to whistle through.

Stillness enveloped, and once again, the corn stood tall, but for only a few casualties, its leaves unfurled into welcoming fronds.

The grass was no longer thirsty.

Quieter rumbles continued in the distance as the storm retreated.

Mary Kathleen heard no thunder, saw no lightning, nor felt the sting of the torrential downpour that fell upon her, mixed with churning oak and maple leaves while the rivers of mud traced their own path around her knees firmly planted in the sodden earth.

When her nephews rescued her, wrapped her and carried her inside the farmhouse, she had no recollection of anything—fire, storm or otherwise that took place that day.

Michael, William and Andrew knew she was sad, even depressed, but until now they had no idea of its severity, nor did they know exactly what had happened for all that was left of her arson showed only scorched brush and blistered paint on the wooden siding.

Sobs were rampant, almost uncontrollable until she had none left to muster.

She thanked them as they held her close, and she promised to call Maggie Fischer the next day to help her to find a good doctor.

They took her for her word, but decided to each take turns keeping a closer watch on her.

# CHAPTER SEVENTY-EIGHT

❧❧❧❧

$\mathcal{M}$ary Kathleen felt weak and exhausted the next morning remembering some of what had happened at the barn, but most of it had left her in a fog.

In the past, she had never been the one to address severe problems. Thomas, her rock, was always there.

Her mind was processing things illogically, but to her they made perfect sense.

She said aloud, through sobs,

"Michael and William approached me for the keys to open the padlocks bolting those barn doors. I know their request was valid, one of sheer need. The combine is parked inside—like they said—next to the antique tractor."

Then anger surfaced,

"I didn't budge, and I ain't gonna'. I don't care what happens, don't want ever, to see inside that monstrosity again, and I'm not gonna let it swallow up my nephews, like it did my Thomas. No, that barn will never again be opened. I don't care if all the farm machinery in the world is in there.

"Don't want to look inside and see the spot where all the death and destruction of my family took place."

She exclaimed,

"What a horrible accident!

"Michael wouldn't let me go inside to see, but I heard him and William discussing it, and in my imagination, it will forever be!

"And when I told him about the padlocks . . .

"I can hear William saying, *but* . . .

"I can hear William . . .

"I can hear . . ."

Her brain was spinning again.

"No buts about it," she squealed out loud, "The answer is no. And if I get any back talk about it, I told 'em, I'll take a match to it!"

She heard herself—really heard herself—and then remembered trying to do just that, the day before.

I must be going crazy, she thought.

Her body was quivering. She had to think. Who can I turn to? Who will listen? Who will help me?

Hands trembling, she held the base and picked up the thick, black handset of the telephone and dialed Maggie Fischer's number as she had promised her nephews.

As soon as she answered, Mary Kathleen pleaded,

"Maggie, please come over. I need someone to talk to, and I feel you will be the only one who can share my grief. I feel all jittery. Can you please come over?"

Maggie heard the raspy sound of her voice, as if she had been crying, and sensed the urgency of her request.

"Of course, Mary Kathleen, I'll be there as fast as I can," she said as she sighed into her own emotions.

She had been sitting at the desk in the grooming salon staring into the empty rooms and wondering how it all could have happened. Getting up to help Mary Kathleen gave her a reason to get out of there for awhile. Before Maggie left, she tossed some special tools in a black bag along with several towels and a tray.

When Maggie arrived only twenty-five minutes later, Mary Kathleen heard the gravel scatter before her car engine was turned off. She prepared to meet her at the door.

Both women had become immediately closer since the tragedy in the barn.

When the door opened, Flurry was the first to greet Maggie. Her long, fluffy tail not only went side to side, but up and down, and when it got into full motion, it looked like an old airplane propeller spinning around.

"You keep swishin' your tail like that, and soon you'll be takin' off," she said, trying to find something humorous to say.

As she scooped her into her arms and received wet kisses anywhere Flurry could land them—neck, chin and cheeks—Maggie accepted each one, needed each one, to relieve her own sadness.

"Missed you little girl. Yes, I did. I know you remember me, don't you sweetie-pie," she continued while the little puppy responded with even more intense affection. That brought Maggie back to the memory of Thanksgiving and the trip Gretchen first made to this house—*this* house with *that* barn. And the last time she had seen Flurry, safely inside the travel crate, just before Jim and she found Gretchen.

As she nuzzled the furry little one, her eyes focused on Mary Kathleen, a woman who, though now in her mid-sixties, was looking much older than usual. In fact, Maggie thought, she looked completely frazzled.

Her hair was rough and separated, no waves followed any particular pattern, and the edges were split and frayed. Her face was dry and weather-beaten, and Maggie could feel the tension in her body as her friend hugged her with a squeeze that took her breath away.

The tears flowed easily and often as she shared the scenario with Maggie who listened to each and every word describing her physical and emotional turmoil.

She had remembered the fiery baton, the hallucination of seeing Thomas, and rolling up into a ball on the ground to escape the fury of the storm, and all proved to be overwhelming.

It caused her to become embarrassed and ashamed as she retold the incident recalling her nephews caring for her that day. As Maggie listened, she also began to cry, but, earnest in her efforts to be a positive influence, held back more tears. One of us has to be stronger than the other, she thought.

Mary Kathleen left to retrieve another box of tissues, and Maggie put Flurry down on a rug nearby with a rawhide chew she had brought along to keep her busy.

She had to get Mary Kathleen to see a doctor, to get a handle on her erratic behavior, but first she wanted to calm her down and help her to relax.

There was one escape Maggie could always count on.

She began pulling out her implements of magic, as people had named them, from the large bag that she had brought.

A puff of air exploded as she released the old folded sheet up in a snap letting it float to the floor. One of Mary Kathleen's kitchen chairs was called up and dragged to the sink. Next, she folded several towels to create a soft, lean-to, to fill the gap between her chair and the rolled ceramic edge of the antiquated porcelain.

Just then, Mary Kathleen was returning from the upstairs bathroom.

"Why, what is all this?"

"If you'll let me, I would like to share my talents with you. I'll gently color, wash, cut, and style your hair after I give you a facial. Actually, I only do this for my special friends, since I've retired from behind the chair."

She knew she would enjoy it, but hesitated, concerned that Maggie might be overly generous in her time and trouble.

"I don't want to inconvenience you, Maggie. I know how busy you are, handling the business by yourself now . . . since you lost . . ."

She cut her off mid-sentence, not wanting to think about all of that, knowing she would also cave-in emotionally and said,

"Mary Kathleen, let me do this for you. It will help me to relax too, and right now I need that more than anything else."

She agreed.

Maggie began twisting the woman's hair back into a figure eight, attaching only two pins to secure it before wrapping it with a towel, turban style. She slathered cleansing cream onto her face and neck and removed it with a damp, warm towel. Her skin was exfoliated with a deep pore emollient to soften the coarseness created by years of neglect, and the residue was rinsed away with moist terrycloth.

She couldn't help it. Mary Kathleen started to weep, thinking of the comparison of the warm, moist towels and her and Thomas' relationship over the years—the fields, wiping his face, neck and hands, those strong, yet gentle hands.

Her partner was gone, and she missed him so.

Maggie sensed she was releasing the incredible tension from within, but of course, didn't know the tender story behind it all. She allowed her to cry, gently dabbing the tears away until Mary Kathleen fell asleep while lying back into the nest of thick towels, which Maggie had created for her. Although her friend had drifted off, she continued, knowing her touch would help the woman to let go, to become limp and relaxed.

After applying the moisturizer, she massaged it onto her skin using all of the most beneficial manipulations she had remembered from her training at beauty school. A mask was next, and as she finished, she heard a faint snore. After twenty minutes, she gently touched Mary Kathleen's shoulder, gradually adding more pressure to awaken her without a startle.

She removed the mask, and as Mary Kathleen opened her eyes, Maggie could see a more relaxed person; but the best was yet to come.

The tray Maggie had brought, allowed Mary Kathleen to lean back on a regular kitchen chair while she applied a temporary color, waited a few minutes then poured tepid water onto her hair and scalp. Bubbles exploded as she massaged a luxurious shampoo, twice through her strands and rinsed allowing water to trickle down the tray and back into the sink. After the conditioner, the entire combination of all three steps imparted a sunny hue into her wavy tresses, and now it was ready for the transformation. She positioned the chair to a central spot on the old sheet.

Maggie was back in the saddle again—combing, sectioning, snipping and checking. Rollers were next, and a plastic bonnet-style hair dryer was used. While the air flowed through each little roller-tunnel, Maggie filed Mary Kathleen's nails and did a hand and arm massage.

Like so many of her former customers had done, Mary Kathleen began to pour out her emotions. She told her of the fears, the uncertainty of each day and the loneliness she felt.

Maggie understood and shared her loss, wishing and hoping that the clock could have been turned back.

She began again, relaying the story of the supply company and the padlocks she had installed, the argument with the "boys" and the baton and matches, only to begin stirring up hostile feelings. Not wanting to feel stressed again, she paused and unhooked the hose attached to the plastic bonnet with elasticized edges. Mary Kathleen slowly walked up the creaking wooden steps to her bedroom and reappeared in a few minutes, bouffant plastic atop her head covering the rollers.

"Maggie, please take these," she said, as she handed her four, flat, steel keys. "Put them up on your walls, but hide them in between the others. They belong to those padlocks that I told you about, the ones from the barn doors, and I don't want anyone to be tempted to open them."

Funny, Maggie thought, keys from the Franks', but not the one I really wanted. Who knows, maybe one day I'll discuss that one with her, the one that Great Uncle Thaddeus had on his ring of keys from Abraham Lincoln's funeral train.

She visualized talking to Thomas about it, several months ago and realized how immaterial it was now.

That was before all of this . . .

She took the keys from Mary Kathleen's grasp and promised no one would ever know where they were.

Maggie knew that Michael, William or Andrew would only have to use a hacksaw, or extra heavy-duty snips to cut through the shackle of each padlock if they wanted to get into the barn. She felt, however, that their respect for their aunt's wishes would prevent that from happening.

Her hair was now completely dry. Maggie removed the rollers and pin curl clips, exposing small tunnels and flat O-shaped designs of crisp, gelled hair which she brushed vigorously into strong waves ending in soft curls. She applied a light shade of lipstick and let the natural glow of her cheeks project through her newly hydrated skin.

Mary Kathleen walked toward the mirror at the end of the hall, and as she got closer, she could hardly believe her eyes and said,

"Maggie, you *are* a miracle worker! I can't believe how much better I look and feel! What do I owe you?"

"This is on me today, but only if you promise to see your doctor and tell him you're having a tough time and need a little help. If you will let me take you, I'll set it up."

She embraced her with all of her strength and smiled into Maggie's eyes as she said,

"Oh, yes I will, and I thank you from the bottom of my heart. I'll pray for you. You are a special friend, and I'll never forget this."

And Maggie, looking at her friend and seeing the change that had come over her, knew why she had always loved her profession. She had always found satisfaction and comfort when giving to someone else and thanked God for her ability to change people's lives by her touch.

Although these feelings of happiness caressed Maggie, her own sadness did too after all that had happened, and she wished that her own life could be changed as if by magic.

# CHAPTER SEVENTY-NINE

❧❧❧❧

## 1983

## SIXTEEN YEARS LATER

"Yeah, that new Monsignor is proposin' that we build a bigger church," said William. Did you see the newspaper last week, The Catholic Review?

"It was announced in there, even had a picture of the old church on Main Street. Told the story about them havin' to tear her down after the fire."

Michael replied,

"Didn't see that, but I saw it mentioned in the bulletin from church. Said about the same thing, that some Masses are standing room only, and ya' know that's on a regular Sunday not on a holiday when the two-timers come on out."

"What? What the heck are the two-timers?" asked William.

"Only come to church on Christmas and Easter. Sure wish they'd catch-on and try to come on a regular basis. You'd think they'd at least wanna' take time to say thanks. Know I got special blessings to be thankful for. Can walk and talk, can't I? Can think, too. Now the rest is up to me, but I gotta' say thanks."

"You got that right," said William, while shaking his head at his brother's humor.

"So, a bigger church, huh? Wonder if they'll build it up on the hill over-lookin' the highway?"

Michael said,

"Actually, the way this town's growin', it's no wonder. Ever since they've proposed that new, Route 795 interstate, we've had more and more people headin' up here. Have you seen the traffic at Englar Road and Route 140? They're settin' up three lanes. Why, I remember when it was only one."

Andrew walked in, ready to grab his morning coffee and said,

"What'r you guys chewin' the rag about now?"

"Hey, pour me another cup, while your there," said Michael.

"Talkin' about the growth up here. It's only a matter of time, with this much expansion, you know, our taxes are gonna' double."

"I was tellin' William," Michael continued, "Noticed for the second week now, in St. John's bulletin, that new Monsignor's article said we might be buildin' a new church, somethin' big and tall and traditional, more along the lines of old St. John's Church on Main Street."

Andrew froze. He swallowed deeply. The pictures flashed before him in a slide show, one right after the other—St. John's Church on Main Street.

Even though he confessed twice, once in the war and again in the confessional, and heard Uncle Thomas say he forgave him, he still had a hard time with it in his heart.

The smoke, the fire, the lies and then those deaths—yes, those deaths—maybe they weren't all related but everything seemed to pile, one on top of the other.

Michael spoke into the silence of Andrew's mind, halting the projector,

"Ya' know if they're serious about doin' just that, I wonder if Father would want to use those pieces Unks stashed in the barn, from the old church?"

Andrew was still silent, he only listened.

William spoke,

"Hate to say it, but first, Father will have to coax, Aunt Mary Kathleen into openin' her up again. She sure has stuck to her beliefs keepin' it locked up, these past fifteen, what sixteen, years.

"Boy, I'll never forget that day. Comin' home and tryin' to get inside only to find the biggest locks—slam, bang, right on the very middle of both barn doors. And then the next week, findin' her at the same spot—kneelin' in all of them streams of mud, soaked to the skin, her hair hangin' like rags, soppin' wet.

"Nothin' could budge her. Remember we kept callin' her name, and it was like she was someplace else, like she was possessed, starin' straight ahead and hatred pourin' out of the depths of her eyes onto those barn doors and the locks.

"Whose gonna' talk to her? Personally, I think the Monsignor might just be the only person that she'll listen to on that account.

"Would you have believed Auntie would lock up that thing and decide never to let any of us inside again? And how about the combine and the antique tractor? Can't wait to see if those things still run.

"She certainly can be mighty forceful. Never could understand why in the world she would close 'er up like she did. I mean, Michael, did she ever let on to you, why?"

Michael said,

"Never said a word, never even let on a little, as to why. But, I got my theory 'bout it. As I think back, every time she needed Unks, one of us had to run out and get him from the barn. And many a time he'd say he was just too busy with somethin'. And you know he'd be manipulatin' one or another of his engines or boxes, heavin' things up and over from one side to the other with his pulleys and levers.

"Course, that's when we saw how angry she would get. Remember? We'd have to high-tail it outta' her sight 'til she'd calm down? Hair trigger temper—I think that's what they call it.

"So, my thought is this. She hated that barn like it was some other woman he was courtin'.

"Thinkin' back, she probably would've liked to lock-up the barn when we were growin' up, so's he would be spendin' more time with her and helpin' her to raise us.

"Now, we all know she's got that temper I mentioned, but, this time, she never softened. Sometimes, I'd see her workin' out front, or swingin' on that porch swing, lookin' at that barn. I've heard her swear, low and under her breath at it, and I've even seen her look at it and cry."

"Yeah, Michael, I'm sure you're right. Never did put it all together like that, but the more I'm thinkin' on it, you sized it all up alright."

# CHAPTER EIGHTY

## 1983

Mr. Codday knew it was time to move on his client's wishes. He had been following the weekly church bulletins, The *Catholic Review* and *The Carroll County Times* newspapers just like Thomas Frank had instructed him to do, looking for any signs of impending growth, and there it was, following the headlines—

**CATHOLIC CHURCH PROPOSES EXPANSION**

> The parish of Saint John's Catholic Church may be expanding. The former church, circa 1860, was originally erected on Main Street in Westminster, Maryland, and was razed, May, 1958. It is now replaced by the Carroll County Library.
>
> A meeting will take place on Monday evening at seven o'clock at Saint John's Parish Center, 43 Monroe Street. Reverend Monsignor Louis Paplana, Pastor and Reverend Valentine Adeo, Associate Pastor will be welcoming all who wish to attend. This is the first of a series of meetings to discuss building a larger church that could accommodate the growth of the parish. Your attendance would be greatly appreciated.

The article continued posing questions as to where money could be procured, perhaps through donations and fundraising.

It highlighted the statement from Monsignor Louis as he closed his previous week's column in the bulletin by saying, *if we all pull together, through prayer and God's grace, we will be shown how to accomplish this—if it is His will.*

ᔕ᷎ᔕ᷎ᔕ᷎ᔕ᷎

After flying into, Baltimore/Washington International Airport, Alex Codday, the attorney and Bill O'Reilly, the financial advisor, drove one hour to Westminster. When they arrived, Mr. Codday called Mrs. Frank and asked if he could visit with her, and also, could he see the farm and the barn that her husband, Thomas, had told him so much about.

"You're sure welcome to come over, but nobody's goin' in there," she said, emphatically. "Barn's closed up."

He didn't broach the subject any further.

Alex Codday told his associate what she had said and after debating with himself said,

"I'll touch on that face to face, and Bill, I need to meet with her alone. Seeing both of us, in these dark suits, considering her age—she'll think we're here to plan her funeral."

Although he had yet to see her, he knew exactly how she was doing. He had continued to keep a very strong relationship with the nurse assigned to the Frank home to care for Mary Kathleen. Initially she needed less care but she was presently assisted in her every day routine. All of the bills were sent monthly to Mr. Codday's office, and working with the accountants, covered any and all of her expenses, just as Thomas had arranged through, Codday & Codday, Chartered.

ᔕ᷎ᔕ᷎ᔕ᷎ᔕ᷎

She was frail, but he noticed that her mind was sharp, as they exchanged pleasantries.

"Mrs. Frank," he began, "I've been keeping up with the growth of your very special town, through various periodicals, and it seems there is an exodus of sorts—people who want the clean, fresh air, schools instilling good Christian values, and friendly, warm neighbors.

"St. John's Parish has grown by leaps and bounds. And, there have been articles stating that they will have to build a larger church.

"Father Valentine Adeo, is heading the proposal under Monsignor Louis Paplana's lead. They are sending out flyers, putting articles in the local papers and *The Catholic Review* and creating notices in the church bulletin—all asking for information about artifacts from the original church that was on Main Street, dating back to the eighteen hundreds.

"I have heard that when they tore it down in 1958, some families retrieved items that had been donated, and others took things into their homes for safekeeping.

"Thomas told me he had several artifacts, including, fourteen Stations of the Cross, marble praying angels, a Nativity set and even the wrought-iron votive holders, all stored in your barn."

The barn and its contents conjured up heavy thoughts from the past. Actual tears welled up in her eyes as she thought of them, and she was shocked to hear that Thomas had shared all of that information with Mr. Codday. Her husband had always been afraid that if the wrong ears would hear that all of it was stored in the barn, and that person would try to break in, maybe even try to destroy some of it.

"Mrs. Frank . . . Mrs. Frank," he repeated, breaking her stare, and pulling her attention back to their conversation. "I'll be proposing to Monsignor Paplana that you have all of those items, and according to Thomas' wishes, all of them should go back to St. John's Parish, if and when they build a new church that will be big enough to accommodate them."

"He told you all of that?" she asked, stunned.

"Yes, and after speaking to your nephews, I have been forewarned that you have locked up the barn, never to want it opened again."

"Mr. Codday, it's true. I said I will never open it again—and I meant it—but if Thomas let his wishes be known to you, I will honor and respect them. If St. John's wants whatever Thomas has stored, its okay by me."

He was surprised that she relinquished her vow so easily, but he knew it must be because the church would need all of the artifacts, and her beloved Thomas' wishes would be fulfilled.

# CHAPTER EIGHTY-ONE

ରୁକ୍ଟର୍କର୍ଜ

$\mathcal{B}$oth Mr. Codday and his associate sat in the back of the room taking notes and compiling figures that were being discussed by Monsignor Louis, as he had asked to be called, and the Parish Council and its President—the position Thomas Frank had held during the last five years of his life. He had taken the post very seriously, as a patriarch to the parish nurturing it as much as he would have a son.

On one of Thomas' visits to Mr. Codday's office he had laid the beginning stages of his grand plan for St. John's, a plan Uncle Jay and he had not had a chance to finish before his uncle's death.

Thomas had told Mr. Codday about the old church from Main Street that he loved so much and showed him photographs he had brought from home, encased in a brown Naugahyde cover.

Thomas had said, *Now, this is the way a church should look. See those high ceilings and the roof peaked even higher, a 'liftin' up toward God? Stained glass windows full of people, not just pretty colors, but tellin' a story, each and every one of 'em?*

*And look here, ya' see those things hangin' on the walls? Well, they're the Stations of the Cross. Talk about tellin' a story—why they show the entire story all about Christ bein' condemned, carryin' His cross, bein' crucified and bein' takin' down from the cross—and they do it without ever sayin' a word. They were made somewhere in Germany in the 1700's. Shipped to the U.S. and were brought down from New York harbor by horse and cart, probably a whole wagon train of 'em. Were put up on St. John's walls in the 1860's and stayed there 'til just before they tore her down.*

*I trust you, Mr. Codday and I'm tellin' you I've got the complete set, all fourteen of 'em in my barn, high up in the rafters where nobody can touch 'em, 'cept the boys, Michael, William, Andrew and Jonathon. They're the only ones that know how my levers and pulleys work to go quite that high.*

*Other things are packed-up in boxes, there, in the barn—Nativity set, complete with ox and ass, is there too!*

*Metal rods that are packed-up are part of a votive holder-contraption, even got all the red, glass cups that hold the candles in place, once it's put together.*

*Now, there are two other very important things—marble angel statues. Got 'em angled, facin' each other, but they're not squarin' off to fight. No, these are prayin' angels, hands folded— one bowin', one kneelin'—in frozen stillness. You call the monument company to move 'em out when you're ready if my nephews or if I'm not around when the new church is built.*

*Some things about me you need to know. Just like my Uncle Jay, I like a good riddle, an interestin' way to tell a story. Like to make people think a little, gets 'em all excited, and they treasure the outcome that much more. Puzzles, love puzzles.*

*Before Jay died, he and I got our heads together— got started anyway, like I said before—came up with a plan. I'm about to lay it all out for ya', so's you'll understand just what we want to happen. Everythin' must be written out.*

*So . . . question is . . . do you really trust that Mr. O'Reilly ya' got coverin' the money Jay earned?*

*I trust him with my own money and my children's money,* Mr. Codday had said.

*'Nuff said then. If you trust him that much, it's good enough for me. Have to say, I got good vibes from him . . . seemed like a good family man . . . said he loved his wife. Heard him say that the first or second time I talked to him, so my thoughts were right. Sure don't want some fly-by-night, some run-around, takin' care of my money.*

*Needed to ask that 'cause he was talkin' about some investments, he'd like to try. My only question is—how will Mary Kathleen and the boys be taken care of, if I'm gone?*

*Wanta' make sure whatever I got to leave behind, gets taken care of by somebody honest and with a good conscience . . . and a good mind, 'ah 'course.*

*So—that's that.*

Then Thomas laid out a grandiose plan that had Mr. Codday raising his eyebrows and shaking his head and laughing, every now and then. He had told Mr. Codday, *now remember, one of your parts of the bargain that you must promise me you'll do, no matter how long it takes, is to subscribe to St. John's weekly church bulletin,*

*the local paper and The Catholic Review, our Catholic weekly
newspaper. Lots of people do, when they move away. Gives 'em a
way to keep up with what's goin' on back home.*

*And I expect you to read 'em, cover to cover, always lookin' for
that sign that'll say that they're gonna build a new church.*

*But Thomas, what will happen if they don't build a new church?*
Alex had heard himself say it, and was immediately sorry that he
had.

Thomas had looked at him sternly and had said, *Codday, ya
know, just last spring, I planted six new cherry trees on my property.
And when I did, one of the men from the Grange said to me—ya'
know Thomas you're gettin' mighty old and there ya' go, plantin'
bare root cherry trees, no bigger, no thicker than my leg— skinny
though it might be. Don't cha' know you'll never get to see the fruit
of those cherry trees?*

*And do ya' know what I told 'em? I told 'em—it don't matter if I
get to eat the fruit of those cherry trees. I'm plantin' 'em for the next
generation and the next and the next. It don't matter if I get to eat
even one cherry.*

*So don't ya' see, someday down the road, Codday, they'll be
needin' a bigger church, and I'm only hopin' to be plantin' the seeds
with this money from Uncle Jay, right now. Patience is somethin'
that comes with farmin'—patience and prayers. And, maybe—just
maybe, Codday— you could do with a little of both!*

Mr. Codday had apologized to Thomas and told him that now,
he had understood.

Actually, after he had heard Thomas' story, he did!

# CHAPTER EIGHTY-TWO

ॐॐॐॐ

## MAY 7, 1983

The convoy of pick-up trucks followed Father Valentine's lead as it made its way to Mary Kathleen Frank's farm in Pleasure Valley.

The air was cool and crisp as the sun shone brightly through cumulus clouds dotting the blue sky.

It was eight a.m.

An inclined gravel road presented occasional potholes. Trees, large and small, were intermixed on the terrain and fern, ivy and underbrush created a dense forest-like impression on both sides.

As they passed through, the farmhouse became visible. The vehicles slowed as they drew near.

Ahead and to the right was a charming cottage with a perfectly manicured lawn, surrounded by a white, picket fence. Off in the distance flanking the back of the house were dogwoods presenting their delicate blossoms from knarred branches.

Inside the fence and to the right was a large circular flowerbed edged out with natural stone, both large and small. Within it, tulips, numbering about two-hundred and fifty in shades of dark royal purple encircled by shorter white specimens, all raised their heads toward the sun. A flowering cherry tree, farther right, bloomed in multiple shades of pink and fluttered to a soft breeze.

To the left, on each side of the walkway and assembled at the mailbox, more tulips were rising, and their colors were duplicated.

Farther left, a crab-apple tree blossomed, its twenty-foot height and fifteen-foot width showed a profuse bloom of delicate, white clusters—its petals floating gently to the ground, having been forcefully kissed by the wind.

Close to the house were clusters of medium pink azaleas dotting the mulch-covered flowerbed, some in bloom and others about to break open, flanked by larger pure-white double-trumpeted rhododendron.

The porch swing gently swayed, beckoning someone to sit a spell and use their senses to take in the sight, sound and smell of the picturesque scene.

All in all, it looked like a Norman Rockwell painting which might have been entitled, "Spring Delight".

Off to the left of their vehicles and down a dirt lane, Father Valentine could see a barn which seemed to be summoning him.

He pondered . . . inside, could there really be the artifacts from the church built in the 1860's, the very artifacts that he had been searching for?

And, if they were there, in what kind of shape could they possibly be? What kind of protection, if any, did they have during the past fifteen years? After all, barns aren't waterproof, and the articles inside had been subjected to rain, snow and hail plus sweltering Maryland heat.

He stopped his car, gesturing to the others as he stepped out to wait where they were.

As he walked toward the house and smelled the bouquet of the garden he touched the velvet edges of the tulip's petals and said a little prayer.

Father Valentine knew what he must do first.

When the door opened, a nurse clad in a white uniform welcomed him, then escorted him to Mary Kathleen's bedroom.

In a quavering voice, steeped with age, Mary Kathleen Frank welcomed him,

"Hello Father, please come in and be comfortable."

She knew he was coming and regarded their meeting with uncertainty.

The barn, her nemesis, would be opened, and all of those memories that she had squelched for so many years would come pouring out.

"Mrs. Frank," Father began, "I wanted to see you first before anything transpired. I understand you've been ill and wanted to be sure that today was a good day for us to enter the barn.

"I've been told that . . . err . . . ah . . . that it's been locked up for some time now?"

"Yes, Father," she said weakly, "After my husband, Thomas, died I couldn't bear to ever go into it again, or, have anyone else go inside. Of course, I still had to see it every time I looked out my window.

"See, Father? Walk over there and peek out. Just push the curtains over to the side, after you pull the blind."

The sunlight streamed in as he did so.

Down below, he saw the flowers, and outside the fence, he saw her nephews and the visitors from Pittsburgh patiently waiting, exhaust billowing from the vehicles they stood near or sat within.

But straight ahead loomed the barn, and he had a different perspective of it from this second floor vantage point, realizing the massiveness of it as it towered even higher.

"Yes, Mrs. Frank you're right, there would be no getting away from it from this spot," Father Valentine said.

"Now, Father, inside that barn, Thomas stored some very special items, I know for a fact, he did. He's got two marble praying angel statues leadin' the way, one on either side, as you walk in. And, there are boxes filled with the old, outdoor Nativity set . . .

Her voice trailed off for a minute, as saying that brought back the memory of how it must have looked. Michael had told her a less gruesome version of how it was after she had insisted—the bodies lying there surrounded by wood shavings, straw and Jesus, Mary and Joseph.

A single tear delicately rolled down her face catching in the wrinkles of her aged skin. Another came and another. Her lip caught one, but she didn't taste its saltiness.

Father put his arm around her and said,

"Mrs. Frank, I sympathize with you for your loss. Even though I wasn't assigned at Saint John's then, I've heard the story and realize how much you had to rely on your faith to get through it all."

"Yes, Father, if I didn't have my faith . . . and my memories," she said.

She couldn't continue to think about the scene from so long ago and changed the subject,

"Getting back to the barn, there is also a box of religious calendars although they're not from St. John's, but you may want them—could sell them if you're tryin' to make money for the new church. Is that right? You're gonna' build a new church?"

"Just as big as we can afford, Mrs. Frank. We are in the hypothetical planning stages right now, finding out what kind of pledges we can get, and collecting the odd pieces that were scattered throughout Carroll County. I had heard that people gave offerings that would be used for the new building for some of the artifacts that they took from the old church, when they were going to raze the building. Of course those were the things that wouldn't fit into the new more modern church or in some cases the items had been donated by the parishioners' ancestors and suddenly those people had something back, something that they could cherish. But, once we had gotten the word out that we wanted to use those artifacts in the new church, everybody gave it all back. Pieces of artwork, marble and stone held in attics, basements or sometimes, even buried, are now being housed in the Parish Center.

We've got a committee overseeing the project. Articles are being cleaned, repaired and polished, while being evaluated as to whether they can be added to the proposed new design. Everyone wants to see all of it in the new church. I'm amazed at the positive response we've had."

"Pardon me, Father, pardon me—but I must say this now, else I might forget—when you said that about the families removin' items from the old church, I mean. Well, that's what Thomas did. They couldn't use the angel statues and the other things in the more modern church, which was built up on the hill, so Thomas wouldn't let anythin' happen to 'em. He was determined to save them.

"Why, I remember it so clearly.

"I knew he was bringin' things from St. John's, to store away. I remember the day . . . Cully, his best friend, and some of his other friends helped him. He had been workin' and workin' out there in the barn, after they left and for days later.

"Then his Uncle Jay came, and Thomas and he installed the stained glass roof out there in the barn and . . ."

Father stopped her.

"Did you say a stained glass roof?"

"Sure did Father. Oh, and there are lots of religious things out there. I think you'll be surprised, and pleased.

"So then, the next day, my nephews, Thomas and his Uncle Jay hung all fourteen Stations of the Cross up there in the rafters. I didn't get to see anythin' that they did during that day It was nighttime when they finished, and his aunt and uncle left, kinda' late, headin' back to Pittsburgh, and all. See, that's where they lived.

"But the very next day he called to me from the barn, *come on over here, Mary Kathleen, I've got somethin' to show ya'.*

"Well, he stood before the huge, closed barn doors. Sometimes, we would go inside through the smaller door, within the big one, but, not this time. He made me close my eyes while he opened one door. I heard a creak and a squeak, and then he opened the other.

"Took me by the arm, *now, keep your eyes closed,* he said, *no peekin'.* Led me inside and told me, *okay, now, open 'em'.*

"It was no longer dark, thanks to the stained glass roof panels, and up there, hangin' in the rafters—seven, on one side and seven on the other—he had hung those Stations of the Cross, from the old church.

"*Oh, my, oh my,* I had said.

"*Thomas. They are beautiful, but what, I mean, what are you gonna' do with 'em?* I'd asked.

"*Honey,* he had said, and I remember word for word now, he said, *I'm gonna' keep 'em here until they come for 'em.*"

Father pulled back and said in an elevated voice,

"He said that to you? Is that right? He'd said, *I'm gonna keep them here until they come for them?*

"Wow that almost sounds like a movie plot."

"Sure did, and ain't that exactly what's happenin' right here, right now, today? She mused, smiling a big, broad smile.

Father Valentine was mesmerized and gathered his thoughts. He said to her,

"Thomas was right. He saw the value of the old, and he knew one day, we would too—would value and cherish those old Stations of the Cross, the Nativity set, and the angels and realize that they were priceless and irreplaceable."

"Father, it goes without sayin', but, I'm sayin' it anyway. Everything in that old barn, I'm donatin' to St. John's building fund. The artifacts, I know you'll use, but, anythin' else you find, you can sell or have to use anyway you like. I'm havin' the boys tear the barn down once you get all of it outta' there so's I won't ever have to look at it, ever again.

"Now, about the Stations of the Cross that are hangin' way up in the rafters—my nephews, Michael, William and Andrew will help you. You see, there are pulleys Thomas put in, and the boys can help you maneuver 'em to get those items down. They're experts at using those and the tall ladders . . . wouldn't want anyone to get hurt. Why they've been scurrying up those ladders since they were . . ."

Again, her mind reverted back to seeing the *boys* when they first came to live with her . . . Michael . . . William . . . Andrew . . . and, of course, Jonathon.

She saw herself picking Jonathon up and holding him like he was her own, the baby she would never have. But now she thought, I can never hold him or touch him or kiss him—ever again.

The tears flowed freely, and Father patted her back gently, as he held her and let her weep on his shoulder, unaware of the trigger.

෧෨෧෨

Both of them heard it at once—gravel kicking up—as a car slammed on its brakes.

The screen door whacked shut, and soon pounding feet were heard climbing the stairs to Mary Kathleen's room.

Air and vibration made the bedroom door move on its own. Fingertips appeared followed by a little knock, and then it opened slightly, as Maggie Fischer peeked her head in.

"Sorry I'm late, but . . ." she blurted and stopped as she saw Mary Kathleen crying and Father Valentine comforting her.

"Jim needed me. He's working on some paperwork. And there was heavy traffic. You know how it goes . . . one cog in the wheel, and the whole day is off, and you're behind."

She walked over to them and Mary Kathleen leaned away from Father to give Maggie a hug and a kiss.

Maggie gave her, her signature squeeze and pulled a tissue or two to sop up the tears.

"C'mon now, you're gonna' get me started, and then between you and me the whole dam will burst."

Maggie winked at Father, who realized how she was trying to make Mary Kathleen laugh. They knew each other and exchanged non-verbal hellos and friendly smiles.

Mary Kathleen looked at her as she shook her head and said,

"Maggie, Father is here to . . . we're gonna . . . er . . . Father's gonna . . . open the barn today."

"Now, sweetie, that's why I'm here—look," she said as she held up four flat steel keys. "Remember, you called me the other day?"

"Oh my, oh my, my brain seems to go in and out," she said sadly.

"Mary Kathleen, you've just got a case of *sometimers*— sometimes you remember, and sometimes you don't," said Maggie, getting her to chuckle and to forget about her memory loss.

Maggie, on the other hand, had no one to make her giggle, to make her feel differently.

And, of all of the keys on Maggie's wall these flat steel keys had brought it all back—all the tragedy, the sadness, that horrible visualization of that day—a day that she would never forget.

She almost didn't add them to her collection, but remembering her promise to Mary Kathleen, she had hammered the little white nails into her wall just like all the others and downheartedly hung both sets. And with that solitary ceremony, the knowledge was reinforced that this tie would be the connecting thread forever linking the Fischer and Frank families to share their depths of despair.

Even though sixteen years had passed, Maggie thought, it was as if it had happened yesterday.

She shivered and shook off the memory.

"I'll stay with you today, while all of this is going on," she told Mary Kathleen, who squeezed her hand and smiled gratefully.

Father Valentine promised to stop by later and left the cottage.

# CHAPTER EIGHTY-THREE

የትታ ኈተ

$S$ix men walked toward the barn. They could see that part of the roof had been elevated slightly when a tree had trailed one of its branches through a knot-hole in the siding. It looked jagged and broken but there was so much debris from neighboring trees that small branches had hidden the view of the exact problem.

Michael and William were anxious to find out if that branch might have broken the stained glass at the roof or, at the very least, affected its molding.

They saw that no grass had grown around the barn's perimeter, only weeds that had flourished up to three feet tall. Dandelion puffs had burst forth toward the front, mixed with a few flowers which had sprouted sporadically—seeded, most probably, by birds passing over.

The path to the barn's entrance, normally clear and unobstructed, proved that sixteen years of neglect can produce a covering of overgrown morning glory vines, thick with funnel shaped-flowers and heart-shaped leaves. They circled round and round, twinning up the sides of the silo that was attached to the barn, wrapping it in tight buds from top to bottom. An unbroken pattern of dense green moss had spread all over the wooden barn siding that stretched across the larger and smaller doors. It proved that no one had entered since its growth began.

Father Valentine, Michael, Andrew and William Frank, as well as Mr. Codday, the attorney, and Mr. O'Reilly, the financial advisor pushed aside the remaining brambles at their feet. After using a sickle and scythe to sever the tallest weeds, they walked closer and closer to the massive doors.

William looked at his brother, Michael, and asked,

"Are you gonna' be okay to go back in there?

"Michael . . . Michael!" William said, seeking to interrupt the deep thought he was in—Michael standing there, staring straight ahead.

"Oh . . . yeah . . . okay, I'll be okay," he answered.

The scene Michael's mind had been surveying from so many years ago was horrible, revealing his brother, Jonathon, pierced completely through by the metal rods from the wrought iron votive holder . . . and the blood . . . and then there was Gretchen.

It had been sixteen years since those barn doors had been opened, and each year marked his furrowed brow, like aging is marked by the number of circles on the stump of a cut tree.

Not one year passed without him dredging up his unanswered questions. Even now, after having tried over and over in his mind to piece it all together, he remained unsure.

The police called it accidental and closed the book on it, but Michael knew Jonathon owed some money to several people—word had gotten back to him—and then there was the assault on Mr. Angelo's daughter. He wondered if . . .

His thoughts were interrupted by William scraping the wooden rake on the ground near him, displacing the underbrush and weeds that they had cut.

Michael motioned to him and gestured toward Andrew.

Both of them turned toward Andrew and could see he was visibly shaken. His pallor was ashen, his mind regressing to his own scene, many years before, by the railroad tracks with Jonathon when he first saw the smoke . . .

*We should go . . . tell the Monsignor . . . we should get help.*

The words resonated in his mind. If only we had—knowing if they had, if he had—none of this would be taking place.

"Hey, Andrew," they said in unison, while Michael wrapped his arm around him, and William patted his shoulder.

"C'mon, we're gonna' deal with this, together. All for one and one for all," said William as they all turned to face the barn.

Andrew heaved an unresolved sigh and began by putting one foot in front of the other.

The iron padlocks and chains on the latches were straight ahead. Rusty, burnished and intertwined with vines which now wove through the eight links on each, they would need additional coaxing or some lubrication from the oil can Michael had brought to turn the cylinders as the keys entered and twisted. He snapped off the ivy, the vines and the honeysuckle that had crept up the wooden siding and suppressed a few drops of liquid onto and into the locks.

William said,

"Ya know, we *can* grab hold of them snips we've got and forget about the oil can and the keys altogether."

Father spoke,

"We could, but I promised your aunt that we would use these keys to open the locks. She mentioned something about ending the ritual she had started."

Father Valentine was getting more anxious, wondering just what incredible finds were inside this enormous building before him. He said another quiet prayer.

The keys from Maggie Fischer had to be forced to turn the cylinders, jimmied back and forth allowing the oil to moisten. Finally, the locks popped open.

At last, they were ready to enter.

As the doors opened wide, they creaked and groaned like a sound effect from a horror movie. A dank, musty smell permeated the air, and they just stood still for a moment gazing into the cavernous expanse.

Cobwebs were everywhere. William found a broom and began swishing it in front and to the sides of the group to clear the area and create a web-free path. Dust was covering the machinery, including the combine, although canvas tarpaulin and burlap partially covered most of the pieces.

The antique tractor sat as Uncle Thomas had always kept it, lined up with the nose of it pointing to the exact middle of the center beam and the large wheels directly across and centered from the corn crib.

Suddenly, just over their heads, about fifty pigeons fluttered their wings and took off in unified flight, leaving through the wide-opened doors, startling Mr. Codday, Mr. O'Reilly and Father Valentine.

Michael said,

"They must've gotten in through the opening that the tree branch created at the roof and then began nestin', here in the barn. See, there's the evidence—droppins' over everythin'—provin' that they've been livin' in here for quite awhile."

As they peered up, they were amazed that the tree branch that had busted through the barn must have gradually sprouted offshoots, creating its own covering for the small hole. All of them saw that it resembled a roof on a thatched hut, weaving onto and into it. They couldn't see through it, even on this bright day, except for one, tiny hole that the birds must have used.

William said,

"Man, will ya' look at that . . . looks like God didn't want to stand in the way of Mother Nature, yet He coaxed her to soften her edges to protect all of these items that were *from* the church, and now, *for* the church."

He pointed to marks on the inside of the barn,

"Look over there—see what I mean. It's obvious from those signs of scorchin' that this barn has been struck by lightnin'. I'd be thinkin' it looks like it mighta' happened several times by the angle of the marks. Lucky she didn't burn to the ground, but I guess God had other plans."

They began to investigate. On the walls were assorted pitchforks, horseshoes and chains. A mirror hung with most of its silver-backing missing. Cans sat on shelves, holding twenty-penny nails and ten, twelve and some thirteen inch spikes about three-quarters of an inch wide. Twisted sisal rope looped around bales of hay exposing jute fibers.

A peg rake leaned against a rabbit hutch, long since vacated. Model-T Ford parts and license plates saved from the Thirties were tacked up on the walls near a vintage Zenith Victrola, still holding its crank, just like the one in the farmhouse.

Balanced over high ceiling beams were zinc-grade 30 chain link that could easily be used to hoist up to thirteen-hundred pounds.

Most of the items housed spider webs of assorted sizes featuring the remaining carcasses of captured moths and gnats and dust close to an inch thick, which conjured up several sneezes as they unveiled it all.

Many farm items seemed to be in like-new condition but they knew that they would have to jump start the engines of the tractor and the combine since they had sat unused, enclosed within the barn for sixteen years.

Father Valentine had heard that her nephews tried to talk Mary Kathleen into letting them move both pieces out to use and relock the barn, but she had said that she didn't care and wouldn't budge.

She just wanted the place sealed off and forgotten. He asked Michael if that were true.

Michael said that she had told he and his brothers, in no uncertain terms, *everythin' is to remain exactly as it is, or, the other option is to light a match to it.*

"And, to tell you the truth, Father, she tried that once. So, ya' see, everythin' just sat here, waitin'."

Father nodded and explored further. There were wooden boxes and their busted lids lying about, cellulose packaging material encasing a plaster star and a baby lamb with a chipped tail.

"Must be part of these other Christmas Nativity pieces that have been unboxed and layin' over here," said William, surveying the area. "Michael, the crosses, and the spires from the stations are in this box. Unks showed me once how the cross fits in the center top. There's a hole in there, and here's one of the little towers—spires, Unks called 'em—that fit on each side of the top. All the finishing touches are right in here."

Father Valentine gazed at the Nativity pieces and lifted the statue of the Baby Jesus above his shoulders. He closed his eyes, hesitated, and then laid it down gently and said,

"Do you suppose even these pieces—this entire Nativity set—are from the 1860's when old St. John's was built?"

The priest continued and gave his own answer.

"You know, they just might be. Back then, just about all of the churches had the complete Nativity displayed just outside their doors.

Gently, he picked it up again and turned it over to look for the designer's name or an imprinted date, but saw none.

He marveled at the sight of the angel statues that were in kneeling and bowing positions. They looked unharmed except for pigeon remains which were old and hardened all over them.

William and Michael took turns telling the others how they were exposed to many of the old artifacts on the barn floor, but were never to play with, or around them.

As William saw all of the pieces lain before them he couldn't help thinking that Uncle Thomas must have unpacked them, never suspecting that it was Jonathon who had, just before his death.

"It just wasn't like him," said Andrew suddenly, thinking of his uncle, "To rip everything apart and just leave it all. Do ya' think?"

William said,

"No, it wasn't like him to do that, but maybe he was gettin' into somethin' when he started to feel bad and then went to the farmhouse to rest. It's the only explanation I can come up with."

Michael nodded and sighed.

"Although," William continued, "He would pull apart the covering, the cloth sacks that he got from the mills, from certain stations that he wanted us boys to see—remember? Had one or two of 'em open for all to see when he called us in to teach us about the workings of the machinery, but before long, he would be sure to point out the part of the story that the station had represented.

"Sometimes, he would let us climb part of the way up the ladder to see the figurines. Always said, *see boys, all hand-carved in realistic detail—now, take a good look at 'em, and don't forget what you saw.*

"I can hear him sayin' it just like he was standing here, right now!"

As they continued to move the items on the floor to go deeper, retrieving the ladder as they went, Father Valentine counted off twelve covered items up high, inside the roof of the barn.

Michael noticed the priest squinting and said,

"Years ago we couldn't have seen 'em even this good, but thanks to the stained-glass roof panels that Uncle Jay installed back then, we can see 'em now. And, ya' know what Father . . . thankfully, when the tree grew and lifted up the roof, it missed that area completely."

Andrew saw the other two shapes in the corn crib leaning up against the wall and each other, with extra layers of burlap from the potato sacks covering them, and he was sure that they were the missing stations. They lifted out the closest one, tore back the top of the covering and saw the Roman numeral, XIII.

Father saw part of the face of it and was thrilled.

Bird excrement was on the front, top and sides inside the loose topping. Mice had created nests in the back within the caverns that were created by the four hollow statues. Straw, mud, and tiny shredded bits of some sort of greenish paper encircled their nests.

They moved it out into the entry way of the barn while trying to remove the debris very carefully, using a screwdriver that Father Valentine had brought in from the glove box of his car.

William pulled out the other tableau that was sitting on the dirt floor, Station number XIV, and brought it next to the one that was being worked on by the priest.

He leaned it over forward while protecting the protruding, delicate faces, hands and feet of the characters in the design.

On this one only the bottom half had what had been open space but now it was tightly packed with thick, almost cement-like mud, overlapping plastic and straw. It housed a nest of some sort, too, a small one, in the bottom left corner,

Andrew let it lean back again and walked away to help Father Valentine clear off their first find very thoroughly, using his pocket knife.

Mr. Codday smiled as they began fitting all the pieces into Thomas Frank's puzzle with some variation—he realized, even he wasn't aware of—but not enough that would have offended Thomas.

Father Valentine couldn't wait to uncover all of the tableaus and thought even though they were wrapped with burlap, they must be magnificent. He said,

"Andrew, will you work on this one by yourself?

"I've just got to get all of them down, right now!

Swallowing hard Andrew said,

"Sure Father . . . I'll do it."

The Priest climbed the huge ladder, one of two that Thomas had kept at the barn. The first had snapped in half the night Jonathon died.

As he removed some burlap, there it was, Roman Numeral X, in all of its magnificence, just as he had imagined.

His main concern was to see what kind of shape they were in after sixteen years in a barn that had open spaces between the lumber. Temperatures fluctuating season by season—below zero and over one-hundred plus degrees—with rain and snow seeping in could have possibly ruined them beyond repair.

Michael walked back into the barn and saw Father Valentine on the ladder. Immediately concerned for his safety, he told him that it would be too difficult to uncover them at that height.

"Let's bring 'em down, as they are. We'll tear off their coverin' and lean 'em against the outside of the barn. Seein' them flankin' each other—their story will come to life."

Father was excited. It was as if Michael had read his mind.

The men knew they would have to use Uncle Thomas' apparatus to gently lower each one. As Father came down, Michael climbed up and hooked a twisted piece of rope through the wire hanger at the top and back of the oblong slab. Wanting to firmly secure the piece, he cut another hank of rope, wrapped it around and securely tied it. As he tugged at it, the station should have given way, allowing the mainstay rope to glide through the system of levers and pulleys.

It didn't budge.

There was mud caked all around the horsehair and wood paste slab. Michael grabbed both sides and tried to loosen the suction that the mud mixed with cellulose fibers and straw had created. He came down and grabbed a butcher knife and carried it up the ladder to cut behind the piece and crack the seal, prying it from the side of the barn.

Michael yelled down to the others,

"Uncle Thomas locked this one in mighty good, wanted to protect it, and not allow it to move at all. It looks like he put layers of actual mud onto the back of this and pressed it onto the wall. Pretty unique idea, and I gotta' say, it really worked. I'm glad of one thing, though—the station didn't break in half when I pried it from the wall."

As he lowered it to them he could see layers of the thick mud in different colors mixed with plastic, signifying that his Uncle Thomas must have stacked onto it at different times.

It was safely down now. They tore off the burlap from its front, and it looked great, except for the dirt accumulation of sixteen years.

Mr. Codday and Mr. O'Reilly each held lanterns and watched, saying nothing.

"There are eleven more to bring down," said Father. "What a gift it will be to have all fourteen stations cleaned-up and hung in the church, if we can afford to build it. I just hope all of them are intact. Their paint is chipping, and I'm sure restoration will be necessary, but, so far, so good."

Both of the angel statues remained as sentinels, blocking the way to put the ladder up to retrieve another station. Before they could bring another down, William was inspecting the first angel statue, deciding how to move it and clean it.

"Let's put these angels on the back of my pick-up truck and take 'em to the self-serve car wash they just opened last week over on Railroad Avenue. Has them pressurized hoses . . . should shoot the debris right off of 'em, and if it works we can hoist each station onto the truck and take 'em, two by two, to wash 'em, dry 'em and deliver 'em to the Parish Center."

Father said,

"The angels are solid marble. How will we ever move them?"

William and Michael looked at each other and grinned.

Michael said,

"Back up the pick-up truck, Will, and let's show 'em."

After coiling them with the heaviest rope, they hoisted them onto the truck using the compound pulley system and fastened them securely. William's truck sank heavily in back, just barely able to handle the load.

"Won't take us long, Father. If this works, every bit of gunk will be removed. It'll save time, and it'll be great!"

Father Valentine and Mr. O'Reilly waited at the barn discussing their find, and they continued to get to know each other better.

William and Andrew followed Michael and Mr. Codday, who asked to tag along, to the car wash. They began hosing the angels down, while both statues sat on the flatbed. Mr. Codday moved, just out of the way so that his suit would stay dry, but remained within earshot.

A Ford pulled into the line, and its passengers' eyes almost popped out of their sockets.

It must have looked strange squirting two angels.

They all laughed about it, making jokes about the, *heavens opening up* and *their dates dropping down.*

*Yeah, they sure were havin' a good time with us, before they got stoned,* one of them said.

One-liners just rolled off their tongues, and as they laughed out loud, the people in the Ford were crackin' up, too.

Mr. Codday was howling while thinking how much Thomas would have liked to have been there.

As the water continued, grey, black, brown and tan muck that had been caked at the base loosened, dissolved and began to pour off while plastic appeared.

"Just like that same plastic that Unks had used that he mixed with the mud on the stations," William said, completing the rinsing of the first angel.

While they leaned the second angel on its side to clear the base of mud, a plastic bag holding another plastic bag fell to the ground. It had been stuffed underneath and inside the hollow part of the statue. The mud continued to rinse off. They saw a small, tan leather book inside which was addressed—Mary Kathleen Frank—and scooped it up immediately.

"Hey, it's for Auntie," Michael said. "It looks like one of Unk's journals that he carried around for years in his back pocket."

Andrew said as he squirted,

"Nothing would surprise me if Uncle Thomas was involved, him and his jokes."

They used a shammy to wipe the book off, keeping the layers of plastic intact and finished their project.

William said,

"Now's there's a lovely sight to behold, two solid, white marble angels, praying, or maybe giving thanks for being found, cleaned and then dried."

They both realized that they would need more help to lift them off the truck and went back to the farm to meet Father Valentine, who was patiently waiting. One of them would have to call several friends to meet them at church to lift off the heavy marble or they'd have to contact the monument company.

Father Valentine had brought the garden hose around and hooked it up near the station that had been leaned against the barn.

"Here Father, let me do that," William said as he stepped back and took the hose.

He began squirting if off, using gentle pressure especially on the delicate, protruding fingers and toes of the statues.

Some of the droppings were coming off and layer by layer the thick mud was as well.

The dimensional figures on the stations usually were hollow, but these were filled with gunk. This one had five people depicted on it. They were standing and kneeling, and their bodies jutted forward the full six to eight inches, which was the thickest depth of the figurines. Each seemed to reach out to you and pull you into their place in time.

Grey, brown and tan dirt turned to mud that looked like lava streaming down a hillside after a volcanic eruption, as it slipped off the statue's posterior.

Plastic started to appear, and several bags encircled with twine dropped out of the back and hit the ground. He continued squirting.

Father Valentine, William and Michael all saw it at once and took turns saying,

"Wait! What is . . . what is that? Is that money? It's money!

"Uncle Thomas hid some money back there!

"It's a one-hundred dollar bill. No wait, it's a bag of money!

"And there's a fifty and a twenty and another one. Look, another and another!" William said, his voice jumping up two octaves.

They kept rinsing, and bags of money poured out. And all of them had, twenties, fifties and one-hundred dollar bills inside.

Suddenly, they looked at one another inquisitively, did double-takes, and ran for the inside of the barn.

In a flash, Michael went up the ladder and quickly attached a rope to the second piece as he had done before. This one, too, had mud caked onto it, sealing it to the wall.

He used the knife to cut away some of the thickest parts, but couldn't pop the seal it had on the wall.

Michael looked down and surveyed the barn floor, saw it, hesitated for five beats, sighed and then said,

"Andrew, hand me that wrought-iron rod from the open box layin' over there."

He remembered seeing one just like it through his brother, Jonathon's body and shuddered as he took it from Andrew, who had climbed halfway up the ladder.

The edges of the station gradually loosened as he jimmied the bar cautiously, yet firmly, on the bottom left and right and finally popped the seal. Andrew guided the hook over using the levers and pulleys, and Michael attached it to the wire hanger after securing it with sisal.

They began to lower the station.

On its way down he saw plastic and mud, just like before. Both of the men were shaking as they rushed it outside. William rinsed. The back oozed mud and more mud and plastic bags emerged.

"Rinse 'em quickly!" Father Valentine ordered, not even hearing himself utter the command.

Sure enough, there were more plastic bags, and as the mud rinsed off they could see the twenties, the fifties and the hundred dollar bills in each one.

The men took turns climbing up the ladder to probe each one, disengage them with the rod, wrap them with rope and lower them into each other's gentle hold. One by one, as they brought them down to the barn floor and squirted, each revealed the same.

They removed the bags and stacked each slab against the overgrown brambles outside, letting them drip dry.

Andrew and William looked at each other, both puzzled. Where could all of this money come from, their eyes seemed to say, as if they could read each other's mind. Finally William said,

"Uncle Thomas was a farmer, a successful farmer, but still, a man of the soil. The only farmers, that I know, who got really wealthy were those who sold their property to developers for shoppin' or medical centers.

William knew he couldn't have saved it from the produce route business—not this much money. Even though it wasn't yet counted, these stations were holding hundreds, no hundreds of hundreds of dollars. He continued,

"I don't understand, why would he put money here and not in a bank?"

As the fourteenth station was rinsed, the plastic bags fell, filled with money, and yet another bag enclosed a book which dropped out.

They carefully removed it from the wet plastic and read the cover—

## WHEN THIS IS FOUND AFTER MY DEATH IT IS TO BE READ BY THE PASTOR AND THE PRIESTS FROM SAINT JOHN'S CATHOLIC CHURCH IN WESTMINSTER, MARYLAND

## THOMAS FRANK

Michael looked at Andrew and said,

"Incredible!

"But, Uncle Thomas died sixteen years ago. He must've expected that the barn would be sorted through if something were to happen to him. Never in a million years would he have expected Aunt Mary Kathleen to lock her up, leavin' all this money out here, to just sit."

William exclaimed,

"Oh my God! . . . Oh . . . my . . . God!

"That's what he meant! . . . That's what Uncle Thomas meant at the hospital!

"Michael, Andrew . . . remember he made us promise *to keep 'em there until they come for 'em?'*

"And then he said, *and mark my words . . . someday they will!*"

"And we all promised, but later, while goin' over everythin' that he said and did, all of us agreed he must have been talkin' out of his head!

"Well I think these stations are the *them* he was referrin' to and all of us includin' Father Valentine, Mr. Codday and Mr. O'Reilly, are the *they who will come for them*, and today is that *someday* to take 'em back to Saint John's Church which is where they belong and are goin' . . . for everybody to see!

Father Valentine was filled with excitement, and Michael, William and Andrew were too as they realized that they were fulfilling their uncle's last request.

The other two men were totally delighted.

After securing some of the fourteen stations, the two angels in layers of burlap and the bags of money they had filled all three vehicles' interiors and their trunks completely with the bounty.

# CHAPTER EIGHTY-FOUR

ॐঔॐঔॐঔ

William had called from the farm to alert Monsignor Louis Paplana, Saint John's Pastor that they were on there way and that it was crucial that he should meet them when they arrived.

Father Valentine was shaking as he steered his car. They sandwiched him between both of the trucks as they drove, as a buffer against typical road traffic. The last thing any of them would want would be an accident along the way.

Mr. Codday and his associate followed, and as they drove up, a puzzled Monsignor Louis met them.

When the emergency brake engaged Father Valentine popped out of his car grinning from ear to ear and hugged his superior. Monsignor Louis pulled his head back in surprise but could tell Father was ready to burst with anticipation as he squealed,

"I can't wait to tell you what has happened."

The Monsignor saw Father's obvious excitement and followed him as he walked to the back of the vehicles. He was astonished while glancing at the magnificent pieces of artwork and the angels on the pickup trucks.

As Father Valentine proceeded to tell the story, the Monsignor's eyes grew wider and wider. Then they popped the trunks and showed him the bags of money they had found which practically knocked him off his feet.

After the explanation was somewhat complete, they showed him the book they found inside the fourteenth station, the last one.

Michael, William and Andrew had recognized it as one of Uncle Thomas' small notebooks that he was always carrying around in his back pocket noting just about everything that took place in a day—the tallies, the weather, and even when he took apart an engine and what he did to fix it.

He saw Mr. Frank's request on the cover of that book and decided to grant that request immediately.

All of them could wait no longer.

It began . . .

Most probably when you
find this book, I'll be dead.
You are no doubt, amazed
at the amount of money
you're seein before you. If I
had seen all of it together,
I'm sure I would feel the
same, 'cause I felt that
way every time I added
more money to what I had
already stuffed away, bag
after bag.
I came by it all very
honestly—want ya' to know
that. And here's how . . .
My Uncle Jay lived in
Pittsburgh and worked
very hard all of his life
and he had a dream.
I think they'd a called
him an industrialist who
made a fortune creatin'
a new invention in the
bottling industry for
a wonderful company,
H.J. Heinz, ya know, the
ketchup king and pickle
man who started that 57
variety company. He liked
what that man stood for
and how he treated his

employees. Hoped to start
his own company like Mr.
Heinz did. And he did,
only smaller
Now Uncle Jay really believed
in banks, unlike me, and
before he died he set up
some kinda trust fund for
my future. I had no idea he
was worth so much money.
Every month his lawyer, Mr.
Codday, would release some
of it to me from that trust
fund. Offered to put it all in
the bank for me, but I liked
goin' up there and gitten it
in my hands. Never saw so
much of it.
I loved Uncle Jay and
looked forward to the days
I shared with him once
a month. (Musta' been
hard on my nephews and
Mary Kathleen coverin
for me every month.) Even
though he could no longer
walk toward the end,
he always had a great
outlook on life. Asked him
to move in with us after
Aunt Rose died but he
always said no—wanted
to stay as independent as
possible. I've always tried

*to follow in his footsteps, specially when it came to my marriage. I saw him treat Aunt Rose with more respect than most men gave to their mothers. He taught me that and told me to be a lovin, faithful husband and that's what I've tried to be.*

His next submission was dated three days later.

*In case you haven't found it, I have more money buried in the ground inside the barn. I usually keep the antique tractor parked straight in. If it's there just move it back 4 feet and you will see a blue marker just barely stickin out of the ground. Dig 3 feet down at that point 'til you hit a metal contaner. That box is for Mary Kathleen in case the money I hid for her in the house ran out. What's buried should take care of her very comfrittably if she should need somethin' else. Mr. Codday, my lawyer, advised me to use the bank*

*for it but I decided against
it. I just don't like banks.
Don't trust 'em since my
Daddy lost 'bout every cent
when everything crashed
in the '30's. I remember
how he almost lost the farm
and his mind.
Packed inside the kneelin
angel is a book for Mary
Kathleen. If for some
reason it gets lost, please
tell her she was the only
woman in my life and that
I loved her from the very
moment I met her.
Dag-nabbit, I'll right more
later again. That dawg-
gone farm is callin' me.*

He had started writing again, this time in ink . . .

*Since you are readin
this I feel fairly sure you
have come across all of
the money I hid in the
stations. It's quite a tidy
sum, but there's more.*

All of them looked at each other, their jaws open in amazement.

*Years ago, after the fire,
when the old church
on Main Street was*

condemned and a new
one proposed, all the
parishioners tried to raise
enough money to build a
traditional style church.
But we just didn't have
enough to do it. So we
built the round one that
everybody goes to every
week.

I made a pledge back then
between me and God. In
my prayers I said, —"Oh
Lord, how I wish I had the
money. If I did, Lord, I'd
give it to St. John's so they
could build a church in
the old style like the church
from Main Street was. Only
it would have to be a lot
bigger than before. Dear
God, I pledge to you here
and now that's what I'd
do."

When I wished that wish
and prayed that prayer I
never dreamed someday
I'd be a rich man. But
thanks to Uncle Jay that
has come true.

My promise still stands to
the church.

All the money you have
found behind the fourteen

*Stations of the Cross I want
to donate in honor of
Uncle Jay and Aunt Rose to
the next St. John's Church
'cause I know we will soon
need a bigger one since
our little Westminster
town's a growin' faster and
faster.
When the time comes to . . .*

He had stopped again, but added words dated the next day-

*build it I only have
one request. Have some
arckiteck make a little
prayer chapel off the main
church and put a couple of
soft, easy chairs in it. Add
stained-glass windows in
there, maybe Jesus talkin'
to the little children and
make sure those windows
get afternoon light, so the
sun shines in with them
pretty colors. The original
windows are in Lester's
barn, or should be—at
least they were.
Make some kind of marker
of sorts to read—
THIS SPECIAL LITTLE ROOM
IS DEDICATED TO THE*

SCHOOL SISTERS OF NOTRE DAME.

Ya' see, they're the ones that taught all of us here in Westminster and I want them to be honored in a very special way, 'course I only went up to the sixth grade—the farm, you know.

People can stop in for a visit and just sit down and talk to God like they are visitin with a friend.

Other than that, please make it as big as the money will allow it to be and try to keep it more like the old church.

Make sure all fourteen stations are securely fastened to the new walls. After so many years of bein' up there on the walls in my barn, I surely don't want anythin' to happen to 'em, though it seems to me God's been protectin 'em all along.

I know it might seem odd but whenever I had problems and didn't know how or where I would find the answers, I would climb up on my ladder, pull back

the burlap and tarp and
say my special prayers.
Sometimes, I would open up
two or three at a time and
leave them exposed while
I did my work. Every once
in a while I'd look up there
and see one of the figures
lookin' down my way and
when I realized His pain, my
problems sure seemed small.
In fact, all my problems
then seemed lighter and
I figured out how to deal
with 'em, one by one. I'm
not sayin' there's any
special magic to 'em, just,
that it sure worked for me.
Why, when the bank was
gonna' foreclose on the
farm because we had a
bad run of luck with the
weather and our crops
dried up, I didn't know
where to turn. I went out to
the old barn and climbed
up on my ladder. Put my
hands straight out and
settled them right on Christ
and His Cross. Stayed there
for a few minutes and told
Him all my troubles. Told
Him about the bank and
the foreclosure notice.

Always thanked Him, too.
Just knew He would help
me know what to do.
Well, the next day, Uncle
Jay calls me to come
see him —talk about a
surprise!
He handed me an envelope
with $20,000 in it. Didn't
know anythin about my
problem, just handed it to
me and said—
This is for the farm
Saved the farm, he did.
Now, just how could
somethin like that come
about? When I told Uncle
Jay about my prayers, he
just smiled and shook his
head. 'God's will,' was all
he said.
After that, every time I
went to see him, Uncle
Jay gave me an envelope.
Always gave it with a
special purpose. Amounts
were always different.

Now where was I?
Oh yeah . . .

Said, this one's for Mary
Kathleen. This one's for a

new piece of machinery.
This one's for St. John's.
He must've known he was
close to dyin' and wanted
to see the smile on my face
each time he gave me one
of em.
Now, I ask you to explain
how all that happened.
Bet'cha can't.
Ya know, when I was a little
boy, it was Uncle Jay who
would hide little treats for
me and then set up a riddle
or bunch of riddles that I
had to figure out before I
got my toy or candy.
He taught me how to
do that and I must say
I always enjoyed it. My
nephews were usually
the ones who I got to use
my riddles on, or Mary
Kathleen, but, Uncle Jay
and I worked this one out
together from his home in
Pittsburgh. Hope your sense
of humor kicks in. It's just
our way to bring a smile to
an ordinary day!

On a separate sheet Thomas boldly printed . . .

*IF YOU ARE STANDIN'*
*WHERE THE LAST STATION*
*WAS FOUND*
*LET THE STREAM SHOW YOU*
*WHERE THERE IS*
*PROSPEROUS GROUND.*

*TO COMPLETE THE RIDDLE*
*WHICH MAY SEEM FUNNY,*
*MAKE SURE YOU DO THIS*
*ONLY, ON A DAY AT*
*NOONTIME, WHEN IT IS*
*BRIGHT, CLEAR AND SUNNY.*

*BEST OF LUCK,*
*THOMAS FRANK*

"Now you know what this means," exclaimed Michael. "Uncle Thomas and Uncle Jay were partners in a follow the riddle, find more money for the church scheme. And men, all of us will have to solve the puzzle."

In the past few hours it had begun to rain, a strong, steady downpour.

It would be a safe bet to say that on the next bright, clear and sunny day all of the key players would meet at noontime at Thomas Frank's barn to play his *game*. They were tempted to pull out the tractor at that very moment, but remembered the note which had said, *make sure you do this only, on a day at noontime, when it is bright, clear and sunny.*

Of course, no one could be told of this incredible find and no one would be. All vowed a solemn oath of silence and prayed for sunshine.

Father Valentine came by to give Mary Kathleen the book from Thomas. He saw that she was asleep and he asked Maggie to come back the next day—*to keep Mary Kathleen company*—was all he said.

# CHAPTER EIGHTY-FIVE

🙠🙠🙠🙠

## May 8, 1983

$\mathcal{R}$ight on cue, the next day the sun was shining brightly, and there were only a few clouds in the sky. It was perfect weather to follow the clues.

This time, Monsignor Louis went along. He wanted to try to piece together the hints and find more answers.

Even more than usual, he had been constantly praying knowing how tough it would be to meet the goals for the church building fund—a massive undertaking. This treasure from Thomas Frank was a windfall he had yet to comprehend.

They all arrived at 11:30 am with adrenalin pumping. Michael held Thomas' riddle and note and climbed to the loft. He was sure he wouldn't see a stream, but he had to check all possibilities. Looking out of a small window that Thomas had added, he saw that no stream was in sight.

Next, each of them stood directly beneath the place where Station XII had been found and tried to discern what the riddle could mean.

First, William moved the antique tractor outside. They scratched the ground and saw it, just like Thomas Frank had said, *a blue marker just barely sticking out of the ground.* Very carefully, they dug down three feet, while not using a pick ax for fear of destroying the metal box Thomas spoke of in his letter. A blue, red and gold circular tin from the Esskay Meat Company was visible. They retrieved it, opened it and saw inside a small tin and inside it, another. Finally, inside the smallest tin from Loft's Candy Company was a small circular wad about six inches in diameter. He had rolled up and rubber-banded, one-hundred, hundred dollar bills! Included was a note which read—*This money is for Mary Kathleen Frank.*

Thomas' nephews started to giggle and Michael said,

"This is his best one yet!"

The priests just shook their heads in bewilderment, trying to understand. Father Valentine asked,

"Why a bright, sunny day versus a dreary day and why at noontime?"

They pondered and talked about other possibilities but none seemed right.

Monsignor Louis wanted to know exactly where the twelfth tableau was found.

William pulled the tall ladder over and set it up just so, for the Monsignor to climb, to observe the spot. The nail was still in place to mark the location.

He touched his hand to the spot where it had been hanging and said another prayer just like Mr. Frank's letter had said he had done on various occasions when he needed answers.

As he finished, he looked down and saw it all, just as plain as could be—five streams of light coming through the prisms of the stained glass roof, at exactly high noon, and the small areas on the ground that they illuminated. The Monsignor asked,

"Can you see it? Could this fit the puzzle? Could it be the answer?"

Mr. Codday watched and waited; Mr. O'Reilly smiled.

Monsignor Louis yelled down to the others,

"Mark all five spots that are illuminated on the ground, and grab a shovel. Grab as many shovels as you can find!"

Andrew began digging fast and furiously. So did William, with the second shovel they found. Michael gently used a pick ax and only dug eight inches down in an eighteen inch circle when he saw a tiny piece of plastic sticking out of the ground. As he dug further, just as he suspected, he found plastic bags—bags full of money.

Dirt began to fly everywhere. Plastic bags surfaced, filled with money from all five holes. At the time they didn't know it but all five spots uncovered over a million dollars in hundreds, fifties and twenty dollar bills.

All seven of them were incredibly joyous, laughing, giggling and smacking each other on the back.

Father Valentine said,

"I can't believe this just happened."

Tears of joy streamed down Monsignor Louis' face.

Mr. Codday re-introduced Bill O'Reilly, the financial advisor who had been a silent bystander throughout all of this, yet offering his muscle as they cleaned and transported the artifacts.

Mr. O'Reilly said,

"So far, this *is* incredible, but there's more to it all, much more. I must say Mr. Jedidiah or Mr. Jay Frank, as we called him, was very wise. He knew his nephew, Thomas, was a good, kind, hard working man who loved his church and his family. But he also knew that Thomas had one flaw, he didn't trust banks.

"In fact, Jay told me that Thomas had a lofty mattress, and at the time that didn't make sense, but after seeing this barn I'd say that we may find some cash—he pointed to the loft—up there too.

Michael, William and Andrew all looked at the ladder and the loft making a silent plan to check it out later.

He continued,

"Jay, on the other hand, realized how money put into the correct investments can compound and grow exponentially over time. Working together he realized that he could rely on me, implicitly, and he knew I would never do anything to betray him.

"Together, we established several trusts to be in force long after his death. He said that he wanted me to invest any and all money that he had earmarked to be willed to Thomas with some cash, actually only interest, coming his way. When Thomas was told of his deceased uncle's wishes, he agreed.

"Somehow, he didn't connect the fact that these investments would be through a banking facility. Just as long as he could, literally, pick up some cash each month, he gave me free reign to invest and manage the trust assets.

"There were some investments that I believed in, and I watched over them like the money was my own. Bought and sold the commodities again and again, as necessary, over the past fifteen years, and I'm happy to report, Monsignor Louis, that the money, totally separate from that which is in this room is nearing the three million dollar mark."

Monsignor Louis' mouth dropped open as he stepped back in shock, clutching at his heart.

"Michael, William and Andrew—there is a special trust for each of you besides the money you received immediately after your Uncle Thomas' death, each totaling one million dollars. It was to be given to each of you at this time when the church representatives were being told of their good fortune. And although there was money earmarked for Jonathon, because of his untimely death, his share will go into a trust fund, an educational fund, for the grandchildren of Thomas and Mary Kathleen Frank"

They were all shocked and looked at each other in total disbelief as they all realized how close they came to seeing all of it destroyed, going up in flames.

Monsignor Louis knew he had been praying quite fervently and specifically for help with the building fund, and he had tremendous faith that God would provide, but never could he believe that it would come in such a unique way and all at once.

"God bless Thomas Frank, God bless Uncle Jay Frank, and may God bless all of you for your commitment to our church and to God. I guess I want to say, God bless you to everyone. I'm so happy right now!" said the Monsignor, full of exultant praise.

Father Valentine said,

"Where is Mary Kathleen Frank? Is she aware of this? Do you think this is her money?"

Finally, Mr. Codday spoke up,

"No, Thomas Frank wrote in a note that Mary Kathleen would be financially looked after through money he had hidden in their house. I know for a fact that we have a trust for her that we set up when she actually found that money, years ago, and called me. He even used his little notes for her hidden treasure, quite a jokester, that Thomas."

He continued,

"Monsignor Louis, he totally and legally willed this money to St. John's and, ironically, for a future building fund he only surmised would happen."

Mr. Codday went on,

"Thomas was adamant about not using banks, but he loved St. John's Parish and was determined his money and his Uncle Jay's would someday build a new church, and now it will. I was not at liberty to speak before, but I have his written instructions and a map as to where every dollar he hid was buried, just in case his riddle wasn't understood.

I had to promise Thomas to let you all play along.

To tell you the truth though, even we, Mr. O'Reilly and I, didn't know about the amount of money he stuffed into the backs of the stations. I get the feeling he's, *up there,* smiling down at us right now knowing he's ambushed us too, and he's as happy as a lark.

# CHAPTER EIGHTY-SIX

ప్ర్ప్ప్ప్

$\mathcal{M}$aggie came back the following day but she didn't see Father Valentine or any of the nephews, only their cars and trucks parked near the barn.

The nurse met her at the door and excused herself.

While the ladies had lunch together, they talked about anything and everything. As the afternoon edged-on, Mary Kathleen's young cat curled-up in Maggie's lap as she fell asleep in an easy chair. Her friend decided to sit quietly nearby and reminisce.

At ninety-three, Mary Kathleen was frail and delicate, and her body was gradually deteriorating as each year came and went. The one thing she had hoped old age would not steal from her she had retained, her mind and therefore, her memories.

Because her recollection was keen, she would often relive the wonderful times in her life when she had been a younger woman caring for her husband and her home.

Happiness surrounded her as she thought of the special times she had shared with Thomas and the holidays they had enjoyed with their nephews, especially the dinners she had prepared for them, so delicious and plentiful.

Of course there were the games that Thomas loved the best. How I loved to watch him as the little ones used their imagination to follow his clues, and then I'd see his thorough enjoyment of it all.

She thought about their picnic lunches that she had prepared and the five bells she had rung.

Our time, our special time . . .

Mary Kathleen remembered how she had saved some of his little notes he had hidden away in the pocket of her dress or in the picnic basket, especially the one he rolled up ever so small and had tucked into the handle.

Releasing a deep sigh, she thought how much she had missed finding his notes.

While she was recalling her past, a strong knock on the door to her room startled her and frightened Maggie causing her to jump up and out of her nap sending Torpedo's offspring scurrying.

It was Monsignor Louis and Father Valentine coming to visit her, but their knock was not as gentle as it was earlier, the day before.

His voice was bubbling out, his grin expansive. Monsignor Louis began,

"Hello, Mrs. Frank . . . Maggie. I hope I didn't overwhelm you. I have quite a story to tell."

He received permission to include Maggie then relayed the tale—the riddles, the streams of light reflecting on the barn floor, the angels, the Stations of the Cross and the huge amount of money uncovered for her and her nephews and for a new church.

It made her happy to hear that her Thomas had been so generous, and she laughed as she thought of him creating the riddles.

"And Mary Kathleen—something special for you to enjoy—he left a book addressed to you."

She abruptly stopped him, "A book?

"Thomas left a book for me?" she asked as her excitement rose.

Her cheeks flushed, and her eyes sparkled once more as she slid on her glasses, ready to read it immediately.

"Pardon me Father . . . please. May I have the book you referred to just now?

"I'd like to . . . no . . . I *must* read it at once. Will you excuse me?" Mary Kathleen said breathlessly.

"Thank you for understanding."

Both of the men backed out of the room and quietly closed the door.

Maggie tucked Mary Kathleen into bed under the brightest light in the room. Whenever she read, magnifier in hand, it was the place she could best see the print.

They said their good-byes. Maggie kissed her forehead and excused herself.

# CHAPTER EIGHTY-SEVEN

∂∽∂∽∂∽∂∽

Mary Kathleen fondled the compact leather-bound book that Monsignor Louis gave to her from her love, Thomas.

It had been over sixteen years, and she almost jumped out of her skin when he mentioned it as part of the story of the bounty left by her husband in the barn.

Everything else that they told her had happened, *out there*, had made her feel great, especially knowing that she hadn't burned the barn to the ground destroying her book from Thomas. For when she heard Father say that there was a book—this book that she now held close to her heart and before reading even a single word—her heart pounded, and she was exhilarated. It was as if he actually stood before her, saying what she was about to read.

She cherished the thought that this was one of the journals he had carried and kept with him and between this book's covers he had penned the words, only for her to see. As she read it through ten times and held it near, she began to add her own thoughts to each scenario that he had written about.

Once again, she read it.

> *Hello, my sweetie. You will be reading this after I've gone.*
> *Please don't be sad.*
> *As I write this I'm thinking of some of our most special times together, that only you and I know the details of—no one else, but you and me. Keep them in your heart forever.*

*First I must thank you for
puttin' our home together.
Know you worked real
hard to make it just so. I'm
thinkin' of all the parts
of it you touched. Made it
look so cozy, like a cottage
in a storybook. And those
meals . . .*

Mary Kathleen wanted to relive every moment she could remember, and she started with the first thing he had mentioned, their farmhouse where she now sat. She visualized it all . . .

The white clapboard siding dotted with so many windows edged with our deep green shutters, still workable, at least they were the last time I attempted to close them, years ago.

Within each porthole I hung a set of white sheer curtains tied back on each side with a finely braided rope that I, myself, made from yarn I had bought at the dry goods store. And the blinds that I had found at J.C. Penney's, which Thomas had installed, were finished with scalloped edges, and each had twine attached to a ring, centered to assure a smooth pull.

Her thoughts danced in her head, and she could see it all . . .

Only four steps led up to the floor of our porch that I had painted battleship gray, the treads too. On it, white wicker chairs and rockers sat to the right, always waiting for the moment when we both could sit and rest awhile. To the left, a swing was suspended by white chain link. She sighed remembering that many a warm night they used that swing and cuddled . . . early on.

Mary Kathleen pictured all of the railings and columns painted glossy white, matching the wooden frames, the gingerbread areas and the rain spouts. Thomas had said he liked how all of that white set off the green roof, she remembered.

Inside the foyer area, she envisioned the stairs, but without her newly added chairlift. The room into which she and Thomas had put their first TV, with the rabbit ears antenna, was directly to the left and straight ahead, the kitchen with the dining room was off to the right.

How glad she was that he remembered that she loved creating in the kitchen, as his note went on to tell her. Every day she put together wonderful meals with five men to feed . . . she longed to do it again.

He had mentioned the wonderful memories of the holiday dinners and two came to mind—Christmas with a sirloin tip beef roast, gravy, mashed potatoes, and fresh green beans and, of course, her special stewed tomatoes. Then there was Easter with its ham, pineapple sauce, corn swimming in melted butter, spinach or collard greens, red parsley potatoes, yams and her own secret recipe for corn bread.

And, oh, she thought, what desserts we had. Thomas' favorite was my strawberry shortcake with real whipped cream or that hot apple pie and, of course, the *boys'* favorite—chocolate pudding.

Reality told her that she couldn't have actually prepared those feasts anymore, but in her imagination she could envision the entire event from planning and shopping to the preparation and presentation.

Thomas' *ohs and ahs* were ringing in her ears exactly as she had heard them, sixteen years earlier.

Before today, before his note, she had only *her* memories that filled her days and nights which were dragging-by ever so slowly, but now, she felt new energy as she read about *his* memories again . . .

> *Am lookin' back over*
> *those holiday meals*
> *specially Christmas and*
> *Easter. You were able to*
> *put it all together so well.*
> *Great food and lots of it.*
> *You sure are a good cook.*
> *Young brides should take*
> *lessons from you.*
> *Can ya remember when*
> *I set up all the flowers out*

front for you? When they
bloomed I loved seein'
you out there surrounded
by the petals of them
flowers. You was like a
dream, my dream, cuttin'
and bringin' in some of
them tulips to put around
inside.

Remember you and me
lookin out the window
and seein both of them
bloomin cherry trees like
the ones in D.C., bustin out
them pink ruffly flowers
you liked so much?

And how about them
white tulips and dark
purple ones in the circlebed
and down both sides of the
steps, anchored by them
big, ol stones I carried up
from the stream.

(Honey-I got a
confession to make.
Did hire a landscapin
company. Told em you
said you wanted your
house to look like those big
old Victorians —over near
Court Street. Had em show
up when you went on that
bus trip to Mount Vernon.
After they dug the holes, I

*did, by myself, work in the
bone meal and place em
just where they told me.)
        Crazy, shoulda told you,
I know it, but you were so
impressed in the spring
when over one thousand
tulips showed up.
        And each day for three
weeks you'd look out
them windows and watch
everything changin.*

Thomas was describing the scene directly outside her window that her nephews had maintained, year after year. But tonight in her mind this entire scene was in her bedroom, surrounding her—so much so—that if she had reached out her hand she would have felt the delicate softness of the azalea trumpets, the silky-satin texture of the tulips, and she could have dusted the pollen from the very fingertip that touched the stamens.

Sleep evaded her. All of these exciting words from her Thomas. But, when did he write this?

So many unanswered questions, but she told herself to be satisfied, after all the book took her back to times before. It had enlivened her spirits and gave her a sense of strength that lately came at a premium. Many things had changed . . .

Mary Kathleen's hair, previously full of copper and blond highlights, had gradually faded into drab pewter. Her ears had lost the keen cat-like hearing that age robs. The once strong back that lifted heavy items now had a crooked bend to it, and her eyes were gradually degenerating, leaving a hazy visualization of the world around her.

Fortunately, while some of her old cronies were drifting in, and out of the throes of Alzheimer's, her mind remained empowered with a sharp memory, and his book stimulated that.

She stopped and said the prayer she prayed each day and added a few new words . . .

> *"Dear Lord, please allow me to keep my wits about me. I might continue to have my problems, can't walk alone anymore, can't hear very good and my eyes seem to be failing me, but Lord, please let me keep my mind rememberin', especially all that I read tonight.*
>
> *Thank you for all you've given' me, nephews honest and true, a long life and, of course, my dear departed Thomas, my one and only true love."*

She looked down at his notes, smiled, and read—

> *Remember the night we went to Beard's and were dancin' up a storm. I couldn't take my eyes off you. You were the prettiest lady there and I loved hearin' that clickety-clack of those high heels you always wore. But what I remember most- I couldn't wait any longer and I said to you—let's get out of here. Remember what happened next?*

Her lips curled up at both corners as she remembered . . .

> *Then in winter we would slide down the chute from the grist mill after it was frozen over. I couldn't wait for you to come slidin*

*down into my arms. You
knew I'd always be there
to catch you, and I did,
didn't I?*

She said aloud,
"Yes, yes Thomas you always did."

*Course I loved takin you
to the State Movie Theater
especially when there was
a love story playin . Why
it'd be givin me an extra
special reason to be able to
put my arm around your
soft shoulder. Seems like
the evenin' turned magical
for us, just like the magic
happened on the screen.
Do you remember?*

Tears came to her eyes as she reminisced.

*But, my most favorite times
with you were when we had
our picnic lunches out in
the field. You were so sweet
to prepare it all and bring
it on out to me. Sometimes
I'd hear our signal, the
five bells, and I'd turn
the tractor so's I could
watch you walkin across*

*the wheat field—coverlet,*
*picnic basket and a big*
*smile.*
*Like I was seein an angel,*
*my angel, walkin towards*
*me.*
*I always liked seein how*
*happy you got when I wrote*
*one of my little notes and*
*hid it for ya.*

Mary Kathleen shifted in her bed and laid the book aside. She began to shimmy to its edge and dropped her feet over the side without calling her nurse to assist her by ringing the bell at her bedside as she was instructed to do.

As her feet hit the floor, she staggered, waiting for better balance. Her toes just missed Flurry who stretched and sauntered by, giving up a waggle, relocating to a soft pillow sitting on the rug. Grabbing onto the bed for support, she inched her way to its bottom and shuffled four steps to the chest of drawers that had an attached mirror edged in wooden trim.

As she gazed into the looking glass, her eyes saw a shriveled woman, but her heart and her imagination were about to show her a different mental picture.

In the top drawer near the back she retrieved the wooden box with the lid that he had carved a heart onto. Somehow, she balanced it haphazardly while she carefully made her way back to her bed and sank into the down comforter with a noiseless plop.

Opening the box, she saw before her bits and pieces of paper, some flat and neat, some crunched and then straightened. There were match packs, napkins, even a tally from the Tractor Supply Company and one note on the back of an International Harvester receipt.

All of them shared the same legible handwriting—that of Thomas Frank. She read each one . . .

*Sure looked pretty today*
*honey.*

*Ham is always sweeter*
*when you fix it.*

*Movie at the State tonight?*

*Got an extra special twang*
*from that hot mustard*
*today.*

*Sorry for the quick lunch.*

*Wanna' kick up your heels*
*at Beard's on Friday?*

*I'm lucky to have you,*
*dearie*

*Can't wait to hold you*
*again later.*

*Can we tuck in early*
*tonight?*

And at least twenty pieces of paper with the words-

*Honey, I'll always love you.*

As each paper piled on top of the other she began to paint a picture of what had been—the kitchen, the picnic basket, the sandwiches and both thermos bottles. Mary Kathleen's memory heard all five bells ring just outside the kitchen door. She imagined her back, strong and straight, lifting the picnic basket and the blanket and her legs, firm, scampering down the back steps and lilting through the field. Her blue eyes, now bright and clear, watched the cloud of dust subside as Thomas parked the tractor across the rows of corn, creating a private, open space. She saw herself wearing that short-sleeved, rayon dress, in shades of azure blue with buttons all the way down its front, the one he liked best.

And there in her mind's eye was Thomas greeting her warmly as his muscular frame shook the blanket in the air and guided it to the earth. She smiled as she motioned for him to recline.

The steam from the thermos rose as she opened the lid, but she wore no glasses that could have become fogged.

Fantasizing, Mary Kathleen poured the water on the first cloth. She saw herself soft-skinned and unwrinkled, gently caressing Thomas' face and tanned neck with the soapy cloth and then rinsing the lather from him with another hot, wet towel. Taking his hands into hers she looked down at them—neither set were veined, spotted or withered. Lovingly, she pictured how she wiped each hand and all ten fingers separately, allowing him to feel the gentle sensation of her touch. First she kissed each finger, and then she tasted his kiss with younger lips, full and supple. His caress was firm, yet tender, his arms encompassing and strong.

The slide show of the afternoon progressed, and she relived each and every wonderful detail as if it were happening at that very moment.

Immediately she inhaled and imagined that she could smell the green stalks holding un-ripened corn and the wonderful fresh scent of wheat grasses as she had remembered them while walking back to the farmhouse towing the coverlet and basket. She could feel the wind ruffling through her wavy, shoulder-length hair. Reaching her hand upward she used her fingers to re-create the ruffles, and she was sure that her amber and gold highlights were glistening in the sun.

Once in the kitchen she saw herself searching for his note, and upon finding it and reading it, she remembered how she had pulled out the heart-carved wooden box from the oak kitchen cabinet with the porcelain top and stacked the newest words onto the existing pile.

A big smile emerged as it always did when she had closed the box, had hooked its latch and had stashed it away.

In her visualization, when Thomas had appeared in the kitchen, later in the day or sometimes into the early evening covered with the farm's soil, she thought that he looked as young and as handsome as ever. A warm blush colored her cheeks as she conjured up what she would have said—*I found your note. Oh Thomas, it sounds so wonderful.*

Painting a picture of it all, she imagined and then remembered that although a kiss might have been on his mind, instead he'd have reached for my fingertips preparing to spin me around like his own Dresden doll while humming our song, "Stardust".

Craggy sounds of the tune emerged from her throat, but her ears heard only the perfectly pitched melody, and she saw herself as always, on tiptoes, as she'd spun like a ballerina. She saw him wink and heard their laughter. And ever so clearly, she heard him say . . . *honey, I'll always love you.*

Tears came to her eyes as they always had whenever she played out this fantasy, this youthful dance of love and affection. But now, she had his book to reread each day. Even though she missed Thomas desperately, because of her strong faith she knew in her heart that eventually they would always be together.

Someday, she thought, they would have their own special picnic again, and afterward he would take her fingertips, gently into his, and he would lead her twirling on tiptoes while he hummed a love song to her. Then he'd stop her and watch as her hair would spin and caress her cheek.

Thomas would look into my clear, blue eyes and he'd say—

*Honey, I'll always love you . . . always love you . . . always love you . . .*

# CHAPTER EIGHTY-EIGHT

ॐॐॐॐ

*E*arly the next morning, the knock on the door startled Mary Kathleen, jolting her out of her dreamlike state.

Flurry snarled, kept her chin to the floor and gave up a weak bark, and then a waggling tail forgave all.

Her nurse apologized for the interruption as she checked her vitals, using a stethoscope, a blood pressure cuff and fingers at the wrist.

"So, am I still alive?" Mary Kathleen kidded. "If you say yes every time I ask, I'll believe ya."

They started their morning ritual—toothbrush, face cloth and towel, cleanser and the moisturizer that Maggie swore by.

"A note I got in the mail, years ago, from one of Thomas' friends said, *as long as I don't see my name in the obituary column, it's a good day.*"

Both of them had a good laugh, and they heard a gentle knock.

Pushing open the door revealed William, full of smiles.

"You two are just havin' way too much fun . . . without me, that is."

"What's this about a good time, I'm hearin?" Andrew asked, sauntering into the room with his young son, Johnny while walking past William. Behind his back he held a huge bouquet of flowers. Before he could surprise her, William grabbed them out of his hand and said,

"These are for you, Aunt Mary Kathleen. Picked 'em myself."

"Hey, wait a minute, William," Andrew said, reaching for them as he clawed his way onto William's arm and shoulder. Both of them tussled with that Frank family playfulness.

She smiled as she said,

"Some things never change, and I'm sure glad for that."

Her nurse had finished and as she left, Andrew and William blew her a kiss, then gave all of their attention to their aunt.

The two of them gave Mary Kathleen a group hug, as they mimicked fighting over her for individual heed, then took their turns one by one.

Did she love it when they fussed over her?

She appreciated each and every moment they spent with her, and replayed them as little children under her watch, when she saw them clowning around.

God chose not to send her infants of her own, but instead opened the door to four youngsters she could parent and love. Sometimes, she wasn't as patient as she had hoped to be, but she did her best, and saw them grow into young men, full of love and appreciation for their life and their faith.

She thought of Jonathon and wondered why his life had to end so young and so tragically, but, knowing she had no answer, she said a quick prayer for him and encouraged his namesake,

"Johnny, come on over here, I need one of your hugs!"

As he walked toward her, she remembered . . .

The book! It had slid under her coverlet next to her. She had wanted to protect it, and she wasn't thinking as she turned away from him, hastily, and hurriedly tucked the book into her pillowcase, safely nestling it behind her.

He was puzzled by her action and stepped back from her.

While she wriggled her back deeper into the pillow—knowing what treasure she guarded—suddenly there was a sheepish knock on her bedroom door. All heads turned toward the sound. Then another and another, until she heard three distinctly different degrees of tapping.

She became preoccupied and forgot about Johnny and the hug.

"Come in," she said.

As the door creaked open, in came three boys, stair steps in height, weight and age. They all ran to, Auntie, as they called her and smothered her with kisses and hugs, each of them offering a little homemade package to her while Johnny just stood there.

Kory, Kacy and the youngest, Lee, who was named in her honor, all proceeded to unwrap their gift to her, cookies, cookies and more cookies—all different, all unique.

As they each sampled their offering and shared them with Mary Kathleen, Uncle Willie, Uncle Andy and their cousin Johnny, passed over the cookies and said,

"No thank you."

Mary Kathleen was oblivious to it all.

The door creaked open again.

"Daddy," the three boys squealed.

"Mommy," they screeched, as they saw Michael and a very pregnant Gretchen using two canes as she ambled in.

"News flash," Gretchen said, as she hugged, Mary Kathleen.

"We just came from the doctor, and you were right, Auntie, the sonogram showed twins, and girls at that, two little swimmers, full of energy, finding their spots to nestle into for the next few months."

Everyone celebrated with hoops and cries of delight, except the little ones who didn't quite understand it all.

"My Mom and Dad don't even know yet, but I heard they were coming over here today and . . ."

"Hello . . . What's this I hear?" Maggie asked as she and James popped their heads in just then and joined the festivities.

Gretchen was bubbling over and giggled out their news, as she hugged her parents.

Maggie yelped,

"I had a feeling! You were getting very big, very quickly.

"And girls—wow—now that will be a big change around here, eh, Mary Kathleen. The boys will be movin' over when the princesses arrive."

Johnny's eyes grew as big as saucers, trying to understand where he stood in it all.

"Jim did you hear that? We're gonna' have one for each knee!"

James just grinned from ear to ear!

Gretchen said,

"Michael and I have already picked out their middle names —Elizabeth and Lorenna!

Mary Kathleen shook her head as she said,

"Your Uncle Thomas would be so happy, but, then again, I'm sure he is lookin' down on all of us celebrating right here, right now.

"That reminds me—just last week, Andrew and William brought various mementoes down from the attic, which Thomas had pigeonholed. He had Civil War memorabilia laid-out up there with everyone's name attached, as not to forget anyone, seemed to be sortin' through old clothes, too, they told me.

"Kinda' surprised me. Makes me wonder if he had an idea that his heart was gettin' bad. Never did tell me anythin'.

"Now, Andrew, fetch those boxes from the closet holdin' all of those things you and William were droolin' over.

"Those are the items that Uncle Thomas wanted each of you to have. He also listed 'em in the book he left for me, the book from the angel statue out in the barn."

She retrieved it to ensure accuracy and held it out at arm's length to read the smaller print.

"First of all, Michael, he wanted you to have the Confederate sword, inscribed with an artillery scene and the name, Johnson, on it, captured at Gettysburg and a Union Cavalry officer's saber, with scabbard.

"William, he listed a Bowie knife, sheath, belt and belt plate with the initials, C.S.A. on it and Andrew, because of your military experience, a Colt revolver, holster and a cartridge box and a bullet mold.

"Now the tassel, the ribbon and the original black, crepe rosettes from the funeral train—you'll all have'ta divvy 'em up amongst yourselves."

Michael spoke up,

"Mr. Codday told us that Uncle Thomas and Uncle Jay put aside money for us, money that we could only dream about. And now, these things too! We never—and I'm speakin' for all of us—never expected anything like this.

"Aunt Mary Kathleen, you took us in when we were so needy. And you and Uncle Thomas, worked so hard to put a roof over our heads, to feed and clothe us, to teach us right from wrong and to give us a Catholic education. At that point, the rest was up to us to make whatever . . . to be whatever, each of us decided. Yes, the rest was up to us!"

"Oh, now hush Michael, you're gonna make me cry. I know you appreciate it all and even with all of my mistakes, I did my best, and I love you all!

"Now let's just move on. That reminds me, Andrew, get me those smaller boxes that were up in the attic."

In a flash, he was back and handing his aunt the parcels.

She called Maggie over and gave her an embrace this time and then handed her an old tin.

As she opened it, her eyes filled with tears.

"My, oh my, this is the key from Great Uncle Thaddeus' key ring, the one that was in the photo from your album, Mary Kathleen!"

"Yes it is . . . Thomas wrote a special note to be sure you would have it."

"Oh, thank you, I'll cherish it," she said as she clutched it to her heart.

"But, I know how much it must mean to you—your heritage, and you've got, your nephews—its part of your history."

The thought popped into Maggie's head . . . could it really have been the key to the safe on Mr. Lincoln's funeral train?

"Hush now, its fine. They're okay with my givin' it to you, want you to have it. In fact, these are for you too."

Mary Kathleen handed Maggie a larger box. In it was a ring of keys. She smiled at her as she said,

"Maggie, this is the actual ring holding the group of keys that you had seen on Thaddeus' belt in the old photos."

She was stunned, never knowing for all of these years that Thomas had that ring and these keys. Scratched on them were dates and the initials of the railroads that they were from—B&O, NCR, PRR, PW&B, WMR and USMRR. Full of exuberance, she envisioned another project, as she marveled at their similarity, yet their uniqueness. Maggie put that project on hold for the moment and said,

"Wow, just look at this wonderful gathering, this family, so strong, so full of love. Isn't it amazing that all of us, the Franks and the Fischers, originally came together because of a key to an old church, now gone forever but kept alive in our memories."

Michael spoke,

"And now, there'll be a new church, built much like the original—the original that my great-grandfather baked all the bricks for and then delivered 'em to the masons. Course it will be larger, much larger, thanks to Uncle Jay's generosity and Uncle Thomas' foresight, keepin' all of the artifacts safe.

"And inside that new building," Mary Kathleen began, "As I close my eyes, here and now, I can visualize it all, the stained-glass windows, those two marble angels, the wrought iron votive holder and, at Christmas, the Nativity figurines, the evergreen trees and the swags. On each side of that consecrated building, I can see seven Stations of the Cross—incredible relics, facing each other and keeping alive the most important story we will ever be told.

"Yes, I can see it completed as Thomas wanted it to be."

Maggie reached in her purse and opened the black velvet fabric surrounding the old key, inscribed with the date, 1865, and held it up for all to see.

"Don't usually carry this, but something told me to pull it off the wall.

"This is it—the key that started it all. I'll always remember the generosity of Cully Anderson through his granddaughter Theresa, who gave it to me, and I remember when he first told me that it was from Saint John's Church, right down on Main Street.

"Little did he know it would unlock hidden treasure in the lives of two families, allowing them to intertwine and grow for generations to come. If I could see him today, I would thank him and tell him, it was truly a key to love."

# CHAPTER EIGHTY-NINE

❧❦❧❦

## DECEMBER 1983

$\mathcal{E}$veryone was in what seemed like controlled chaos. Michael announced that it was time to leave as William flicked off the lights and the radio, squelching the strains of 'Every Breath You Take' by the group, Police.

As the last car left following the pick-up trucks, a procession was formed leading back to Route 140 and Sullivan Road. All arrived safely and scurried inside.

This week between Christmas and New Years had brought distant relatives to visit, and therefore they would be able to attend the ceremony, and later, the celebration.

❧❦❧❦

The lane leading to the church withstood the wind blustering through, as if on a camera's rolling tripod. Trees were bowing, and leaves scudded. Its intensity rolled onward toward the masterpiece, and as it neared the heavy glass doors at the Narthex of the Church, it blew them wide-open.

The parishioners, feeling the accentuation of its power, turned in awe to see the debris it was bringing—the vortex splitting and depositing it into three piles just outside the open doors as the air current progressed alone and into the church.

It accompanied and almost encompassed the entire Frank family—William, Michael, Gretchen, their three boys and Mary Kathleen, holding both girls and being wheeled in by Andrew, flanked by his son, Johnny. They proceeded down the center aisle.

The soft chiffon of Gretchen's dress caressed the back of her legs and wrapped her canes while her hair feathered forward. The men's suits plastered against their backs while the little boys were turned sideways from the tremendous force of the draft. Mary Kathleen shrugged her shoulders higher to screen the wind from her neck and wrapped the blankets tighter around the little ones. Andrew and Johnny locked their legs and stood firm.

They all protected the Offertory Gifts they were carrying, first and foremost, as they approached Monsignor Louis at the altar. His Alb and Chasuble fluttered from the ongoing gust.

Although they all felt the cool edge of the wind touch them, they continued on as if nothing unusual was happening.

James and Maggie Fischer sitting in a nearby pew witnessed it, and they too, saw the vestments of the priest and the altar boys sway. They felt the icy breeze touch them, occasionally edged by a warm blast, and sensed what was happening.

Maggie looked over at Cully Anderson and his now adult granddaughter, Theresa. They all smiled, and he winked hello. Maggie knew that because of them, this day was taking place, and that although he may be old and frail, he looked alert and aware. Later, both of them would join in the festivities at the farmhouse, for today, following the Mass, would be the first, actually the first *two* Christenings to take place in the incredible edifice that Thomas and Jay Frank's money had funded.

The timing was a bit unusual for the twin's Christening, normally it would have taken place only a few weeks after their birth, but Gretchen had to undergo surgery, and her recovery was slower than expected. While she recuperated, her mother and father kept her abreast of the development of Saint John's Church, and she hoped it would be ready in time for the girl's first Sacrament.

⊱⊰⊱⊰

The dedication of Saint John's Church took place at the opening of the Advent season, four weeks before Christmas. Mary Kathleen was not able to attend, she was ill. Today was her first glimpse of the interior and its incredible splendor. Great attention to detail—just as it had been done to its predecessor, the original church from the 1860's on Main Street—was lavished on this new building.

Tall and stately evergreens flanked the interspersed small and medium Scotch pines, which set up the backdrop for the resplendent white marble altar, pulpit and two praying angel statues facing each other. The evergreens' graceful branches gently swayed, kissed by the touch of the breeze.

Above the parishioners, high in the eaves, were swags of pine, spruce and fir, wired and draped from one side to the other, precariously placed there by a devoted team of Sacristan volunteers. As the puffs of air blew, the swags swung tenderly—their fragrance crisp, clean and distinct as it filled the church.

Candles, hundreds of candles of varying heights and widths were positioned throughout the Sanctuary, the altar boys having started thirty minutes before the service to light the abundance of tapers. Flames flickered, but none went out!

Crimson poinsettias and bows punctuated the setting, adding a brilliance of color that finalized the overall scene. Petals, of both red and green, fluttered.

On its walls, in all of their incredible beauty, hung the fourteen Stations of the Cross that were kept in Thomas Frank's barn for sixteen years enduring rain, snow and sleet and sweltering heat. Thomas had saved them from their demise, sheltered them and then housed the bounty he packed within each one.

And the stained glass windows, stored at Lester's barn diffused the sunlight, which showed them in all of their magnificent color and their depiction of a place in time, long, long ago.

The Crèche and its inhabitants, no longer hidden away in boxes filled with excelsior, were here today, the predominant focus of the Christmas season. All of the characters previously displayed on the outside of the old church because of their large size, were now dwarfed by the sheer dimension of this new building. They fit perfectly inside, in a cave-styled stable, to the left of the altar.

After the Consecration and the Communion, but before the final blessing, the twin girls of Michael and Gretchen Frank would receive the Sacrament of Baptism before the congregation, naming them Madison and Mackenzie.

It seemed fitting that the wind would make its presence known—the dueling gusts dancing, touching the highs and lows of the interior as it snuck through a sliver of opening between the doors—displaying its sheer power while creating a slight whistling sound. It was a sound that blended to make the music seem sweeter as notes bellowed from the original pipes that had been saved from the Main Street organ much like the one before it, glorious, both inside and out.

Wind and music danced in unison until the ushers secured the main doors, putting an end to the opening, and therefore the wind that the catalyst had created.

As the Frank family handed the unconsecrated bread and wine and the parish offerings to Monsignor Louis and turned to take their seats, they faced the rear glass doors, hearing the strains of 'O Come All Ye Faithful' being sung by the choir.

The sun gleamed through those doors, one of the strongest statements that God sends, its rays emanating to the earth like straws that He uses to pour down His goodness to us all. These were glorious rays of sunshine, like those slanting through the stained glass roof panels of Thomas Frank's barn to point out each hidden bounty, a bounty which allowed this building to come to fruition.

Although Mary Kathleen's eyesight was challenging, she could see the majesty of the structure she was in and knew her husband must be content to see that his oath to God had been fulfilled.

As she sat in the pew, she could touch the solidness of the oak, smell the aroma of incense, hear the strains of the music but, most of all, feel the presence of her love, Thomas, who made it all possible.

On her lips she could taste his ever so tender kiss generated by the friskier breeze that had touched only her. In her ear she could hear him whisper, just as she had heard him whisper in the fields, in their home and now, here, in the new church . . .

"Honey, I'll always love you."

## THE END

ॐ๛ॐ๛ॐ๛

# THE HISTORICAL
# CHRONICLE

**The following is the actual story of Saint John
Catholic Church as it relates to my novel.**

**I researched it to the best of my ability.**

**Any error or omission of information was purely
unintentional.**

 codebase·ନ·ନ·ନ·ନ·ନ

This is the oldest photo of the parish buildings that I was able to acquire. It pictures Saint John Catholic parish, circa 1910, located on Main Street in Westminster, Maryland. From left to right are the rectory, church and school sitting on a dirt road, with a horse and carriage parked in the front.

John Orendorff, a stone mason, donated over 500,000 bricks, baked on his farm on Bachman Valley Road for the construction of the church building. The bricks were hauled to the site by a six-mule team. The cornerstone was dated April 18, 1865.

"Courtesy of the Historical Society of Carroll County, Westminster, Maryland"

Saint John Parish, circa 1950. The vintage cars, cement road, paved schoolyard, parking meters and electrical lines attest to the era.

"Courtesy of Saint John Catholic Church Library, Westminster, Maryland"

The next two photographs show the interior of Saint John Church, both taken during the Christmas season. The first photo, circa 1900, is displaying the numerous evergreens and their proximity to the candles. There were so many candles that the altar boys began lighting them thirty minutes before Mass.

After a repainting in the 1930's, the interior and the decorations were more simplified . . .

St. John's Catholic Church Westminster, Md.

As recounted by editor, Deacon Mark Ripper in his book, *Our History . . . Our Legacy,* this is the actual story of what happened to the church on Main Street, as described by Reverend Stephen D. Melycher—

"On Thursday June 19, 1952 at 4:45 p.m., "The Storm" hit Westminster. The weather had been unusually hot, up in the ninety degree range. Then the temperature dropped several degrees within a few minutes. Heavy rain moved in from the west. High winds followed the rain and with them came a spectacular play of lightening and a twister.

"Simultaneously, a bolt of lightning struck our once beautiful steeple and broke it in half, and the twister picked up the top half and threw it upon the roof of the rectory next door. The steeple's bottom half, torn from its foundation and pushed off balance, tottered and fell through the roof of the church."

The story continues as recounted by Lester Stem, now deceased, who had been a devoted parish historian and whose family has been active for eight generations in St. John parish. His great grandfather was John Orendorff, a stone mason, who in the 1860's baked 500,000 bricks that were to be used to build the church. He transported them, trip-by-trip, to the Main Street location using a wagon and a six-mule team—

"Another priest and pastor from 1950-1953 was Reverend James A Dwyer, whose mother was sitting on the front porch of the rectory as the storm was approaching. As the winds grew stronger, Mrs. Dwyer decided to go into the rectory and back into the kitchen. Just minutes after she had left the porch, the strong winds of the storm toppled the steeple which crashed through the porch and the front part of the house where she had been."

Amazingly, no one was injured.

Destruction caused by the windstorm . . .

"Courtesy of the Historical Society of Carroll County, Westminster, Maryland"

Parishioners viewing that destruction . . .

"Courtesy of the Historical Society of Carroll County, Westminster, Maryland"

Saint John Church on Main Street was repaired and many blessed events continued to take place until architects found the church to be structurally unsound.

Following this discovery (the cost estimates and the possibility of expansion) several meetings were held and a vote was taken by the parishioners.

It was decided that the church was to be torn down.

During the interim, and until a new, more modern church was built, the congregation worshipped at Mass at Baker Chapel located on the Western Maryland College campus (now known as McDaniel College) and the Saint John School Gymnasium.

Although the new church had its own advantages, many of the parishioners pined for the traditional church that had been built in 1865.

The following photo shows the more modern structure that became Saint John Catholic Church on Monroe Street in Westminster, Maryland. It was dedicated in 1972 . . .

Although some of the original artifacts were too traditional in style for the new building, many proved to be timeless. The following three statues continued to be used in the more modern church on Monroe Street.

This example is made of solid marble and portrays *the Sacred Heart of Jesus* . . .

This statue of *Mary, the Blessed Mother of Jesus Christ*, was original to the Main Street location . . .

"Courtesy of James Buckley, Manchester, Maryland"

Saint Joseph, the husband of Mary, was also an original from the Main Street location. He is shown holding the Christ Child. Notice the innocence of the baby as He pulls on Joseph's beard . . .

"Courtesy of James Buckley, Manchester, Maryland"

⤜⤛⤜⤛⤜⤛⤜⤛⤜⤛⤜⤛⤜⤛⤜⤛

# THE
# "MIRACLE"
# BEGINS

⤜⤛⤜⤛⤜⤛⤜⤛⤜⤛⤜⤛⤜⤛

Part of this incredible story was told to me during a four-hour interview with Mary Elizabeth Crone, at the age of ninety-three.

Her memory was razor-sharp!

❧❧❧❧❧❧

Lawrence Crone and his family were living in the parish of Saint Lawrence Catholic Church, located in Jessup, Maryland, when interstate highway Route 95 was proposed by the government. It was to run directly through their property. Lawrence and his wife, Mary Elizabeth, fearing their land would be taken from them and realizing they could not impede progress, decided to sell their property.

Mary Elizabeth stayed in Jessup while her children continued studies at the parochial school. Her husband ventured north and purchased land, including a house and a barn, in Westminster, Maryland.

In 1969, St. John Church, located on Main Street, was being readied for tearing down. The last Mass had been celebrated on February 4, 1968.

Lawrence Crone, not yet a parishioner and with no knowledge of what was taking place, walked into the church with the intention of signing up to become an usher. Instead, he found himself witnessing an exodus, with items being carried past him. Curious, he asked what was happening.

He was told that parishioners were allowed to purchase old church articles that were not to be used in the new, more modern church at the Monroe Street site. The money raised would be used to purchase items needed for the newer church.

Lawrence had always cherished religious articles and, noticing that no one was addressing the tableaus on the walls, he asked the pastor if he could have the Stations of the Cross. Reverend Francis McGuire agreed.

The stations were four feet by six feet tall, with finials, a centered top cross and ornate carvings across both the top and bottom. Up to six characters had been placed in each scene, all molded of horsehair and wood paste, creating a three-dimensional design. The depth including the body of the stations and the figurines totaled about eight inches. Looking at one of the stations from the side you would see heads, hands, arms, noses and even toes jutting forward, which made them more realistic, their story, more heart-wrenching.

Because of their delicate design, he had to wrap them securely as he transported them, one-at-a-time, by truck to his new farm.

Lawrence fastened some of the stations to the flat portion located inside the rafters of his barn. Still other stations were stored, back-to-back, in the corn crib within the barn. Some were protected by burlap he had carefully wrapped around them.

About two weeks after the stations' relocation, the Crone family moved into their new home on the farm.

Lawrence asked his wife to come out to the barn.

Mary Elizabeth told me,

"He opened up those barn doors, and I saw the Stations of the Cross hanging up there. I just stood there in awe as he told me how they came to be there, and I said, Oh, my God, Larry . . . why, they are beautiful! And before I could say another word, he said, 'Honey, I put them up there and I want 'em to stay there until they come for them.'"

When she said that to me, I was amazed! I couldn't believe what I was hearing. It reminded me of a movie, so I asked her,

"Did he really say, 'I want to keep them there until they come for them'?"

Mrs. Crone said,

"Sure did, and that's exactly what happened. It was three years after my husband died when Father John DoBranski and Jim Judge came with the other men. They made a vehicle caravan, and they took the stations back to St. John's, just like my husband said they would—back where they belong!"

The parish of St. John will be eternally grateful to Mr. and Mrs. Crone and the entire Crone family, who followed their father's dream by caring for and preserving all fourteen of the Stations of the Cross for twenty-six years. The stations survived rain, snow, sleet and sweltering Maryland heat, safely housed in the Crone's barn until they were returned for all of the future parishioners to use in devotion and prayer.

There was the distinct possibility that the set of fourteen tableaus could have been divided, never to be reunited, if Lawrence Crone had not intervened!

This photo was taken in December of 1999, twenty-six years after their initial placement. Father John DoBranski and several men went to the barn and opened the doors. These are but a few of the artifacts that they saw, safely nestled among the hay and straw. The boxes may have stored the crosses and finials for the top of the tableaus.

"Courtesy of James and Mary Jo Judge, Westminster, Maryland"

After removing the fourteen stations from the barn, a photo of each of them was taken in the light of day. They were then placed into temporary storage in the basement of the parish center, prior to restoration.

As well as the deterioration, hay and straw can be seen jutting out in various places behind the statues. Obviously, over those twenty-six years, birds and mice found comforting homes nestled around these figurines.

"Courtesy of James and Mary Jo Judge, Westminster, Maryland"

ॐख़ॐख़ॐख़ॐ

In April of 2000, I went to the parish center to complete an errand. A secretary told me that the fourteen Stations of the Cross and several other items were being stored temporarily in the basement before they were to be moved for the restoration process. I just happened to have my camera in my car. Reverend Monsignor and Pastor, Arthur Valenzano, granted permission to me to photograph them.

I took the following photos of the stations in their deteriorated condition never dreaming at the time that I would use them in my book.

There were no windows in the room. The lighting came from a few overhead bulbs and typical flash photography.

God placed me at the right place at the right time because this is what I saw when I stepped into the room . . .

The intricacies of the figurines amazed me, and the emotion captured on the faces by the original designer, who created them around the mid-seventeen hundreds, was astoundingly realistic. They are a combination of wood paste and horsehair. Wood paste offered excellent molding and sculpting properties and the horsehair was used as a binder due to its strength, elasticity and durability.

The elaborate detailing in the design, sometimes called 'gingerbread', was topped off by a cross inserted at the centrical crown of each station . . .

Finials are shown in their deteriorated state. They were restored and attached by sinking their fitted rods into holes at the top-sides of each station . . .

Additional pieces of the puzzle that had been stored in the basement of Saint John Parish Center . . .

Some of the paint has been removed showing this station's original neutral base color . . .

Other artifacts from the Main Street church had been stored by parishioners. Announcements were made including articles in the Carroll County Times newspaper announcing that Father John DoBranski hoped to get original pieces back, should a new church be built. The congregants' unselfishness proved true as numerous items were returned. This photo shows a portion of the marble that had been retained in attics, basements and garages. Some pieces had even been buried.

Finials, center crosses and Nativity pieces as they were being separated during the restoration process.

Before and after the restoration of Station IV, entitled *Jesus Meets His Afflicted Mother* . . .

"Courtesy of James Buckley, Manchester, Maryland"

The multi-dimensional figurines are so realistic that it is difficult not to be drawn into the passion of the scenes . . .

"Courtesy of James Buckley, Manchester, Maryland"

"Courtesy of James Buckley, Manchester, Maryland"

"Courtesy of James Buckley, Manchester, Maryland"

Before and after of Station XIII, entitled *The Body of Jesus is Taken Down From the Cross* . . .

"Courtesy of James Buckley, Manchester, Maryland"

This is station XIV, which was found to be the most damaged. It had to be restored first to ascertain whether it would be feasible to refurbish the entire set of fourteen.

After it was repaired, it was hung in the Monroe Street church, which is where I saw it and became mesmerized.

As I stood looking up at it in amazement, Jim Judge, a parishioner, told me that he was the one who told Father John DoBranski where the stations were (under Mr. Crone's care).

∂∽∂∽∂∽

It was the beginning of a journey of a lifetime for me!!!

"Courtesy of James Buckley, Manchester, Maryland"

# THE STATIONS OF THE CROSS

❧❧❧❧❧❧

The Stations of the Cross are iconographic depictions of Jesus Christ's last hours on earth.

Father John Dietzen (now deceased) of *Catholic News Service* had written the following in his newspaper column, *QUESTION CORNER*,

"For those who are not familiar with this Catholic devotion, the Stations of the Cross is a series (today, usually fourteen) of images from the Good Friday journey of Jesus from Pontius Pilate's headquarters to the crucifixion on Calvary. The person or group 'making' the *Stations* prays and reflects briefly on each incident."

© *Catholic News Service, Reverend John Dietzen Reprinted with permission of C.N.S.*

In recent decades, stations often have been abstract, but the Saint John stations depicted characters realistically, presenting each step along the "Way of the Cross," as they are sometimes referred.

"We believe that they were created in Germany around the mid 1700's in a factory that produced many of what we now call *'the last of the quality handmade wood paste art work in the world,'*" says Joseph A. Bahret of *Bahret Church Interiors and Liturgical Design of Harrisburg, Pennsylvania.* This company was contracted to complete the restoration of the stations and was quoted in an article for the book—*OUR HISTORY . . . OUR LEGACY*, produced by Deacon Mark Ripper for the one hundred and fifty year celebration of St. John Church, Westminster, Maryland.

Mr. Bahret continues, "The factory produced statuary of all types and sizes along the religious line for over 100 years prior to the date of these pieces. By the 1900's, the political agenda and the modern world had changed focus to other areas and the industry suffered greatly."

The stations remained in the Main Street church "hearing" devotional prayers of parishioners until a violent storm wreaked havoc on July17, 1952.

The storm brought the ninety-foot steeple crashing to the ground, missing Mary Dwyer, the mother of the pastor, the Reverend Father

James A. Dwyer. She had been sitting on the front side porch and was called to come into the house which inevitably saved her life, as the back upper wall of the rectory toppled in a delayed action after the original impact. Amazingly, the stations and the stained glass windows were untouched, although the steeple and its pinnacles created a hole about one-hundred-fifty feet deep in the body of the church.

The church was repaired, and the congregants continued worshipping there.

In 1969, architects were inspecting churches that had a history of major repair. They found the St. John Church to be eleven inches wider at the top than the bottom. It was most probably caused by structural damage as a result of the storm in 1952 and vibration created by the Western Maryland Railroad trains passing nearby for over one hundred years.

A decision had to be made—fix it at great expense or build a new one.

Discussions and meetings were held and the parishioners voted—the original Saint John Catholic Church at the Main Street location was designated to be torn down.

As reported on prior pages (see *THE MIRACLE BEGINS*), Lawrence Crone took the Stations of the Cross to his barn and protected them for twenty-six years. His barn was built of wooden planks, that were, in some areas, about one inch apart.

The stations were retrieved and returned to Saint John Parish Center.

After careful evaluation, it was established that all of the stations had to be restored.

According to an artist who specializes in religious art restoration, this barn was a good place to have stored them because it allowed for air flow, without which the horsehair and wood paste plaster would have turned to powder.

They were treated for mold, and layer after layer of paint had to be gently chipped off before restoring them to the original colors hidden beneath. The artist, who chooses to remain anonymous, had an assistant who spent more than two years of Saturdays on the project.

Each time I look at the stations, I say a little prayer for both the artist and her student, without whose talent the artifacts may not have been restored to the quality they possess.

They have come home, and after their extraordinary restoration they have "come-to-life", in spite of their incredible journey which only God can decipher.

ॐॐॐॐॐॐ

Please accept my invitation to visit Saint John Catholic Church at 43 Monroe Street, Westminster, Maryland, to see these incredible designs. Please call to verify the times of the church services at 410-876-2248.

ॐॐॐॐॐॐ

To help worshippers devoutly journey through the devotion of the Stations of the Cross, many pamphlets are available at Catholic book stores throughout the world. Another option is an eight page booklet, written very beautifully, entitled, *"The Way of the Cross,"* by Father Joseph Breighner.

Since 1977, Father Joe has been the host/creator of the nationally syndicated radio show, *"The Country Road,"* through *Paulist Media-Works* which can be heard on *WPOC HD2.*

He was the Coordinator of Evangelization for the Archdiocese of Baltimore from 1979 to 1989 and serves as pastoral counselor, writer, retreat director, and presenter of various parish missions, workshops, keynote addresses and days of recollection.

For the past thirty-five years he has been writing a weekly column in the *Baltimore Catholic Review,* the archdiocesan newspaper.

Father Joe received the Pope Paul VI award in evangelization for his service to the people of the United States through his radio ministry, preaching and writing.

My personal opinion—Father Joe is a gifted author and guest speaker, who spends countless hours helping the most humble and "ordinary" people to believe that their lives matter and each life is connected to God's life.

For information about any of Father Joe's publications, as well as audio and video or to view his schedule, visit—
**http://frjoebreighner.com/**

ॐঌ৵ॐঌ৵ॐঌ৵

My initial meeting with Father Joe Breighner and beyond . . .

I had promised God that if I won the Mrs. Maryland Pageant in 1985, that I would do my best to help others. Then, having won the competition I was frantic—after all, I had made a promise to God, and I felt that I wasn't moving fast enough to fulfill my vow!

I attended the parish mission at Saint John Church to ask for guidance through prayer. Father Joe was moderating in his unique way—light, bright and always with interspersed humor while bringing God's message to all.

He announced that he would be happy to talk with anyone who wished to stay . . . little did he know I was about to have a meltdown.

I waited until the mission service ended and the other parishioners had left the church before I approached Father Joe.

Then I started to cry, after all . . . a promise to God!!!

Father Joe saw my anxiety, listened to my story, and helped me to calm down. He was instrumental in suggesting the power of prayer, emplacing a positive direction—dreaming my big dreams, yet always letting God show me the way in *His* time and not *my* time.

I can't help but think that God had my book in His plans.

As I have worked on **A KEY TO LOVE,** I have been led in so many directions.

It began with the initial information derived in Westminster from a local, Charlie Brown, whom I met while I was eating a hot dog at Harry's Lunch counter. Then there were breakfast meetings at the Purple Diner with Charles Swinderman or luncheons at Baugher's Restaurant with the parish elders. Parishioners invited me into their homes to reminisce and display their photos. There was also research with Archivist Father Paul Thomas at the Catholic Center of Baltimore and hours of delving into the past at the Historical Society of Carroll County and the Carroll County libraries. I found the archives at the Hays T. Watkins Research Library which is part of the Baltimore & Ohio Railroad Museum, Inc. fascinating as I researched President Lincoln and his connection to Maryland, relative to the trains.

While traveling through the eastern United States into Quebec and Montreal searching for information about the tableaus, I found my way into the office of Rev. Claude Turmel, Director of Sacred Art and Construction Committee. That experience was incredible. His enthusiasm and his suggestions were greatly appreciated.

Meeting the Crone family was a highlight, as was sharing time with the descendants of John Orendorff—Lester and Irene Stemm, Sharon and Tom Peeling, Bud, Nancy, Jim and Ellie Clingan and their families, Dot and Sterling Shipley, Jean Zepp and Ken and Fran Wetzel. Devoted parishioners—Charles O. Fisher Sr., Joseph Beaver, Becky and Mr. and Mrs. Paul Martin, Charlie Swinderman and Bucky Zentgraft and many others brought the Main Street location of St. John Church back-to-life for my research.

And the stations . . . I remember meeting usher Jim Judge in the rear of the "old" round church after Mass. I was staring at the recently restored Station XIV hanging on the back wall. We both marveled at its beauty. He began telling me about the stations coming from the barn and that he was the one who told Father John DoBranski where they had been. The next day I found thirteen more in the basement of the parish center and photographed them (in the year 2000), never dreaming that I would add them to my novel this year!

To illustrate how this project has encompassed my life and how it has led me on quite a journey, I will explain one more ironic set of details.

While working on my book, I thought that I had compiled everything and was strictly editing my manuscript, I peeked in to say hello to Jean Bouvy. At that time, she was the director of the Saint John bookstore and has been a loyal supporter, anxious to sell my book as soon as it would be ready. She kindly asked once more,

"Should I make room on the shelves?"

I told Jeannie that I had been busy editing, but every time I thought I was finished more information had been falling my way, important things that would make my book more complete.

Just then Mary Jo Judge, a parishioner and the wife of Jim Judge, "just happened" to be shopping in the back of that store and heard us talking.

Mary Jo said,

"I've been planning to call you because I've uncovered photos of the Stations of the Cross that were taken in the barn and outside of the parish center over ten years ago!"

She had been sorting through photos, found them, and wanted to give them to me!

"They show bits and pieces of straw, straw used as nesting material by the birds and the mice," she said.

I couldn't believe it!

Of course, I told her that I would make them available to the church library, as well as the Historical Society of Carroll County archives, after the book is finished.

They were so important that I couldn't turn away from them. My book editing had to wait, and time continued on as I had the photos scanned and compiled into a disc to insert into my manuscript.

My project has fallen into place, piece by piece. As I marvel at the interconnection of the puzzle pieces, and these are but a few, I ponder whether to present the intricate story in detail someday, as a complete book.

I will see if God sends me in that direction.

As for this book, although it took over ten years to complete and much of that time entailed "learning the computer," it truly was in His time and not mine, just as Father Joe suggested.

I am convinced—when God wants it to be done it will be done!

# A UNIQUE RESEARCH OPPORTUNITY

## THE HISTORY OF "THESE" STATIONS OF THE CROSS

ॐॐॐॐॐॐ

Although a complete history of these stations and exactly how they came to St. John Catholic Church has not been completed, the last known pieces of information were compiled in April, 2002, by the Archive Office of the Catholic University in Washington, D.C.

(Be sure to note the information in the section, *The Stations of the Cross*, previously reported).

It was suggested to me by Rev. Claude Turmel, director of the Sacred Art and Construction Committee of Montreal, Canada, to offer a request to a serious student of the arts or religion to expand the quest.

When you view the expression on the faces of the characters that the artist created, it is difficult to walk away.

If anyone would like to research them, perhaps for part of a thesis, please share any information with me, Mary Jane Buettner, the author, in care of St. John Catholic Church, 43 Monroe Street, Westminster, MD 21157, or contact me—

**http://www.akeytolove.com**

I guarantee it will be a labor of love, and God will surely bless you!

# THE CHRONICLE CONTINUES

Additional items made their way back to St. John Church. These angels were donated by Walter and Elizabeth Reed, who had stored them in their barn in Greenmount, Maryland.

"Courtesy of James Buckley, Manchester, Maryland"

The bowing cherubs now stand on either side of the St. John Sanctuary . . .

"Courtesy of James Buckley, Manchester, Maryland"

When articles were removed from the Main Street church prior to its demolition, this statue of Saint Thérèse, formerly in the Baptistry, found its way to the bottom floor of the rectory on the Monroe Street campus.

In 2001, it was restored by Michael Corsini, Jr., and now resides in a place of honor in the St. Thérèse meeting room.

The original Sanctuary lamp is from St. John Catholic Church on Main Street. When the artifacts were being taken from the condemned building, Mr. and Mrs. William Leister acquired this lamp. They donated it to Saint Bartholomew Catholic Church in Manchester, Maryland, where it hung in the parish's historical chapel until their new church was dedicated in 2006. A decision was made to have it cleaned, polished and restored, which brought back its original luster. It now hangs in the new Saint Bartholomew Sanctuary.

St. Bartholomew website: http://www.stbartscatholicchurch.org

This ornate wrought iron pulpit was donated from Saint John Catholic Church, Main Street. Both the pulpit and the votive stand can be seen at Saint Bartholomew Catholic Church in Manchester, Maryland, in the historical chapel. That parish was established in 1864.

Six of the ten stained glass windows are shown from the Main Street location. It is also a miracle that they were protected.

ॐॐॐॐॐॐॐॐ

Monsignor Joseph C. Antoszewski, Pastor of Saint John Church from 1971-1992, was very generous. He knew that the traditional stained glass windows, crafted in Munich, Germany by the Franz Mayer Stained Glass Company, circa 1865, would not be used in the modern church on Monroe Street.

He offered them to a church being built in southern Maryland, who sent their representatives to retrieve them.

Years had passed, and Monsignor Joe received a call asking if he wanted the stained glass windows returned to use at St. John's, unbeknownst to the caller that the parish had been contemplating the building of a new church.

Monsignor Joe thought that they had been placed in the walls of that southern Maryland church, but actually, only some had been installed. The remaining ten had been boxed away for years and were being stored in that caller's basement.

The Reverend asked parishioners, Terry Jones and Ed Gregg, to recover them. The windows were carefully wrapped in paper and cloth, then placed into pick-up trucks that were barely able to hold the weight. They transported them back to the parish.

Terry and his son Sean inventoried the items and transported them to a storage room in the school, where they remained in sturdy boxes until they were sent for restoration.

❧⌘❧⌘❧⌘❧

The ten original stained glass windows can be viewed in full color and each is described at the Saint John website—
**http://www.sjwest.org**

Reverend Monsignor Arthur Valenzano, then Pastor, was responsible for completing the beautiful Saint John Catholic Church in 2003. Terry Jones (not shown) had been elected as committee chairperson. He retired from his secular job to oversee the huge undertaking.

Three of the churches of the parish of Saint John . . .

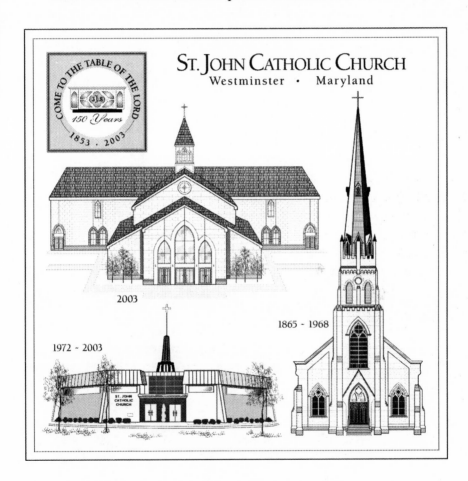

Courtesy of Norma Perron, Westminster, Maryland

## MY SUMMATION

It seemed very obvious to me that God wanted many of the original pieces that were part of the former parish to come together again. He placed just the right people at just the right places and at just the right time to bring all of the unique items back where they belonged.

After more than twenty-six years, the stained glass windows, the statues, the pieces of marble, and the entire set of fourteen Stations of the Cross have come full-circle.

They are restored and cherished, now residing in the parish of St. John. By my estimation . . . the miracle is now complete!

# THE EVOLUTION OF THE COVER

৵৵৵৵৵৵

The original artwork was designed and donated by Clara Nash, renowned artist, having galleried in Baltimore, Reisterstown, and Tilghman Island, Maryland, and whose mediums have included oils, watercolors, and pastels. Clara, a resident of Ocean City, Maryland, chose to create her statement for **A KEY TO LOVE,** in acrylics.

She agreed that I could watch as she composed, something I had never had the privilege to do although I already own several of her original pastels.

I vigilantly became the spectator following her every move, and she was incredible!

Her thoughts were spinning as she planned the best course of action . . . to sketch the church, a masterpiece—it too being an original, built in the 1860's amidst the backdrop of the Civil War.

A ferrotype or tintype reproduction of Saint John parish and original sketches by Norma Perron and Charles Swinderman were her inspiration.

The church sat on a dirt road, hence the clay-like tones as its base.

The body, the windows, the front door and, of course the over-sized steeple with louvers and pinnacles—each awaited a turn in the sweep of her *magic wand*, which would make them come-to-life on the canvas.

After a tedious taping to protect her design, the backdrop was begun—a wash of yellow, orange and a touch of red.

As I read the story aloud to her, especially the words describing various characters' strong agitation and emotion, more and more intense shades of red and brown were applied, each in its own unique glory. Amidst the turbulence of the story, her intensity and passion heightened. The colors were repeatedly layered until a magnificent explosion appeared and the true design that Clara envisioned was born.

Though the palate was vivid, she cleverly omitted an area to apply a pastel application illustrating the sun glistening through, as if the heavens, an almost celestial presence, were watching over the edifice, protecting it from the conflict that she was capturing.

Trees, light and airy, immediately grew from her paint brushes and nestled around the building, coddling Clara's straight lines and almost whispering in the wind—the secret they were keeping, about to be told.

And, about the key . . . I purchased it at an antique store, flea market or tag sale in the Westminster area. What secrets, what history does it truly hold? It was one of many in my huge collection of keys that grace the walls in my home. I snatched it off to give it to Clara, as the key of honor for the cover.

There was no fanfare, no planning. The key was very old and worn, and had an ever-so-subtle indication of a heart shape at its bow, the end that would protrude from the keyhole.

It spoke to me when I walked over to my key gallery.

Months later, at Clara's studio while she studied original photos and began sketching, she asked me,

"What is the significance of the shape of the small windows repeated again and again in the old church? They have a three-leaf clover-like-shape repeated throughout."

I said,

"They probably signify God the Father, God the Son and God the Holy Spirit—the Trinity, or Faith, Hope and Charity. Actually, there are several references of 'threes' in the Catholic Church. Why do you ask?"

Clara responded,

"Because, that old key that you decided upon for the cover has that exact same shape. See? 'Course over time the edges were softened by wear, but you can still see the three circular parts that make up the clover shape down here, carved into the key's cleft protruding from the throating, at the pin."

"Oh my God, Clara," I exclaimed, "Wouldn't that be incredible if the key that you are sketching could be the actual key from 1865, from Saint John's Church!"

Is it . . . is it???

It is only *one* of the mysteries in the story that we will never truly solve . . .

During this beginning sketch, Clara noticed the correlation between the shape within the windows and that which was within the tine of the key . . .

After covering the church and the key, Clara layered the backdrop. The dirt road came alive in a clay-like depth of color and the passion began—tumultuous swirls and volcanic excitement of reds, browns, and oranges evolving into an escape of yellow overlooking, protecting the main focus.

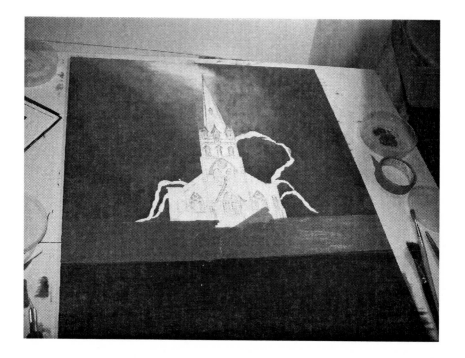

Unveiling the church and visually preparing to add the softness of
the trees and shrubs.

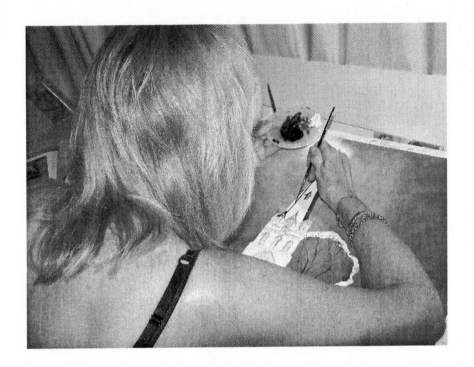

Detailing . . . etching . . . delineating . . .

## A KEY TO LOVE

To view these photos, in color, and her incredible collection of designs, visit Clara Nash's website
**http://www.claranash.com**

# BIBLIOGRAPHY

❧❧❧❧❧❧

Archives, The Lincoln Highway National Museum *The Greatest Funeral in the History of the United States—Twenty Days—April 15 to May 4, 1985. The Lincoln Highway National Museum & Archives,* Ohio Publisher, Date—unknown. Print.

Ashcraft, Mary Ann. *The History of St. John Catholic Church. The Carroll County Times* [Westminster] 2 July 2006, daily ed., sec. Publisher, The Carroll County Times, 2006. Print.

Baty, Catherine, and the Historical Society of Carroll County. *Images of America-Westminster.* Charleston, South Carolina, Chicago, Illinois, Portsmouth New Hampshire, San Francisco, California: Arcadia Publishing, 2009. Print.

Books, Time-Life. *Arms and Equipment of the Confederacy(Echoes of Glory).* Virginia: Time-Life Books, 1996. Print.

Books, Time-Life. *The Civil War-The Death of a President.* Virginia: Time-Life Books, 1996. Print.

Catton, Bruce. *American Heritage New History of the Civil War.* New York: Viking Books, 1996. Print.

Clark, Champ. *The Assassination: Death of the President(Civil War Series).* Rev. 1988 ed. New York: Time-Life Books, 1987. Print.

Elkins, Joby, and George Welty. *St. Johns' Goes Down. The Carroll County Times. Article March 14, 1977. Print.*

Gunnarsson, Robert L. *The Story of the Northern Central Railway.* Maryland: Greenberg Publishing Company, 1991. Print.

Long, E.B., and Barbara Long. *The Civil War, Day by Day, an Almanac 1861-1865*. New York: Da Capo Press, Inc., 1971. Print.

Meredith, Roy, and Arthur Meredith. *Mr. Lincoln's Military Railroads*. Toronto, Canada: W.W. Norton and Company, INC., 1979. Print.

Mitchell IV, Alexander D. *Baltimore Then and Now*. Ohio: PRC Publishing Ltd., 2001. Print.

Monk, Eric. *Keys: Their History and Collection (Shire Library)*. 2nd ed. Princes Risborough: Shire, 2009. Print.

Ripper, Deacon Mark, and Bahret, J. Bahret Church Interiors and Liturgical Design. *"About the Stations of the Cross." Our History . . . Our Legacy*. Baltimore: self, 2003. unknown. Print.

Ripper, Deacon Mark, Norma Perron, and Contributing Editors and History Committee Members. *Our History . . . Our Legacy. Celebrating 150 Years 1853-2003 A History of Saint John Catholic Church, Westminster, Maryland*. Baltimore: self, 2003. Print.

Sheads, Scott S, Scott Sumpter Sheads, and Daniel Carroll Toomey. *Baltimore During the Civil War*. 1 ed. Baltimore, Maryland: Toomey Press, 1997. Print.

Spalding, Archbishop Martin John. "unknown." *Excerpts from the Honorable Archbishop Martin John Spalding's Diary*. Baltimore: Unknown, 1865. unknown. Print. Excerpts were acquired under the direction of Father Thomas at the Catholic Center Archives, Baltimore, Maryland. Approximate date 2000-2001

Starr Jr., John W. *Lincoln and the Railroads: A Biographical Study*. New York: Kessinger Publishing, Llc, 2008. Print.

Varhola, Michael J. *Everyday Life During the Civil War*. Cincinnati: Writer's Digest Books, 1999. Print.

Warner, Mary. *The Patriot-News. Harrisburg, Pennsylvania. Article November 28, 2003. Print.*

Weber, Thomas. *The Northern Railroads in the Civil War 1861-1865*. Bloomington: Indiana University Press, 1999. Print.

Welty, George. *The History of St. John Catholic Church. The Carroll County Times* [Westminster] 1 Jan. 2000, daily ed., sec. unknown: unknown. Print. Article was separated from newspaper, no dates available.

MLA formatting by—http://BibMe.org

# SPECIAL APPLAUSE

❧❧❧❧❧❧

Without God, none of this would have been possible.

My unending thanks, love and devotion to my parents, Frank and Margaret Trachta. Together they created a loving home environment. They told me I could be anything that I wanted to be, encouraging me to be thankful for my many talents. After nurturing me and teaching me my ABC's, they gave to me the advantage of a Catholic education at Sacred Heart of Jesus Parish in Baltimore, Maryland. There the School Sisters of Notre Dame taught me how to rearrange those letters, giving me the building blocks to tackle this project.

Henry, my love, you're simply the best! Honey, without your continual support I could not have devoted hour upon hour to this vision. Thank you for keeping everything working, believing in me and calming me down when I had computer jitters.

Jennifer, Michael, Mackenzie and Madison—how blessed I am to have such a supportive family who trusted me all the way. I love each one of you.

Much love to my sister, Diane and her family—Joe, Kory and Kacy who continually heard the snippets change as I created and re-created and who willingly and patiently awaited the finished product.

Lee, although you are not here, I felt your energy and know that you were my intermediary. I will never forget you, my loving brother.

Clara, my wonderful and talented friend, former business partner and confidant who sometimes played 'Lucy' and other times 'Ethel' continues to encourage me to reach higher and has always been an inspiration to me. She is the only person that I know who accomplishes more in a week than some people do in a lifetime.

Reverend Monsignor Arthur Valenzano, who listened patiently as I shared my dream to write this novel and constantly kept me in his prayers!

Sister M.Charlotte Beierli, SSND, my special angel through it all!

Reverend John DoBranski who shared his enthusiastic efforts through God's graces which allowed him to 'find' the artifacts, the pieces of the puzzle, and pull them back to St. John Parish were they belonged. Amazing!

Mary Jo Hutson who possesses the innate ability to see all of the pieces of a project, balance the pros and cons of each scenario and verbalize what needs to be changed through a constructive process. How lucky I am to have you share your talent with me!

Helen Milano, SSF—my love and appreciation to a special friend and a true blessing for skillfully formulating the adult book club questions!

Francis J. (Frank) McGrath—you graciously offered your time and technical skills to delete the "goblins" in my computer. What an unselfish gift! What a remarkable contribution!

Sister Reginald Gerdes OSP, who so graciously verified the culture and cultural significance of the arabbers as a contribution to the history of Baltimore, I offer special thanks!

Charlotte Rajotte—tirelessly you turned my initial scribbling into beautifully entered type, long before my digits touched a keyboard. Continued encouragement to me just reinforces your unique talent of seeing the positives. My everlasting gratitude!

Cecile Pickford who called from Malibu, California, to reference the comparison of Jonathon and Andrew to Cain and Abel, then followed with, "You've hit a home run—first time out!" I really needed the reassurance that I was on the right track!

Charles (Charlie) Swinderman who shared his life, both verbally and visually, as well as his love of the St. John Parish with me. Through his eyes, the church, Westminster and Civil War history came to life. I enjoyed our breakfast meetings at the Purple Diner . . . a unique way to do research!

Cheers to my twenty "first" readers, their pros and cons!

Angie, Barbara, Cecile, Debbie, Gail, Mary Jo and Pat—you remembered the tiniest of details long after your initial reading and could discuss specifics of places, scenes and each character and their emotion—so helpful, so incredible!

Nancy Latini, an accomplished writer of her own merit who came to my assistance professionally with more than one perfect word pulled from thin-air during the various editing phases—all proved invaluable. And as a friend, you faithfully presented an encouraging ear and unwavering belief in me as you continued to inspirit me to reach my goal. My unending applause and hugs to you!

Anne Mc Mahon, godmother to A KEY TO LOVE, or perhaps *fairy godmother* waving her magic wand to make it look easy as she offered me her inexhaustible editorial eye, devoting hours and hours and hours of proficient detailing. Dear cousin, my deepest thanks as you meticulously hovered over my 'semi-colonitis' and eradicated my quotes within quotes within quotes. I appreciate your expertise, your patience and your keen ability to teach as you edited. What a joy that we have found each other!

Jim Buckley, who did an outstanding job, capturing the intensity of the artifacts throughout the St. John Church, deserves a special thank you. Although not a parishioner, his was a donation of time and talent. He shared his gift and through his professional eye the items graced his camera lens allowing all of their magnificence to be presented to you!

Tom Diehlmann, for his gift of time and expertise while masterfully assisting at the computer, diligently preparing literally thousands of names and contact information for potential book buyers. Behind the scenes, but a shining star!

Naida Burkholder Scaggs, my dear friend who dreamed my dream from the initial conception, hearing me edit and re-edit the tale always in awe of the way it came together. I feel that you will read the finished copy over my shoulder and watch out for me as angels do. I will miss you!

Continued appreciation to Iris Wingert for opening her heart as she used all of her Media-Specialist skills to show me what could be expected from a Power Point presentation and a Video Story.

My personal adulation to one of the master storytellers and one of my heroes—Mr. Walt Disney—who taught me that the antagonist and the protagonist must be present in any story to ensure its success. Thank you for having the tenacity to forge ahead through the tough times. You have been an inspiration to me and if you were here, I would repeat your quote—"All our dreams can come true . . . if we have the courage to pursue them!"

# Your Prayers and Support Have Been Priceless

૭ન્ડ્રૅ૭ન્ડ્રૅ૭ન્ડ્રૅ

About Faces Staff Members
Rev. Larry Adamczyk
Brittany Alms
Danielle Alms
Debbie Alms
Steven Alms
Sydnee Alms
Victoria Alms
Joseph Matthew Azersa
The Baltimore and Ohio
    Railroad Museum, Inc.
    Baltimore, Maryland
Bahret Church Interiors and
    Liturgical Design,
    Harrisburg, Pennsylvania
Mary Jo and Don Bankard
Catherine Baty
Marilyn Beach
Mr. and Mrs. Joseph Beaver
Bonnie Becker
M.Charlotte Beierli, SSND
Joy Beyer
Rev. Louis A. Bianco
Lauren Blanchard
Barbara Block
Rev. Bonnie Block
Janice and Francis Bocek
Susan and Ed Bollinger
Jean Bouvy
Kim and David Boucher
Doris Brackney
Rev. Joseph Breighner

Eric Brennan
Patrick Brennan
Patricia Brink
James and Doris Buckley
Jennifer and Michael Buckley
Mackenzie Buckley
Madison Buckley
Brian Buettner
Joe and Mary Jo Buettner
Judy Buettner
Julie Buettner
Leroy Buettner
Mark and Jennifer Buettner
Steven Buettner
Joyce and Herbert Burk
Theresa Bohli Burns
Monica Calwell
Joseph Caouette
Susan Bratten-Capute
Christie Cartomany
The Carroll County Library
The Carroll County Times
Debi and Steve Cesenaro
Anna and Roy Chiavacci
Susie N. Chung, MD
Christine and Chic Cieslik
Deacon and Mrs. Joseph Cinquino
Ginny and Stan Citko
Marilyn Clements
David (Bud) and Nancy Clingan
Jim and Ellie Clingan
Pat and Richard Clontz

The Knights of Columbus
Karen and John Cooney
Mary and Barbara Cooney
Rose Ann and John Cooney
Deacon Jack Coster
Carol Cox
Theresa and Shawn Cox
Ed Craig
Anthony Crone
Lawrence Crone
Mary Elizabeth Crone
Mary Tansil-Crone
The Lawrence Crone Family
Vivian Crutchfield
Paul and Pina Culotta
Emy Damberg
Michelle Dapelo, SSF
Karen Davis
Lesley Desautels
Pat and Pete Devereux
Brian Dick
Angie and Tom Diehlmann
Craig Diehlmann
The Thomas Diehlmann Family
Dwight Dingle
Rev. John DoBranski
Cathy and Brian Dolan
Margarete Doyle
Valentina and Bill Dragen
Walter Dreschler
Katherine Dukehart
Pamela Dupree
Janice Earle
Terry Eckard
Tony Eckard
Beth, Randy and
    Danielle Essenwine
Deacon and Mrs.William Fallon

Linda Fay
Robin Ferro
Terri First and Quint Kessenich
Charlene and Fritz Fischer
Charles O. Fisher, Sr.
Neal Foore
Linda Frisch
Leslie Gabler
Paul Gallagher
Brenda and Ray Garner
Christopher Gaul
Savitri Gauthier
Reginald Gerdes OSP
Jackie German
Dr. Rosalyn Ghitter
Christine Glavaris
Gail Glick
Sue Glick
Rachael Glick
Valerie Glick
Debbie Gotshall
Greater Pittsburgh Chamber of
    Commerce
Greater Pittsburgh Convention and
    Visitors Bureau
Dianne and Steve Grubb
Krista Grubb
Cathy Hagey
Daniel C. Halvorsen
Phillip (P.T.) and Tamara Hambleton
The Hambleton Families
Melanie Hampton
John Hanson
Harry's Main Street Grille
Colleen Hattrup
Robin Heart
H.J. Heinz Company,
    Pittsburgh, Pennsylvania

The Heinz History Museum,
Pittsburgh, Pennsylvania
Joy Hess
Loretta and Harold Hicks
The Historical Society of Carroll
County, Westminster, Maryland
Wendy and Bill Hoff
Karen Hoffberger
Ann Horvath
Mary Bell and Bill Howser
Carol Huber
Donald R. Hull
Hull Company Accountants
Mary Jo and Clark Hutson
Melissa and Bill Hyde
Joanne Izzo
Ginger and Rob Jefferson
Loni and Mike Jones
Terry and Cathy Jones
Judy Joyce
Jim and Mary Jo Judge
Ruth Kantor, MD
Howard Kapfer, Jr.
Diane and Joe Kapinos
Kacy Kapinos
Kory Kapinos
Anna Kehring
Catherine Broome-Kelly
Chris and Joe Kolodziejski
Tetyana Kovrizhenko
Mary Jo Kotwas
Karen Kuessner
Jacqueline Lambert
Miriam and Jim Lane
Nancy and Rick Latini
Stephanie Latini
Lois Leasure
Trudy Leister

Christopher Leppert
Ellen Levin
Amanda and Micah Lewis
Melissa Little
Bernadette and Randy Loiland
Debra A. F. Love, DDS
Anna Ludwig
Mary Luht
Dot and Walt Machener
Deacon Robert A. Malinowski
Jean Maloff
Kathleen Malstrom, SSND
Marlene and Fred Manfra
Cookie and Danny Margiotta
Becky Martin
Dorothy and Paul Martin
Rev. Raymond D. Martin
Rev. Hector Mateus-Ariza
Elizabeth F. Mathias
Terry Mathias
Francis J. McGrath
Janet McKercher
Brenda McKinney, Fancy Paws
Grooming Salon
Anne and Bill McMahon
Lucy McNeir
Monica Metzger
David Meyerson, MD
Helen Milano, SSF
Deacon and Mrs. Donald Miller
Louise and Chuck Minchik
Rosalie Mislowsky, DDS
Pat Mueller
Mollie Mulligan
Michelle Murphy
Gail and Don Myers
Clara Nash
Cathy Neubauer

Barbara and Joe Neukum

Anne Nevin

Monkton Train Station, NCR Trail,
    Monkton, Maryland

Rev. Brian Nolan

Michele and Bryan O'Connor

Karen and Mark O'Donnell

Omni-William Penn Hotel, Pittsburgh,
    Pennsylvania

Geraldine Palese

Mrs. Gerry Palese

Parishioners of Saint John Church

Rev. Leo Patalinghug

The Patriot News, Harrisburg,
    Pennsylvania

Mary Carol and Mark Pearce

Sharon and Tom Peeling

Ashley Peeling

Norma Perron

Carolyn and Ralph Peters

Photo Magic, Ocean City, Maryland

Javier Pica PT

Cecile E. Pickford

Anne Marie and Monique Pierson

Joe Pitta

Greater Pittsburgh Chamber of
    Commerce

Greater Pittsburgh Convention and
    Visitors Bureau

Reba Poole

Kathleen Pusheck

Charlotte and Lucien Rajotte

Brian and Darlene Raver

Reese Fire Department

Michelle, Scott & Zachary Richards

Deacon and Mrs. Mark E. Ripper

Rev. Michael J. Roach

Fran Rock

Ron's Automotive

Trudy Rosentrater

Jae Lynn Ross

Pastor Herbert A. and Mrs. Shelley
    Ruby

Bernard B. Salzman

Janice Salzman

Naida Scaggs

Shari Scheuermann

Donna and Bill Schmidt

Billy and D'Anna Schmidt

JoAnn and Don Schmidt

Linda Schmidt

Grace Schnauble and Family

Lew C. Schon, MD

Janice Schreck

Denise Schumann

Debbie and Alan Schwartz

Joe and Deborah Seeberger

Joe and Marge Seeberger

Alain and Mary Sellem

Christy Shaffer

Ella Shinkar

Sterling and Dot Shipley

Jennifer Shores

Reed Shusterman

April and Ryan Sigmon

Harry Sirinakis

Kyparissa Sirinakis

Zoe and George Sirinakis

St. John Ladies Sodality

Former teaching Sisters of Saint John
    School—

M. Rosalia Auth, SSND

Mary Charlotte Beierli, SSND

Mary Cassia Schneider, SSND

Marie Bernadette Fields, SSND

Edith Ann De Giosio, SSND

Mary Agnesita Klug, SSND
Mary Ita Lashley, SSND
Mary Monaghan, SSND
Frances Marie Usher, SSND
Paul Skotarczak and Bruce Perna
Charlotte Smith
Chester Stacy of MBC Precision
    Imaging
Kay Stefan
Rev. Gerard Steffener
Mr. and Mrs. Lester Stemm
The Stemm Family
Helga Surratt
Charles (Charlie) Swinderman
Pat Tate
Rev. Paul Thomas, Archivist, Catholic
    Center, Baltimore, Maryland
Shirley Thomas
Catherine Trachta
Joyce Trachta
Margaret and Frank Trachta
The Trachta Family
Tractor Supply Company
Rev. Claude Turmel
Marguerite Twist
Rev. Msgr. Arthur Valenzano
Pat Vega
Dana Villarte
Mary von Paris
The von Paris Family
Carol and Bud Walderman
Harriann Walker
Carol and Bob Wallace
Lisa and Michael Ward
Hays T. Watkins Research Library
Dorothy Webb
Anna Weinfield
Annette Welsh

Melissa Welsh
Ken and Fran Wetzel
Peggy Wheeler
Catherine Whitcomb
Iris Wingert
Mary Ellen Winter
Bea Wolfe
Josephine Wood
WTTR Radio
Lynn Yurfkowsky, DPM
Jean Zepp
Stewart (Bucky) Zentgraft
Katy Zouck

# A KEY TO LOVE

❧❧❧❧❧❧

## READING GROUP DISCUSSION QUESTIONS

## ADULT FORMAT

❧❧❧❧❧❧

1. Why, or why do you not think the title **A KEY TO LOVE**, fits this story?

2. What did the story unlock for you about life and love?

3. Discuss the relationship between Thomas and his father, and Thomas and his Uncle Jay . . .
   What part does their religion and faith play in the relationship?
   What parts do games and puzzles play?

4. Traditions: The keeping of photos, letters, written records, lists, and keys, etc. provide information that changes our perception and understanding about the characters and events in the story . . .
   How is Maggie Fischer affected by her collection of keys?
   Do you think it is important to collect or keep things?

5. What did Mary Kathleen hold near and dear to her heart?
   Did Mary Kathleen collect something?
   What did Maggie and Mary Kathleen have in common?
   Were they a healing presence for each other?

6 After spending time with the boys Michael, William, Andrew and Jonathon, how do you interpret the death of their parents?

7.  What does the care of their Aunt and Uncle have to do with their formation and transformation? You might want to take a real good look at Jonathon's short life.

8.  How does the family history of Thomas Frank and Cully Anderson affect the history of Maryland and the United States?

9.  What do their families bring to the growth of a nation?

10. The building of a family, a church, and a nation is woven with trials, questions, doubt, sadness, laughter, planting, cooking, work, holidays, love, etc . . .
    As the families and parishioners of the new St. John Church feel 'the wind whip and wrap around them', what and how are they gifted?

11. How did they 'taste the kiss' of love and life?


**Prepared by Helen Milano, SSF**

# A KEY TO LOVE

꛰ঌ꛰ঌ꛰ঌ

## READING GROUP DISCUSSION QUESTIONS

## YOUNG ADULT FORMAT

꛰ঌ꛰ঌ꛰ঌ

1.  What did you think about Maggie's key collection? Could you visualize it? Were you surprised that it took you on the journey that it did?

2.  Did you think that Aunt Mary Kathleen had favorites? How should she have acted differently to make her relationship better with her nephews?

3.  Should Uncle Thomas have offered more attention to his wife? How could he have done so?

4.  How did you feel about Jonathon? What three words would you use to describe him and why?

5.  What did you think that Jonathon thought about his brothers? Why does he feel the way he does toward them?

6.  What emotions does Jonathon display throughout the book?

7.  What did you think about Jonathon buying the bike? Should he have tried to prevent Andrew from buying it? At the drag race, what should Jonathon have done to help his brother, Andrew? What would you have done?

8.  What did you think of Jonathon and the way he treated the animals?

9. Who or what could have possibly prevented Jonathon from becoming a destructive person?

10. Why did Uncle Thomas ask him to leave and should he have done so?

11. The main characters-Jonathon, Andrew, William, Michael, Uncle Jay, Uncle Thomas, Aunt Mary Kathleen, Maggie and Gretchen–how do they differ? Who do you feel that you identify with? What part of their personality do you possess?

12. Did you like the character, Gretchen, and if so, what did you like about her? If you were she, would you have handled the confrontation with Jonathon any differently? If so, how?

13. Was Uncle Jay a character that you would like to have known? Why?

14. What does the word "treasure" mean to you? Did you think there was hidden treasure? Where did you think it was? Were you surprised by the locations for the treasure? How did you feel about the choices for the protection of the treasure? Should Thomas have done something differently? What?

15. What did you feel was going to happen when Aunt Mary Kathleen lit her makeshift torch?

16. If you could, how would you rewrite the ending? What would happen next year?

17. If you witnessed that life altering event, what would you have done?

18. Did you feel a sense of obligation to learn more about the history of the actual church?

**19.** Did you like having the real story attached and enhanced with pictures?

**20.** For you, what is the take-away message of the novel and that of the historical story?

**21. A KEY TO LOVE** was a 'dream project', yet a long term commitment. What are you passionate about that you would be willing to commit to for ten or more years?

**Prepared by Mary Jane Buettner**

*Dear Readers . . .*

*Thank you for sharing your valuable leisure time, perusing* **A KEY TO LOVE**. *I hope that you have enjoyed the characters, their down-home flair and flavor, and that they have come alive in your psyche, satisfying your personal investment in their lives!*

*Could you see Maggie's keys and dream with her?*

*Could you smell the aroma of Thanksgiving, get ready to lick the cupcake batter from the spatula and taste the peanut butter cookies in Pittsburgh?*

*Could you visualize the farmhouse and the barn, touch the warm, wet cloths in the field and hear the music playing in the background?*

*Could you feel the emotion within the family, experience the tension building, sense the helplessness and hopefulness, mourn their losses and feel contentment at the outcome?*

*If so, and if I stirred your memory historically, then I am delighted.*

**Mary Jane Buettner**
**http://www.akeytolove.com**

# ABOUT THE AUTHOR

Mary Jane has accomplished many things in her life; her 42-year marriage to Henry takes precedence. Daughter Jennifer, son-in-law Michael and granddaughters Madison and Mackenzie sum up the ingredients that make her whole.

She was born in Canton, in the heart of the city of Baltimore, Maryland. Fort McHenry, birthplace of 'The Star Spangled Banner,' stood majestically nearby.

Blessed with a vivid imagination, she utilized it with a variety of mediums: writing, producing, directing, and performing numerous creative endeavors. A 'Master' hair designer, color specialist and image consultant are just some of the accolades she achieved locally, nationally and internationally!

After winning the coveted title of MRS. MARYLAND AMERICA 1985 and competing in the MRS. AMERICA CONTEST in Reno, Nevada (promoting volunteerism), her creative writing talents surfaced with passion.

**A KEY TO LOVE** has been a labor of love. It has coupled her new-found delight in story telling with her devotion to her religion.

છ્જ્છ્જ્છ્જ્છ્જ